GINGERMAN

IN SEARCH OF THE TOYMAKER

TONY BERTAUSKI

Copyright © 2020 by Tony Bertauski

All rights reserved.

No part of this book may be reproduced in any form or by any electronic or mechanical means, including information storage and retrieval systems, without written permission from the author, except for the use of brief quotations in a book review.

PROLOGUE

The desk was cut from a fallen cedar.
Its surface was scarred and discolored with blots of ink and coffee stains. It was cluttered with sentimental things. An ugly mug with #2 pencils. A red wallet. An etched metal ornament that was as heavy as it looked. A gnarled branch hooked on the end, good for scratching between the shoulder blades.

The old man dropped a cane in a metal cylinder, the shaft polished hickory with a sterling silver handle. He leaned back slowly, waiting for the day his chair would collapse.

Today was not that day.

There was a sturdy chair across the room. It was more of a throne, the cushion dusty and worn. But it was too heavy to move. Even if it wasn't, he'd decided, long ago, he wouldn't sit in it. He'd considered having it removed. Instead, it held boxes of things he couldn't bring himself to throw away.

The room was a maze of collectibles. Stacks of wooden boxes and towering shelves filled with carvings and sketches, glass lamps and wind chimes, metal ballerinas and clay sculptures. It would be a treacherous journey for a man his age just to get to the throne. The chair at his desk was simple. It would live another day.

Just like him.

He pulled the leather strapping on a large book and cracked it open, pushing a can of potpourri next to a bag of hard candy. The pages were thick and yellow. The surface coarse. Feathers were displayed on a block of lacquered spruce with holes drilled in a line. He found them on hikes and never failed to bring them home. His students knew his habit and picked them up, too. Somewhere in the clutter, there was a box of them.

On this day, he chose a snow goose feather. It was only fitting. The vane unblemished. The downy barbs fluffed at the base. The hollow quill stained. It felt as light as a, well, as a feather. He slid a small tank across the desk and removed the ornate lid. The ink was a stark contrast to the feather.

The blackened tip hovered over the page.

A brisk winter breeze blew through the open window and rattled the pages beneath a googly-eyed rock. Somewhere, far below, children were shouting. The old man smiled. He wouldn't be long. It was just this day was a good day to start. He'd been putting this off long enough.

A gingerbread man was at the back of the desk, leaning against the stone wall. Arms and legs stiff, eyes of white icing round and expectant.

"Where to start?" The old man grunted. The gingerman stared. The quill scratched the page. "Mm. The beginning it is."

It was almost winter.

1

"You didn't fix it?"

"It's fine." Dad pointed at the dashboard like there was a gauge pointing to *fine*.

"It's not fine, Henry," Mom said. "What if it breaks down? Here. No reception, no directions." She shook her phone. "What are we going to do?"

Chris watched the trees. The window was icy on his forehead, soothing the nausea that had been stirred up by the never-ending curves in the road. The smell of Mom's cold coffee. He was glad he hadn't eaten breakfast. Or lunch.

"What's this?" Mom said.

The road slanted toward a tunnel. A gate blocked the entrance, steel bars that were once bright yellow now a dull mustard with patches of blue-green lichen. They stopped short. The parking brake wrenched into place.

"Do we have a pass or a code or something?" Mom said.

"We don't have a pass."

"How are we supposed to get through? Is there a guard?"

"There's no one."

"We can't just stop in the middle of the road, Henry."

Mom sounded like an animal in distress. Chris knew what she looked like when she made that sound—lines across her forehead and lips creasing a sharp line above her chin. Yu called it muppet lips.

Dad rolled the window down. Autumn snuck inside the car. Yu tapped Chris's leg.

What's happening? she signed.

We're lost.

She looked through the rear window and quickly spoke with her hands.

"Yu says we missed it," Chris said.

"Missed what?" Mom said.

"There was a guy back there."

It was eerie when his sister did that. She'd slept the entire way, impervious to the asphalt roller coaster. But somehow she saw a guy.

Mom took her seatbelt off. "Honey," she said, signing her words, "what did the guy—what're you doing? We can't back up."

"We can't turn around." Dad threw his arm across the seat. His glasses slid down his nose. Chris couldn't watch.

"How far do we have to—oh!" Mom snapped the seatbelt in place. "Ask your sister how far."

Chris half-opened his eyes. Yu's hands made soft sounds in thick cotton gloves. Chris didn't bother telling his dad what she said. He was already cruising. Mom dug into the vinyl seat like a cat. They coasted back a quarter mile. There was a guy.

"Could use a sign," his dad muttered. "Or a light or an arrow or a—"

"That's enough," Mom said.

The Visitors' Center was built into the side of a mountain. The windows were as black as swamp water. The car's reflection pulled into the empty lot. One of the headlights was out. The guy pointed at an empty parking slot. They were all empty.

The car died into silence. They sat quietly for a moment; then Dad climbed out. He unloaded two duffel bags from the trunk.

This is it? Yu signed.

Chris nodded.

Mom looked over the seat. Her smile was brave. "You ready?"

No. He wasn't. But when did that matter?

"Hello!" Mom turned on her happy voice reserved for strangers and phone calls. "We almost missed you."

Her laugh was shrill and embarrassing. She was nervous—she was always nervous—but this trip was an anxiety thrill ride. Her pills kept her from falling through what she called thin ice. When it cracked, there were dark days below. Sometimes weeks. Chris didn't want that to happen. Not now.

You getting out? Yu signed.

Chris didn't have the strength to pull the handle, even when Dad pointed. As dad-looks went, it wasn't scary. But it was serious. *We drove all this way.*

His sister crawled out. Chris was frozen. *Fear is like jumping into a spring-fed stream,* his grandma used to say. *Cold at first. Then fun.*

Sometimes, though, it was just cold.

"There he is." The guy held out his hand. "I'm Kogen. You're Chris." He looked at a clipboard. "Christmas White Blizzard. I don't think I've ever met someone named Christmas before."

"It's a family name," Mom said.

No. It wasn't. She lied when she was nervous. Exaggerations, she called it. Words came out to fill the empty spaces. Christmas was what you named your kid when you were a seventeen-year-old mom who gave birth on Christmas Day. Yuletide was what you named the twin sister.

"Let's go inside. A little brisk for September, yeah?" Kogen pretended to shiver, even though he was wearing a black jacket. The slacks were sharply pressed. Too thin for the weather. Maybe he was cold.

He held the glass door open. A small sculpture watched them from the corner. It was a fat man with a round face and small eyes. The arms were strangely short. It was carved from granite. The belly had been worn smooth for luck. Long locks of hair cascaded over the shoulders, the details finely chiseled.

It was staring at them.

Dad gave a duffel bag to Chris. His dad was tall and skinny, not made for cold. Chris was short, thick and doughy. Built to play offensive line. If he cared about sports. His face was long and his nose a skinny slope that turned pink in the cold.

Someone dressed like Kogen took the duffel bags—the thin black slacks and dark jacket. She threw them on a gold-plated cart, the kind at expensive hotels where tips were expected. Dad didn't reach into his pocket. She didn't seem to care.

Mom announced how warm it was inside. And how lovely the drive was. And how tall Kogen was. And good looking. He smelled good, too. Did he see them drive by? Was he hungry?

It was dim and open inside. Clean. And empty, really. Just a large circular platform behind Kogen and his beautiful teeth. The place felt expensive, like the minimalist décor at an art gallery. There were rooms around the perimeter, little glass library cubicles. A girl about his age was talking to a computer.

"Welcome." Kogen clapped his hands. "This is the Visitors' Center for the—"

"Did you hurt yourself?" Mom said.

"I'm sorry?"

"You look sore. I don't mean it that way, just—" she laughed nervously "—we can sit down if that's better for you."

Kogen stalled. His introduction was thrown off the tracks. Mom could do that. Her mouth was a shotgun loaded with words; her mind a hair trigger. Then he clapped his hip.

"This? No, no. It's fine. Skiing accident." He had a short hitch when he walked. "Gets a little stiff when the weather changes."

"Have you tried ice?"

Yu tugged Mom's sleeve. Dad put his arm around her and nodded. Kogen's introductory smile returned.

"This is the Visitors' Center for the Institute of Creative Mind. You, sir, are the recipient of prestigious acceptance. Congratulations."

Chris looked at his shoes. The rubber was peeling off the toes.

"We're so proud." Mom started again. How the letter came late, they were so excited, they were so sure he didn't get in when the deadline passed, but they still submitted the application because you never know.

Kogen kept eye contact with Chris. It was strange. Not that he was looking at him. It was just Chris was accustomed to his mom taking over conversations, like going to the doctor and her explaining how he felt and the doctor sort of forgetting he was there.

"What's your passion?" Kogen said.

"Cooking," Mom said. "He's a master chef. You should see how he—"

"Cooking? Well, well." He didn't consult the clipboard. "This school has a rich history of some of the most creative minds in the world. For over two hundred years, the Pelznickel family has selected only those with the most potential. You are one of them, Chris."

What family? Yu signed.

"The Pelznickel family." Kogen's sign language was fluid.

Mom covered her chest. "You know how to sign?"

"A little. This is your sister, yeah? Yule Logan Blizzard. Pleasure to meet you." He continued signing.

Yu was often left out of conversations. She was good at reading lips, but when people started talking loudly, it made her uncomfortable. She usually waited for Chris to fill her in.

"The institute is family owned. It was started in 1805 by Lord Kris Pelznickel."

"Did you hear that, hon?" Mom said. "A lord."

"Yes." Kogen chuckled. "He saw the intrinsic value of the creative process, how it is the very backbone of the arts and sciences, the fabric that creates the world around us. Graduates have won Nobel Prizes and Pulitzers. I can attest to the school's brilliance." His smile grew impossibly brighter.

"You went here?" Mom said. "Did you hear that, hon? Kogen went to school here, too."

"And there have been multiple failures," Dad said. "I mean, the dropout rate is, you know." He tipped his head back. "High."

Kogen was ready for it. He said to Chris, "We'll challenge you to discover your true nature." Then he turned his attention to his dad, his tone softer. "But failure is part of the creative process. That said, it is a tough curriculum. And not everyone makes it. You know what they say about omelets."

"You have to break the eggs," Mom said, too cheerfully.

Kogen was strangely comfortable and flawlessly hospitable. But Chris sensed discomfort beneath the veneer. Like old wood with a new coat of paint. He hobbled up three wide steps that led to the circular table. Warm light illuminated his approach.

"Whoa. You see that, hon?"

It was a model of inconceivable detail. Gravel paths crisscrossed a glittering white ground like snowflakes after a cold night. Figurines with painted shoelaces had bookbags as large as rucksacks. The buildings were castles made of chipped rocks with mortar pasted into the seams.

Kogen pointed out the dormitory where Chris would live, the halls where he would take classes, and the cafeteria where he would eat. Of course, there were classes in nutrition and organic gardening, all the tools an aspiring culinary artisan could want.

Each one of the buildings was unique in their blocky style, the walls varying slightly in tones of granite, sandstone and limestone. They were arranged around the tallest building—a castle with toothy steeples that, perhaps in mythology, would keep giants from stepping on them.

"It started there." Kogen saw Chris looking at the castle. "The family's home. They were wealthy, of course, but chose not to spend their lives in the solitude of comfort. They wanted to contribute. To educate. The path to human freedom is paved with other."

"Other?" Dad said.

"Creativity." Kogen smiled. "So they built this campus and for the past two hundred years have operated as one of the most esteemed schools in the world."

"Why is there a wall?" Dad said.

"Privacy, hon," Mom said, shaking her head. The parade was just beginning. Don't call for rain.

The wall, however, was daunting. Even in miniature scale. It looked hand-built, as if each stone had been laboriously lugged into place, and circled the campus, the light casting dark shadows around it.

"The family owns the mountain, Mr. Blizzard. The wall, however, remains from the early days when walls were necessary."

Given how many times he'd given this speech, the answer was lame. Chris could see the symbolism. It was dark outside. But on campus, the light of creativity was bright. But that wouldn't satisfy his dad. Kogen probably knew nothing would. The hard truth about walls was that they were built to keep things out. Or in.

"And it gets cold," Kogen said. "The wall helps break the wind. But you don't mind the cold."

He winked at Chris. Like he knew. He was right. Chris slept with his window cracked in December. His dad kept the house so warm that guests fell asleep. The air conditioner had broken three summers ago, and he refused to fix it. Fans were good enough.

What's wrong with her? Yu pointed.

The girl in the library cubicle had her face in her hands. Her shoulders were quaking. It was soundproof, but Chris imagined her sobbing sounded like wet hiccups.

"It's an adjustment for some." Kogen observed her with what seemed like real compassion. He turned to Chris. "You can write as many letters as you want. But once a month, you can come here to virtually visit your family if you choose to."

If I choose to?

Kogen didn't consult the clipboard. Like he knew Chris might not. Chris spent summers at his grandparents' farm, where he built forts in the trees and stacked stones in the streams. At night, he made supper, and in the morning he'd have breakfast ready with eggs taken from the chickens and greens from the garden.

He hadn't called his parents once during those visits.

"Of course, you'll come to visit." Kogen flashed polished whites at Mom and Dad. "Parents' Day is the week after Christmas. The Visitors' Center will be staged with all of the semester's accomplishments. You'll see how much your little genius has grown."

"Visitors' Center?" Dad said. "You mean here?"

"Hon, the campus is exclusive. But that's all right. Right, honey?" Mom rubbed Chris's shoulder. "You can send pictures."

"I'm sorry. He won't be able to take pictures. Our facilities are proprietary. It was all in the application guidelines. Did you read them?"

"Of course we did. Of course. I just meant, well, the…" Her words trailed off a cliff. She twisted her fingers into a nautical knot. "It'll be nice."

"Parents' Day is a celebration," Kogen said, then signed for Yu, "And there will be presents."

"Presents?" Mom beamed. "Did you hear that, hon? There'll be presents."

Yu deadpanned a nod. It sounded dreadful, coming here over break. Presents might work for a five-year-old. It wouldn't matter. The family cruiser wasn't making it up the mountain in winter.

"There's always presents," Kogen said. "So, questions?"

Of course not. All the questions had been answered in the detailed packets Mom had showed her friends. She just didn't think Chris wouldn't be able to take pictures. It sounded absurd.

"In that case, hand it over." Kogen put out his hand.

Chris knew the deal. It had been explicitly laid out in the guidelines. No electronics of any kind. He could write all the letters he wanted, but no texts. No pictures. *We value the mind uncluttered.*

Chris gave up his phone.

"It'll be stored in the Visitors' Center. Any other electronics? Laptops? Tablets?"

The bags were probably searched. Maybe Kogen was giving him a chance to lie.

"It was wonderful to meet you." Kogen extended his hand. Mom hugged him instead. He laughed, patting her back. Probably wasn't the first time a parent clung to him.

I don't like him, Yu signed quickly.

"I didn't catch that," Kogen said.

"Don't do that." Mom grabbed Yu's hands, her friendly façade crumbling. *Don't embarrass me.* "They just sometimes... never mind. It's very nice to meet you, Kogen."

He paused, thinking, then said, "We'll take good care of him, rest assured. I'm proof good things happen here. Take your time saying goodbye. I'll wait here."

A cubicle lit up on the opposite side of the room from the sobbing girl. Dad had a last few words with Kogen. He tried to sound stern, but he could never find the words or tone to pull it off. It was bad acting, but he tried. He always tried. They'd driven up a mountain in a car that struggled on flat road. No turning back now.

The cubicle smelled like cleaning supplies. There was a table with a monitor. One chair. Mom was shaking. Her hands felt like knobby sticks on his cheek.

"We're so proud of you." She meant it. She would tell everyone at church about him, insert it into conversations at the checkout aisle, post on social media. If there was a gift shop, she would buy one of every item. But she really meant it.

"Do us proud, son." Dad's hug was stiff. A quiver melted the crusty exterior he tried to maintain. A man who pretended he didn't cry at movies thumped his back. "Okay?"

"Okay."

Chris hadn't hugged Yu since they were eight years old when Mom wanted a Christmas picture of them in matching pajamas. Their haircuts were similar back then. Now his hair was long and Yu's head shaved. Who was going to eat all her cereal before she woke up? Who was going to fix his computer?

I know, he signed, answering what Yu had said earlier.

They left him in the cubicle. He was alone with a blank monitor. In that moment, he figured, yeah, he'd come back to call.

Kogen waited.

He had his back turned, in case Chris needed to dry his eyes. It was a kind gesture, but he didn't need to. Chris was nervous, yeah. No, he was scared. The kind of scared that accompanied the unknown, the stranger waiting at the end of a dark tunnel, the ice melt in his legs.

The model of campus was dark again. An electric golf cart was behind it. The seats were buffed to a slick shine. The grainy floorboards clean. A double set of doors opened at the back of the room like mandibles. A dank, musty breeze exhaled.

"Ready to grow?" Kogen said.

THE WALLS of the tunnel were rough-hewn and supported by cedar beams. It smelled like wet rock. The road stirred his stomach, transforming butterflies into seagulls.

They emerged in dappled sunlight. Autumn's leaves cascaded in a slow dance, carpeting the path and crunching beneath the tires. Birds watched from above, their feathers black and shiny like they'd been freshly oiled. The lane was as winding as the mountain road, hemmed in by massive tree trunks with an understory of ferns.

The forest ended abruptly. The pathway led down a steep slope toward a stone wall that grew twenty feet. The details were exactly the same as the model—the seams dirty between a patchwork of rounded stones.

"Intimidating, I know," Kogen said, the crisp breeze turning his cheeks a deeper shade. "Nothing prepares you for it, even the model. But this is our home. The wall provides us with the solitude to foster growth. It's a symbol of our connection, a circle with no beginning or end. But I think you knew that."

He winked again. It was supposed to reassure him. It needed work.

"You're going to love it here, Chris."

They were greeted, yet again, by slacks-wearing men and women. Mid-thirties, Chris guessed. Forties, maybe. Kogen could be fifty, even though he sounded like a fraternity president. Chris had no idea how old adults were.

He hadn't noticed the gate on the model, but it was exactly what he would've guessed. Something a child would draw. Big iron bars flaked with age. A blocky lock for a simple but heavy key.

"Are those ornaments?"

Big red ribbons with wide bows were attached to the gates. Silvery coils of garland wound through the bars, the ends gently dancing. Decorative orbs dangled. It was September.

Chris heard the key turn in the lock. The metal hinges swung with an unnerving squeal.

"Thank you, Pierre." Kogen turned to Chris. "This is it."

They left the cart with Pierre and company. Chris stood on newborn legs. Kogen grabbed his arm with a steady hand. At least he didn't wink.

The gates clanged behind them. The campus was relatively flat with subtle slopes. The hills rose in the distance, as if this place had been scooped from the mountain. The courtyard, or quad as Kogen called it, was laid out like a university campus with raked gravel paths.

People stretched on the manicured lawn. In the model, it was covered with snow, which was probably the case for most of the year. They looked to be about Chris's age, some slightly younger or older, and dressed in sweatshirts and denim, cargo shorts and T-shirts. Chris was relieved. He didn't recall uniforms but started to worry after seeing all the formal attire. He wasn't a slacks person.

Among the people stretching were giant reindeer and snowmen, elves holding boxy presents, nutcracker soldiers, and dogs with floppy red hats. There were Christmas decorations that swayed back and forth. Some were steady, made of metal or glass or stone. Others were inflated.

"You missed the hike," Kogen said.

Chris nodded. He had no idea what he was talking about, but he'd learned from his mom to just go with a conversation until you figured it out. Like Christmas ornaments in September.

"All newcomers take a trip in the first week. It's a ceremonial hike, a celebration of nature."

"Where?"

"Where?"

"Like, where to?" Chris wasn't a nature lover. He liked stainless steel countertops and gas ranges with removable griddle plates. Wandering through trees without a destination was pointless.

"It's a special mansion, not far from here. You'll see next year." Kogen punched his shoulder.

The gravel crunched firmly beneath their shoes. The sky was the color of the stone castles and just as heavy. They walked through the middle of the students, who were moving in slow motion like the inflatables. Chris could feel them looking at him. The new student who skipped the first month. And the hike. None of them were physically imposing.

But sharp tongues hurt worse than biceps.

THE DORM WAS TWO STORIES, the walls a patchwork of granite squares and rectangles with white seams. Gold strands of garland hung over windows. The steps were bullnose bluestone, depressions worn where footsteps had eroded the surfaces. A keystone arch framed the entrance.

The door was made of heavy planks stained by time and preservatives. A grapevine wreath stuffed with holly leaves and clusters of red berries was hooked to the center of the door. Kogen held it open. The building heaved a breath of warm air. The interior, however, was modern—walls of painted sheetrock and ornate shoe molding. They were white with a fresh coat and the beginnings of graffiti done with marker and acrylics.

An announcement board was mounted inside the entrance. It was outlined with red and white borders and intricate three-dimensional snowflakes. Pinholes dotted the corkboard, a row of thumbtacks lining the bottom. A banner was posted at the top.

Welcome Gifters!

There was a checklist of hiking supplies. *Don't forget,* the announcement read. A photo of a strange mansion was at the bottom. The porch slanted, strings of old-fashioned Christmas lights hung from the eave. Large colorful bulbs dulled with dust.

"Is that it?" Chris said.

"Yes. The place was owned by an eccentric entrepreneur, once upon a time. The family rarely visits."

"The Pelznickel family?"

"No."

"Isn't that trespassing?"

"Trespassing? Why would it be trespassing?"

"I mean, it sounds like someone else owns it."

"It's a walk in the woods, Chris."

Kogen's hard-soled shoes clapped the pinewood treads of the stairwell. The bannister was slick cherry with thin ribbons of red and green. Shiny bows were randomly stuck to the walls like colorful stars. Kogen's strides echoed unevenly. The skiing hip was stiffer.

The second floor was the same as the first—white walls with outlines of murals between decorated doors, as if creativity was germinating.

"Here it is."

Chris's duffel bags were nestled on a bare mattress next to a square stack of neatly folded linens. The walls smelled of fresh paint and cleaning supplies. A long desk was at the window. The glass old and wavy from a time when it was blown the old-fashioned way, the view of the quad slightly warped and rippled and obscured by an empty wreath attached to the outside.

"Everything you need, supplies, stationery for letters, notebooks." Kogen dropped his hand on a three-foot-tall stack of hardbound textbooks. "Don't highlight or write in the margins. We like to keep these fresh. A list of rules is here." He tapped a sheet of paper. "Your assignments here. You're a little behind."

He smiled. Winked.

The students in the quad had finished their exercise. Chris watched them through the wreath as they walked in small clusters. He could hear laughter. He'd never belonged to a group. He had friends, but not really. He walked to school alone, walked home alone. Never went to a football game or pep rally or chess club after school. Some days he never talked to anyone. He just didn't know what to say.

"This is a big change." Kogen put a light hand on his shoulder. "And change is frightening. I know. You're young. You don't know who you are or where you fit in. But we're going to find out who you are."

Kogen smelled like mint. He smiled again. A little too intense.

"There's something in your teeth," Chris said.

Kogen didn't break eye contact or pick the little flake from between his teeth. He lifted his hand. A round wristwatch was ticking.

"Supper's in Bixen Hall. There's a map." He pointed. "Read the rules."

He left the door open. Chris stared through the window. A bruise moved across the sky. The muted colors of shadowless figures walked the pale gravel paths. There were voices in the hall.

He closed the door.

The assignment list was long. Deadlines underlined in red. He slid the first book off the pile. The binding glue crackled. He sat down to do what he did best. At some point, the quad was busy again, people making their way toward Bixen Hall, wearing sweatshirts and jackets in their little groups. Laughter found its way into his room. When it grew quiet, he reached for another book.

When the quad was lit only by the Christmas sculptures, he saw one person going into the tall, pointy castle, bundled in a heavy coat. Just before entering, the person put on a stocking cap. It wasn't that cold outside. But that wasn't the weird part.

They were bundling up to go inside the castle.

SCRAPS OF TINFOIL littered the desk.

Mom had tucked snacks into his luggage. Homemade granola bars, chocolate chip cookies, and sticks of celery. He rooted through the side pockets and found a baggie of carrots.

A subtle glow of orange bled into the sky. A few lights were on across the quad, vague silhouettes moving behind thin curtains. There was no way to know the time without his phone. There were no clocks. There was a bed, dresser and homework.

His fingers were stiff.

He'd filled an entire notepad. The mountain of reading had been chiseled down to one textbook. *The Creative Flow.* Two chapters had been assigned. A short essay was due. His nerves were firing as his body burned the last dregs of sugar. He reached for his phone, wondering if there was enough time to run over to Bixen Hall in search of coffee. Wondering if they had coffee. Wondering if they were open or if he could even find the building.

But he didn't have a phone.

He cracked the book and started in, following the words with his finger as they swelled in delirium. His notes trailed off the lines into scribble. He didn't know if he could make it without caffeine. He rubbed his eyes.

Someone had underlined a letter.

It was a faint line under the first letter of a paragraph. There was another one near the bottom of the page and another one a few pages later. He jotted them down and flipped through the chapters. They were hard to catch. No one would see them with a cursory glance.

They ended two-thirds through the book. The last letter was in a chapter on *The Art and Craft of Christmas Pastries.* He looked at his notes.

UNRUAFASASUCN.

He had never finished a crossword puzzle in his life. This was someone who was in the room before him and flunked out. Although who would flunk out in one month? *Someone who saw the stack of books and decided to underline letters.*

He was jittery, his head pulsing. Yellow light suddenly splashed across the quad. It shrank into darkness. Four or five people walked toward the castle, dark lumps cutting across the lawn. The yellow light sliced through the dark when the door opened. They were wearing puffy coats and wool hats.

He put his hand on the glass. It wasn't that cold. His heart began thudding. He closed the textbook and hid the word scramble. He needed to erase the lines in the textbook before Kogen thought he did it.

"Relax," he whispered.

His clothes were piled on the mattress after the food raid. He found a towel and Ziploc of bathroom necessities—toothbrush, toothpaste, and soap—and threw the rest of it into the dresser. The hallway was quiet. Someone was snoring.

The bathroom was empty. A dozen porcelain sinks were against one wall. There were shower stalls with plastic curtains rather than one giant sprinkler with multiple showerheads. He took a cold shower to wash the sleepy dregs off. He brushed his teeth and pushed his hair back. His reflection looked back with roadmaps in different-colored eyes. One green, one blue.

Christmas colors, Mom would sometimes say to explain his name. Yu's eyes were blue. But they were twins, so Yu was Christmas by association. Most people didn't tell her blue and green weren't Christmas colors. Most.

"Okay." His whispers echoed off the tile. "You can do this. It's a marathon."

His bare feet were clammy against the floor. The snoring was louder. It was joined by a voice in the room next to his. Yu would sleep-talk when she ate too much sugar. The floor, mercifully, did not creak outside the door. Chris heard a deep voice, the kind incapable of whispering. He couldn't make out the words. But someone was taking long pauses. No one was answering.

He's got a phone!

Chris was talking to his own reflection, but this was a conversation. Someone was talking *and* listening. The voice rose an octave.

"You said that last time... *look what happened.*"

Chris leaned closer. His ear was almost against the door. The conversation was heating up when Chris felt a strange wave of pressure pass through his forehead. He nearly bumped into the door.

It opened.

The boy was slightly shorter than Chris. A chubby roll of neck meat pinched his T-shirt's white collar. His hair was coarse, black and pushed to the side. He wore cargo pants, with his hand clenched at his side.

"S-s-sorry. I, uh, thought I heard something..." Chris looked over the kid's shoulder. The room was dark and messy. "Do you have aspirin?"

The boy stared with big brown eyes with dark rings beneath them. Chris really wanted aspirin. And he'd just got caught standing with his ear against the door. The kid put something in his pocket. Then closed the door.

That was weird. The whole thing was. Standing in the hall, staring. Whatever he'd put in his pocket was too small to be a phone.

"Just relax."

2

"Missed you at supper."

Chris shot up. A paper was stuck to his face. He was asleep at his desk. The page dislodged from his forehead. Daylight filled the room. Several people mingled in the quad.

Kogen was next to him. "How was your first night?"

Chris rubbed his face. It felt like a rubber mask.

"Looks like you got some work done."

Kogen looked at the page that had been stuck to Chris's head. The underlined letters were across the top. And the textbook was open. Kogen didn't notice, looking at the mess of wrappers and a half-eaten baby carrot.

"It's time to exercise," Kogen said. "Everyone is due in the quad at seven thirty. Got to stay in shape. Can't sit all day. Your body is your mind."

"I, uh, I don't have a watch."

A veneer of forced patience hardened the corners of Kogen's mouth. He shuffled the papers and found a list under a collection of crumpled plastic wrap. He brushed off the crumbs.

"Did you read the rules?"

"Yeah, no, I looked them over, but"—he cleared his throat—"I didn't make it past the assignments. So behind, you know."

"The first assignment is the rules, Chris." He tapped the sheet. "If you read them, you'd know there is a watch."

He opened a desk drawer. The round face of a wristwatch was inside. The thin needle ticked off the seconds toward seven thirty. He placed it on the desk like a jeweler displaying his finest diamond.

"Yeah, um." Chris looked up. "It's just, you know, I didn't sleep much, and it looks like the, uh..." He found his class schedule on stark white paper. "My first class is at nine, and there's no break, so maybe, you know, can I skip this morning?"

Kogen stood taller. He took the class schedule like it was the first time he was seeing it. He handed it back.

"I understand."

He reached inside his jacket and produced a red card. It was the size of a poker card, stiff and plastic. It was as red as the queen of hearts. No queen or king printed on either side, though. Just red.

"Don't be late for class."

Kogen left the door open, his uneven footsteps receding. Chris closed it and went back to his desk. He was awake now.

A SYNTHESIZED BEAT COURSED through his body. It had an energized sweetness to it and enveloped him, carrying him in a throbbing flow of darkness. It was hard on his back.

He pried his eyes open.

It took a moment to recognize the wall across from him: a collage of black musical notes swimming in a colorful current where silhouettes of graceful dancers played. The music was coming through a metal door.

He climbed off the pinewood with dead legs, lugged his backpack onto his shoulder. He'd gotten to his last class at 2:45. It was 3:15. He'd just closed his eyes for a second.

The rhythm pulsed through the doorknob, his hand suddenly

wet with perspiration. He held it there, felt the music ride up his arm, considering his options. Music escaped into the quiet hallway. He peeked in then clumsily tried to slide in sideways, the hefty backpack catching the doorjamb.

Everyone noticed.

They were sitting on the floor. They didn't have to turn their heads. The opposite wall was a mirror. His reflection was attempting to sneak inside. Chris stood still, as if his gray sweatshirt might blend into the door. A tsunami of heat prickles flooded his back. Beads of sweat wet his lip.

A boy was dancing.

He was the size of a high school defensive lineman, but like a real football player. Not soft like Chris. His pink shirt exposed his stomach as he raised his arms. His footsteps were light on the bamboo floor. He spun on one foot, twice, then bowed on one knee. There was no applause. He stood up, hands at his sides. His eyes found Chris, who quickly looked at the floor.

"Ms. Jansen." The teacher, Ms. Taiga, a bent flagpole dressed in black tights, looked at a girl sitting in front. "Critique Mr. Chetty's performance, please."

The girl's response was sharp and speedy. "Mr. Chetty was fluid through the intro, but his movements were jerky when the chorus changed rhythm. The transitions were awkward, but he recovered with impressive balance, and at one point during the climax, he seemed completely absent."

Ms. Taiga listened without response, standing in the corner next to a Christmas tree smothered in tinsel. A tight smile pierced a deep valley of wrinkles. Her back was slightly stooped. If he were a Boy Scout, he would help her cross the street. She looked like she would shatter both hips if she tried to run. But her eyes could weld sheet metal. Her voice would scare monsters.

She offered a single nod when the girl finished. Then she focused her laser beams across the room. A fresh sheen of sweat broke across Chris's forehead.

"Mr. Blizzard, you are late." She held out a card. The students began to whisper. Chris waited, then realized it was for him. It was red. "Put your bag over there and have a seat."

Chris took the card and tossed his backpack in the corner. He sat cross-legged next to a girl with tight curly hair, cinnamon brown like her skin, with the tips dyed Kool-Aid red, wearing baggy pants and a white tank top.

"Ms. Bykov," Ms. Taiga said.

A waifish girl sprang from the floor, wearing a lime green leotard and soft-toed shoes, her hair coiled on the back of her head. She took Mr. Chetty's position in front of the mirror. Sweat tracked Chris's ribs. Ms. Taiga's look was turning him into a puddle of saltwater.

Mercifully, she went to a radio. All attention was sucked into the vortex of Ms. Bykov's performance. Chris tried not to slouch. He was panting like a cornered rabbit. The girl next to him was picking chips of putty from the edges of her fingernails. Black lines swirled around her brown forearm in an intricate pattern that covered her shoulder with prickly foliage and round berries. The lines were blurry and smudged from a Sharpie.

Ms. Bykov's dance ended with a student critique. It was followed by ten more performances that ranged from mediocre to expert. The critiques were insightful. Chris memorized their words and prepared a loosely assembled response that wasn't obvious plagiarism. He snuck peeks at his watch when the teacher wasn't looking.

"Mr. Tanaka, critique Ms. Taylor's performance, please."

"It was good."

"Good?" She nodded sharply. Waiting.

"I mean, she was fluid and her transitions were smooth, and the, uh, climax part had a lot of, you know, emotion." He was doing the same thing Chris was planning to do, but his brain had turned to sludge under Ms. Taiga's glare. "It was really, really good."

"Two whole reallys, Mr. Tanaka?"

Chris glanced at his watch. He closed his eyes and held his breath as she boiled Mr. Tanaka into overcooked noodles.

"Mr. Souza, take the floor, please."

Chris exhaled. Sweat stung the corners of his eyes. This was the last one.

The boy was knobby-kneed and lanky; he danced like a marionette doing his best to bring a puppet to life. Chris crafted a complete and smart critique as the boy tapped out his finale like a sprinter running in place. No applause. No groans. Just silence as Ms. Taiga's crosshairs glassed expectant faces. Chris felt the thousand-watt spotlight sweep over him.

"Ms. Oliveira, critique Mr. Souza, please."

Yes.

The red-tipped girl next to him lifted her chin. There was a long pause that stretched the tension. For a moment, he thought she had nothing. And then she spilled the best one yet. It wasn't a regurgitated mishmash or memorized from a textbook. It was poignant, insightful. She propped Mr. Souza up with heartfelt admiration and cut with stinging accuracy. The teacher didn't seem impressed, holding her craggy mask intact. But she nodded more deeply when Ms. Oliveira finished.

The students shuffled. They were sneaking looks at their wrists. Appetites were on the prowl, and the instinct to escape the glare grew taut. The bell sounded like a hammer striking a church bell.

"Class!" Ms. Taiga raised her hands.

Everyone was on their feet. They were as confused as they were hungry. Slowly the room settled back on the floor. A cold premonition reached for Chris.

"Mr. Blizzard?"

The people nearest him turned. The rest of the class stared at his reflection. Chris's legs were numb from sitting cross-legged. Now they were petrified. He had been hoping for something else. A public scolding, perhaps. Run a marathon in flip-flops.

"Take the floor, please."

"I, uh." He cleared his throat. "I just got here." If someone wasn't looking at him before, they were now. "I mean, today is my first day."

"Clearly. Take the floor, please."

"I don't know the assignment."

She offered an icy smile. "Isn't it obvious?"

Chris felt his eyes balloon in their sockets. He wasn't a crier. If he were, now would be the time. Something sharp poked his knee. The girl next to him jabbed him with her fingernail. It released the bone-frozen lock in his legs. Then she nodded. Just a nod. That was it.

It thawed him just enough.

He put the red card in his front pocket and saw his reflection rise. Dark patches circled his armpits. His shirt stuck to his back. His boots were clunky, but he was afraid to take them off. It could only get worse. He tried not to look at his reflection.

There was something about standing in front of a crowd that blew a flame into a forest fire. Now that he was up there, the room had become a pottery kiln. Paralysis locked him in place. Carbonated bubbles fluttered through his chest, into his head. He closed his eyes.

The music started.

It was one thing to formulate a critique. That was just words. Thoughts. And thoughts were safe. This was different. He had never danced. Not even in his room alone. He didn't feel comfortable in his body. Like it didn't fit. Like it was allergic to expression.

But this was why he was here. At this school. To do this. Not just the things he was good at. And he didn't know any of these people. So.

It started in his knees.

The tendons creaked in time with the bass. A slight bend at first. Up and down. Up and down. His head joined in. Boom. Boom. Boom. It loosened him up, not enough to move his feet, but enough to feel the rhythm. Up and down.

Listen. With each bounce, he repeated the thought. *Listen. Listen. Listen.*

Behind closed eyes, he felt the music wrap around him. It didn't feel like it was out there, coming through a speaker, bouncing around a room. It found its way inside him. That was how the others were doing it. They weren't dancing to it. The music possessed them. The flow took them. Their bodies were the expression. His mantra began to shift.

Listen. Listen. Listen. Feel. Feel. Feel.

He heard his boot clop on the hardwood. It went out to the side and back. God, he felt so stupid, but he did it again. Out to the side and back. Then the other foot.

Feel. Feel. Feel. Be. Be. Be.

And then he turned in a circle. It felt like stepping off a cliff. Eyes closed, he turned around. Then lifted his hands like he was conducting a symphony. Sweat cascaded down his stomach. His shirt was a damp rag. But once he took the turn, he didn't fall into oblivion. He heard someone snort, but it didn't stop him. The laughter was cleansed in the music's current.

He forgot where he was. Just in the dark, by himself, alone with what he was feeling. A trace of freedom cut the outside world away. He didn't dare open his eyes. He stayed in the flow and was moving now, turning wider circles, arms doing strange things like an airport worker with glowing lights. The clopping of his boots synchronized with the beat. It was just him and the music, a thin barrier separating them. He wanted to be it, the celebration, to forget who he was.

And then came the bright light.

It was followed by dull pain across his face. His head jerked back from the mirror. The heel of his boot caught the floor. He landed on someone's lap. A girl with black lipstick shoved him off.

"Ugh, he's wet."

He was staring at a swirling pattern on the ceiling. The music stopped. His heart continued the beat.

"Sorry," he said.

Quiet resumed when Ms. Taiga shuffled onto the floor. Her scanning look settled the laughter. Chris stood up, pulling his shirt down. The room felt so small.

"Mr. Claibourn, critique Mr. Blizzard, please."

The boy in the front leaned back, his eyelids heavy. "Terrible."

"Terrible?"

"No rhythm, not even close. He just jumped around and swung his arms. His finale was running into the wall."

Laughter scurried through the room.

"It was an ode to a scared bunny."

Laughter bravely reared its head. The teacher didn't stop it. They started muttering to each other, adding their own interpretations of the scared bunny. Ms. Taiga looked at Chris.

"Were you scared, Mr. Blizzard?"

He nodded.

"What did it feel like?"

"What?"

"The fear. What did it feel like?"

"Um." He cleared his throat. Shook his head. He didn't understand.

"Close your eyes again. Tell us what you felt."

Chris was glad to close his eyes. He recalled it from the very beginning, from the moment she called his name.

"Well, I was afraid everyone would laugh."

"Those are thoughts, Mr. Blizzard. Describe the bodily sensations. Don't label it. Just tell us your physical experience."

He took another deep breath. He described the flutter in his chest. The walnut in his throat. The cold water in his thighs. How his skin tightened like plastic wrap. The quiver of his bones.

There was silence. The teacher was nodding when he opened his eyes.

"Why are we here, Mr. Claibourn?"

"Uh, to dance."

"To dance," she said flatly, pacing with short, tentative steps. "We are here to express ourselves. Completely. Whatever it takes, whatever stands in our way, we aim to be present. Art is work."

She held up a crooked finger.

"To work, we have to fail. If we are not willing to fail, we will never create. That first step, for some of you, will be terrifying. It takes courage. Absolute daunting courage. Your critique, Mr. Claibourn, missed the point entirely."

She tugged the red card out of Chris's front pocket.

"Class dismissed."

His classmates got up quietly and retrieved their bags. They would wait till they were out of the building to talk about him. The room emptied out. The teacher held Chris's attention, then took the red card back to the radio.

"Don't be late again, Mr. Blizzard."

Brown and reddish foliage had collected on the steps. A crisp breeze chilled his damp T-shirt. He felt weak, post-catastrophe adrenaline dump still coursing through him. Like he'd narrowly outrun a mountain lion.

"So you're a culinary artist?"

The girl with red-tipped hair and baggy cargo pants watched students gather on the quad and begin to stretch.

"And you're a dancer," he said.

She snorted. "No."

"You sound like one."

"My dance wasn't much better than yours."

"Did you run into the mirror?"

She snorted again. "I think that saved you. Never seen Ms. Taiga pull a red card back."

"Yeah. What, uh, what are those? The cards."

Her mouth fell open. One of her bottom teeth sat crooked in an otherwise straight row. "Serious?"

He reached into his back pocket. The card Kogen gave him that morning was slick. He'd sweated through his pants. She frowned. Chris explained.

"A slacker gave you that?" she said.

"Slacker?"

She pointed. One of Kogen's wardrobe clones was leading the quad in the slow-moving exercise. He wore a V-neck sweater and a collared white shirt with creased slacks.

"Do we have to..." He nodded at the group.

"Do tai chi?" She shrugged. "If you want. I'd rather drink coffee."

It was a small group compared to the one that morning. Kogen wasn't out there.

"There's coffee?" he said.

"Yeah. You could use some."

She walked with her bag over one shoulder. It was half the bulk as the one weighing him down. His shoulders were sore. But then she didn't have to catch up on a month of assignments.

Her dorm was next to his, identical in size and color with twice as many Christmas decorations. Inside, the doors were open. There were mostly girls inside the rooms. A few of them he recognized from dance class. One of them said she liked his dance. He wasn't sure if it was ironic, but she didn't laugh. He didn't say thanks.

Her room looked ransacked. Clothes were on the floor and bed. The walls were covered with three-dimensional cutouts like paper nightmares. Quite the opposite of the festive decorations on campus. Beaded fishing lines hung from the ceiling, sunlight reflecting off the colored orbs like it was raining jewels.

She unpacked her bag on a desk with mounds of clay shaped into unfinished mythical creatures, some stabbed with paintbrushes and pencils. A coffee machine was in the corner. The red light was on.

"Don't close the door," she said.

His hand was on the knob. "Sorry, sorry. I just, I thought—"

"No closed doors if someone's in your room. That's a red card."

"Yeah, no. Right. I thought you meant... never mind. What do the red cards mean?"

She turned holding a book. "You haven't read the rules?"

"Yeah, yeah. Sort of."

"Sort of? Dude, three cards in a semester and you go home. Like, forever."

"Oh. Really?"

"What did you think they were?"

He was too embarrassed to tell her he thought it was like soccer or something. A red card meant he didn't get to play the game. Not kicked out of the sport for life.

He scanned her desk for a list of rules. A notebook was covered in viney doodles like the ones on her arm and shoulder.

Joli Oliveira was in big bubble letters.

"I'm Chris."

"I know."

"How did you know I cook?"

"This is a small town. Everyone knows everything. Peek your head out there. You'll hear them. Probably talking about your dance." She shrugged. "But who cares, you know? Help yourself."

The coffee pot was filled with steaming tar. Worse, it was hazelnut. She either forgot to turn it off or brewed espresso in bulk. He sloshed it around. Coffee grounds stuck to the glass.

"I'll make another."

"Coffee snob?"

"No, I just didn't want to take all... this."

There was a kitchenette down the hall. He washed it with soap and water, scrubbing the stains off the rim. The coffee grinder was out when he returned, a bag of beans next to it. She was searching through a pile of shirts. He sniffed the beans. He would drink broccoli if it had caffeine.

"Where'd you get this?" he said.

"The Tree."

"Tree?"

"Sorry. The *Christmas Tree.*" She rolled her eyes.

He'd seen a dozen Christmas trees that morning. None of them had presents. "Which one?"

"Which what?"

"Which Christmas tree? I mean, they're, like... everywhere."

At first, she looked angry, wrinkles folding between her eyes. "Oh my God."

"What?"

"He really did throw you to the wolves."

"Who?"

"You're so innocent." She looked adoringly at him. "And weird."

He stepped back. "What're you talking about?"

"What did Kogen tell you? Because he's your guide. Your *advisor*." She rolled her eyes again. "Did he just open your bedroom door and wish you good luck?"

"Sort of." *After I pointed out the green stuff in his teeth.*

"Did he even show you the rules?"

"Well, technically—"

"He should've told you about the Tree. At the very least. It's the best thing about this place. We get monthly credits, buy whatever we want. Money from mommy won't get you anything. Keeps the richies from hoarding everything." She smelled a sweatshirt. "Socialism at its finest. Except for the king."

He waited. "Who?"

She mouthed a word. He shook his head. "The guy who owns this, that, you, me. Everything inside the circle."

"Is he, uh, the guy who lives in the castle?"

"Yeah. Kings live in castles."

"I thought he was a lord?"

"Whatever."

He ground the beans and looked inside the reservoir, thinking he should've taken that down to the kitchenette to powerwash. It would still produce caffeine. He poured the water.

"You know, I saw a bunch of the, uh, the slackers going in the castle."

"Uh-huh."

"What do they do?"

"Watch us." She searched her dresser. The drawers were empty except for socks. Everything else was on the floor. "That's what they call themselves. Watchers. We all have one. Kogen is yours, and he's card happy. Can't believe he redded you after you stayed up all night."

"How did you know I stayed up?"

"You look like a corpse."

The coffee began dripping. He wiped the lip of a mug with a clean-looking shirt. The one he was wearing was damp. She didn't seem to care.

"They all went to school here," she said.

"Who?"

"The slackers."

"All of them?"

"Yup. School then work. Like a religious cult following the gospel of Pelz the Great. They didn't used to. Like, twenty years ago they went out and spread their genius. Ever hear of Andrew Miniski?"

"Didn't he—"

"Win a Nobel? Yup. And Greneda Popavich. Loretta Kingowicz made the—"

"The famous mural at the national capital. She went here, too?"

"They all did. But now they just stay here. I won't. Promise you that."

"How do you know that?"

"Didn't you research this place before Mom and Dad dropped you off?" She tied a paisley blue handkerchief around her head. It was smudged with paint. "This is a controlled environment, Christopher."

Christopher. She didn't know everything.

"This is the ultimate dichotomy. Be creative and free. But follow the rules or go home. Be who you are but not totally or go home. There's a brainwashing room in Glitzen Hall that makes you want to iron dress slacks."

"There is?"

"No. But maybe. Who knows." She shrugged. "I plan to red card my last semester before they dress me up." She bent her pinkie. "Promise you."

He watched the last drips send black ripples across the coffee pot. He poured a cup into a mug that someone had molded into a snarling face. The coffee was bitter and hot. The artificial flavoring made him cringe. But the caffeine instantly engaged a higher gear.

"They were wearing coats and stuff." He watched her sort another pile of clothes. "When they were going into the castle. You know, like hats and mittens and stuff. Like it was winter inside."

"Pelz likes it cold. Why do you think we pretend it's Christmas?"

"About that."

She shook her head. "Serious? You really didn't do any research?"

"I mean... my mom did."

Chris had glanced at the literature. It was a long shot to get in. And when the deadline passed, he forgot about it. Then everything had happened so fast.

"Okay. Well, it's Christmas here all the time. I mean, Christmas-Christmas, at the end of the year, is a really big deal. But the other eleven months is still a bang. Why do you think the gift shop is called the Christmas Tree? Right. You don't know."

She dropped clothes like a child tossing a forgotten toy, then changed the paisley handkerchief for a red one, fixing it in the window's reflection, tugging on the tight red-frosted curls.

"You've been inside the castle?" he said.

"No. No, no, no, no, no. That's like a prince or princess thing. Pelz finds the ones he likes and lets them kiss the ring. I'm curious, though." She held a wad of paint-splattered sweatshirts. "Like death, you know. What's beyond the door?"

"Heaven or hell."

A serious look took her. "Yeah, but no one knows, do they. Until you go. It's all guesses till then."

"You don't believe in God?"

"Like Ms. Taiga says, this moment is all there is."

She emptied a strange-looking mug of markers and filled it with coffee. She smelled it. "Oh yeah. You are a cook."

"I cleaned the pot."

She spilled the sip. It stained her white tank top. She dropped a cuss word and wiped it with a sock. He sat on the bed, where the fitted sheet had exposed the mattress. His dull headache was replaced with a warm buzzy surge. Still, if he laid his head down, he would be asleep.

She observed him over her mug. "You Swedish?"

"How'd you know?"

"Pale skin. Doughy, no offense. Built for cold. Shouldn't you be taller?"

"They make them short, too."

"Yeah, well, I took one of those DNA tests. I'm 43% Brazilian. 20%

Irish, 10% Swedish and something. And 0.1% *unknown*." She sipped and sighed. "Mom thinks it's alien. She watches a lot of TV. Thinks humans were seeded. She also thinks the world might be flat."

Chris's great-grandfather was from Sweden. Had immigrated when he was two years old. Chris had taken one of those tests a month ago. His mom had ordered the kits. The whole family had to spit in a tube and mail it back. His and his sister's DNA were close. They weren't identical, obviously.

"You took a test, didn't you?" she said.

"How'd you know?"

"We all took one."

"What's that mean?"

"I'll bet you got a small bit of unknown in you, too, don't you?"

He didn't know. He didn't really look at it. His mom had told him about the Swedish part. He didn't so much care about that either.

"But that stuff's private," he said. "They can't just know. You know?"

"You're cute. The Pelz family has been around foooorever. You think they can't buy a database? Please. Listen, I don't really care. This place is free. Food and room and all the art supplies I want." She kneaded the clay lump on the desk. "Fair trade, as far as I'm concerned."

She scooped a bundle of clothes into a towel.

"So now I'm going to shower, and you're going to leave. Take the mug with you. Later this week you bring it back with some of your gourmet coffee."

"I don't have a, uh…"

"Shhh-sh-sh-sh. This is the circle, Christopher. Anything is possible."

He smiled. Maybe for the first time in weeks. By the time he got to the door, he was laughing. It had been months since he'd done that.

3

"Think of the circle as a pie," Joli said. "There are four slices. We stay in the east slice. This is the north slice. And that"—she pointed behind them where the castle loomed—"is the big fat cherry."

Chris recalled the model in the Visitors' Center and the equidistant sidewalks that divvied it into quarters. Kogen hadn't said anything about it. Joli's analogy was much better than equidistant pieces.

There was clanging in the distance. It was slow and methodic. The sound of metal meeting metal. The temperature had dropped several degrees over the two weeks since he'd arrived. Chris was still sleep-deprived but had learned to catch naps in between classes without being late. Everyone was wearing coats now, even during class. Some of the buildings were colder than outside. Chris still wore a T-shirt.

"So you have a sister, then?" she said.

"Yu."

"Yu? Like Yoo-hoo?"

"Like Yuletide."

"You have a sister named Yuletide?"

He turned away and smiled. "We were born on Christmas, so my mom, you know…"

"Twins. Okay." She hooked her thumbs under her backpack straps. He could hear her feeding the gossip machine. "So what's it like?"

"To have a twin?" He'd heard that question a thousand times.

"No, I mean sibling."

"Oh. Well, I mean, I don't know. Okay, I guess. It's not like we share clothes or anything. She's like any other sister, I guess, just five minutes younger."

The clanging grew louder. They took a gravel path that went in front of Lasher Hall.

Joli picked a three-leaf clover and chewed on the stem. "What happened to her hearing?"

"So you knew?"

"Well, I knew you had a deaf sister, but I didn't know her name." He stared. She minced the green stem and spit. "Okay, yeah. I knew it was Yu. Not Yuletide, though." She pointed with the clover. "I swear. It's better, you know, to have a conversation."

"Even if you already know the answers."

"So what happened to her? I swear I don't know this part."

They rounded Lasher Hall. Someone was wearing a thick apron and swinging a mallet on an anvil. Black goggles were pushed on her forehead and fanned her hair like a peacock.

"She got sick before she was a year old. A rare disease."

"What was it?"

He shook his head. He always felt a little guilty he didn't know. Like he didn't care. That wasn't it. It just didn't matter what did it. He could feel the noise with each swing. It tickled his eardrums. Yu could feel sounds. She noticed some things better than he did.

The clanging stopped. She took her work clamped at the end of long tongs through a wide opening. Trupid Hall was posted over it, the letters ornately cut from black sheet metal. There were glass ornaments hanging from mounts on the building, swinging on thin wire, and iron stakes out front with elaborately welded work.

He could hear distant chimes.

"So can you teach me sign language?" Joli said.

"What do you want to say?"

"How about bring me coffee?"

He chuckled. She was good at that. He made two fists, put one on top of the other, and ground them in a circular motion.

They ventured off the gravel path between glassy orbs displayed on iron rods. Some were stretched like solid flames, others dripping with colors. They walked through a field of curling glass dyed pink, yellow, blue, red, and violet, like a prairie. The clanging started again, but the chimes had grown louder.

A titan tree was ahead.

It was a giant among trees. Almost as tall as the castle. A Norway spruce, he knew from botany, with enormous pendulous branches that swayed gently in the cool breeze, each one singing with silver chimes. Glass orbs from Trupid Hall dangled like miniature planets, reflecting tiny points of light. And all the way at the top, shining with its own light source, was a three-dimensional star of multiple sharp points.

The Tree.

It serenaded their approach. He hardly noticed the squat building tucked beneath its raised limbs, hidden in the shadowy bed of needles. It looked like a mound of boulders from a dump truck. Round portal windows were set deep in the sides, and a thatch of tarred straw thickly padded the roof.

Someone came out with a gift. It was wrapped in glossy green paper and a wide red ribbon. The door was made from thick slabs of gray cypress, the grain stained with black sealant. Joli pulled the iron ring, and a little bell rang. A vapor cloud of spices escaped. It was cloves and cinnamon, a hint of hot chocolate and burning wood.

"This is it," she whispered.

He could feel the chimes singing above them. Inside, the soulful sound of a violin played a familiar song. It took a moment to recognize. *Chestnuts roasting on an open fire...*

The cobblestone floor was uneven where the Norway spruce had uprooted them. Its massive trunk anchored the center of the circular hut and rose through the thatched roof. Flakes of bark were streaked with gray sap. Christmas ornaments hung from the ceiling. Reindeer weaved from twigs, snowflakes of beaded glass, clay stars cooked in a kiln, and holly branches heavy with red berries.

"Over here."

Joli walked along the wall. Shelves made from rough-cut wood were anchored into the stone. They were deep and loaded with a strange collection of radio clocks and remote-control cars, jars of cat's-eyes marbles, folds of silken fabrics, boxes of googly eyes, a mini telescope on a sprawled tripod, clay pots of succulents, whistles on braided string. An ice-cream machine.

There was no organization, like a pawnshop stocking the shelves with whatever came through the door. Original coffee mugs were next to a netted bag of jacks. A Ziploc of loose tea leaves was on top of a box of yo-yos. Chris pulled a coffee cup off the jacks. It looked like the ones in her room. It was stout with a bulbous nose and buck teeth with bulging eyes. The cherub cheeks were round. A white tag dangled from the misshaped handle.

5c.

"That's mine." Joli was still whispering. It felt like church.

"You want it?" he said.

"No, I mean I made it. That." She stuck out her teeth. "Not bad, yeah?"

"What's 5c?"

"Five credits. You get a hundred credits a month. No rollovers. Someone buys that, though, I get the credit."

The brass bell over the door rang.

Her eyes went wide. The sarcasm was back. "Oh. My. Gah," she whispered. "It's a prince."

A slender boy had entered. He wore a silk robe with embroidered designs on wide sleeves and designer jeans ripped at the thighs. His hair was as sleek as the robe, a white band around his forehead. He walked with the grace of a ballerina, his toes finding perfect balance on the wobbly floor.

"Kumiko, hi." Joli waved. "Remember me? Ceramics, Tuesdays, Thursdays. Mr. Gregor. I made this." She held up the ugly mug. "I got an A."

Kumiko's expression didn't change. He examined a jar of incense sticks, sampling them like cigars. He slid a wooden box of teabags off the shelf and waved them in front of his face like a hypnotist, closing his eyes to inhale.

"Try the cascara," Joli said. "Helps with constipation."

He was unperturbed, wrapping three teabags around his finger. There was a counter on the other side of the room. An old man cut a sheet of paper.

"They get like that," Joli said.

"Who?"

"The chosen. Kumiko used to be cool, you know. Smiled. Talked. Now he's got that, you know—" she swung her hand around her head "—and the you know." She looked down her nose. "He's a pet. Pelz skims the talent, sweet-talks them in the tower, and they come back like that. See the headband?"

The white band was knotted at the back of his head. The ends were plated in silver.

"I'll bet he's hiding a crown. Serious. There's like a gold thing they put on, like superhero stuff. Turns them into wayholes."

Kumiko left with a small, smartly wrapped gift. The paper pearl white with a thin band of red.

"Next time you poop," she said to him before the door closed, "you're welcome."

They went past popcorn machines and Frisbee sets. A section of spices and herbs, bottles of olive oil. A set of plastic syringes used to apply dye, something he'd used in grade school to color a white T-shirt, next to a small bottle of supremely insane hot sauce with a label of a reindeer with flaming antlers and smoking nostrils.

Reindeer Breath.

"You want this," she said.

An entire section was dedicated to coffee. Beans of every flavor and various models of coffeemakers. The simple ones were on the floor, the kind Joli had in her room. But the real ones were on the top shelf. A Breville Barista. It didn't just make coffee. Espresso, too.

And 130c.

"I like your style," she said. "But out of your price range."

With one hundred credits a month and no rollovers, it didn't make sense. "How does anyone buy it?"

"You put your stuff on the shelves. Oooor," she slurred, "you make a deal."

"What kind of deal?"

"I float you the balance. You make me coffee for the rest of my life."

He cringed. "For life?"

"Hey, that or that." She pointed at the Keurig.

This was all so new. But if he was going to make it at the Institute of Creative Mind, he was going to need coffee. And not the cheap stuff. He pulled the Breville down. Joli shoved a bag of hazelnut on top. It wasn't even whole bean.

"You made the right choice."

They went around the tree, ducking under a bobsledding dog with a red floppy hat. "This feels weird," he said.

"Being an indentured coffee servant?"

"I mean, it's free."

"Oh, it's not free. Everything costs something."

That was what bothered him. What exactly was he paying with?

An old man was at the counter. He had the posture of a question mark. A thin-skinned centenarian who had shrunk under a hundred years of gravity. He looked like an overbaked human with faded gray eyes and a wispy field of thinning white hair. He wore a wool sweater with a turtleneck as thick as a tire that appeared to hold up his pointed chin.

"Hi, Mr. Kramer!" Joli waved.

"Ms. Oliveira." He squinted his glassy eyes at her.

"I'm Chris Blizzard."

Mr. Kramer put his hand to his ear. The ring finger was curled against his palm, the tendon pulled down in advanced Dupuytren's contracture. The fingernails long and yellow.

"You have to shout," Joli said.

Chris yelled his name. Mr. Kramer's brow furrowed. His chin disappeared into the turtleneck and he turned around. A big book with pages as yellow as his fingernails was on a walnut shelf. He licked his finger and turned the pages. One at a time. Groaning with each one.

Chris looked at his watch.

Twenty pages later, Mr. Kramer reached for a feathered quill and dipped it into an inkwell. He turned around to squint at the coffeemaker.

"Use my credits for the balance!" Joli shouted.

Once again, his chin buried in the collar. He went back to the book. Fifteen pages later, he returned to the counter. He pulled a sheet of blue sparkly wrapping paper off a roll.

"No, I don't need it—"

"Let him," Joli said. "It's part of the deal."

His shoes scuffed the gritty stones, past a small wood burner with a black stovepipe that exhausted out the side of the wall. He laid the wrapping paper on a waxed board and smoothed it with gnarled hands, wiping bits of debris that seemed to continuously float off the tree trunk. Then back to the desk for scissors specially made with wide handles to fit his fingers, and a metal yardstick. He struck a line with a black marker, carefully slid the scissors with his eyes six inches above it.

It reminded him of how his grandfather opened presents. Peeling the tape so it wouldn't rip, carefully creasing the paper into a neat square so it could be used next Christmas.

The bell above the door rang.

Someone went near the Reindeer Breath hot sauce, his back to them. He was short, black hair.

Mr. Kramer tore three pieces of tape from a dispenser, the same length, and plied them to the edge of the counter. He placed the coffeemaker in the center, his breath crackling as he carried it, adjusting it half an inch to each side before making the first fold.

Chris felt dizzy.

His head suddenly felt heavy, a queer sensation like the time he'd had his tonsils removed and came out of surgery. The anesthesiologist had put the mask on him, and then he woke up hours later, like time had been clipped from his consciousness. But unlike the anesthesia, this time he heard a voice. It was garbled and strange, distant.

"You all right?" Joli said.

Chris was leaning against the tree. Mr. Kramer was pasting a bow on top of the giftwrapping. He was already done. Chris couldn't remember stepping back. Like a piece of time had been clipped away.

The bell rang. The door closed.

"Merry Christmas." Mr. Kramer nudged the gift.

Chris felt wobbly. He took the present. There was a smaller one on top. "Thank you."

Mr. Kramer lifted his misshaped hand. Joli elbowed Chris. "Say merry Christmas."

"Oh. Merry Christmas."

"Louder."

"Merry Christmas!"

Mr. Kramer nodded into his sweater and went to the big book. The quill scratched the page. It felt strange carrying a big present outside. It was almost October.

That was the kid who was in the room next to his that had come inside as Mr. Kramer performed the wrapping ritual. The boy who had caught him listening outside his door.

The chimes were singing in the tree. They stepped out of the shade, the ground soft with fallen needles. Chris looked around. There was a thick stand of trees near the far wall. The path that separated the north and west quadrants went straight through the middle of it. And farther out, past the wall, a white column of smoke rose beyond the trees.

"I got you something."

Joli pulled the small present off the box. It was tightly wrapped. He watched her rip it open.

"A wallet?" he said.

"It's for your red cards." She opened it like a book. "You only need three slots. Get it?"

"Thanks?"

"I knew you'd love it. Gotta go." She hiked her backpack up and started jogging backwards. "Acrylics in five."

"Wait. What do I do with this?"

She ground her fists together, one on top of the other. Chris looked at his watch. There wasn't enough time to go back to his room. He started running. There were stranger things in this place than bringing a present to class.

4

"Have you lost weight? Is the food good?"

Mom's face filled the monitor. Her lips were painted red, her church pearls around her neck. He didn't miss Sunday mornings on the hard, creaky pews, staring at religious scenes in stained glass that confused him, the angular faces of apostles and saints who looked glum and serious. *Life was hard,* Mom would say. *Sit up straight.*

"It's been over a month." She carefully wiped her eye. "You look so grown-up. Are those whiskers? Henry, look." Mom leaned in. "Your father wants to talk to you. Henry, it's Chris."

"Sport." His dad's tie was loose. He called him sport, which was hilarious. The only time Chris had ever played a sport was when he broke his nose trying to catch a baseball. "How's school?"

"Good."

"Yeah? You doing good?"

"Pretty good."

The Blizzard family small talk was on display. They were nodding, fidgeting. Trying not to look at the clock when they talked at the same time. *You go. No, you go.*

"Ask if his classes are hard," Mom's voice whispered. Dad

repeated her questions. Chris answered. Then she nudged him to the side. He stood behind her, pulling his tie.

"Do you have any pictures of your work?" she said.

"I don't have my phone."

"Well, can you, I don't know, ask them if you can just use it to take a picture? I'm sure they won't mind." She laughed nervously, asked his dad if he wanted to see his work.

"They don't do pictures, Mom."

"I know, but you know it doesn't hurt to ask. Wait. Your sister wants to say hi."

Yu had already shed her church clothes. She seemed happy to see him. He felt the same. It was easier to talk to her. Not really a twin thing. Just easier.

I moved into your room, she said.

I knew you would. You feeding Baby? His pet tarantula was a year old. Mom and Dad wanted to set her free.

"Ask if he made friends," Mom whispered.

So what's it like? Yu turned so she wouldn't see her signing.

Chris told her about classes, the Christmas Tree, the ornaments that were everywhere. He could hear Mom repeating it to his dad. Chris told her about the dance class. Yu laughed into tears.

Kogen was outside the cubicle, talking to another slacker. The Visitors' Center was filled with them.

"People are waiting. I gotta go. I'll call you next month."

"Okay. Write a letter," Mom said. "And see if they'll let you use your phone. Be assertive. Right, Henry?"

They waved. She blew kisses. The monitor froze their images. Mom's lipstick smudged on her fingers. He had started to write a letter a few weeks ago. His hand was sore. But that wasn't why he stopped. Writing a letter wasn't any easier than talking. Maybe he could just make something up that made his mom feel better. Just tell a story. He was good at that.

"How was it?" Kogen said.

"Good."

"Seems like a long time since you saw them, right? You'll get used to it."

Boys and girls were silently talking inside their soundproof cubicles while slackers waited outside, checking their watches. *Watchers watch,* Joli would say. Their expressions varied from excitement to boredom. October had replaced their jackets with winter coats and scarfs. But they still wore the slacks.

Chris wore a flannel shirt.

"Can I walk back?" he asked.

He wanted to take his time before being locked in the zoo of creatively gifted young adults. It was easy to forget about the walls once he was inside, but it was different on the outside. He could feel the freedom. The sky looked different.

"No."

They took the electric cart through the tunnel. Kogen wore fur-lined leather gloves, tapping the steering wheel.

"You cold?" he asked.

Chris was still sleeping with the bedroom window cracked open. It kept his room from feeling stuffy. He didn't feel so trapped.

Kogen dropped the cart off at the gate. Joli was bundled in a heavy coat with an old rucksack over her shoulder, the fabric decorated with a black mosaic. She blew into her hands decorated with new thorny designs.

"Did you check the lock, Kogen?" she said. "Don't want anyone to escape."

"You're funny," he deadpanned. Walked off. The cold had stiffened the hitch in his hip. Chris wondered if they would go skiing. He hoped not.

"Where's your stuff?" she said.

"Room."

"Good. I need coffee."

The quad was scattered with students. They sat on blankets, chatting and laughing. Some were alone with their books, taking advantage of the last few snow-free days. It was cold but tolerable. Chris actually looked forward to an empty quad. He felt less guilty for wanting to stay inside.

"How's the Ps?" Joli asked.

He shrugged. His parents were parents. "You don't call your parents?"

"We got cut off."

"They can do that?"

"I might have been talking about Pelz. Not in a good way." She shrugged. "They said something was wrong with my mom's connection. That sort of thing. Just as well."

Her parents were divorced. Her mom had another family with little kids. Her halfbloods, she called them. Her dad was doing real estate. Joli wrote letters. Mostly just sent journal entries she penned late at night. It was therapeutic, she said. Got the thoughts out. She wondered if her mom read them. She never wrote back.

"You ever see Pelz?" Chris said.

"He walks around at night sometimes, I think. It's hard to tell if it's him."

He wondered if she was jealous of the princes and princesses. The specials, she called them. He wasn't about to say that out loud. He thought maybe she wanted to be one. Maybe not. *People keep secrets from themselves all the time.*

The path felt harder, the soil firmer beneath the gravel. Halfway across the quad, a pack of students watched them from a wool blanket. The lanky boy with loopy curls of reddish-brown hair began to dance. He jerked around and smacked into an invisible wall, falling rigid on his back. The others laughed.

"Hey, Claibourn," Joli said, "the Tree is out of diapers. You'll have to use the plastic bedsheet again."

Claibourn didn't seem fazed. He was in a fit of tremors.

"Diapers?" Chris said.

"I'm getting a bedwetting rumor started. He's a turd."

It was the third time Chris had seen someone doing the dance. The other two times were in the hall when they didn't see him. Chris pretended not to see it. It would go away. It always did.

Slackers were clearing the announcement board in his dorm, moving sign-up sheets for club activities and tossing handwritten trade requests in the garbage. It was the third week of October, and most of them had spent their monthly credits. *I've got forty Ho Hos. Make an offer. No clothing.*

The second floor was filled with classical music and hip-hop. Josie Merelus's synthetized club mix was loud. She and others sat on the bed while they took turns dancing, tapping each other in. It was a weekend ritual. Sometimes Chris watched from the hall. They'd invited him in once. No sarcasm. He left.

"It's freezing in here." She closed Chris's window.

His desk was a clutter of notebooks, textbooks, projects and snacks he'd snuck out of Bixen. He considered the Ho Hos but didn't have anything to trade except textbooks.

Joli inspected the sketches he had taped to the window. The gesture drawings of still lifes weren't half bad. He poured water into the Breville as she inspected the piece he'd created from a sugar block in culinary. The spires of the castle had been carved, and the stone walls etched and dyed with food coloring. A glob of clay, which they were supposed to use, somewhat resembled what he was going after. Clay just wasn't inspiring. What was he going to do with clay when he was done? Look at it?

He could eat a sugar castle.

The coffee began dripping. "My oils are over there somewhere." He pointed. "Throw them in your bag if—"

"Run, run as fast as you can."

"What?"

Joli dusted sugar off a notebook she'd dug out from beneath the oil paints. It was spattered with primary colors and smudged with clay, forgotten beneath an onslaught of schoolwork. Letters had been jotted across the margin.

UNRUAFASASUCN.

"Word scramble?" she said.

Those were the letters he'd found in the textbook on his first night. He'd forgotten about them. He shuffled around the desk, found the art book under a loose pile of sketches, looked at the open door. Joli poured a cup of coffee while he flipped the pages.

"Look." He put his finger on a word. "The letter, it's underlined."

"Yeah?"

"There's a bunch of them." He turned to the next one. "See?"

"So you wrote them down?"

"Yeah. It seemed, I don't know. Like a message."

She leaned over the textbook.

"No one would see them if they were just flipping through the book. Only if you were reading it." He studied the notebook. "Maybe I missed a few."

"Or Bobby was bored." She sipped and closed her eyes. "You can really make coffee."

"Who's Bobby?"

"He was in this room before you. Nice kid. Sort of quiet. Stayed in his room mostly." She casually flipped the pages. "Always reading."

"What happened to him?"

"Red cards happened. I mean, that's what the slackers said. He must've gotten all three in one night. He was here one day and then bye-bye."

"They can do that?"

"They can do anything, Christopher."

"So he just moved out?"

"Well, *they* moved him out. Loaded his stuff on a cart and drove him out the gate. Didn't say goodbye or anything, but then he didn't talk a lot anyway. Rumor was he got caught sneaking into the castle, which is bonk. I think he just cracked. This place isn't for everyone."

She sat on the bed and leaned against the wall, cradling the mug near her chin. She'd made ten goofy-face coffee mugs. Half of them were in Chris's room. He held the notebook.

"He was a culinary artiste, too," she said. "He made this stack of pancakes once with this impossible lean. The colors were squeezed from blueberries, raspberries, cherries and whatnot. He got honorable mention. I don't know how he didn't win, probably lost points when he ate it. I thought it was more like performance art, but what do I know."

Chris searched the textbook. He found the first letter, U, and went back to the beginning of the chapter. There it was, a wispy strike of graphite. He jotted it at the start of the line.

"He wasn't the same after getting lost," Joli ruminated.

"He got lost?"

"Mm-mmm."

Another letter. It was just a small dot under an S. He wasn't sure that was intentional, but he inserted it anyway. It seemed to fit.

"The hike, yeah. He wandered off. Not supposed to. Supposed to stay with the group. But I get it. The house is bizarre, man. It's haunted by M. C. Escher. Had all these strange corners and creepy rooms. Staircases that went nowhere and doors on the ceiling. Sometimes you climbed rope ladders that went down hallways that got smaller. A bedroom had a vault door. Toys were, like, everywhere. Like the old-fashioned stuffed ones sitting around with shiny eyes, watching."

"Who owns the house?"

"Some family. They don't go there anymore, I guess. Some recluse built it back in the day. Slackers say we have permission to look around, but it doesn't feel like it."

He added a *T* with a faint line under it. "So why do we go up there?"

"Inspiration. If we find something interesting, we're supposed to tell a slacker. That's a hard rule. Can't take anything without showing it. Three-card special if you do, call mommy and daddy to pick you up. At least that's what they say. The slackers watch us like spies when we're there, keep asking if we feel inspiration every time we walk into a room. 'You feel inspired now? How about now?' Don't get me wrong, I'd totally live there."

"Maybe Bobby took something."

"I doubt it."

"Why?"

"He was too scared." She topped off her mug and filled one for

Chris. "He wandered off into the trees. We had to do a big search party for him. Found him in this open field next to one of those towers, you know the ones they used to watch for forest fires? He was leaning against it, sort of staring out. He looked cold."

"How'd he get away from the slackers?"

"I don't know. There." She put her finger on a lightly shaded letter. Chris inserted it toward the end of the line.

RUNRUNASFASTASUCAN.

The headwave returned. It wasn't a headache. More like a magnetic rope wrapped around his head. The pages turned blurry. Joli nodded. Someone was at the door, his coarse black hair undulating. Big brown eyes growing larger and smaller.

"Hey, Sai," Joli said. "Want some coffee?"

"I want to be on your team."

"Okay. What team?"

Chris swiveled his chair, forgot he was holding a mug. Black coffee sloshed over the notebook, staining the lined paper with muddy watercolors. He slumped over the armrest.

"Whoa, whoa." Joli held him up. "You all right?"

And then it was gone. The vertigo vanished. His head was clear. Chris took a shaky breath. He felt perfectly fine.

"You got to stop the all-nighters," she said. "Here. Water."

Sai was gone. But he had been holding something, Chris was sure of it. Just like that first night when he got caught outside his bedroom. It was cupped in his right hand. And that feeling he had at the Tree, when Sai arrived, was exactly the same. Joli cracked a bottle of water.

"I think he's got a phone." He nodded at Sai's room. "I hear him sometimes late at night. He's talking to someone, but I never hear anyone talking back."

"First of all"—she sopped up the spill with a rag flaked with dried bits of clay—"he doesn't have a phone. Even if he did, there's no reception. Secondly, everyone in this place talks to themselves."

"He's having conversations. Like, long ones."

"What's he saying?"

Most of the time, he couldn't understand them. It was just muttering, and Chris was in the habit of turning on music when he heard it. It disturbed him. Sounded like rambling. But she was right. Chris talked to himself all the time. *It just isn't a conversation.*

"Sai's a sculpture guy," Joli said. "Pretty good one, too. He almost won a challenge last year using paper straws, made this thing that looked like a tree with branchy arms and twiggy hair. Sort of dark, but good. I'll be honest, I was jealous. He always works alone, though. Maybe he's starting a club."

Chris took a swig of water. "Was he on the hike?"

"Everyone was on the hike."

"So was he with Bobby?"

Joli shrugged. "Who knows. You ready?"

"Did you see what he was holding? He had something in his hand. The first night I was here, I saw it then too."

"Did it look like a phone?"

Chris hesitated. "A cookie."

She started laughing. Maybe she thought he was going to say something else, or he sounded far too suspicious about a cookie when there were snacks all over Chris's room. But that was what it looked like. A round cookie. It was just the way he was holding it. Not like a good luck charm or something he was going to eat. He was holding it carefully. Like a teddy bear.

Chris packed his paints in her bag. They were going to Gromet Hall to work on an assignment. Joli was good with the brush, and he needed help with blending.

Sai's door was closed. It was quiet inside his room. Chris wasn't listening for voices. He just wanted to see if the brainwave would return. He went down the steps. The slackers had rearranged the announcement board. Joli was in front of a poster.

"So he wants to be on our team."

5

It looked like a mountain of cupcakes dumped on a snowy sheet of ice, a collage of pink, cream and chocolate cakes with colorful candy sprinkles, orbs of jellybeans, and gooey sugar bombs drizzled with white icing. Silhouettes climbed the sides with icepicks and cleated boots toward a brilliant star spiked on top.

Fall Challenge was stenciled at the top. *Clancer Hall.*

"Looks like a Christmas tree." Chris slid the poster across the table.

Joli doodled on her forearm, a spiral design that circled around her arm, the ink bleeding across the soft flesh of her elbow. The table was long with benches, scarred with names, faces and graffiti. The clatter of aluminum trays echoed with conversation.

"But it's almost Halloween," Chris said.

"In the land of Christmas, there is only Christmas."

She put the marker down to pop a purple grape in her mouth and chased it with a handful of chocolate drops. That was lunch. *Highly recommended,* she said.

"We build up to Christmas, and then, when it's over, we start over."

"All the competitions are about Christmas?"

"Surprised?" She funneled a fistful of chocolate into her mouth. "Last summer's challenge was interpretive dance. It was called Santa Off-Season. We had to design our costumes and perform on the quad. I got paired up with Sheena Mallifort. She was a potter. Did some cool stuff with glazing but not with her feet. We took a half ration cut after that performance."

"Cut on what?"

"Our credits got docked for the semester. It could've been worse. The losers got shut out. No credits at all. They had to eat the cafeteria junk for, I don't know, two months or something."

"There's losers?"

"Can't be winners without losers. We did suck, though. And she's gone now." She took to designing an angry flower on the table. She nodded at the kitchen. "You can get more credits if you do that though."

The slackers were running the food, but students were helping. Chris forked a bite of cheesecake. It was better than he expected. He didn't know when anyone would have extra time to work on top of everything else.

"It sort of goes against the spirit of creativity." He sipped from a short carton of milk. "Winners and losers."

"Charles." She looked up. "Want to tell Christopher about the challenge?"

The slacker stopped with a tray of cottage cheese and salad. His haircut was a blond buzz. "Did you take that poster from a board?"

"This?" She spread her hand over it. "We found it. It was on the floor."

He stared a moment longer, then went to another table with a group of identically dressed thirty-something slackers. Or were they forty? It was so hard to tell.

"Charles didn't want to tell you." Her tone turned stiff. "Growth, Mr. Blizzard, isn't about the warm and fuzzy, young man. No, no. It's about pushing the boundaries. The creative waters churn greatest in the rapids. Nothing comes from stagnant pools. You must rest in the chaos of discomfort. Why do you think we're in the coldest part of the country?"

She popped another grape and chocolate combo.

"You ever hear the one about the Buddha? No? Well, it goes something like this. The biggest jerks are the best teachers. They push your buttons, compassionately revealing your deficiencies, forcing you to grow. Hugs are fine. But when you're comfortable, you're stagnant. And speaking of great teachers."

She slowly waved. Claibourn walked past, sitting with friends who looked over their shoulders. Joli smiled sarcastically; a thick film of chocolate smudged her teeth.

"Honestly," she said, "I don't entirely disagree. I mean, I hate the edges of creativity, but discomfort works. Think about that dance you did. It was awful, no offense, but Ms. Taiga was right. You learned more from taking that leap than if you sat in the back with your thumb in your mouth."

"You drank the Kool-Aid."

"I didn't drink it." She brushed the cherry red tips of her hair. "Pauline!"

Joli looped a grape over Chris's head. Pauline, a chubby girl who ate white icing from a jar during pottery class, caught it in her mouth without slowing down, went to the end of the table by herself. Joli raised her arms.

Chris flipped the poster over. The back was blank. "So what do we do?"

"Won't know till we show up. The rules, how much time we get, all that at showtime. No practicing. It's raw creativity. You know, drop into the flow, that sort of thing. Last fall we each got a block of granite and two weeks. I slept, like, two days and got bonus creds. Did this weird little elf holding an ornament. It sucked, but it was better than the others."

Chris remembered the squat sculpture outside the Visitors' Center. It was chiseled from granite. Sort of looked like an elf.

She took his hand, her fingers warm in his palm, and traced an inky star over the back of it, dotted it with dark sparkles flaring from the points. It felt good, the wet tip of the marker, her warm fingers.

"It shows up so good on white skin," she said. "You have any black friends?"

He shook his head. "I don't have any friends."

"Not true."

He shrugged. Maybe she was right.

Charles had returned with his tray and took the poster. He waved a yellow card at her. She acknowledged the warning with a nod. First yellow card Chris had seen. *This is soccer.*

"I got a bunch of these," she whispered.

She put a smiley face in the middle of his star with a hanging tongue. Dotted the eyes.

Sai sat several feet away from them. A mound of yellowish sauerkraut rested in a pool of clear liquid. They watched him slide down the bench a little at a time, stopping to pluck strands of kraut off the top until he was next to Chris.

"Hi, Sai," Joli said. "Want a chocolate with your... *sauerkraut*?" She put a small chocolate in an empty cell on his plate. "That's a lot of kraut."

He ate like he didn't notice them, picking at it like a bundle of straw. He wiped his mouth with the back of his hand.

"Three-person teams," he said, not making eye contact. "We choose team members."

Joli and Chris looked at each other. "The challenge?" she said.

"A twenty-four-hour event. Open competition. Access to a full kitchen." He slurped the juice. "And double stakes. Winners double credits. Losers go empty."

"How, uh, how do you know that?" Joli said.

He slurped a string through plump lips like spaghetti. Juice spilled on the chocolate Joli gave him. He moved it a few inches. Maybe he was going to eat it. Chris was beginning to feel nauseous. Grapes and chocolate were one thing.

Sai looked around then reached into the front pocket of his military green jacket. He pulled out a folded sheet of paper. As he opened it, golden cookie crumbs fell from the folds and sprinkled the chocolate drop.

He flattened it on the table. The creases bent a detailed sketch, moisture from his fingers dabbing the graphite lines. It was a cubist fortress with three spires and a porch that wrapped around it. Dimensions specified the walls.

"Looks like the mansion." Joli spun the plan around. "Did you do that from memory?"

"We're going to make it," he said.

"What do you mean?"

He nodded. Chris and Joli looked at each other. Then she snorted, covering her mouth.

"You serious?" she said. "We can't build this, Sai. There won't be enough time. Even if we had a week. I mean, that's a sweet drawing and everything, but we'll be broke if we try that. I'm not going six months without credits or, or working it off."

"He can do it." His brown eyes looked at Chris.

"Me?" Chris said.

"Nope. Nope, nope," she said. "No offense, Sai, but hard no."

Chris slid the bent paper closer. There was more on the back, a sketch of the front of the mansion. The front door was askew with a porch swing.

"What is that?" Joli tapped the figure on the steps. It looked like a headless cartoon cutout. "Is that a Halloween twist or something? How do you even know the rules?"

He went back to slurping. She regarded Chris with wide eyes and shook her head.

"Chris is the chef," she said. "So if we are a team, then he calls the shots. You and me, Sai, we follow."

"Live in the current," Sai said.

"Yeah, well, live another day with credits."

She brushed the sugar crumbs off the table and folded the paper into a neat square, handing it back to Sai. He snatched it from her and slid down the bench, a little at a time, until he reached the end of the long table. Just past Pauline. The two of them picked at their food. Chris thought Joli had hurt his feelings.

Someone was behind her.

"Trade?" Claibourn took a chocolate from her tray. He popped it into his mouth before she could stop him. He had a handful of grapes, the same purple ones she was eating. She didn't notice him put one on her tray. One grape for one chocolate.

"I didn't mean to scare your friend off."

"You have that effect." She moved away from him. "What do you want?"

He ate one of his grapes, chewing it slowly. Smiling at her. One of his teeth was chipped at a sharp angle, chocolate gathered in the corner. He looked at Chris.

"Listen, I just want to apologize. What I was doing on the quad, making fun of your dancing, that was uncalled for. Really. We're a family. Even you, Oliveira. You know, brothers and sisters give each other a hard time, but in the end we're a happy family."

"Happy?"

"Well, yeah. Like, I like the way you stain your hair at the ends and, you know, the way you play the rebel. You're the little sister who doesn't take crap. I appreciate that." He held out his hand. She looked at it. "Anyway, yeah. I just want to say sorry to Blizzard."

He offered his hand across the table. Chris didn't know whether he should take it. But Claibourn held it with a sincere smile. The awkwardness hardened until Chris couldn't take it anymore. He shook his hand. Claibourn squeezed.

"Go eat your lunch." She pushed her tray before he took another chocolate.

"Yeah, well, I apologize." He finally let go. "Have a nice lunch. Enjoy your grapes."

Chris watched him go back to his table. His friends muttered. They avoided looking.

"You should wash your hand," Joli said.

Sai was gone. His tray was at the end of the table, a pile of sauerkraut still in a sad mound. Chris lost his appetite. His stomach knotted.

"Do you think Sai was right?" he said. "About the challenge?"

"No one ever knows the rules ahead of time, trust me. I think he was just guessing. I mean, teams are probably likely for a culinary challenge, but the rest of it, I don't know how he would know." She broke a chocolate between her teeth. "If something like that got out, I would know. The slackers keep that stuff super-secret so no one goes in prepared. Like Sai, with the drawing and everything, that's unfair."

She held a grape between her finger and thumb.

"But if he's right, you think you could do that?" she said. "His drawing?"

Chris wasn't sure what it was, really. The walls would have to be thin and sturdy, not to mention edible if it was truly culinary. It was basically a building. They'd have to make it from scratch, he assumed. Even if they had all the parts preassembled, to put that together would probably take eight hours. But, guessing from the level of talent, it would be more like twenty-four.

"We need to think of something else." She bit the grape in half. Juice spurted out like a tiny water balloon. "Even if it's—"

She spit the pulp out. Her complexion went from brown to burnt scarlet. Her eyes filled with water. She began scraping her tongue, ejecting little bits of purple skin onto the table.

"What is it?" Chris said.

She waved her hands, grabbed a bottle, and began chugging. The plastic collapsed as she sucked it out, and water spilled down the front of her pink sweatshirt. Eyes tightly closed, tears seeping from the corners.

"You all right, Oliveira?" Claibourn put his hand on her shoulder. "You get a bad grape?"

She shook him off, wiping her tongue with her sleeve, the ink bleeding on her arm. Claibourn's friends laughed, half hiding their faces. Joli tipped the bench over. She snatched an orange juice from someone. Her face resembled a swollen radish.

And Chris sat there. He watched like all the rest of them. Frozen in his seat. He didn't know what to do. How to help. Guilt filled him like a concrete mixer dumping its contents into his stomach, the slurry hardening in his veins. Just like the time he'd been shoved outside after gym class, left to get back into the school through the front door with only his towel. Like the time someone threw dog crap across his back at the bus stop and he had to sit there smelling like a toilet.

He watched Claibourn stand back, his mouth wide with laughter, telling her not to touch her eyes.

Chris wished he could do something. Just something. His head filled with humming, like a metal mixing bowl struck with a spoon. His gums felt like a visit to the dentist's office. That magnetic wave pulsed through his head.

Then Claibourn's head snapped back.

A howl eclipsed the sounds Joli was making. He put his hand to his eye. Something had bounced off him, a ricochet of dark brown. It rattled on the table.

A chocolate chip.

"What happened?" Charles said.

Joli was chugging a small carton of milk, white streams flooding her chin. Chris was holding the chocolate drop.

"He did it!" Claibourn cried.

"Come on, let's go. You too, Joli. Come on."

"You gonna let him get away with this?" Claibourn shouted. "He hit me in the eye with-with-with that!"

Chris was holding the evidence. He looked like he threw it. But he hadn't moved. It came from somewhere else. He just couldn't say it.

"Someone want to tell me what happened here?" Charles said.

Everyone shrugged. Claibourn's friends played idiots to the grape that had started the whole thing. But they didn't know where the chocolate bullet had come from. Chris wanted to confess. *He put a grape on Joli's tray, Charles. Claibourn did something to it. That's why he was laughing out of that big dumb mouth when he caught one in the eye.*

But Chris's throat was coated in ice.

"I'm fine." Joli gasped, her sweatshirt dripping.

"Listen, Joli." Charles reached for her. "You were just—"

"I'm fine."

She jerked away from him and left. Embarrassed. Angry.

"You gonna red card him?" Claibourn said with one bug eye. "He tried to blind me."

"With a chocolate chip?"

"Yeah, a chocolate chip! Let me throw one at you, right in your open eyeball, man. From-from-from five feet away."

Charles sighed. "Did you throw it, Chris?"

"You're going to ask him?" Claibourn looked around for support. "Just look!"

"Chris?"

Chris couldn't explain why he was still holding the evidence. He couldn't put it down. Couldn't answer. This was the worst part. Just sitting there like a snowman with no feeling. His face had molded into a plastic mask of stupid confusion. He could feel his chin begin to quiver and hoped—for the love of all that was good—no one could see it.

"He didn't throw it." It was Pauline. She was watching from the end of the table with a half-eaten apple. "It came from down there."

She gestured with the apple to the end of the table. Claibourn frowned with his good eye. Charles asked who threw it. She took another bite and shrugged.

"All right," Charles said. "Come on."

"That's it?" Claibourn shrugged sarcastically. "That's all you're gonna do? He's guilty. Look at him."

Charles dragged him out. No one protested. They didn't see who threw it. Pauline said it came from over her shoulder and that was all she knew. Not until the room settled down, when everyone went back to eating, did Chris finally drop the chocolate chip. He felt the heat of their gossip. Pauline looked up from her tray, an apple core sinking in a glob of tapioca pudding.

Sai's tray was still there.

Chris thought maybe Sai had thrown it when no one was looking. Because the chocolate drop Joli had given him had been in an empty cell with cookie crumbs all over it.

Now it was gone.

6

The sky was cracked.

Bits of rain streaked the window, blurring the people in the quad. There was only three of them. One was a slacker. Frigid air huffed through the raised window, rattling the pages on his desk.

Dear Mom and Dad.

That was as far as he got. The pencil was useless. There were no words left in it. His knuckles ached from filling notebooks. Calluses had developed. He found himself doodling in the margins. Helplessness rested in his stomach like a tub of ice cream.

Run, run as fast as you can. He wondered if Bobby Kelly had felt the same way. Did he stare out the window? Did he leave clues so someone would know what he was feeling? Chris couldn't outrun it. It was there. It was always there.

Helpless.

"What was that?" Joli shouted.

The pencil bounced across the desk. He spun in the chair. She was in the doorway, red-frosted hair peeking from the plaid head scarf.

"Hey," Chris said. "You okay?"

"Yeah. You look like your dog ran away."

"Oh, yeah. No. Just, you know… I mean. You okay?"

She snorted. Her smile melted the lump in his stomach. He hadn't seen her in days. He thought she would never talk to him again. She walked into his room, bright and bouncy, fresh paint on green cargo pants and a puffy red sweatshirt that read DORK ON BOARD.

"Everything tastes normal again." She poured the remains of cold coffee. "Slept in for two days while you froze your nose off in morning exercise." She closed the window. "You see what Claibourn did?"

"Uh. I don't know." That was as close as he could come to admitting it. The grape. The hot sauce. *Reindeer Breath.*

"I had it on my fingers, got it in my eyes," she said. "It was like putting out a grease fire. Water made it worse. I snotted for half an hour. Milk and bread, man. That's the way you put it out. I'll know that next time."

"Next time?"

"Just in case." She flopped on his bed.

"You mad?" he asked. *At me?*

She shrugged. "I'll be honest, that was a good one. I don't know how he did it, but it was good. He got it worse, though. Haven't seen him since. Probably hiding in his room with an eye patch. That was a good shot, by the way." She raised the mug. "Were you aiming for his eye?"

"It wasn't me. I swear."

She nodded, squinting. "Sai, I'll bet."

He didn't tell her the chocolate chip was missing. Or the strange way he felt when it happened. He'd convinced himself it was Pauline, that somehow she'd flicked it without notice. That was possible. He'd seen people shoot pennies with a snap of their fingers. In a strange way, he felt guilty. Because he'd wanted it to happen.

"Where's Sai?" she asked.

"Haven't seen him or heard him. He wasn't at exercise, either." Chris looked outside. The quad was empty. "You think he's still here?"

"One way to find out."

She downed the coffee and dropped the mug. The remnants leaked onto his pillowcase. She went into the hall.

"Sai?"

She knocked again. Chris put his ear to the door, remembering what had happened the last time. Joli turned the doorknob slowly.

"What are you doing?" Chris said.

"Shhh. Sai, you there? Buddy?"

She cracked the door. A fierce shiver struck Chris in the stomach. The hallway was mostly quiet except for the mourning of classical music. Only one door was open, people quietly talking.

"Sai," she said again, swinging the door open. "You not feeling well?"

He thought, for a moment, he was in bed. There was a lump of pillows beneath a soft beige comforter with a high-top shoe, the laces knotted. Joli was just pretending for anyone listening.

"Just stopped by to see how you're doing." She nodded, her colorful mop bouncing.

Chris was bolted to the floor. She grabbed a handful of his shirt and pried him loose. Then she swung the door to a small gap. It wasn't exactly following the rules.

"He's worse than me," she said.

It looked like a storm blew through a library. Sheets of paper littered the floor. They were taped to the walls and window, covered the desk like an understaffed newsroom. Pillars of textbooks were stacked in the corners. Some of the papers were torn from sketchbooks with abstract drawings Chris recognized from class, but most of them were architectural drawings of odd-shaped structures.

Most of the pages were ripped from Blueline notepads. They were filled with run-on sentences without paragraph breaks or punctuation. It wasn't homework or letters to his parents. Just streams of thoughts spelled out in squiggly lines. Chris picked one up. Most of it was illegible. Like his fingers couldn't keep up. Chunks of it read like a story that was out of order, or pieces of different plots.

The Toy Collector.

The rest of the page was tiny scribbles, like he was falling asleep.

There was more on the back.

He's looking for something. Someone. He's using them to find him. He's been looking for a long, long, long, long time.

Chris put the pages in his back pocket.

She was moving papers on the desk. Beneath the avalanche were containers of goodies. Gumdrops and chocolates, multicolored sprinkles and silvery beads of candy. Tubes of white icing. It was a crash course in diabetes.

Chris lifted a notebook off a cardboard model. It resembled some of the drawings taped to the wall, an abstract construction of a fun house with crooked doorways and slanting walls. A folded sheet of paper was tucked underneath it. Chris pried it open. Crispy crumbs fell out. It was the plan Sai had brought to the cafeteria. The same crumbs that had fallen on his tray when he showed it to them.

"Check it out." Joli pointed.

A black T-shirt was spread on the desk. The words *Nerd Life* in yellow letters. Cookies had been placed on it. They were generic figures several inches long with wide flat arms and legs. Different patterns had been painted in white icing, embedded with blue gumballs, candy corn or Reese cups. They had one thing in common.

The heads were missing.

Broken off at the rounded shoulders. Dried flakes of icing were pasted like white crusty collars where the heads had been removed.

"You think we should tell someone?" Chris whispered.

"What, that he's eating cookies?"

"No, that he's... he's eating the heads."

Joli wasn't infected with the paranoia squirming through Chris's belly. But she didn't hear the way Sai talked to himself at night. Maybe it wouldn't be so bad if Chris hadn't read that page on the pillow. Joli broke off a foot. She nibbled the toe.

"Not bad." She held it out.

"What are you doing?" a voice boomed.

Chris wet himself a little. The voice had the tenor of trouble, the power of a teacher's voice that struck chords of panic.

"Talking," Joli said. "What are you doing?"

The door was wide open. Kogen's hands were on his waist, his coat unzipped, exposing the gold belt buckle on his skinny leather belt. He looked with heavy eyes.

"I can red card you both."

"For what?" Joli ate the whole foot, her words muffled.

"You're in another student's room with the door closed."

"It wasn't closed, Kogen."

"It wasn't open."

"It wasn't closed."

Chris was hardly breathing.

"And Sai went to the bathroom," she said. "No rule against that."

Kogen nodded slowly. "I'll wait till he gets back."

"Yeah, well, it might be a while." She held up two fingers. "Candy and sauerkraut, you know?"

Chris wished she'd stop. Just apologize, tell him they were looking for Sai, they thought he was sick, they were just leaving. The more Kogen's eyes narrowed, the louder she chewed, the sicker Chris felt.

"I heard you took a poster off one of the boards." Kogen looked at Chris. "That's against the rules."

"We found it in the trash," Joli said. "That isn't. Besides, Charles already yellow carded me. You can't red card a yellow card for the same thing."

Kogen kept his slotted glare on Chris. It penetrated his skull, a tractor beam extracting the truth. Chris looked down. He was still holding the plan that had been tucked under the model.

"Mr. Claibourn might lose the eye," Kogen said. "We had to take him off the mountain last night, send him to a specialist. It could be a detached retina. That's serious."

"No, you didn't," Joli said. "I saw him this morning at Bixen, shoving a breakfast roll in his mouth. Besides, a detached retina isn't that serious. My mom had one from a volleyball accident, and they fixed it the next day. You know how hard volleyballs are?"

Chris couldn't tell if she was telling the truth. It didn't matter. She'd called his bluff and he didn't raise. He walked inside the room, his shiny dress shoes kicking up papers and clapping the floor. He looked around the desk, unperturbed by the headless cookies, and plucked a plum-colored gumdrop from a plastic container.

"How do you think it would feel if I hit you in the eye?" He held it like a dart.

"He didn't do it," Joli said. "There were witnesses. And leave him alone, Kogen. What's your problem? You're supposed to be his guide."

A joyless smile creased his cheeks. His teeth in white rows.

"Stopping problems before they start, molding boys into men. That is guidance, Ms. Oliveira."

"You're not helping."

"Most people don't understand the problem." He turned his sterile smile on her. "And can't recognize true compassion."

"This ain't it."

"What are you doing in here?"

"None of your business, really. We don't have to tell you everything."

"Chris?" He popped the gumdrop in his mouth, grinding it between his molars.

"Um. Just, you know." He held up the folded paper. "Just wanted to show him some ideas."

"Ideas?"

"Yeah. About the challenge."

"Mmm." Kogen tipped his head. "What ideas?"

Joli snatched it first. "It's a secret."

"Give it."

"No. You know the rules. We can talk about it. And we don't want our ideas getting out. I know how you slackers are, all gabby when you sleep in your coffins with the lids open. You can't keep a secret."

Chris cringed. He'd never heard anyone call them slackers. Kogen didn't flinch. Maybe he'd called them slackers when he was a student. Before he became one. He considered the folded sheet of paper. Was there even a way to report a slacker? Could they get him red carded?

"Sai's not coming back," Kogen said. "You need to get out."

"Where is he?" Chris said.

"He's not in the bathroom."

"No, I mean, he's not leaving the school, right?"

Kogen was more relaxed. That was his natural state, having someone on their heels. It was so easy with Chris. He fished another gumdrop out of the container and squashed it between his teeth.

"Out."

"Sure." Joli grabbed Chris's elbow. "You have to leave, too. Those are the rules."

Kogen watched them go. He looked around the room again, stared a few moments at the headless cookies before closing the door and striding unevenly down the hall. The colder it got, the more he limped.

"And you can't take gumdrops from someone's room without asking," Joli called. "Rules, Kogen."

He turned down the stairwell, the report of hard soles fading.

"You almost showed him the plan?" She wagged the paper at Chris.

Chris realized what Sai had told them in the cafeteria. That they weren't supposed to know what the challenge was about. She shoved it in his pocket.

"Give it back to him when he's back," she said.

"What if he doesn't come back?"

"He will."

She sounded like she was convincing herself. Kogen had seeded doubt in her too. Could they all just disappear like that?

Chris grabbed his backpack. Ceramics class would start soon. They were doing teapots that would be graded on creativity and functionality as well as critiquing others.

Chris pulled the paper out of his pocket. The sketch of what Sai wanted to do for the challenge was so detailed. Joli was right. They couldn't do that even if they had a week. But Sai had added something to it. A line written in tiny letters at the bottom. It looked like the scrawl on the other pages he'd shoved in his pocket, but it wasn't strange ramblings. It was a simple statement.

You can't catch me.

7

There once was a boy in a castle.
It was tall. Solid. The stones mined from the mountain and laboriously cemented. In the summer, the rooms were dank and cool. The warm wind would pass through the open windows from one side of the castle to the other, ventilating the stuffiness that filled the dark rooms. In winter, the walls were warmed by roaring fireplaces continuously stocked with wood.

It was any child's dream. But it was all he knew.

The servants chopped wood and tended the garden and stables. Gretchen, his favorite, was a portly woman with a chin that quivered when she laughed. She would wake him in the morning, dress him, and feed him. At night, she sat in a rocking chair and told stories. Sometimes, he would stare out the window as her chair creaked, watching the moon. And she sang to him.

He would watch the gardener in the afternoons and the stable hands tend the horses. Occasionally he would feed them sugar cubes, their rubbery lips on his hand. But he didn't ride them.

He preferred to watch from the castle.

The servants would bring him things from outside. A netted butterfly or shiny beetle, interesting sticks or colorful rocks from the stream. He would put them on shelves. Oftentimes, when he was very young, he would sit in the eastern reading room, surrounded by books, looking out the window to watch the road. He would sing to himself while waiting for his father.

His earliest memory of his mother was when he was three years old. He was sitting in her lap in front of the dining hall fireplace. He remembered the elk head staring at them from above the mantel, its glassy eyes black and bottomless. He was wrapped in a fur blanket, falling asleep as she sang. Her voice was soft. Beautiful. He liked the way it felt against his chest.

Fever took her one day.

Gretchen said his mother was too young. The boy didn't understand. His father arrived a week later. It was the only time he heard him weep. He gave the boy a photo of her, a small colorless photo, to remember her. The boy didn't cry. It was years later that he understood what Gretchen meant.

His mother was twenty-two years old.

His father was a businessman. He made clocks, knives, sewing machines and other things that required him to be in Sweden. This, Gretchen explained, was across the ocean. He took a ship to work. That was why he only came home every three months. That was why he spoke differently than everyone else.

He knew when his father was about to arrive. Gretchen would dress him in a particular outfit, press his trousers, put on shiny shoes, and wrap a tie around his neck. He would stand with the servants out front in the summer, in the dining hall when it was cold. The boy called his father sir. Gretchen said he was a lord. That was important.

His father would take tea in the big room, sit in a red leather chair studded with brass tacks. He would cross his legs and read the paper, small square glasses perched on the end of his nose. On the boy's birthday, his father would give him a card. He would sign his full name, first and last. "Happy Birthday, son." It was always the same. Except when he forgot, then Gretchen signed it. The writing was different. And she would add "I love you."

When his father was away, the boy would fill the endless rooms with the stuff the servants fetched for him. It started with a rock collection. He was fascinated by the different shapes and patterns, the colors that were muted or sparkly, little bits of quartz or minerals. He arranged them on shelves according to their characteristics or size. They brought him new ones daily. And daily he reorganized. Sometimes from the time he woke up to the time Gretchen tucked him in.

He took to building houses with sticks and twine. Elaborate constructions that resembled three-story dollhouses with pointed roofs and arching doorways. He fashioned dolls out of corncobs from the garden and designed clothing from fabric. In the summer, they would bring him berries that he would use to dye the fabric. One year they grew indigo. He would cut swatches and clip them to lines, studying the colors that changed with time.

Before he was ten, Gretchen taught him to paint. She wasn't very good. Her paintings were simplistic, he thought. He would sit at his window and replicate, with impressive realism, the trees and the garden, the horses grazing. Gretchen once sat for him each morning, when the sunlight came through the eastern window, for a month. She was impressed. It wasn't the fake enthusiasm given to children for eating their vegetables. She had no words to describe it. He could tell by the look on her face.

His paintings were displayed around the castle. When his father returned one Christmas, he wasn't as impressed as Gretchen. He made no sounds as his shoes clapped the cobbled floor, his hands locked behind his back, stopping to peer through his square spectacles. Later that week, after he left, a tutor arrived to teach the boy the finer points of painting, introducing him to watercolors, oils and other media.

The boy became quite good.

His fondest memory of his father was the time he saw the rock collection. Of all the things the boy had created, this seemed to be the least impressive. But his father, in his usual candor, perused the shelves and made sounds of approval. "Orderly," he said. "Fine eye for detail, son."

Perhaps it wasn't the compliment that moved him. He'd called him son.

No matter how much the boy painted or built or collected, he could not satisfy the itch. He wanted more. A sign of a great artist, Gretchen once told him. Never satisfied.

It wasn't enough for the boy. He wondered, even at the early age of ten, if there was a way to be at peace. There was something missing, he thought. A hole he couldn't fill. Even when he squeezed the berries of all their juice, when he licked it off the floor, when he wrapped himself in *freshly dyed fabric till his skin was stained, he could not fill the hole. He began eating his creations. First it was berries. Then it was small sticks and pebbles. He would eat them until he vomited. For a brief moment, he was satisfied. But the hole would return.*

At the age of twelve, he took fever.

Gretchen had begun to worry. It had lasted a week. She would wring her hands when she brought wet compresses for his forehead, her lips tight with worry. Wrinkles bunched between her eyes as she fretted in her rocking chair, knitting scarfs and sweaters that would pile up.

She had his bed brought down to the dining hall, and he slept in front of the fire. He sweated through sheets that needed to be changed twice daily. Dreams were vivid and frightful. He would hear his dead mother singing in the night.

"When the cold winds blow and bring the snow. On a clear winter night we will see what it's for. The year may be long, but we can sing this song, and remind us that Christmas is coming."

His father arrived the next week.

He was not due for another month. He pulled his red leather chair with brass tacks next to the boy's bed, read the paper, and took his tea. Sometimes he took the compress from Gretchen to apply it to the boy's forehead.

His father spent time in the western room, a small room with a large desk made from walnut. Sometimes the boy would call out for him. Gretchen would take him to where his father was writing letters, studying documents and other things of business, muttering angrily in another language. He would look over his spectacles at the boy and ask if he was feeling better. Sometimes he would let the boy lie on the floor until Gretchen took him back.

The boy would pretend to sleep, listening to the way his father muttered in a foreign tongue to himself. He liked the sound of it, although he never understood a word. His voice was low and powerful. It was big, like his stomach. Full like his beard. It was impossible for him to whisper.

It was one afternoon the boy fell asleep on the floor. He woke to the sound of his father's voice. He was in the hallway talking to Gretchen, his shadow just past the doorway. He told her about a family who had a boy who was trouble, sneaking out of his room, exploring where he shouldn't. Their nannies would quit.

"We're on the third one," his father exclaimed.

But the tone of his voice was different. It wasn't stiff. He chuckled often, speaking affectionately. Despite the trouble this boy made, he sounded entertained. Envious. The boy could feel the affection in his voice. It felt delicious. He closed his eyes and dreamed it was him he was talking about.

His fever broke after the third week.

The boy watched his father talk to the gardener from a window. His laughter boomed with joyous tenor. The boy could feel it all the way in the castle. His father seemed happy; he wondered why he wouldn't stay. Didn't he want to be happy?

The carriage was in the yard. The stable hands had the horses out, brushing their coats, with feedbags around their heads. The boy knew what that meant. If only he could stay sick, his father would stay. He would be happy.

The boy went to the western room. His father's belongings were packed. A crate with a large duffel bag and a leather bag. The desk was cleared. The boy felt a strange sensation of doing something he wasn't supposed to be doing. It was new. Exciting. And for a moment, it filled the void, which was beginning to return.

He stroked the leather bag, smelled his hand. He unsnapped the gold buckle. A shiver hummed in his stomach. He listened for footsteps, then pulled the flap open. The contents were neatly arranged. Books and binders, a calendar, folders of papers with formal headings and neatly written scripts. The boy memorized the flow of the letters to repeat them later. He would write his father one day, perhaps, and tell him of his feelings.

He laid them open on the floor, occasionally pausing to listen, feeling the coarse paper, smelling the ink. The contents were things he didn't understand, things of business and men. He folded them up and replaced them exactly as he found them.

A letter was tucked into an inside pocket.

It was different than the rest. Smaller, eggshell white, with flowery writing. It smelled sweet like perfume. The waxy seal was broken. There was a lump inside. He pulled out the letter.

Dearest, it started.

It spoke about mundane things, the town where she lived, the people's troubles, and repairs to the house. But then it said, somewhere near the end, I'm pleased to hear you have recovered from your illness. You have been away far too long. We look forward to your homecoming. Nicholas misses you dearly. And I do too, my love.

An object fell out of the envelope. It was attached to a silver chain. An oval locket with a flowery design etched on the front. The boy ran his thumb over the etching, felt the smooth touch of the back. A tiny latch sprang open.

There was a picture inside.

It was faded tones of black and white. He didn't recognize the woman. But he knew the bearded man next to her. Wearing his square spectacles. There was a boy between them with a mischievous grin. He looked to be the same age as the boy.

The boy felt a pressure in his chest. Like a hand had reached inside to squeeze his heart like berries, squeezing until the juice was gone. It hardened into a stone. That warmth he felt in the presence of his father's laughter was swallowed by cold. And fell into the ever-widening hole.

He put the pendant in his pocket.

Months later, in his room one afternoon, he took it out. He painted over the picture with white. Over the next year, when Gretchen wasn't around and the tutor had left, he would pull a single hair from a paintbrush and sit in front of the black-and-white photo his father had given him when he was very young. Little by little, he painted the details of his mother.

When the cold winds blow and bring the snow... Christmas is coming.

8

Chris jolted upright.

Papers fluttered on the floor. He'd fallen asleep deciphering Sai's story, the handwriting fading into illegible script through large sections. The story, however, was good. It felt like more than a writing assignment.

His hair was flattened against his head, the pillowcase printed on his cheek. He had been dreaming of the cold stone of the castle and a rock collection. The sun was up. He jumped out of bed and looked through the wreath on his window. The quad was dusted with snow, off-colored shortcuts carved in the frozen gravel paths.

Three people were warming up for exercise.

He was still dressed from the night before. He put the Toy Collector story on the desk, grabbed jeans and clean underwear and a T-shirt from the floor, smelling it first, then hustled down the hall. Jacob Steyer was brushing his teeth, and Justin Meiers was popping a zit.

Chris pulled the curtain on a shower stall and cranked the handle. The water was straight from the Arctic Ocean. The water heater sucked. The best he could hope for was tepid. He'd given up on something warmer weeks ago and just gave in to cold showers.

He bundled his dirty clothes in the towel and walked back while pulling on his shirt, almost walking into the wrong room. It had been closed for almost a week. Someone was cutting something heavy.

Sai was at his desk, wearing boxers and a black shirt that barely covered his stomach. His arms were ochre in the morning light, his hair a black mop. He didn't turn around.

The floor was still papered. The bed exactly the same. The pages Chris had taken a week earlier wouldn't be missed. Sai worked a yellow-handled pair of scissors through a square of cardboard. The model was twice the size since Chris had last seen it. Windows were outlined with swirly patterns of white, red and green icing. The eaves dripped with white frosting, the crooked door pried open. Gumdrops were inside like sugar-coated presents.

Chris cleared his throat. "Hey, Sai. Where you been?"

He creased the cardboard and made another cut. "Medical," he muttered.

"You, you were at the clinic?"

"Just needed some quiet."

The floor had been relatively silent for the past week. Midterms had dampened the party. Chris had been running a playlist through the night on a little Bluetooth speaker he'd bartered with Shane Barlow. Ten espressos made to order. It was barely loud enough to hear across the room.

"Was it me? I thought... I didn't think, you know, I was playing music that loud."

He used a utility blade to cut a smaller rectangle, then smeared it with black icing. It looked like solar panels. A tower had been erected with wind turbine blades.

"Is that what you want to build? For the, uh, the challenge?" Chris swallowed a knot. "I'll be honest, I think Joli's right. I don't think I can do it. I wouldn't know—"

"You'll know."

"Yeah, sure. But that." He pointed. "You're using cardboard and glue and, and, I mean, the challenge has to be edible. I'm not sure how we're going to do that. The details, maybe, but not the structure."

"You have to."

He pushed away from the desk, his eyes red-rimmed with ashy question marks. His lips moved silently.

"You all right?" Chris said.

He stood like an old man climbing out of a soft recliner, shuffling to the door with joints needing grease. He looked down the hall.

"Wait," Chris said. "I don't think you should—"

He closed the door quietly. Sat on the bed, rubbing his face, running his hand through his thick hair till it stood out like he'd stuck a fork into an electrical outlet.

"You got to help me, man."

"What's wrong?" Ice cubes fell in Chris's stomach. "Is there anything, like, that I can do?"

"You build it."

"That?" Chris shook his head. "I don't see how—"

"I can't do it much longer."

"Do what?"

A long breath quivered. "I can't tell you."

The window was etched in frost. Foggy figures were milling out to the quad, stomping holes in the new snow. The slackers were out front, cranking their arms to the sides, pulling their legs behind them.

"Does this have to do with them?" he whispered. "The, uh, the slackers?"

"Not like that. No, I mean I *can't* tell you. Not you, not anyone."

"What about Ms. Taiga? She's—"

"Nobody!"

"Okay. Okay." Chris shook his head nervously. If Kogen found him in the room with the door closed, he was getting red card number two. For some reason that felt worse than running laps.

"He says you're the one," Sai said quietly.

"Who? Who said that?"

"You're the one who can help him."

"I-I-I don't understand, Sai. Help who?"

He scooted across the mattress, leaned against a wall. A landslide of notes cascaded on the floor. It was more of the story. Chris had the urge to pick the pages up. Sai rested his head on the wall.

"What he's really doing to us."

"Who is doing what?" A magnetic wave hummed inside Chris's brain. He touched his temple and tasted something sweet. *Cloves and sugar.*

"I *can't* tell you, Christmas. But he can."

"How... how do you know my name?"

They stared at each other. Kogen knew his birth name. Joli was still calling him Christopher. The teachers called him Mr. Blizzard. Sai thumped his head on the wall, soothing whatever bothered him.

"Um, here." Chris pulled a page out of his pocket. "I want to help, seriously I do. I mean, I don't know how building that will help you, but we can try. This is yours though."

He tossed the plan on the bed. Sai's eyes darted toward it.

"We were in here a few days ago, looking for you. Me and Joli. Sorry. We were just worried. And I took that." He opened the plan. "I just wanted to have another look to see if it, uh, if it would work. I mean, I still don't know how, and Joli doesn't want to, but I, uh, I shouldn't have taken it."

He put it on his lap.

"The, um, there was something you added to it." Chris tapped the line at the bottom. "It wasn't there before. I was just wondering, you know, what it meant."

Sai thumped his head. "He broke Bobby."

"He did, huh." Chris almost asked who.

Sai deflated. "He didn't mean to. Honest, he didn't. Nothing like that. He was trying to help because Bobby found him, and then there was this whole thing that happened. Now Bobby's gone and I can't do it, Chris. I wish I could, but it just doesn't work."

"Right." Chris knew what not to ask, and that was every logical question. *Bobby found him?*

"I found his clues," Chris said. "In the textbooks Bobby was using, I found them the first night I was here. He underlined letters that spelled a sentence. Joli figured it out, really. *Run, run as fast as you* can." He pointed at the plan where Sai had written the line. "*You can't catch me.*"

For the first time, Sai actually smiled. It was a joyless attempt. He mouthed something like he was talking to himself. Chris could read his lips. He was thinking the same thing.

"You'll understand, Chris. I promise." He opened his eyes. They were clearer than before. A weight lifted, or a burden. "You can feel it, right?"

No. No, he couldn't feel it. There was no way he was going to stop anyone from doing anything or help anyone. If he could, he would've done it in the cafeteria. He glanced out the window.

"When you left and Claibourn, he, uh, you probably heard what he did to Joli with the grape and the hot sauce? She was hurt pretty good, and you know what I did? I sat there, Sai. I saw him put the grape on her tray and didn't do anything. I watched her drink water and Claibourn laugh and didn't say a word. And you."

Chris shook his finger. It quivered like his voice.

"You were the one who stood up for her, Sai. You threw it, didn't you. You hit him in the eye. And what did I do? So-so-so if you or whoever it is you can't tell me thinks I'm going to help someone or stop someone, whoever's doing what, then you're wrong. It's not me."

Sai's eyes fluttered. His lips moved. Then he nodded.

"Flight, fight or freeze," he said.

"Yeah. What?"

"Those are the options. We either fly, fight or freeze. Those are the choices." He crawled off the bed, looked at Chris, then went back to his desk. "You chose to freeze."

"I didn't..." Chris ground his teeth. His hands clenched around his towel. "I didn't *choose* anything, Sai. I just... forget it. Look, I, uh, we should go. Exercise is almost ready to start."

"I'm not going."

"Okay, sure. But I got to."

Chris wanted to turn around, shout at him, tell him those were reactions driven by DNA. He didn't choose to do nothing. The other two options weren't available. He didn't know how to fight or how to run. He was born to freeze. *I didn't choose it!*

Sai measured another piece of cardboard. The truth hurt. Was he really that helpless? He grabbed several pages off the floor and shoved them in the towel. Sai didn't notice or care.

"He was right, you know," Sai said.

Chris opened the door. "Who, Sai? Who's right about what?"

The sound of scissors ground through heavy stock cardboard. "*You* threw the chocolate drop."

Chris didn't know what to say to that.

9

Clancer Hall was the stoutest of the halls.
 Thick columns anchored the building's corners like ancient rooks. Its dome-shaped roof was blocky, something that resembled life-sized Legos. Smoke chugged from chimney stacks. Snow clung to the crevices.

Its wide arching wooden doors faced an open field about half the size of the quad, with an unimpeded view of the castle. Chris stood on the semicircle of bluestone steps. The sun warmed his cheeks; his breath was foggy.

It looked like Mardi Gras crashed into a Halloween party.

Tempest Mallard wore a flowing robe that drifted behind her with sparkles glued to the trim that left uneven trails in the snow as she pranced. Her lips were as black as her eye shadow, but her hair was dusted white. Peter Dervishi carried a broomstick wrapped in electrical tape padded at both ends like a giant Q-tip. The fingers were cut off his leather gloves and his nails glossy red. He wore half a milk jug on his head with tenpenny nails poking out; his face painted with red crossbones. Jacque Moreau wore a tiny bathing suit and a rubber shower cap. His bony chest was bright pink. Katarina Novak trotted around a village of miniature snowmen, wearing pink cowboy boots and a white medical coat with a striped necktie swinging from a cutoff T-shirt that said PARIS.

Chris wore a gray sweatshirt with coffee stains.

He watched them gather and gossip, throw snowballs, wrestle and dance. In the center of it all, Joli had rainbow-striped hair and torn black leggings and combat boots. Her oversized sweatshirt went to her knees. She was with Amoy Russo and Jamee Popa, both of them with safety pins through their noses, their hair gel-stiffened spikes. They were piling snow around a concrete sundial. Its iron fin protruded through wet snow.

She waved at Chris. She was telling the hot grape story, fanning her mouth and running in circles. Amoy and Jamee kept looking at him.

The castle was dark gray and patched with lime green lichen, the grout stained black. It faced south, the wall dripping with snowmelt. It looked like an aberrant pitchfork, a toothy warning to giants not to step this way. The spires were numerous, each poking at the sky with a copper tip. A single window was at the top of each one, lined with arching stone.

Someone was watching from the center spire.

"Hey," Joli said, "we were supposed to meet at the dial."

Inky vines were crawling up her neck and reaching for her eyes, like tortured clown tears.

"Forgot."

"No, you didn't."

He shrugged. "You see that?"

Joli squinted. "Huh, yeah. He likes to watch."

"Pelz?"

"Who else?"

It was a little creepy. Like a grandfather who didn't want to get dirty. He stood back from the window, maybe three steps away, so his outline was barely visible.

She waved and muttered, "Hi, Lord Pelz. It's me, your loyal subject. Joli."

Chris felt exposed. It was impossible for him to hear her. Could he read lips from that far up?

"It's freezing out here." She jumped in place. "Is it time?"

No one was wearing much more than a thin coat. A lot of them were starting to shiver. None of them, though, was Sai. He was supposed to meet them on the steps. Chris had knocked on his door then opened it. The room was a mess, but the desk was cleared. The model was gone. And so were the headless cookies.

"Listen." Joli looked around. "I've been thinking about asking Calista Pocheski to join us. She's with the fairies." A small group of tutu-wearing ballerinas had dragonfly wings strapped to their backs and thorny tiaras on their heads. "There's four of them. If Sai's right, one of them is out, and Calista is a crazy good potter. She did this—"

"No."

Joli frowned. "What do you mean no?"

"Sai said he'd meet us."

"Yeah, well, I don't see him. Besides, he's a little out of sorts, know what I mean?"

"We wait for him."

"No, no, we don't."

"He needs help, Joli."

"That's what I'm saying. He needs help, not to bake a cake."

He didn't know what else to say, how much to tell her. If she would even believe him. "He said..." He cleared his throat and leaned into her. "He said the other day there is something bad happening."

"Um, that's no secret, Christopher."

"No, I mean, something that nobody knows about."

"Okay." The tattooed vines wriggled on her chin. "What is it?"

"He said he couldn't tell me."

"Right."

"No, I mean, he didn't say it like that. It was more like, like..." He shook his head. "I don't know."

Joli surveyed the field. "Sai's got to help himself. You know? We can't, like, save him from himself. This place is hard. You got to have a sense of humor, got to roll in the snow, know what I mean? I got to take care of myself first. He's got to do the same."

A silver-clad trio approached the steps. Tinfoil rattled like sheet metal on their arms and legs; shiny cones reflected sunlight from their heads. They'd painted their faces gray and wore bike chains around their necks.

"Hey, Claibourn," Joli shouted, "you twenty-twenty?"

The tallest of the three turned around. He had two perfectly good eyes. "You feel your lips yet?" he said.

"Better watch it," Joli said, "or I'll have my boy here take out the other eye with a breath mint."

She snapped her fingers. He aimed his middle finger at both of them. Joli thought that was funny. Chris froze to the steps. He took a shaky breath.

"I thought he went to the hospital?"

"Yeah, well, Kogen's a liar."

Chris watched Claibourn tear a sheet of tinfoil off his leg and wad it like a snowball. He threw it at someone near the sundial, as if he'd already forgotten about them. No big deal. Like people eat red-hot grapes and take a chocolate chip to the eye every day.

A bell gonged. Chris felt it in his chest.

The crowd threw snowballs in the air and cheered. Claibourn chucked another tinfoil ball.

"Come on." Joli grabbed Chris's sleeve.

Corroded bull rings were bolted to the center of enormous arching cypress doors, the silvery-gray wood the color of a winter morning. They split open on rusty hinges, sending a squeal through the fading bell. It gonged again. Warm air escaped the building. A bright orange balloon wiggled out the widening door. It bumped across the overhang and lifted toward the sky with a small glossy gift in tow. It was followed by a red one, then a blue one.

Clancer Hall was belching party balloons.

"Oh, yeah." Joli pulled him back. "Gifts to the world. Forgot to tell you. It's, uh, symbolic. Our creativity gives to the world, that sort of thing. Which is hilarious because they all end up stuck in the trees. Which, actually, is more accurate."

When the last one bumped its way out, the bell gonged again and the doors swung wide. Joli was the first one through, dragging Chris by his sweatshirt into a dank atmosphere that smelled like burning cloves.

It was a short hallway with torches anchored in black iron hangers. Oily smoke curled up the curved ceiling, where a gold balloon was stuck, staining the old stone with trails of soot. Shadows flickered across the cobblestone floor, making decorative grapevines dance over the entrance.

They entered a cavernous room divided by a velvet stage curtain. The faculty stood on a short stage, lined up shoulder to shoulder, wearing scarlet robes with fuzzy white cuffs, their gray and balding heads bowed slightly. Ms. Grendel was in the center with a thick wool robe that gathered around her feet. Her saggy bulldog jowls quivered. Lord Pelz might be the warden, but Ms. Grendel ran the joint.

The slackers were lined up, shoulder to shoulder, a step below the faculty in their standard attire, with hands locked behind their backs. They were upright, shoulders back in contrast to the faculty's stooped postures.

The bell gonged again, its tone reverberating in the open space behind the curtain, tickling Chris's eardrums. He followed Joli. They passed a roaring fireplace. The smoke was sweet. The room was thick with spices and yeast.

Chris peeked down the line of costumed students.

"God, they're old," Joli whispered.

The faculty looked like they'd been pulled from crypts and propped up. They were pillars of ancient wisdom. Chris felt a sheen of nervous sweat prick his chest when Joli whispered. His spine froze into an icicle. He was afraid his knees would buckle.

The final bell faded. Ms. Grendel stepped onto a short pedestal and swept a slow gaze down the line, a generous smile buried in her cheeks.

"Welcome, Gifters," her voice boomed, "to the 204th Fall Challenge!"

The students cheered and high-fived. The slackers clapped respectfully. The faculty did so delicately.

"Yes, yes, yes." She put her hands up. "I have the honor of leading you on this beautiful fall day to challenge your vision, your fire, your execution and creativity. And, most importantly"—she held up an arthritic finger—"your taste."

Another round of applause.

"This year you work as teams." She held up three crooked fingers.

"Sai was right," Joli whispered.

"You must choose your partners wisely, to lead. To execute. It is your partnership that will excel, not your individuality. *Lose yourself, Gifters.* You will have twenty-four hours. There will be no limits on ingredients. Your work, however, must excel in appearance, execution, and taste. The winners will receive triple credits until the spring challenge. The losers…"

She held up that long crooked finger, her gray eyes shifting back and forth.

"Will go home."

The panic was palpable. Like a vaporized cloud of pungent perspiration squeezed from their pores.

"What did she just say?" Joli whispered. Chris could feel the temperature drop.

"There is no reward without risk," the old woman continued. "So enjoy the process, be the moment, feel the thrill and heartbreak. The beauty of existence is born of harsh elements and perseverance. You are not here because of your talent but to forge the beauty from your souls. And most importantly…"

Her hands dropped to her sides. A dark pallor shaded her expression. She looked at Chris.

"To create."

The bell reported louder than before, shaking Chris's bones like a mallet striking solid oak. The velvet curtain dropped with a heavy whoosh, fanning the flames in the fireplaces, embers swirling like fireflies.

The room was revealed.

A large dome-shaped hall lined with arching opera boxes, and a tiered chandelier with dripping white candles hung from dull links of iron. The floor was cluttered with individual kitchenettes organized in rows. Pantries were arranged around the perimeter—shelves loaded with sugar and flour, jars of pickled vegetables, baskets of fruit, racks of spices.

"Come on."

Joli dragged him through the aisles. The kitchenettes were identical. Chris could taste the air; it tingled on his tongue, tickled his sinuses—fried onions, banana bread, garlic, ripe tomatoes and bitter coffee beans. They beat Jesse Hoffmann and his rubber-suited teammates, their oversized ski goggles like frenzied insects, to a station in the back.

"We need a third." Joli looked around. It was chaos. Teams were forced to cut down to three. The orphaned teammates were searching for each other, anybody. "Maria!"

Maria Kvaran had shaved her head and drawn crying eyes on the back of her scalp with gold paint.

"No," Chris said.

"Are you kidding me? Sai was wrong. Losers are going home. I'm not ready to go home yet. I don't care how good you think you are, two people aren't going to cut it. There just isn't enough time. Sai doesn't know what he's talking about."

"He was right about most of it."

"Except the going-home part."

"He'll be here."

There was a sketch pad on the stainless-steel surface and a thick wooden pencil. A notebook for ingredients.

Joli tied her paisley scarf around her neck. "Grendel loves pastries. And she loves horses. She's got pictures of them in her office, or so I heard. I've been thinking…"

The room echoed with clanging skillets. Teams were already gathering materials and mixing bowls, big spoons ringing on their sides. Joli made broad sweeping lines of a horse reared up, globs of sweets embedded in the hindquarters, cupcakes on its head. There was scaffolding material in the cabinets—candy canes and cinnamon sticks. She'd done something like this already with clay.

"Where do we start?" She slid the pad at him. "You're the cook. Come on, go. Don't freeze up."

His thoughts stirred like a snowglobe. He closed his eyes. Sweat found a way out of every pore in his body. His head began to pulse. It wasn't the fading tone of the bell, but that wave he felt from time to time. Someone slammed the countertop.

Sai was smoothing out his plan. The creases buckled the sheaf in quarters, the corners bent. He was wearing baggy sweatpants and a tight T-shirt that hugged his belly. He looked weary.

"You can do it," Sai said to Chris.

"No, he can't," Joli said. "No one can. We don't have enough time. You heard what happens to the losers, right? Right? We won't lose credits, Sai. We play it safe; we score enough to not go home. That's the plan."

Chris closed his eyes again. He felt the magnetic wave spread into his chest and thaw his backbone. The chaos of chopping knives and whirring blenders faded.

"I'm switching teams," Joli said.

Pressure inflated his skull. He leaned on the counter, felt the cold smooth steel on his palms. He imagined absorbing the details of the cutlery—the fully stocked cabinet below, the oven door, the iron burners. His body solidified, but something hot was burning inside, like magma at the core. A glass dish broke. He felt the shards scatter on the stones, felt the frustration of the person who dropped it.

"Chris?" Joli sounded a mile away.

He heard someone tell them to say cheese, Joli tell them to stop taking pictures, and where did they get a camera.

Chris was an ice sculpture, his skin cold and brittle. He was doing what he always did under pressure, the fear sweeping over him like polar winds. An avalanche of snow crushing him. Until he couldn't breathe.

And then something broke.

The pulsing sensation in his head shattered the icy grip. The magma spilled out, and he saw the plan. He saw how it could be done.

"Flour, baking powder, ginger, cinnamon, and cloves." He shoved metal bowls at Joli. "Go, now."

She looked around. "What?"

"And salt, brown sugar, butter, eggs, molasses, and water. Sai, I need you to fetch all the candy you can find—peppermint sticks, gumballs, gumdrops, white icing, graham crackers, food coloring, licorice, lollipops—"

Sai scribbled madly.

"Marshmallows, small and large, Life Savers, Smarties, Milk Duds, M&Ms, Skittles and butterscotches."

Chris pulled rolling pins from the drawer, lined up knives, stacked measuring cups and four bowls with large spoons. There was only one mixer. It wouldn't be enough. Joli was still holding the bowls.

"Do I need to write it down?" Chris said.

"No, I, uh..." She shook her head. He scribbled the list and slapped it in her hand. "How much do you—"

"It says it right there." He shook a pastry bag. "Now go!"

The room was a disturbed hornet's nest. There were already gaps on the shelves. He preheated the oven and looked at Sai's plan. He wadded it up. He wasn't going to need it.

He could see it.

Sai returned with an armful of colorful candy. "Not enough candy canes. Get two dozen more. And more Skittles!"

Chris stripped off his sweatshirt and cut the sleeves, wrapping one around his head. There was a ruler in the bottom drawer. He marked lines on paper for quick reference. Joli returned with flour, sugar and water in one bowl. He looked at the other.

"Ground cinnamon! What am I going to do with cinnamon sticks? Read the list, Joli. Pay attention." He scooped flour into a bowl. "Bring back what I need and start mixing. And there's not enough pans over here. I need two more. Find them."

If she protested, he didn't hear it.

He mixed the dry ingredients in one bowl and set them aside, then put butter and brown sugar in the mixer, adding eggs, molasses and water. The flour mixture was added and kneaded until it reached the right consistency. He wrapped it in plastic.

"Refrigerate." He handed the dough to Joli.

"How long?"

He didn't say anything. Just looked at her. She took it to an industrial refrigerator next to the spice cabinet. He started another batch.

"Organize." He pointed at the disarray of bowls. "Candies over there."

Sai followed his instructions, then took the second batch to the refrigerator. After two hours, the first batch returned. He dusted parchment paper with flour and rolled the dough into a thin sheet and cut pieces. The oven was ready.

"Joli, do these." He handed her notes. "I need these dimensions. Get them on the pan. Sai, get the royal icing ready."

Chris checked the oven. The first sheet he'd cut was almost ready. Joli was slicing her pieces. He put the ruler on one side, then balled up what she was doing.

"Wait. What are you—"

"Exact dimensions, Joli. Not sort of, not kind of. Cut them like this."

He took the knife and demonstrated.

"Hey, listen," she said. "You can just ask me—"

"Do you want to do this? Hey, no!" Chris jumped in front of a slacker who had his hands in his pockets and steely glare on the countertop. "You're not a judge. This isn't your business. Go!"

Kogen didn't move. But the faculty was watching. He shuffled away, as if he wasn't interested. Chris turned back on Joli.

"Do it now. Do it right. Please."

"That's all you had to say."

The pieces came out of the oven toasty brown. Sai organized them like Chris told him to do. This continued. Piece after piece, examined, broken, started again until he was satisfied. He needed all of them ready. They would need every bit of counter space.

Chris remembered a time when his parents took them to visit their grandparents at Christmas. The snow had drifted to the eaves of the house. They dragged a toboggan up a hill one morning when the sky was blue and crisp winter air watered their eyes. Chris had a scarf around his face and a stocking cap pulled down so that he was looking through a woolly slot. His dad put him on the front and gave him the reins. The wind bit through the scarf and stung his eyes. He held on tight as the snow slushed beneath them.

The hill was steep.

They were flying before they reached the bottom. He couldn't hear the snow or feel his fingers or his dad's arms around his waist. A powder trail in their wake, Chris didn't know if they would ever stop. And a weird thing happened. Time seemed to stretch out.

They were going so dangerously fast, he wasn't afraid anymore. He was blissfully caught in the magic of the sleigh ride, lost in the moment that he couldn't control. He had let go. And let the toboggan take them where it was going.

Chris took a piece of gingerbread.

❄

He jerked awake at the gargantuan sound of the bell.

He was staring at a chocolate waterfall pouring from a candy vase into the upturned mouth of what sort of looked like a sea monster.

"Hands up," Ms. Grendel announced. "The fall challenge has concluded."

The clatter of cutlery and pots echoed like raining tin cans. It rang in Chris's head as the gong's long tone drifted away. His breath tasted stale; his head was filled with cotton candy. He rubbed his eyes, flakes of icing falling like dried wax. Burnt sugar and cinnamon, nutmeg and ginger coated his nose.

His bottom was sore, like he'd been repeatedly beaten with a rolling pin. He rolled onto his elbows, pushed himself up. Joli was at their station, her hair a matted display of dusty colors. She wore a different shirt—a concert T-shirt with dates on the back and powder on the front, her cheeks smudged with icing.

"This, Chris... this..."

He pulled himself through a fog—the stirring, the baking, the bending, the squeezing. It was a mammoth assemblage of crispy tan walls and white sugary seams.

"Did we..." He leaned on the counter. "Did we make that?"

The porch was crooked, and the doorframe skewed. The bent door was open, the hinges laced with red strings of licorice. He peeked through it to see the slanted floor and fireplace framed with panels of biscotti with cinnamon stick logs in the hearth. A portion of the roof was removed to reveal the foyer—the upside-down staircase, the licorice whip ladders and toothpick chandelier with dewdrops of sugar.

"You did, Christopher."

He wished he could remember. He'd built little cabins from sticks in his backyard with his sister, had carved human figures from bars of soap, and folded canoes from paper to sail across puddles. But this.

"You've been awake for, I don't know. I went back to my room, and you were still going. You crashed. I finished that." She pointed at the lookout tower made with pretzels. "The whole thing, it looks just like it."

"Like what?"

"The mansion. The one we hike to. You weren't even looking at the plan."

It was to scale. A weird complex with obscure angles and warped dimensions. It had a tenuous lean like an old barn. The only thing out of proportion was against the lookout tower—the odd detail Sai insisted they include.

The headless figure.

It looked like a third grader's version of a human cutout. Gumdrops stuck to it like sugar-coated buttons. Red, green and yellow. The head was broken off at the shoulderless neck.

"You talk in your sleep," she said. "You were having a whole conversation—hey, no!" She snatched his wrist before he grabbed the headless figure. "Challenge is over. You can't touch anything till they judge it."

Something about the figure was off. He couldn't place it, couldn't remember. But some details were different. He recalled outlining it, shaping it exactly like the plan called to do. What was different?

"Where's Sai?"

"In bed. That's where we need to be."

Chris looked at the faculty. "Aren't they going to judge?"

"That's tomorrow."

"Tomorrow?"

"Grendel wants to wait a day." She shrugged. "I'm too tired to remember why."

He backed away, scratching for what was missing. They followed bedraggled students toward the door, the costumes half-shed, makeup smudged and faded. Tired eyes hung like bags of concrete. The faculty watched them exit, and followed. They stumbled down the steps.

Ms. Grendel was the last one out. The heavy doors collided into the arched doorway. The iron lock turned with a toothy key on a metal ring. The hall was closed until the judges assembled the next day.

Chris took a deep draught of winter air and blew the webbing from his thoughts.

"I didn't use gumdrops," he said.

"What?" Joli said.

"The headless figure. I didn't put gumdrops on it."

"Sai did, then."

She walked off. He stood on the steps, watching his classmates wander like the undead. Ms. Grendel leaned on her cane, the hickory shaft polished, and told him to get some rest. "Well done," she said.

That was the first time she'd ever spoken to Chris.

Maybe Sai did put the gumdrops on it. But he'd seen that headless figure before, in Sai's room. Did he switch them? By the time Chris made it to his room, he'd forgotten about it. He left his door open.

He was asleep when the waves pulsed through his head. In slumber, it was no longer magnetic waves. He heard a voice.

Hello, Christmas.

10

Chris pushed off the pillow like a deer hearing a twig snap. Light was coming through the window at a sharp angle. He'd slept through the night, his dreams a conversation in a dark room. The voices were familiar, but the words were dusty.

The door was closed. The quad was a trampled mess of frozen snow—the last students clad in gray sweatshirts leaving. He checked his watch.

Exercise was over.

He fell in the chair and grabbed his hair, waiting for Kogen's uneven footsteps and grim smile. A cookie was propped against a *Painting with Oils* textbook. It was in the shape of the gingerbread man he'd prepared for the challenge. Only this one had a head pasted on it. It was the one he'd made—the white lines of a jacket and a bowtie.

Sai had switched them. *What's it doing here?*

There was something odd about it. Not the design. It was the way it was leaning. Like it was balanced on thin legs. Standing there. Looking at him with circle eyes and a narrow smile. Chris reached for it.

Don't pick me up.

The words were in his head like they were spoken through a funnel. He shoved the chair back. The air suddenly felt mountaintop thin. He began gasping. It was like he knew what was coming next. He could feel it just before it happened.

The gingerman moved.

"What..." Chris said.

Breathe, buddy. Breathe. In with the good.

"What's happening?"

Just look at me, all right? Okay? Let it happen. It threw its arms out. *Get a gooood look.*

Chris fell out of the chair and crab walked across the floor, tangling in dirty clothes, slipping against the door. The gingerman watched him scramble for the doorknob, crispy thin arms on its hips. The line on its face bent in a smile. Chris scooted into the hall. His back against the wall. Eyes wide. The air so thin. If he could feel his legs, he would run.

"See a ghost?" Kogen stood over him. A satisfied grin.

Chris muttered. Pointed. Kogen looked inside the room. The gingerman had been on the desk. Chris rubbed his eyes.

You talk in your sleep, Joli had told him.

The stress was breaking him. He'd hardly slept in six weeks. Now he was sleepwalking. And talking to cookies.

"Hey." Kogen squatted next to him. "You stink, Christmas. There's rules about hygiene. You can't smell like hot garbage, son. I could red you for that. But I'll do you a favor this time."

He flicked a red card between his fingers.

"Strike two, bright boy."

"But—"

"You missed exercise. You want to complain, I'll strike you out for smelling like dog turds."

"I thought today, that exercise—"

"Because of the challenge? Oh, no, no. That's the grind. It doesn't excuse you from the daily. You do that no matter what. Fine job with your gingerbread house and all."

Kogen brushed his slacks like Chris's body odor stained the

fabric. He posed like a supervillain who'd just thrown a caped crusader in a shark tank.

"You lied about Claibourn." Chris stared at the plastic card, the edges biting into his fingers. "He didn't go to the hospital."

"You're not ready for the truth. You're a kid. A baby. Can't shower, can't exercise. You need guidance. I'll say whatever I want to help you grow. You understand? If you can't survive a little lie, you won't last." He ruffled Chris's hair. "Don't be late for class or you know what's next."

He walked off holding up three fingers, whistling a song. It was a great day in Kogen's world. Chris stared at the card, imagining how far it would fly if he threw it like a ninja star. If it would strike the back of Kogen's head, it would make the trip home worth it. There was only one reason he didn't do it. He would miss.

Sai's door opened a crack.

When Kogen's whistling faded down the stairwell, Sai stepped out. He looked good. Rested. His eyes bright. Gently smiling as he slid next to Chris. The world was spinning. He sat there, staring into his room, waiting for the ride to stop.

"You did it, Chris."

Something moved on his desk. The cookie in the shape of a gingerman climbed up. Chris shook his head, his heart surging in his throat. He waited for reality to snap back.

"Do you..." Chris pointed.

Sai went into Chris's room.

"Hey." Michael Wagner stepped over Chris with a towel around his neck. "Good challenge, man. Hope you win."

Michael didn't look in the room, didn't see the cookie waving. Chris pinched himself, closed his eyes and opened them. Then he got up. He went in the room.

And closed the door.

※

HAVE A SEAT.

The voice was a strange sensation, like eavesdropping on someone else's thoughts.

Tell Sai to sit. The cookie aimed its arm. *He can't hear me anymore.*

Chris stood numbly. The words fell off his tongue. "It said to, uh, to sit."

Sai nodded like that made total sense. Not like a cookie told him to do it.

It? Did you just call me it?

Chris grabbed his hair. There was a legit voice in his head. Like he was talking to some guy. *He broke Bobby,* Sai had said. *He didn't mean to.*

Your head feels tight, the gingerman said. *That's me.*

"I don't... how..."

I don't know how it works, either. It just does. You know how vibrations work? Strike a tuning fork near a glass, that sort of thing? Don't like that one? How about this. You know how a radio works? Me neither. But it does. You're a good receiver. Sai not so much. He did good enough, though. Tell him he did good.

Chris shook his head.

Tell him. He can't hear me anymore, so you got to tell him. Tell him I'm proud.

"He said he's proud."

The gingerman saluted. *He looks good, right? You helped him, Christmas. That's all you.*

"Helped him? How did I... what did I do?"

This, buddy. The gingerman strutted across the desk, showing off his toasted body like a runway model. *I'm loving these stripes, the bowtie.*

He brushed his stomach. Crumbs dusted the desktop.

So Christmas, huh? Never heard of anyone named Christmas.

"What's happening?" Chris asked Sai.

"Bobby found Gman at the house, the one we hike to."

"Gman?"

"That's what Bobby called him. It was just the head. He showed it to me, thought it was cool. We're not supposed to take anything, but, you know, it didn't seem like a big deal. Then he said he heard him talking. I didn't believe him. But then, you know." He shrugged. "Yeah."

"Bobby found the head?"

"Show him," he said to the gingerman.

You're not ready for that, Christmas.

"Ready? Ready for what."

"He can sort of play things for you," Sai said. "Make you see it."

"Oh, man." He paced back and forth, pulling on his hair. "I'm talking to a cookie."

Remember, breathe. Panic starts with shallow breath. His cookie chest bowed out, the icing cracking.

"You breathe, too?"

I know stuff. Trust me.

Chris crossed the room and stooped to eye level. The cookie backed up, the circle eyes narrowing. He moved like Claymation.

"Is this the, uh, the help you needed?" he asked Sai. "You were hearing what I'm hearing?"

Sai nodded. "It didn't work so well with me. Gman said you were the one."

"The one for what?"

"To hear him. And make him a body."

Listen, we got off on the wrong foot. I'm sorry about the don't-touch-me thing. There's only one reason why someone picks up a cookie, know what I mean? There's just no easy way to break the ice with a cookie without a few crumbs. But Sai is sitting right there, and he's not freaked out, right? He stepped to the edge of the desk and poked Chris's nose. *This is happening, buddy.*

"How are you possible?"

Did you make yourself? Decide to be a boy? Be named Christmas? You were born. You didn't ask questions.

"I have blood, cells, organs, DNA. You're a cookie."

If you took an airplane back ten thousand years, you think it would blow minds? I don't know how this works. I'm here, you're there. Accept it —the big man works in mysterious ways.

"God?"

No.

"Pelz?"

No, no. We'll get to him. First things first. He climbed a stack of textbooks and tapped the window. *We need to get rid of him.*

Students were on the crisscrossing paths with heavy bookbags on their shoulders. The inflated Christmas figures moved like bad dancers stuck to the ground. Someone was cutting through the snow, walking between an inflatable dog with a nodding red hat and a leaning metal Christmas tree with glowing glass ornaments; his hands in his coat, shiny shoes stepping unevenly.

"Kogen?"

The gingerman turned. *Kogen.*

"You want to get rid of him?"

Bobby was a good kid. He was delicate. Emotional. Needed more hugs. Kogen broke him like a cookie. He's got to go.

"Get rid of him?"

Yeah. Rid of.

"Like rid of-rid of?"

Yeah, no. What? We're not going to hurt him. Just get him out of the way. He swiped his generic arm. *You like him?*

Chris shook his head. No. No, he didn't like Kogen. But he never entertained the idea of Kogen leaving. He'd accepted him as part of the school. A sadistic card-throwing egomaniac was part of the tuition. *Nothing's free,* Joli had said.

It's you or Kogen, Christmas. One of you is leaving.

"Can you just stop calling me... it's just Chris, okay? What do you mean?"

Why do you think I had you build the house?

"Build the house?" He looked at Sai.

"What's he saying?" Sai said.

"He said he wanted me to build the house."

"Yeah. That was Gman. I just drew what he showed me."

"How'd he show you?" Chris imagined a giant pencil wedged between the generic arms like two thumbs.

All you need to know is this. I needed you to build a body for me and a house for Kogen.

"How'd you know about the challenge?"

"He knows stuff," Sai said.

A lot of stuff. Listen, how do you think you built it? Huh? Think.

The details were still fuzzy. It was sleep deprivation, sure. But it was something else. *You flipped a switch,* Joli had said. He had felt different right when Sai showed up. That pulsing headache had returned like a balloon in his skull. And then he knew exactly what he needed to do. He saw it all, every detail exactly how it needed to be done.

And he'd blasted Kogen. When he'd stopped by to look, Chris had grown fierce. He'd totally forgotten about that. The look on Kogen's face. He was itching to give out another red card. Chris didn't need to give him another reason.

"That was you?" Chris said. "Inside my head."

Not exactly. But sort of. I needed this. He curtsied. *And you need Kogen out of the way. I do, too.*

"So this is about Kogen?" He looked at Sai. Sai shrugged. It was hard having a two-way conversation with three people.

It's way bigger than that, buddy. He swung his legs off the desk. *Way, way.*

"What's that mean, it's bigger? Bigger than what?"

Baby steps, Christmas.

"Chris!"

Gingerman fell like he had been hit with a fly swatter. He rolled himself upright. For a baked cookie, he was surprisingly pliable. Then again, the laws of physics weren't applying to this situation.

Turn it down. He scratched his head, crumbs sprinkling the floor.

"Sorry." It wasn't the volume that did it. Chris felt the thought ring in his head. He meant it, felt it hum like the gong on top of Clancer. The tuning fork nearly broke the glass. In the last thirty minutes, he went from sleeping to having a conversation with a cookie to plotting Kogen's expulsion.

"Bigger than what, Sai? What's he mean by that?"

Sai stopped smiling. "I don't know exactly. Bobby said there are bad things going on. Gman knows."

Chris tangled his fingers in his hair. "This is crazy."

Is it crazy if everyone is doing it? Yes. But you're not. Yet.

"What does that even mean? Forget it." He looked at his watch. "We got to get to class, Sai."

He threw books in his backpack. There'd be no time to shower. Whoever sat next to him would have to suffer. He couldn't be late. Gingerman dodged the books and leaped onto the bed next to Sai. They watched him sweep his desk until his bookbag bulged.

I get it. I'm just a cookie. That's okay. But here's the deal. This isn't a dream. You'll go to sleep tonight, wake up, and I'll still be here. And so will Kogen. And you know what happens the next day? Me, Kogen, you. You know what happens—

"Okay, all right. I get it."

Chris slung his clothes into the corner and found less offensive ones. He sat on the bed to tie his boots.

Chris, hey. Chris! He felt a coarse nub on his arm. *I don't want you to go home, buddy. I just met you. Besides, you made me whole again. I'm here for you.*

"I don't need your help."

Yeah. Yeah, you do. Because I know what Kogen's about to do. You'll go home. Sai will go home. So will Joli.

"What?"

Yeah. Bye-bye. He's like that.

"How do you know about Joli?"

"He knows things," Sai said.

"What's Kogen going to do?"

Sai looked at Gingerman first. "I swear I don't know."

Listen, Chris. There's no time to debate. You're talking to a cookie with your thoughts, remember? This is real. And so is what I'm telling you. Just do it. If I'm wrong, you can throw me over the wall. But I'm right, Chris. I'm right.

He looked at his watch. "I can't miss class."

You won't. Here's what you do, and repeat after me so Sai can hear. It's very important you do exactly what I tell you or else it doesn't work.

He gave the instructions. It was an animated explanation. Lots of bouncing on the bed, loud thoughts in his head. He made him repeat everything back.

Don't screw it up, Chris. He scaled the pillow onto the desk and looked out the window. *This isn't just about you and me. It's something that's been happening a long time. It's bigger.*

"Something bigger, right."

Chris opened the door. Joli had her head turned. She had been listening.

"What are you doing?" She looked at Sai. "Closed door will get you card number two, Christopher."

Hahahaha... Christopher.

Chris didn't tell her he already had number two. Sai walked up to her with his hand up. She high-fived him, confused. He went to his room with a smile. Even if everything went totally sideways, at least Sai looked normal.

"What's with him?"

"I'll tell you later."

Chris couldn't walk to class with her. He would have to run if he was going to make it in time and do what the gingerman asked.

11

"What did you tell him?" Joli said.

Chris watched Sai from the top step of Clancer Hall. Sai didn't take the shortest route across the yard where snow had frozen footprints. He walked along the gravel path with Ms. Grendel. The old woman stabbed the gravel with her lacquered hickory cane, the glossy finish catching the sun.

"That someone cheated," Chris said.

"In the challenge?" Joli blew in her hands. "Who?"

Chris checked the time. Five minutes till eleven o'clock. Sai was late. He knew it, too. Ms. Grendel moved like a wind-up toy on its last turn.

"It's gonna be close," Chris muttered.

"Close to what?"

He hopped down the steps. Ms. Grendel was startled by his approach. Her eyebrows looked like two bushy caterpillars greeting each other. The cane struck the gravel like a pickaxe. She rested both hands over the sterling silver handle and regarded him down the bend of her nose.

"This is a very serious accusation, Mr. Blizzard. You realize this?"

"I do, ma'am."

"These doors are not to be opened until the bell strikes noon. You have irrefutable proof?"

"It's inside."

"Ah, inside." Her mouth hung open. "I am not opening the doors without sufficient evidence. We watched the event very closely, you understand? We inspected each piece before locking the doors. Did you see something we did not?"

The first bell rang. Chris looked at his watch. Her coarse words drowned in the slow-fading gong.

"... integrity of the students. There is no tolerance for falsehoods here." She waved her hand. "Or bitter rivalry."

The second bell tickled Chris's eardrums.

"Mr. Blizzard?"

"You have to see it, ma'am."

"I see." She shuffled onto the first step and looked down on Chris. She smelled like spiced apples. "Do you want me to go through with this?" She dug into the lining of her wool overcoat and displayed a trio of plastic cards. One for each of them. "Are you positive, Mr. Blizzard?"

A card slipped from her trembling hand.

"I'm sorry. I was just..." Chris shook his head. "Yes, ma'am. The proof is—" The third bell rang. "There will be no doubts if you open the doors. We just have to be quiet."

She grunted. "Would you care to explain?"

"You'll see."

The fourth bell sounded. Sai handed the fallen card back. Joli stared with wide-eyed confusion, mouthing words he couldn't understand.

"You are in agreement, Mr. Laghari?"

"Yes, ma'am," Sai said.

"Ms. Oliveira?"

She looked at Chris. It was one red card for her and Sai if the gingerman was wrong. Chris was going home.

"Yes. There's definitely something in there."

Ms. Grendel looked up. The tower castle cast sharp shadows the length of its rough walls. Chris didn't need to turn around. Someone was watching.

The fifth bell rang.

A cold, cloudy sigh escaped her. "Very well. But I must warn you not to touch a thing. You will be disqualified, all three of you. Understand?"

She jabbed the steps one at a time and shrugged off Sai's help. The sixth and seventh bell had struck by the time she reached the last step. Chris waited at the doors. She had difficulty unlatching the iron ring of keys from her belt. She handed the cane off and sorted through the metal skeletons, counting them with stiff fingers. They slipped from her grip and clattered to the stone.

The eighth bell.

Chris swept them up. She snatched them back. Her rebuke was swallowed by the ninth bell. Gruffly, she sorted a key, the stem shiny with wear, and stepped into the shadow of the arching doorway. The ninth bell was nearing the end as she drove it through the keyhole.

"Ms. Grendel?" Chris said. The old woman paused. Perhaps Chris was having second thoughts. "You won't be disappointed."

The sound of the lock's tumblers disappeared in the ten bell's thunder. Even Chris couldn't hear it. She dialed the key and pulled it out. This time she deftly latched it back onto her belt and reached for the metal handle.

Chris grabbed it first. Her frown drove wrinkles deep into her saggy cheeks.

"Mr. Blizzard, you are not—"

The final bell of the eleven o'clock hour struck.

Chris snapped the handle down and leaned into the door. The creaking hinges were lost. She stood with disapproval. The bell was waning. Chris waited with it open. His heart thudded. There were only seconds left when she stepped inside. Sai and Joli quickly followed.

Chris shut the door. The creaking was barely audible. Still, it might be the last sound of his enrollment.

The torches flickered on the walls. The smell of oil haunted the cramped space. The scarlet drapes at the end of the short hallway were closed. Shadows leaped among the folds. Chris tiptoed with the cane in one hand. The metal tip would have signaled their approach.

Ms. Grendel grumbled, "Your performance is tiresome—"

Chris held a finger to his mouth and parted the curtains. Across the room, a figure was hunched over a station. It was too far away. Ms. Grendel would barely notice. Chris pulled the curtains a bit more.

Ms. Grendel was not entertained. Her annoyance was overcooked. Anger boiled in her gray eyes, turning them a sharper hue of steel. Deep tracks carved her forehead like eroded channels in soft clay. She drew a breath as the final bell gave way to silence, flicked a glance into the room.

Her color changed.

Curiosity seeped into her expression. She tilted her head, mouth falling open on stubborn hinges. The room was supposed to be empty.

"Stop!" the old woman's voice bellowed with surprising steam. "Remain where you are. Do not move."

The intruder spun around and dropped what he was holding. He was rigid, the headlights of shock freezing him in place. Ms. Grendel held out her hand. Chris gave her the cane.

It spiked the stones like a spear.

They followed her like ducklings, passing impeccable creations— a theme park of taffy and cotton candy, a dragon confection with a toothy mouth holding a blue flame, a chocolate tower with staircases that merged in a never-ending spiral. Ms. Grendel was singularly focused, her cane echoing like the strokes of a pendulum.

Kogen had turned the color of bleached flour. "Ms. Grendel—"

The old woman held up a gnarled hand. She pointed the cane. Kogen stepped back. She fixed him in place with the well-practiced glare of a tenured professor. She pointed to the objects on the floor. Chris picked them up. The old woman examined them.

A utility knife and plastic syringe.

White shavings were swept into neat piles. The syringe contained water. Ms. Grendel observed the gingerbread house from three angles. Kogen's jaws clenched. She held the cane with both hands and lightly tapped one of the load-bearing walls.

The roof collapsed.

The structure had been weakened. The seams diluted. Kogen was going to be long gone when the house failed for the judges.

"What possessed you..." Ms. Grendel stood inches from him.

"My apologies, ma'am. I—"

The hand went up. Kogen bowed his head. She gestured with polite and profound disappointment. Kogen led the way, head still down. They fell in behind Ms. Grendel's steady pace. The metal tip marked each step.

Kogen pulled the door open. Sunlight filled the short entry hall. Ms. Grendel stopped him on the top step. Students were watching. Ms. Cebotari was there with long white braids swinging from her headscarf. Mr. Faber was next to her, his dark shiny head steaming in the sunlight.

Ms. Grendel waited for others to arrive—Mr. Vukovic, Ms. Dekker, Mr. Kostovski, and others lined up as students gathered. Chris, Sai, and Joli stood behind her like administrators of a catastrophic announcement.

"Witness!" Her voice cracked. "We hold honor in the highest regard. It is the pillar that supports our endeavors, the foundation upon which we build character, the very fabric of our being. Without honor, we are no higher than the animals outside the wall." She pointed the cane. "We have betrayal among us."

"Confession!" Zack Lund shouted.

Others joined in. The calls grew louder. The teachers did not stop it. Ms. Grendel looked up at the castle.

"What's happening?" Chris said.

"I don't know," Joli answered.

Kogen turned his head. He wasn't looking at Chris or Sai or Joli. For a brief moment, his shame receded. He hissed at Ms. Grendel, "You did this."

"Come." Ms. Grendel waved at the slackers who had assembled. "Dishonor will stain us no more."

Three red cards were fanned under her thumb. Kogen took them in shame. The slackers stood aside. Kogen walked through the human corridor. In silence, they watched him enter the castle. The mob dispersed in an undercurrent of gossip.

The old woman turned with a stiff neck. "He sullied your creation, Mr. Blizzard. The judges will take that into account. And I must offer gratitude." She bowed slightly. "It was a great risk. Such courage is noted, for each of you."

"What's going to happen to him?" Chris said.

She smiled weakly. "I am curious. How did you know?"

"Kogen hated him," Joli said. "He's been after him—"

Ms. Grendel raised her hand, not taking her eyes from Chris. "Follow me."

"What about class?" Joli said.

Ms. Grendel patiently walked away. A trail of frost crept over Chris. A winter stream filled his stomach. Reluctantly, they followed the old woman stabbing the gravel path, students watching from a distance.

"Did Gman say anything about this part?" Sai whispered.

Kogen had been disgraced. But Chris didn't think the gingerman had this ending in mind. They went where none of them had been before.

12

The doorway was deep, the shadows cool and dark.
The door was metal with rounded bolts hammered into place. It swung slowly without a sound. Ms. Grendel used both hands to pull, passing her cane to Sai, mopping her forehead with her sleeve before taking it back.

The hallway was wide and high and long. Yellow sunlight bled through a window at the far end but didn't quite fill the length of the hallway. When the door closed behind them, the details dimly vanished—the rough texture of the walls becoming smoother.

There were wooden doors on both sides with rustic iron rings. Ms. Grendel went midway and pushed one open. She stood aside to let them pass.

It was a large room with a round table and high-back chairs milled from dark wood. Leather upholstery studded into hand-carved trim. Their breath trailed in wispy clouds. There were no windows, just candles tossing dusky light.

Her pace was slowing, her joints beginning to rust. A long, narrow table was against the wall. A white candle, the size of a soft coffee can, flickered over an open book, the pages thick and rough at the edges like the one Mr. Kramer had leafed through at the Tree. She offered a quill.

"Sign."

Joli went first, dipping the feather in a black well. The tip scratched the page. Chris scribbled his name under hers, the ink pooling where he started. Ms. Grendel pulled her coat aside, finding the metal ring on her hip.

A black door was on the far side of the room. A massive rack of antlers spread over it, the bony points once possessed by a great buck, its shadows dancing like a ghost trying to flee. Orange light flickered from a large gap below the door.

"Are we..." Chris swallowed. "Are we in trouble?"

He wished he hadn't said it out loud. The words came out guilty.

The lock sounded like a hammer. A torch made the stony staircase jitter. "We will be with you shortly."

She closed the door. The lock clanged into place. The tip of her cane slowly faded.

"Where's she going?" Chris asked.

"I don't know," Joli said. "But there's no way she's climbing those steps. She barely made it across the room."

Sai didn't seem bothered. He was flipping through the ancient guest book. Chris was afraid the ink hadn't dried. *We're already in trouble.*

"This place is a dungeon." Joli walked around.

Chris's eyes had adjusted to the candlelight. The air was cold and dank, almost wet. The kind of cold that sank to the marrow. It did feel like a dungeon—a dungeon with oil paintings framed in copper, brass and pewter. He pulled a chair out to sit down. It felt like a boulder and propped his head up.

It felt like the time Mike Jankowski tripped Jenny Cruz after third period, kicked her leg while she was walking. Jenny was carrying a stack of books and didn't land gracefully. Her glasses broke. A bloody garden hose poured from both nostrils, soaking the frilly edge of her blouse.

Chris saw the whole thing.

Mike didn't mean to hurt her. He panicked, told her Chris did it. His parents had to come to the principal's office. They couldn't understand why he would do it. Chris didn't say anything. Telling on Mike was worse than apologizing to Jenny. He was sorry, he truly was.

"Look at this," Joli said.

The oil paintings might have been done by former students from long ago, the finish dull, the colors muted. There were black-and-white photos, too. Smaller than the paintings, in simpler frames. There was the quad with the same gravel paths. The buildings hadn't changed, but the trees were smaller. Students were sunning on blankets, wearing long dresses and collared shirts, flat caps, boater caps and pillbox hats. There were no ornaments. No inflated snowflakes or dancing Christmas dogs. Just festive sculptures of iron, glass and stone.

"The Feast." Joli pointed at a more recent one.

It was a long table filled with dishes and candles. It looked like students standing with raised goblets, their expressions as muted as the colors. A large man sat at the far end, his details hidden in shadows. Ms. Grendel behind him.

The oldest of the photos was a grainy black and white. The masts of a ship pointed at a white sky. The name was painted on the side. The crew was hauling cargo aboard the *Alexander*. Two men stood near the plank. They were the same build—heavyset, bulky—wearing dark peacoats and short-billed caps.

"There's Kogen." Sai was still leafing through the book.

He'd flipped back a few pages, his finger on an ink-blotted signature. The letters were blocky, but legible.

"Probably got caught stoning a bird's nest," Joli said.

"And look at this."

Sai turned several pages. He went back and forth, sliding his finger down the brittle page. The first name wasn't familiar.

"Grendel?" Chris said. "Is that what it says?"

"When was it?" Joli said.

There were no dates or page numbers. But there were other names they recognized. Ms. Haberdashy, Mr. Morozov, and Ms. Balog.

The lock turned with a cold echo, punching Chris in the chest with adrenaline. The room was flooded with torchlit warmth. Two figures crept out of the stairwell. Each of them carried a heavy book bound in leather. The second one locked the door.

They wore gray wool coats and trousers a shade darker. The smaller one had thinning white hair as brittle as the guest book. Her mouth was a cave of wrinkles, puckered like she was holding a lemon. The other one wheezed as he locked the door. Blotchy spots on his scalp and the posture of a giant tortoise.

They didn't look up or even act like anyone was in the room, sitting at one end of the table, opposite each other, placing the books in front of them. They sat with long expressions, their cheeks pulled under the weight of gravity and long lives. They smelled like a basement.

They didn't teach any of Chris's classes. They looked too old, like talking would be exercise. And no one dressed like that. They each wore something that contrasted with the colorless drab. Around their foreheads was a thin band.

Made of gold.

"Hi," Joli said. "Do you, like, work here? In the castle?"

Their stares were long and unfocused. Maybe they were deaf. Joli was thinking that, too, and made the sign for coffee. Chris shook his head.

"Is there a bathroom somewhere?" Joli said.

Chris could use a bathroom, too. Hide in a stall for five minutes or an hour. But he just wanted to get this over with.

The lock turned again. "Have a seat."

Ms. Grendel was missing her cane. She gingerly pulled the chair out from the end of the table. The legs scraped the bumpy floor. She dropped a small velvet bag with a gold drawstring on the table. It thudded like rocks. The grays opened their books when she sat, holding pens like a raven would clutch a twig.

Chris felt dizzy.

Ms. Grendel called out the date and incident of Kogen's dishonor. The grays began to scribble, the points of their utensils sounding like matchsticks. Ms. Grendel covered the velvet bag with her thin-skinned hands thoughtfully, then pulled the string. A dull metallic ball rolled into her palm, a large ball bearing that tossed candlelight from its polished surface. She passed one to the gray with collapsing cheeks, who gave it to Chris.

It was warm like a biscuit straight from the oven.

"How did you know?" Ms. Grendel said.

"What... what is this?"

"How did you know about Kogen's betrayal, Mr. Blizzard?"

The ball bearing vibrated. He felt it hum. Like his bones had been jumped to a car battery, that sensation just before surgery happens. His voice sounded funny, tickled his ears, as he explained how Kogen had been acting during the challenge. He wasn't sure if he was making sense.

The grays transcribed like machines with scritching chalk sticks.

"He gave you two red cards," Ms. Grendel said. "Did you want to get rid of him?"

Get rid of him. That was what the gingerman said. Chris stiffened. The ball bearing hummed louder. He took a deep breath.

"I didn't want to fail."

"You seemed very precise with our entrance into the hall, timing it with the bells so he would not hear our approach. Correct?"

An intuition to tell the truth possessed him. The words nearly raced from his tongue. He swallowed them. "A creative hunch. I went with my gut. Like we learned in class."

"You gambled, then?"

"The judging was going to start soon. I honestly didn't know he was there. But I knew he was going to do something." That was the truth.

"You took a risk."

"It wasn't much of a risk," Joli said. "It was a matter of time before Kogen gave him another red."

Ms. Grendel stared at Chris, her eyes shallow pools of turbid water. The grays stopped scratching, pens hovering. She fiddled with the velvet bag, poured another ball bearing out. This one to Joli.

"How did you know, Ms. Oliveira?"

"Like he said, Kogen was acting strange. He was up to something. Chris knew it, told me to meet him outside the hall. I trust him."

"Enough to fail?"

"Nothing is created without risk."

Touché. The foundation of what they taught at the Institute of Creative Mind. Ms. Grendel didn't react. It was clever, perhaps. Questionably convincing. The third ball was passed down the table. Sai was hunched over, cupping it with both hands.

"Place your hands on the table, Mr. Laghari. How did you know?"

"Chris asked me to get you." He sounded feeble.

Chris could sense the truth trying to escape, how a gingerbread cookie told them what to do.

"You were willing to fail?"

"Yes."

"So you knew, the three of you, that Mr. Archelleto was sabotaging your challenge. Is that what I am to believe?"

They looked at each other. Joli said, "No. We didn't know. But we believed. We took a risk. That's what I'm trying—"

Hand up. "Do you know what I believe, Ms. Oliveira? Mmm?" She shook her head, the hand still up. "You are not telling me something."

The old woman looked tired. She sighed and seemed to shrink. The grays held their hands over their pages, heads down. The thin gold bands around their foreheads, tucked under dead-end hair, reflected candlelight. The bands looked tight.

"Empty your pockets," Ms. Grendel announced. "Your bookbags, now. All of it on the table, please."

They looked at each other and then, slowly, pulled their pockets out. Pencils and pens, a shiny black rock, a crusted tube of acrylic paint, a paintbrush, a note from class with assignments, the wallet Joli gave him. Her yellow card from Charles. They were told to open their textbooks and dump their supplies. Sai dropped a button that read *Happy Now?* Crumbs sprinkled from his hand.

Ms. Grendel muttered to the grays.

She sorted through the debris with the tip of her cane, poking like it was radioactive. She walked around the table, leaning over them, pressing against their chairs, smelling like bath salts in a musty cupboard, and called out the items. The grays wrote down each one. She licked her finger and dragged it through the crumbs, put it on her tongue.

Joli made a face.

Ms. Grendel nodded at the grays. They recorded whatever that meant. She fell back into her chair, slightly out of breath, closed her eyes. The room was silent.

"Dreams," Ms. Grendel said. "Tell me what you remember."

"Um, dreams?" Joli said.

"You do dream, Ms. Oliveira?"

Joli frowned, stammered, looked at the ceiling. "Pick up the sphere, Ms. Oliveira. Hold it in your hands."

Joli had put the ball on the table, absently. The one in Chris's hand felt heavier than before. It was uncomfortable. His palms glazed the surface with sweat. He was afraid to look at it.

"Just, uh, candy canes," Joli said. "Dancing sugarplums. The usual."

Sai said something about a car with doors made of cake.

"Mr. Blizzard?"

"I don't remember."

"You don't remember," Ms. Grendel repeated. Chris figured it didn't matter what they said. "Very well. One more thing before you go directly to class." She paused. The silence trickled down Chris's back. "Tell me how you threw it."

They were confused by the question. Even Joli's sarcasm was foiled.

"Threw what?" Chris said.

"The item that hit Mr. Claibourn in the eye," Ms. Grendel wheezed. "The chocolate."

She was looking at the items on the table. Like the answer had been revealed.

"Oh, that." Joli explained what Claibourn had done to her—the grape, the Reindeer Breath—and how Pauline had said someone threw it from behind her. Sai was gone. Chris was across the table. "I'll be honest. I'm glad someone did it."

"Is that so?" She turned her tired eyes on Chris. He shook his head. *You threw it,* Sai had told him. But he couldn't have. He didn't move.

The grays closed their books with heavy thumps. They moved with tiny steps to the door. Ms. Grendel held out her hands, the folds deep and weathered, the knuckles swollen. They passed the spheres, as she called them, to her. She tied them in the bag.

"Hand me your red cards."

"Wha-why?" Chris said.

She gestured with her claw. Joli handed her the yellow card. Sai didn't have any. Chris opened the wallet. Both red cards were in the pockets.

"On your way. You're late for class."

"Is that, is that it?" Chris said.

Joli didn't need a reminder. She and Sai swept their belongings into their backpacks and hiked them on their shoulders. Ms. Grendel followed the grays to the door, the climb inside appearing impossible.

"What about Kogen?" Chris said. "What'll happen to him?"

She paused in the doorway. Then locked it behind her.

13

Chris's bedroom door was open.

Joli and Sai were still at the cafeteria. He'd seen them on his way out of pastels lab. Maybe Sai had stopped by to see if he was there and forgot to close his door all the way. Chris's room was a mess.

But a different mess.

Papers scattered on the floor, clothes lumped in piles. He'd stopped putting them in the dresser but still organized them in piles of socks and shirts and pants. Now they were mixed. The handle of the coffee pot was pointing straight out. He always left it to the side.

A bitter breeze rustled a note stuck to the desk. He'd left himself a reminder to submit homework. The window was cracked, but that was the way he always left it. It was dark outside, the colorful glow of blowups dancing in the quad.

"Hey," he whispered. "You here?"

There were crumbs on the desk, the same ones that came from Sai's pocket. Chris looked under the bed, in his drawers, kicked the clothes. Music was in the hall. People were milling back and forth, casting a second glance when they saw him peek out.

Sai and Joli exited the stairwell.

She was cordial, joking with people she passed, shouting inside the room where the dance party had started.

"Is he in your room?" Chris asked Sai.

Sai frowned. He didn't understand. That worried Chris for a couple of reasons. One, Gingerman was missing. Two, and more importantly, he wondered if Sai even knew what he was talking about. Like none of that had even happened. Chris opened Sai's door and went in to look around.

"What. Was. That?" Joli closed the door to the allowable limit. "I mean, those metal balls? What were those, like, true-tellers or something? Did you feel them get hot? Honestly, if that meant we were lying, I don't know how we didn't get burned."

Chris shuffled things on the desk. The stack of headless gingermen was under a shirt, but none with bowties.

"And the gray ones? You know, they invented tape recorders, like, a hundred years ago. Those poor people with the ugly robes and brittle bones. I thought one of them would just, you know, like, turn to dust before it was over. They smelled like, like... I don't know. Feet? Did you get that?"

"You in here?" Chris whispered. "He's not answering."

"Who you talking to?" Joli said.

Chris and Sai traded knowing glances. It didn't feel safe, even with the door almost closed. "Come on."

"Where?" she said.

"We got to go outside."

"It's freezing, Christopher. I'm delicate."

"Listen." He peeked into the hall. "We got to go where no one can hear us."

"Okay. Aaaaaand why?"

Chris started pacing. He couldn't say it out loud. Even in a whisper. For the hundredth time that day, he grabbed his hair.

"Bobby found a gingerman," Sai said.

Joli looked back and forth, waiting for the punchline. "I don't get it."

"He found it on the hike. Well, it wasn't a gingerman. Just the head."

"Huh." She watched Chris. "Is that why you ate the heads?"

"It talks," Sai said.

"What does?"

"He, uh..." Sai waved his hands around his head. "It's like he can—"

"He's alive." Chris said it too loudly. They would hear it down in the bathroom. Sai closed the door a little more. "It sounds crazy, I know."

"Let me rewind that," Joli said. "Sai said Bobby found a gingerman—correction, a gingerman head—and then you said he's alive. Did I hear that?"

Sai explained what had happened. Bobby started to hear the voice in his head; then Sai did, but not so good. Chris, he said, was a good receiver. And he made the head a body, and Sai put it together. And now it was alive.

"Chris?" Joli said.

Chris was pacing, watching his feet. Tugging his hair. "He told me about Kogen. He's the one who came up with the plan, to open the door at eleven o'clock so the bell would cover us."

"The cookie did?"

"Yeah."

"I mean, were you both looking at it when it said this?"

"It walks, too," Chris said.

"Sure. And it told you about Kogen?"

"That's how I knew. I think, I don't know, maybe Ms. Grendel knew something was up. You see the way she licked those crumbs?"

"I saw that," Sai said. "That's when she started—"

"Where is it?" Joli said. "The cookie."

"Gman?" Sai said. "That's what Bobby called him."

"Where is Gman?"

"That's what I'm trying to tell you," Chris whispered. "Someone was in my room. I think they might've taken him. That's why Ms.

Grendel had us empty our pockets, I think. Maybe she thought we had him with us."

"Maybe that's why she kept us so long," Sai said. "To give one of the slackers time to come up here."

Chris and Sai discussed where the gingerman was last. Maybe he was still hiding. Was he scared? But Chris couldn't feel anything in his head, like he did when the gingerman was near.

"That's why she asked about our dreams," Joli said. "You dreamed it."

"Both of us?" Chris said.

"It makes more sense than a talking cookie. And people search other rooms all the time. We don't have locks. I once had a sock full of Milk Duds—"

"We weren't dreaming," Chris said.

"You sure? I mean, you really wanted Kogen gone, right? Maybe you tapped into the subconscious and figured out he was going to mess with the gingerbread house. That's why there's no cookie in your room. Think about it. Why would a talking cookie want to get Kogen?"

"He broke Bobby," Sai said. "And he was going to get Chris kicked out."

"True. Doesn't mean a cookie told you."

"No, it's not just that," Sai said. "He said there was something bigger going on."

"What?"

"He didn't say," Chris said. "But you felt it, right? I mean, those spheres Ms. Grendel had and those gray people. There's something really weird about this place. You told me no one leaves the school once they graduate, not in the last twenty years or something."

"I'll give you that," she said. "But that doesn't mean a cookie—"

"There's got to be a way to find out more about this place. I mean, there's no computers or phones, just mail. And you know they probably read that. We're isolated in here. Pelz's got total control and—"

"Before you tell me the Earth is flat," Joli said, "let's focus on facts. We did good in the challenge, right? We're not going to get last.

Kogen is gone. We don't have any red cards. And Ms. Grendel wanted to know if we dream. Maybe she was trying to tell you that you need more sleep, Chris. I know I do."

She went to the door and looked out.

"So before you both disappear down a rabbit hole, sleep on it. A day, a week. I don't know. Maybe write your dreams down, see if any cookies come up."

"I'm not crazy."

"I know, Christopher. And you make great coffee. I'll be by tomorrow for some."

She left the door wide open. Chris and Sai stood there. Maybe all they needed was sleep. Stress can do strange things to a person's mind. Sai scratched his back with a knotty stick.

"We didn't dream it," Sai said.

Chris went to his room and closed the window. It was getting cold.

14

The temperature had dropped below zero that night. Chris had stared out the window till the early morning hours. Now he was in bed with his clothes on.
Even his boots.

He rolled over, threw his arm over the edge, wondering, for the hundredth time, if he'd checked under the bed. He closed his eyes, wishing to hear that gruff little voice like a speaker between his ears. He'd only just met him.

Every night for the past two weeks, he had the same dream of running over to Bixen to stop everyone from eating dessert. They had crumbs on their faces. Claibourn was munching on a foot. He would sweep all the pieces into a pile and mold it into a lumpy cookie man with dollops of yogurt and pudding, his fingers sinking through the little chest as he administered CPR.

He'd begun to wonder if Joli was right. It was surreal. Given enough time, he knew, he would believe her. There was no way a cookie could talk.

He needed to change shirts and found a relatively fresh one streaked with acrylics but smelled okay. He scraped the window with a putty knife, flakes of frost curling off the edge and melting on the desk. No one had replaced Kogen, and Chris didn't want another slacker watching him. No one said anything.

People were out there in single-digit weather, their breath heaving clouds, their shoulders hunched. They were all walking in the same direction.

"Did you just wake up?" Joli peeked in the room.

"Can you knock? I'm half naked." He pulled on the paint-splattered shirt.

She was in a wool overcoat that swished around her ankles, a big circle painted on the back in red, the paint peeling, with two eyes and a straight-line mouth. Her scarf was purple and sparkly and itchy looking.

"Where's the coffee?" she said.

He handed her the pot. She went for water. Sai moved out of her way, wearing a poofy coat and a thick stocking cap down to his eyes and mittens that folded off the fingers.

"Anything?" he said.

They only talked about the gingerman when Joli wasn't around. They'd made the mistake of doing it once.

Faculty were marching out of the castle. He couldn't see their faces from his window. They were hidden in mounds of winter clothing. But they moved in slow motion, tiny steps testing for ice, clinging to each other in pairs. If one fell, they would both go down. None of them, though, were wearing gray.

Joli returned with water. Chris prepped the coffeemaker and continued staring out the window. The faculty were still making their way out.

"Ever notice how old they are?" Chris said.

"They're wise, Christopher."

"But every single one of them is old. We had a couple of teachers at my school like that, but just a few."

She blew into her hands. "Can you make the coffee go faster? We can't be late."

The great bell over Clancer struck. He could feel it all the way in his room. The coffee wasn't done, but Joli started pouring. Chris cradled a mug with a curling nose and squinting eyes, the chin jutting off the bottom.

"Let's get this over with," she said.

They fell in behind the faculty who were moving faster on the gravel paths. Chris's coffee was already lukewarm. Some of the coffee grounds had slipped past the filter. He had been sloppy that morning. His scalp tightened in the cold. His nose and ears were numb.

A crowd on Clancer's front steps parted for the faculty. They closed in around them like penguins. There were no costumes. That had been two weeks ago when the weather was tolerable, the snow fresh and hopes high. Now they were battle-weary artists waiting for judgment. Joli trotted ahead and squeezed through the crowd.

Chris dumped his coffee in the snow.

"I can't believe this." Joli returned. "We're not on the list."

Sai bit his lip. He started to say something, then shook his head. He did it twice.

"What's that mean?" Chris said.

"It means we're not in the middle," she whispered.

"Hey, Oliveira," Sally Mendittis shouted. "Where'd you get?"

"Okay, yeah." She nodded. Sally laughed. She turned to Chris, whispered behind her hand, "It means we're either top three—"

"Or bottom three," Sai said.

"Shh!" She jabbed him, waved at someone, and fake laughed.

"How do they not know?" Chris said.

"Because they post team names," Joli said.

"We had a team name?"

She looked at Sai. He said, "G Peeps."

"Huh," Chris said. "Good enough."

"Yeah, good enough," Joli hissed. "Better be good enough to not be last. We shouldn't've built the house. Should've played it safe, made a snowman with licorice lips and toffee eyes and, and… I swear to God, if we lose, I'm going to find Kogen and shove a hot grape up his nose."

The last bell sounded. In search of warmth, the crowd tried to enter at the same time. Chris didn't rush. He was one of the last ones in, seeing the list posted on the wooden door. Three blanks at the top. Three on the bottom.

"This could be good." Sai pointed at the top three.

"You're not a half-full guy, Sai," Joli blurted.

There was no curtain this time. The faculty weren't on a stage. They stood behind six pedestals that were hidden behind velvet curtains. The entries that weren't in the top three or bottom three—the middles, Joli called them—had been shoved to the back wall for display. The shelves had been cleared, the kitchenettes gone. Chef DuPont presided over the students' entrance, his pointed chin buried in a bulging neck roll. His stovepipe hat pointed back slightly as he looked down his nose.

Ms. Grendel was absent.

The student body gathered in an arching line. Some meandered near the fireplaces, but when Chef DuPont cleared his throat, they got in line. Nervous chatter fell away when he raised his hands. Only the sound of popping embers echoed.

"Welcome!" he called, his raspy French voice aided by the large room's acoustics. "It's taken a bit longer than usual to finish the fall challenge. My apologies for holding you in suspense."

Chef DuPont pontificated on the value of patience, driving his point home with long pauses and a devilish grin.

"Pelz is lazy," Joli said. "He could've judged this in a day. Now we're standing around until someone has a heart attack—"

"Shhh," Pedro Martinez said.

"You shush."

"I want to congratulate you all, no matter the outcome. You are all gifts, I want you to know that. This was a very difficult challenge to judge. But when you work with the best in the world, you need to be more than remarkable. It requires you to be *impeccable*." His hissed the word *impeccable*. Mr. Chonewski would give his performance a C. "Three of you will go home today. This is no light matter. And we take it as such."

His beefy hands walloped together.

"Without further ado, Ms. Mihalow, would you do the honors?"

The sculpting teacher nodded. Her dull gray hair lay flat against her head. Her tiny frame was hidden in folds of more than one coat, but the tilt of uneven hips was still obvious.

"Third place," she said with a quiver, "goes to…" There was a pause as she reached for a lever, hand shaking. The thick blind fell into a soft heap. "Tin Hats."

The taffy and cotton candy theme park was perched on a mahogany table. The multicolored taffy had wilted some, but the sugary fluff still floated like pink clouds. Applause filled the room. The team at the opposite end—Willie Furudo, Annie Florit and Chancey Willowes—high-fived and hugged.

Joli gagged.

Chris didn't know if they won anything. But not being in last place was enough to celebrate.

A student critique was given. Then Chef Dupont called to a teacher, "Mr. Lhotsky?"

The other sculpting teacher, he specialized in abstract metalwork, stepped to one of the curtains. He was portly, like a clay figure who had been squished before being put in the oven. His bald pate was spotted like a work of art.

"Third last," he said with a tired smirk, "Mink Setters."

No delay with Mr. Lhotsky. He yanked the trigger. It was a plaid wedding cake slumping to one side as if it had been placed too close to a fire. The figures on top were carved from sugar and leaning toward the mudslide. The symbolism was rich. Too bad the design was dull.

Mink Setters quietly celebrated, shaking hands, nodding, to avoid drawing Chef DuPont's ire. Third last was nothing to cheer. But it wasn't last.

"Man," Joli mumbled. "Oh, man."

Sai looked at his feet.

Chef DuPont took the opportunity to request critiques. This went on for ten minutes.

"Ms. Mihalow?" Chef DuPont called.

"Second place." The teacher moved to the next curtain, paused again. Chris was finally feeling nervous. He never believed they would get last. But Joli wasn't helping. He unbuttoned his coat. Ms. Mihalow drew a breath, coughed into her delicate fist, drew another breath, and said, "Picknitties!"

It was the chocolate tower with spiraling staircases. Boris Klemesrud, Geni Hatam and Ally Syndulla were standing next to Joli, jumping and squealing. Joli walked in small circles. Sai put his hand on Chris's shoulder to keep from falling.

"I can't believe this," Sai said. "There's no way we got first."

The gingerbread house was good. But not first-place good. *It's not last, either.*

But what if the judges didn't take Kogen's sabotage into consideration? It would look like a dilapidated home. Worse than the mudslide wedding cake.

Another critique. This one felt like an hour before Mr. Lhotsky stepped up. No pretense. The Band-Aid was getting ripped off. Joli folded her arms and closed her eyes. Sai faced the other direction.

"Second last." The curtain crumpled. "Chip and Tales!"

"I'm going to puke," Sai said.

It looked like a psychedelic cactus in a bed of frosting. A cylindrical cake almost a meter tall with diagonal stripes winding around it—bumblebee yellow, carrot orange, candy apple red, bubble gum pink, and mulberry violet. Red and white candy sticks poked from the sides like thick quills. The frosting was covered in a medley of skittles.

It was a contrasting theme of danger and invitation, summer and winter. A visually jarring head trip.

Paul Struecker, Annie Mcmyne, and Derice Benntt gathered in a circle, heads together. Annie was quietly weeping. They weren't the Chip and Tales team. Which meant they were one of the last two teams left. First. Or last.

Excitement charged the atmosphere. Chris could feel the looks. Everyone knew who was left now. His legs were cold. Sai paced in little circles. Joli stared in shock.

"Ms. Oliveira," Chef DuPont called, "critique, please."

You got to be joking.

It was sadistic. Unfathomable. They were going to ask the last teams to critique. Chris had nothing. Sai could barely talk. Joli stared at the Alice in Wonderland cactus, blankly. The room grew still. The silence erasing whatever thoughts she might've had. Chris hoped whatever thoughts she did have, she didn't say them.

"Ms. Oliveira?"

"Um. The, uh..." She pointed. Her hand shaking. "I find the, um, the composition to be, um... it's..."

He let her dangle, her cheeks flushing burnt scarlet. Firelight danced in the water in her eyes. Chris saw her hands trembling. They were breaking her in front of everyone.

"It's visually jarring," Chris said.

Chef DuPont held up his hand. "Mr. Blizzard, please. We would like to hear from Ms. Oliveira. Although, Mr. Laghari, if you would like to help?"

Sai wasn't breathing. It looked like a walnut was stuck in his throat, bobbing up and down. Chef DuPont gestured for him to step forward. The heat of a thousand eyes was melting them.

"The, um, jarring aspect has a quality that's..."

Sai managed a string of smart words that meant nothing. A skill they had all acquired. Chris could only stand back and watch it unfold. He formulated his own reply. He was ready.

A hand firmly gripped his shoulder.

Ms. Grendel was behind him. Her heavy eyes, unblinking, seemed to look inside him. She nodded once. Chef DuPont wasn't distracted. She pulled him toward the exit. No one said anything. They were focused on the unfolding tragedy as the final teams withstood pressure that could crush diamonds.

And Chris left. Without a word. Leaving Joli and Sai to stumble. He wanted to go back, to say something, to explain what was happening. This could be the worst day of their lives. And then he realized what was happening.

We're going home.

15

They entered the castle's main entrance.
Ms. Grendel brandished an old coppery key worn smooth along the shaft, the coarse teeth with rounded corners. The foyer was a small room with cobbled stones and a high domed ceiling with a naked bulb hanging from the apex. There were three wooden doors, one on each wall.

She pulled the hood back, her gray hair spraying kinked sprigs. Her coat looked like some sort of animal hide, seal maybe, smooth and oiled with white fuzz at the cuffs and the hem of the hood. She worked the large buttons through their slots.

She opened the door on the right, her breath laboring, and retrieved a long wool coat. She held out her hand. He gave her the empty coffee mug. He'd forgotten he was still holding it. She put it in a grapevine basket.

"Empty your pockets."

"Where am I going?"

She lifted the basket like it was made of steel. He gave her the wallet Joli had given him, two pens, and a handkerchief.

"Watch," she said.

He undid the clasp and dropped it in. Then she held up the coat.

He slid his arms into it. It smelled musty. She buttoned the front of it, pulled gloves from one of the pockets and a stocking cap from the other, fitting it on his head.

"Did we lose?" he said.

She wrapped a scarf around his neck and tucked it inside the coat. Heat prickles were beginning to sting. He would be sweating in minutes. She went back to the closet, leaning on the cane, grinding it between stones, and pulled a thin hoop from a shelf. It was gold and didn't connect on the back side.

"Put this around your head."

He hesitated. "What is it?"

It didn't look threatening. Just a gold hoop. He pried it open, took his cap off to slide it over his head. Like a prince. It was cool against his forehead. He felt very stupid.

She reached up to adjust it, centering it on his forehead. Adjusted it again, just right. Her hand smelled like lotion. She stepped back to observe it with a rheumy stare, lips puckered in doughy cheeks, then went to a chair against the wall, slowly lowering herself into it. She pointed the cane at the middle door.

"When you're ready."

He wasn't ready. For any of this. But how long would he stand there waiting to be ready? He wanted to ask, but she hadn't answered any questions so far. And the quiver of his voice drove fear into his legs each time he spoke. The metal knob on the door was large. He stood there with his hand on it. She didn't prod him, just sat there.

"Action," she said, "is not taken because we feel like it."

"What?"

She offered a smile. He knew what she was saying. Duty didn't care about his feelings. It required action. If he only knew what this was.

He cracked the door, the latch ominously clicking. Humid air rushed out. Stone steps led into a dark stairwell. He took a deep breath. His legs were numb. If he didn't move now, he would never move again.

He started the climb.

The handrail was polished wood. He pulled himself up to the first landing, the stairs switching back every ten steps. Sweat dampened the stocking cap. His breath echoed in the narrow space. Halfway up, he was in complete darkness, considered turning around, telling her he couldn't do it. Just call his parents. He was ready to go home.

The climb felt endless.

Eventually, a gray line appeared. It was a horizontal gap. He held his hand out, slowly moving toward it. His fingers touched a grainy door. The gray line suddenly turned white. A light had been turned on.

The gold band felt icy. It felt tighter. A strange vibration filled his face and poured into his body. It wasn't unpleasant, reminding him of a time he'd had surgery to remove his appendix, the buzzy sensation right before the anesthesia put the lights out. He stood still, waiting to see if he would go to sleep.

The door nudged open on its own.

The room was bigger than he expected. The top of the tower, he assumed that was how far he'd climbed, didn't look that spacious from the ground. Frigid air leaked out. His breath became white clouds. The body heat that had accumulated during the climb dissipated.

The room was cluttered. Piles of things stacked against the walls and on tables. On the far side, in a high-back chair with engrained trim, sat a man of significant girth. A wide smooth face and stubbled scalp. His hands perched on the end of a gnarled wooden stick.

The threshold felt like an electric wall. It was like walking into a sunlit room. But there were no torches, no lights on the ceiling. Just small candles with steady flames on antique tables along curved walls where boxes were neatly stacked. There were things nestled on the floor and on shelves, random stuff like empty picture frames, bags of ornaments, deer antlers, blocks of various colors children would stack. There were clocks and chairs, piles of plastic dolls, video cassettes, and balls of yarn. A metronome was ticking.

His footsteps echoed in a strange, distant way. The man in the chair began to smile. It grew as Chris approached. White and perfect.

"Christmas White Blizzard," he said with a voice deeply resonating, "it is a pleasure."

"Lord..." Chris suddenly forgot his name. They'd called him Pelz for so long. "Lord Pelznickel."

Pelznickel nodded with an open, penetrating look and a smile that warmed Chris from the inside. The stick, too short to be a cane, went from one hand to the other.

"I want to apologize for Mr. Archelleto. He is an ambitious young man."

Young man? Perhaps if you were Pelznickel's age, most people were young.

"His expectations are very high. He was a prodigy, a prized Gifter. His talents were some of the most promising the school has ever seen. But his emotions are still unmanaged. You know why he treated you that way, mmm?"

Chris shook his head.

"You threatened him, Christmas."

"I-I-I didn't do anything."

Pelznickel's laughter rumbled. "No. But your potential, young man. Mr. Archelleto saw the very same thing I am seeing right now. To the unrefined, that is a threat."

Kogen was tough. But perhaps he hid something very small and frightened underneath. A front to keep others from seeing what he hid.

"Are you thirsty? Here, please." He extended a bottle of water.

Chris was parched. Pelznickel watched him drink half of it. It felt strangely cool down in his throat and stomach. The plastic crinkled in his hand.

"You are wondering why you are here." Pelznickel waved the stick. "This school has been in my family for hundreds of years, as I'm sure you're aware. Thousands of students have come from afar. Our standards are demanding. Mediocrity unacceptable. Most, as you know, don't make it. We make diamonds, Christmas. And those who withstand the pressure, who discover their true selves, are the true gifters who never leave. They see the value of what we do here, what we offer the world."

He gestured to drink again. Chris finished the bottle.

"Art can be taught. Anyone can learn to paint a picture, to carve a stick or mold beauty. But that does not make a true artist. The true artist, Christmas, is born with something. A turtle can learn to crawl through the sand, its tracks something of wonder. But a turtle will never be a diamond."

Chris nodded. He wasn't following.

"I've been doing this a very long time. I can see the diamonds."

Pelznickel pushed himself out of the chair. His coat was dark fur with dull yellow trim that swayed around black galoshes. His steps heavy, patient. He dropped thick hands on Chris's shoulders. His eyes sharply blue like a clear winter afternoon.

"It is an honor."

Warmth emanated from this large man looking down. It was his smile, the cherub cheeks, the firm grip. The warmth of emotional acceptance. Of real safety.

"Please, sit." He gestured to the throne. "The first time coming here takes its toll. The body adjusts. It's a long climb, after all."

The armrests were wide slabs of cherry wood, the covering padded velvet. It was firm and comfortable. Powerful.

Pelznickel looked at him like a crown prince. The band hummed around Chris's forehead. Pelznickel nodded with satisfaction then walked around the room, stopping at a table to wind a music box.

"I'm not going home?" Chris said.

He laughed uproariously. "On the contrary. This is an invitation, Christmas. I am inviting you to join a select group. Do you know what that means?"

Chris shook his head. He could use another water.

"It doesn't mean you're better than the others. It means you're not the turtle."

His eyes twinkled. He moved crystal figurines on a shelf, took one down to rub his thumb against it. Rearranged them so they were facing each other.

"Do you believe me?"

"Yes. But... but what does that mean? I mean, I'm barely keeping up with homework, you know, and the, uh, the challenge."

"You don't feel special?" Pelznickel turned his head.

Chris thought. "No."

"That's precisely right. This is an invitation. You must choose to accept your birthright. You must be willing. Are you willing to know who you are?"

"I don't know."

"Very good."

It was the truth. The answer was frightening to say out loud. He felt it. But it was a risk to admit it. To lose the acceptance Pelznickel had already given.

"Ask me anything." Pelznickel held a large ornament. It looked heavy, the surface etched with intricate designs. "Anything at all. Don't think. Listen to your inner voice. Do you hear it?"

Chris fidgeted. *Is he talking about the gingerman?*

"Don't be afraid." Pelznickel paced across the room. "Anything at all. There is nothing to hide. Honesty is the foundation of what we do here. It is your path. So please." He began winding a yo-yo. "Ask."

Chris suddenly felt free and blurted out the first thing that came to mind. "Why is everyone so old?"

"There you go." Pelznickel winked. He swung the yo-yo on its string a couple of times before rewinding it. "When you love something, truly love something, you are singularly focused. You lose yourself in that love. Give yourself to it. True love, Christmas, is freedom. The men and women here were once gifters who freed themselves through dedication and the pursuit of truth. They are committed to the work. Give their lives to what truly matters."

"They don't seem happy."

"Ah, happiness. Yes. Why are we here? In this world. Is it to be happy, to avoid sadness? Is the sun happy when it gives light? We exist to create. That is our true purpose. But we can't escape the toll it brings. Age brings aches and pains, but it also brings wisdom. Would you rather be young and blissfully ignorant of your potential for a fleeting moment of pleasure? It is a question youth cannot answer."

He pulled the lever on a clock. A cuckoo popped out of a little door and made a silly sound. Pelznickel smiled and did it again.

"Why is it always Christmas?"

"Ah, yes. Christmas is the spirit of giving. You are the true gifters of the world. I value what you bring to the circle, the work you do. I never saw a reason to drudge through the seasons only to celebrate at the end of the year. We live the spirit of giving every single moment. We embrace joy. Every child in the world understands that feeling. Imagine the world celebrating each and every day like Christmas morning.

"It's not without its hardships, of course. Art is work. But we can recognize the inherent beauty in the struggle." He laughed heartily. "And you, Christmas, you were born for this. Don't you see?"

He continued laughing as he walked among the clutter, picking a glazed chopstick from a cup and running his fingers down its length as if seeing it for the first time. The wonder.

"Go on," Pelznickel called, sensing Chris's hesitancy.

"Someone said you know our DNA, like a test we took at home. There was a part that was unknown. Is that why we were chosen?"

Pelznickel studied another stick, this one royal purple with spots of lemon yellow. "There is no such thing as magic, Christmas. We create to express ourselves. With creation comes understanding. And we seek to understand through science. Our DNA is a magnificent work of art. It is the backbone of our essence. And therein lies your potential. For most, it will lay untapped, unknown. Unfulfilled. But here, you will unearth yourself. This is the adventure of self-discovery. And that, Christmas, that is why we exist. To ask who am I, what is my true purpose? To excavate the unknown."

"Do you know who you are?"

"We all do. Deep down there is that yearning to connect with ourselves. You see, what you do here isn't for me or the world, really. It is truly for you. If I could bring all the people in the world here, all seven billion of them, I would. Science helps us identify those with the most untapped potential. Like you."

Chris nodded. "What were those marbles, the ones Ms. Grendel had us hold?"

"Science. You're young, remember. Growth takes time. You will understand one day."

He had placed the sticks back in their cup and was carefully stacking something on the table. The objects clacked together as he balanced a small tower, then turned. His boots clopped patiently toward Chris. He offered his hand. Chris took it, but, strangely, Pelznickel didn't pull him. Chris stood on his own.

"Ask yourself, what is my purpose? Do I want to know myself? I want you to think about my invitation. Answer when you're ready. You're a good kid. Special. I see you. Even when you can't."

Chris was overwhelmed with emotion. He felt dizzy with goodness melting inside him, thawing the fearful sensations that always seemed to grip him. No more cold legs, no stiff back. As if he could do anything, say anything. He wanted to say yes, right then.

Because he wanted to belong.

"Do I have to wear this?" He touched the gold band around his head.

"Of course not." Pelznickel took his hand away. "Ms. Grendel will take it. I believe now you have some celebrating to do."

"Celebrating?"

Pelznickel chuckled. "It was a pleasure to meet you."

He fell into his throne, balancing his hand once again on the contorted stick, watching Chris walk to the door. He was floated out of the room. The sun was shining inside him. He'd never felt so accepted. No judgment. No expectations to be anything but who he was. And now, for the first time, he wanted something more than anything else.

To know who he was.

"Christmas?" Chris stopped before crossing the threshold. "I have one question, if you don't mind."

"Yeah?"

"There was an incident in the cafeteria. A prank was played on one of your friends, and Mr. Claibourn was struck in the eye." He moved the stick back and forth. "What happened?"

A jolt of fear darkened the sunshine. "Someone threw a chocolate chip."

"Can you tell me what you were feeling when it happened? What you were thinking?"

Chris hesitated. He wanted to exclaim his innocence. It was impossible for him to throw it. But Pelznickel just wanted to know what he was feeling. So he told him. He'd felt helpless. Paralyzed. Like he always did. Sitting there watching Joli trying to put out the fire and Claibourn laughing with his fat mouth.

"You wanted to stop him?" Pelznickel said. "Emotions are like that, yes? Uncontrollable sometimes."

"Yeah."

"You can't control them, though. You can understand them. But they don't change. You are the container of your emotions. Right now you are merely a thimble holding a pebble of fear. Growth will turn you into a barrel. A bigger container. The pebble doesn't change. That is transformation. That is what I offer."

Chris didn't quite understand. It sounded like Pelznickel wanted to know something else. He seemed to think Chris threw the chocolate chip. Or maybe he was just making the invitation sweeter. Chris was going to say yes to the invitation.

"And, Christmas."

"Yes?"

"You can leave the bottle."

He was still holding the empty water bottle. He put it on the table next to the cup of glossy chopsticks. There was a delicately balanced stack of rocks next to it. They were rounded by a river's current, the surfaces worn smooth and black.

"You-you collect rocks?"

"I collect many things."

Chris left with the warm feeling of sunshine. But it was mixed with something mysteriously odd. That the real truth was disguised by another truth. As soon as he left, he was very thirsty.

He could use another bottle of water.

16

It was dark in the trees. And quiet.

Chris wandered into the small forest near the wall in the west quarter of the circle. It was mostly pine and fir. Fallen needles had made a soft bed. More importantly, no one was around. It gave him time to think. He skipped classes. Even lay back with his head on his backpack and fell asleep.

When he woke, it was night. The trees grew closely. Narrow paths and a few wrappers left behind suggested he wasn't the only one to find this hiding place. But no one had bothered him. By the time he wandered out, the campus was empty. Windows were bright. The Tree shimmered with tiny diamonds on its branches, the chimes softly ringing. The star cast shadows over the snow. Below, the windows of the store glowed with warm firelight. The hunched form of Mr. Kramer slowly trudged past.

Chris just wanted to disappear for a while. That feeling came to him every so often. At home, when there was a test or he was in trouble, he would sit in his closet for hours, leaning in the dark corner and counting his breaths. He'd watched videos of how to meditate, but mostly he was just thinking. And it usually put him to sleep. He'd stay in there until he felt better. Sometimes he did.

There was a lot to think about.

What he felt from Pelz was acceptance. It still warmed him like his grandmother's embrace when he was little. Like the safest place in the world. But still. Something was off. And he couldn't quite place it.

The quad danced with the ornaments' jolly light, splashing fractured rainbows on the white canvas of snow. His dorm was a checkerboard of bright windows draped in strings of colored lights. Only one window was dark. He stood on the gravel path, staring up at his room.

Sai's light was on.

He waited to see him in there, wondering if they'd sent him home already, cleaned out his room for the next contestant. Even though Pelz said there was something to celebrate, he didn't believe it. He was beginning to shiver. His nose was runny and his fingers stiff. The numbness moved between his eyes. He could still feel the line around his head where the gold band had been. He pinched the bridge of his nose. Then he heard the ringing. It started as a low distant hum. The ground seemed to fall away and he was floating.

Christmas.

The word whispered inside his head. The familiar gruffness was distant. Weak. He spun around, searching the quad. The windows were closed. But he heard it. It sent shivers through him. He stood under the window of his room.

"Where are you?" he whispered.

Down here.

Chris looked at his boots. They were in a foot of snow drifted against the building.

Warmer.

He took another step, then another, approaching the wall carefully. There was a soft indention at the peak of the snowdrift. A line had been drawn where the icicles dripped from the eave. The snow was up to his knees.

You're burning up, buddy.

Chris fell on his knees and began digging. He found something rigid. It began to wiggle. Chris jerked his hand back. The gingerman paddled his way out like a small critter.

"What are you doing out here?"

Turning into a snow cone. He brushed his shoulders. *Oh, man. The bowtie.*

The white decoration had chipped away. Just a few of the buttons were left. He looked like a cookie left on the counter too long.

"What are you doing?" Bodie Wrenfrow stood in the snow.

A pink glow from a glass hot-pepper display covered half of his face, the other half yellow from an inflatable Labrador. His hands were in the pockets of a thick black overcoat, his creased slacks sharp below his knees. A scarf was around the lower half of his face. He peered through a slot just below the stocking cap.

He didn't take the path, had come directly from the castle, probably saw Chris digging in the snowbank. Chris snatched the gingerman.

Hey, don't—

"I dropped something the other day." Chris palmed Gingerman into his coat pocket and pulled out the coffee mug.

Bodie watched him wipe the snow off. Chris kept his hood up, the fuzzy trim hanging over his face. Bodie looked inside but didn't seem to recognize him. Chris aimed the mug's distorted features at him, proof of what he was doing. Chris noticed the line across Bodie's forehead. *He just came back from the tower.* Bodie took the mug, turned it around, looked inside before giving it back.

"Curfew's in thirty minutes."

"Going up now."

Chris went straight to the front door. It was hot inside. He stopped at the bulletin board. It had been cleared. The fall challenge announcement was gone.

"Be still," Chris whispered.

Gingerman squirmed like a squirrel trying to escape his pocket. *I can't breathe.*

"You don't breathe."

How would you like it if—hey! Hey, don't. Chris put his hand in the pocket and held him.

The second floor was filled with music. Almost all the doors were open. People walking across the hall. Laughing, shouting. The dance party in full swing. A group gathered outside the door. Chris pulled up his hood.

"Blizzard?" Johnny Itokazu shouted. "Hey, man. Congrats."

The others were looking now. Harriet Wexel pushed out of the room. "Where you going? Come on, join in. Just one. Celebrate, man."

Sai heard the commotion. He was outside his door. He wasn't smiling like the others. Arms stiff at his sides. Chris waved at Jonny and Harriet, said thanks.

"Where'd you go?" Sai said.

"Come on." Chris threw his hood back and went into his room. He closed the door.

"You left us there," Sai said. "You just disappeared and—"

Chris placed the gingerman on the desk. Sai's mouth fell open. He rubbed his eyes, looked at Chris and back to Gingerman, stepping forward carefully. Gingerman saluted awkwardly. Chris took off his coat. Sai pinched the back of Chris's arm.

"We're not dreaming," he said. "Right?"

"I don't think so," Chris said.

Who said you were dreaming?

"What were you doing out there?" Chris said.

That. Yeah. FOPs came into the room after you got Kogen, turned the place over.

"FOP?"

Friends of Pelz. What do you call them? Slackers. Three of them. But you with your polar-bear metabolism had the window open. I bailed two stories. If it wasn't for the snowbank, I'd be Humpty Dumpty.

"You've been out there the whole time?"

Two weeks and one day.

"Where was he?" Sai said.

Chris repeated what the gingerman had said. "Why didn't you say something?"

I did! I've been screaming my head off, almost literally, for two weeks and one day. I thought you were ignoring me. Maybe things went sideways with Kogen and you were, you know, not happy talking to a cookie. But then today. He teetered on the edge of the desk. *Something was different.*

"Like what?"

You heard me. And that. He aimed his stubby arm at Chris's head. *What's up with that?*

Chris touched his forehead. He was right, something did feel different. Gingerman was talking, and it didn't feel like an electromagnet inside his brain. No headache, no dizziness. It was like talking to Sai. It sort of tingled across his forehead.

"What's wrong with your head?" Sai said.

"It feels, I don't know... lighter."

"No. I mean that." Sai pointed like gingerman had.

Chris leaned over the desk. His reflection was in the dark window. There was a line across his forehead. It looked like the beginning of a sunburn. He ran his finger over it. It felt funny.

"Oh, man."

"What happened?" Sai said.

Chris told him about Ms. Grendel, how she came for him at the ceremony, dressed him in warm clothes, and gave him a gold band to put around his head. Then he'd climbed the stairs all the way to the tower.

"You met Pelz?" Sai said.

No. No, no, no, no, no. Gingerman's crispy legs clicked across the desk. *Do not tell me you met with him.*

"It's not like I had a choice."

Oh yeah, you did. You could've said no for starters. Your stomach hurt. You personally don't believe in tyrants. You're allergic to fascism.

Chris frowned. "Do you know what fascism means?"

You could've said no. That's all I'm saying.

"What happened?" Sai said.

Chris sat down, stared at the ceiling. He told him about the cluttered room, the throne and the stick, the furry brown robe and musty yellow trim. His round face and the way he smiled.

"He invited me to join some group."

"What kind of group?" Sai said.

"Just, I don't know, something special was all he said."

Something special? Buddy, do you hear yourself?

"He was nice. Like really nice."

Of course he was! That's how it starts. Did he make you a cake? Did he play your favorite songs? He gets you to like him, and then it happens.

Chris didn't want to hear it. He'd spent all that time thinking about how he felt. Pelz was genuine. He cared. He really saw him, that was how it felt. And now he didn't know what to think.

"What happens?" Chris said.

What?

"You said he gets me to like him and then it happens. What?"

I don't know! Something. He climbed onto a book.

"You don't know," Chris said.

"He doesn't know what?" Sai said.

"He doesn't know what Pelz is doing."

I never said I did.

"You said we needed to get Kogen out of the way because something really bad is happening."

There is. Trust me.

Chris leaned forward, eye level with the gingerman's round face. He smelled like burnt cloves. "How did you know about Kogen?"

I don't like where this is going.

"You had the details, every one of them, all the way down to when the bells rang. How did you know?"

I'll be honest. He turned around. His backside was crispy on the edges. *I don't know.*

"What'd he say?" Sai said.

"We could've been kicked out of school!" Chris said.

I was right, though, wasn't I? He twisted around, his midsection crunching. Chris thought he might break in half. *I know things, Christmas. I can't explain it. I just do.*

"Then what is Pelz doing?"

He sat on the textbook, swinging his legs. Crumbs dusted the pages below him. He lifted his arms, started to say something, twice, then dropped his head.

"This is crazy." Chris stood up.

The bedroom door opened. Joli didn't knock. Her cheeks were flush, her boots caked in snow. She threw a bright red scarf over her shoulder.

"Well?" was all she said.

"I, uh, I'm sorry. I was just telling Sai—"

"You're sorry? That's it?"

"Yeah, I didn't want to leave. There was—"

"I had a heart attack. Did you know that? Sai was hyperventilating, weren't you, Sai? We had to stand there, by ourselves under the glare, and try not to wet ourselves. Sai almost did."

"What?" Sai said.

"And you left us, Christopher."

She still thinks you're Christopher?

Chris heard the scamper across the desk, hoping the gingerman was hiding. Now wasn't the time to explain a talking cookie.

"He met Pelz," Sai said.

Joli's creased brow thawed. "What?"

Chris explained Ms. Grendel, the clothes, the stairs, the room.

"You met him?" She stalked closer. "You met Pelz?"

Chris nodded. She looked at the two of them. Chris moved to block her view of the desk.

"What'd he want?"

"He invited me to join a special group."

"A prince?" Her tone was crestfallen. It sounded like a gut punch. "You said no. Tell me you said no."

"I didn't say anything."

"You didn't answer him?"

Chris shook his head. He felt squeezed between rocks. "I, uh, I wanted to... I wanted to say yes," he muttered. "You had to be there. He was so nice, Jo. He made me feel, I don't know, just... not so... invisible. You know? Maybe we got him all wrong."

We don't.

"Just... shut up a second," Chris said.

Joli looked hurt. "What?"

"Nothing. I'm just confused, that's all. Sorry. I didn't want to leave you at the, the thing. I didn't have a choice."

Joli sat on the bed with Sai. She looked at both of them, nodding. Thinking. "That was it? He just invited you to, what, wear the crown?"

"Yeah. And he answered all my questions." Chris told them about why everyone was old, what they were all doing, how important the school was. "He asked me who threw the chocolate chip."

"What's the deal with that?" Joli said. "It's physics. You couldn't have thrown it. Why would he ask that?"

"Gman said he did," Sai said.

You did throw it.

"Who?" Joli said.

Sai exchanged a glance with Chris. Chris shook his head. Too late.

"You dreamed that, Sai, remember?" Joli said.

Is she talking about me? Chris heard the papers shuffle. He was coming out.

"Stop. No, not yet. Just... stay there." Chris sighed. "Sorry."

"You think Pelz knows." Sai nodded at the desk. "About... you know."

"Knows what?" Joli said.

"That Chris threw it. Somehow. I'll bet he knows."

"Look, Sai." Joli grabbed his hand. "There's nothing to know. Chris didn't throw anything. I was there. I saw it. It was physically impossible. You both are acting weirder than usual. What's going on?"

"Something else." Chris walked away from the desk. Joli didn't freak out. Gingerman was hiding. "Pelz was collecting stuff in that room. There was everything up there, all of it on shelves or in boxes. And he walked around admiring it. You should've seen the way he moved these little figurines around."

"I wish we did," Joli said, "but DuPont was busy boiling us alive."

"It was just like your story, Sai."

Sai didn't know what he was talking about. Neither did Joli. Chris searched his desk. Gingerman was sitting behind a textbook like a five-year-old in church. Chris found the notebook paper wadded up. He flattened out the wrinkles.

"What's this?" Sai flipped the pages. It was his handwriting.

"I took it from your room. Sorry."

Sai held up the first page. "I did this?"

"We went in your room, like, a month ago. You weren't there. I just started reading it and then didn't give it back. You don't remember it?"

He nodded. "Yeah, no. I was sort of writing a lot of things back then."

"What is it?" Joli said.

"It's about a boy who grew up in a castle. His mom died when he was little, and his dad would only visit once a month. The boy collected things. Like rocks. I thought it was a story, but it's weird."

"You think it's Pelz?" Joli said.

"No. I mean, it was just a story, but it happened a long time ago. But maybe it had something to do with the family." Chris looked at Sai. "You know what I'm talking about, Sai?"

He was staring at the floor, shaking his head. "I wrote a lot of stuff."

"What does that mean, you don't remember?" Joli said.

"He was, you know... he was telling me things... I would start writing and..."

"Who was telling you?" Joli said.

He shrugged.

"Look, I got to get back to my room," she said. "You two can talk about cookies on your own time. BTW, we won the challenge. You know that, right?" She punched Chris in the arm. "I sweated through my coat while you were getting fit for a crown. Just so you know. So make sure you talk about that, too."

She walked into the hall. The dance party wrapped up. Curfew was a few minutes away. She stopped, thinking. Then said, "I'm glad you're safe."

She left. They heard her talking with people on the floor, heard the clap of high fives and an invite for one last dance. She probably did it.

Sai closed the door.

Can I come out? Gingerman used a paintbrush to climb a mound of clay.

"Sorry," Chris said. "I wasn't ready for her to... you know."

I get it. Is she cool? I can't get a read. He spiked the paintbrush like summiting a mountain. *She's into you, though.*

"What'd he say?" Sai said.

"Nothing."

Chris fell on the chair. Gingerman hopped on his thigh, then leaped to the bed. Chris rubbed his face and pulled his hair. It was like having a secret pet. One made of sugar and flour. *How did this become normal?* he thought. *When nothing is normal, everything is normal.*

"What now?" Sai said.

Good question. Tell him I said that.

Chris shook his head.

For starters, you stop visiting Lord Pelznickel in the luxury suite.

"How do you know?" Chris said.

Know what?

"Kogen, Pelz, everything. How do you know these things?"

How do you know how to breathe? I just do. Something's not right, I can feel it. He's hypnotizing you. No one ever leaves this place.

"Hypnotizing?"

Or whatever, I don't know. But you can't just fly with the flock. They're going in the wrong direction.

Chris paced the room. There were too many questions and not enough answers. It was a giant puzzle with impossible shapes all painted the same color. He didn't know where to start. Sai and Gingerman watched Chris go back and forth.

"You told Sai the Toy Collector story, didn't you?"

I think so.

"You think so?"

Look, it was hard to get through to the kid. He couldn't hear me half the time. So I would just ramble sometimes. I like to talk. Sue me.

"So you told him a story?"

Not exactly.

Chris pulled the chair up like an interrogation. He leaned forward. "What does that mean?"

Well. Gingerman scratched his head. Crumbs sprinkled the bedspread. *Sometimes I remember things. But it's not, like, I did them. Hard to explain.*

"Okay." It didn't make sense. But none of this did. "Is there more to that story?"

Sai was sort of following the conversation, looking back and forth.

I think so. Ask Sai.

"He doesn't remember."

Well, search his room. He wrote it all down.

"Can you just tell me the rest of the story?"

He looked at the ceiling. *Hmmm, no. It's not coming to me.*

"Great. That's great. The biggest clue we have and you don't remember."

You're the one who made friends with the dark lord—

"I'm just trying to make some sense out of something! You're telling me something's wrong, telling Sai that I, somehow, threw a chocolate chip, and now we're staring at each other."

You did throw it.

"How? How could I have done that?"

He scratched his head again. Sai's pants were dusted with crumbs. If he kept doing that, Chris would have to build him another body. Would he just break the head off and reattach it?

"Do you remember where you came from?" Chris said. "Like, how you started?"

Do you remember being born?

"Why do you always say that?"

Because you act like I'm a—

"A cookie?"

Chris ground his palms into his eyes and growled. This was like untangling the longest string of Christmas lights in the world and only half of them worked. He could feel the wall that surrounded the school. He started pacing like a tiger at the zoo, wondering why he was there. And how to escape.

"He needs to show you," Sai said.

"Show me what?" Chris said.

Gingerman walked on the bed, springing on the mattress, mirroring Chris's manic pace. Chris could hear Gingerman muttering. Then he nodded.

You need to lie down for this.

"For what?" Chris said.

Gingerman pointed at the pillow. *You'll see.*

"What's he talking about?" Chris said to Sai.

"You should lie down."

"I got that part. But for what?"

"He'll show you. You'll see."

Chris looked back and forth. They were patient, let him do five, then six walks across the room. Sai went to the chair, and Gingerman pretended to fluff the pillow. *It won't hurt. Promise.*

That didn't help.

Chris lay down. Gingerman walked over his shoulder and sat on his chest. He'd seen a puppeteer work a show in middle school and make the puppets come to life. That wasn't even close to this. Gingerman was like having a kitten plop down and purr.

"Close your eyes," Sai said. "It works better."

Tell Sai I got this.

Chris ignored Gingerman and closed his eyes. A nervous twitter cranked his heartbeat up. Gingerman rode it like a pony.

Take it easy. I'm not going to drill a cavity. Just a little visualization, that's all. Think of my voice as pictures. Easy-peasy.

"It's like dreaming," Sai said, "only—"

The bed disappeared.

Chris was falling through outer space. There were no stars, no light. It was complete black nothingness. He tried to swing his arms and kick, but he had no arms or legs. He had no body. And then he began to swirl. Colors came out of the blender like a video in reverse, splitting off, congealing.

It was a battle. An angry, vicious battle between someone dressed in... a panda costume. He couldn't see who the panda was fighting. There was too much fluff in the room. It wasn't snow.

Stuffing was pouring from the costume.

It went airborne in a vortex that threw furniture against the walls. A staircase was stuck to the ceiling. Someone was throwing a wooden toy at the panda. It moved like a bullet with a spear and had the square mouth of a nutcracker. A toy soldier slashed the suit again. Stuffing fell out and something else. The panda cradled a large metal ornament.

Then shoved it back into its belly.

Chris's point of view ran across the room. He was inches from the floor. The panda held the tear across its belly with one padded arm. It held something in the other arm. It was green and floppy.

Chris jolted upright, taking a deep, hungry breath. His eyes spilled tears, and he gulped for air as if he'd been held under water. The gingerman went tumbling between his legs. He lay flat, arms and legs out. Like a cookie should look. Then his head looked up, the eyes large circles.

"You stopped breathing." Sai was on the bed. "I thought you both were dead, I swear to God."

Chris sat on the edge of the bed. His chest was tight, his throat dry. He stood up carefully, waiting for the floor to stop swaying before grabbing a bottle off the desk. He drank until it was empty.

"What was that?" Chris said.

The gingerman wobbled onto his feet. *That was... that was wild.*

"You didn't know that was going to happen?"

It was like a... like a brain collision. He clicked his hands together. *We melted into each other.*

"You don't have a brain."

Brain. Mind. Whatever.

"What happened?" Sai said.

Chris explained what he'd seen. The upside-down staircase. That was the mansion. The one he'd built as a gingerbread house. The one everyone hiked to see. "There was a fight between a... man or woman or someone in a panda costume and a..." He shook his head. "A toy soldier."

That wasn't a costume.

"What was it?"

Those were toys.

"Toys?"

Toys.

"Toys that were fighting?"

Yup.

"Toys were fighting?" Sai said.

Pando was a bully, and the others were trying to stop him. It's a long story. But yeah. Toys.

It was like Chris was there, lying on the floor, watching it. Trying to get away. It wasn't a dream. He was there. He wouldn't believe it, at all. It was madness. But if a cookie could talk...

"You were there," Chris said.

I was sharing a memory. But that never happened with Sai or Bobby. Not like that.

Chris closed his eyes. It was like his memory now. It was fresh and frightening. He was shaking. The toy soldier was attacking the panda bear, tearing him apart. Something almost fell out. It looked heavy, with patterns etched into it.

"That orb," Chris said. "I've seen that before. Pelz had something like it."

It's what brought them to life, made them special. All the toys had one. Pando's was bigger.

"What about you?"

Gingerman shrugged. *I'm special.*

Chris wanted to know where the gingerman came from, how he came to life. It must have been at that house. Something made inanimate objects come to life. But the gingerman didn't understand it any more than most people understood their own biology. Or being born.

"They were fighting over something," Chris said.

The toymaker's hat. Don't have to worry about that anymore.

"Why?"

Santa has it.

"Who?"

He came for it, took it back to the Pole. Too dangerous for—

"Santa Claus?"

Yeah. Santa Claus. You heard of him?

"Fat man, white beard? Delivers presents on Christmas?"

That one. Gingerman shook his head. *Wait. Don't tell me you're one of them.*

"Who?"

A nonbeliever.

"What's he saying?" Sai said.

"He said Santa Claus took the hat back to the North Pole."

"Santa Claus?"

Santa Claus! What's the confusion here? You're talking to a cookie and you're having a hard time believing in the fat man?

He had a point. If a cookie could talk.

Santa has the hat. The hat made the marbles. The marbles brought the toys to life. It's math. Do we need to mind-meld again?

"Wait, marbles?" Chris looked at Sai. Ms. Grendel had them hold marbles. They didn't look strange. But they felt strange. "Pelz has the marbles."

That's why everyone hikes up there, looking for marbles. He took them.

"For what?" Chris said. "There aren't any toys around here. You see any living toys?"

Sai shook his head.

"What's he want with them?"

Gingerman pointed. *Exactly.*

Chris was woozy and exhausted. The quad shined with ornaments. How many nights had he stared at them? Not once did he see them walk around or fight. Or maybe they only did when everyone was asleep. There were a lot of conspiracies in the world. None of them about living toys.

"What now?" Sai said.

I've got some ideas. Want to know what I'm thinking?

"No." Chris's scalp hurt from grabbing his hair. "I've had enough ideas." He really wished he'd done more research about this place. "What about that story? Can you tell me the rest of what you told Sai?"

Um. I was sort of in a trance. I can't explain it.

"Can you find the rest of it?" he asked Sai.

"I'll look."

He searched the quad for movement. No one was coming or going from the castle. The ornaments were just ornaments. There was something obvious about them. Every possible Christmas ornament was in the circle. Reindeer and snowmen, snowflakes and jingle bells and sleighs and little drummer boys.

"Have you ever noticed," Chris said, "there's no Santa Clauses?"

17

"You've lost weight. Henry, look at him." Mom turned the iPad. Chris's dad was drinking orange juice from the container. "He looks like a skeleton. Are you eating, hon?"

"Plenty, Mom." Which wasn't true. Unless coffee counted.

"Well, you should get plenty of turkey tomorrow. They're not vegans, are they? I didn't see that in the literature. Are you going to make dessert? Look what we did."

She aimed the iPad at the dining room. The table was already set. Candles, plastic placemats and little pumpkins with oak leaves and contorted sticks from the front yard. Same arrangement every year. Name tags, too. One for each member of the family, including Grandma and Grandpa, Uncle Thomas and Aunt Jessie.

Chris's picture was taped to a chair.

He was never a fan of dry turkey and lumpy potatoes. Uncle Thomas would tell a new joke. Mom would laugh. He'd tell her to sign it to Yu. She would say it wasn't appropriate in front of the children. He would say they weren't kids. Dad would tell Yu when Mom wasn't looking. Sometimes Chris would.

Grandpa, Uncle Thomas and Dad would fall asleep in front of the television. Football was on. Chris would help clean up. He made the dessert. There was never any left. Aunt Jessie would make oyster stuffing. There would be plenty put in Ziplocs for everyone to take home and throw away.

"How are ya, sport?" Dad said. "Any news?"

"Not really."

Chris didn't feel like reporting the fall challenge. It felt tainted, for some reason. He'd gone through the entire cycle of emotions—from nervous, to confused, to content, to happy and back to confused.

"You all right?" Mom tilted the iPad.

"Just tired, Mom."

"Oh." Her X-ray vision didn't work as well through the screen. She could tell something was on his mind. If he was in front of her, she would dig the secrets out of him. But it was hard to do it from a thousand miles away on a ten-minute call.

"Your sister wants to talk. Here."

Yu walked off with the iPad.

"I want to say goodbye when you're done," Mom called.

Yu went to Dad's office. Chris could still hear the television in the next room.

Hi, she signed. *How's it going?*

"It's... strange. But okay. You?"

She looked over her shoulder. Mom was watching from the other room.

Want to switch?

"Okay. Why?"

Tell you what I found.

She didn't want Mom to know what she was saying. They'd developed their own signs and signals to confuse her. It started when they were in third grade. Mom didn't like it. *No one likes secrets,* Mom would say. It was the same reason Kogen hadn't understood her when she said she didn't like him at the Visitors' Center.

Your guidance counsellor, she said.

Kogen? It took Chris a few seconds to catch on.

I thought he didn't seem right. I looked him up. He's from a small town. They brag about him, so it was easy to find. He was taking college classes in middle school. Played lacrosse, won a state championship, won some other awards. I did the math. *He's twenty-five years old.*

What? Chris wasn't good at gauging ages. But Kogen looked his parents' age, and they were in their forties. Chris looked through the cubicle glass. There were a few others still on calls, their slackers waiting. No one was outside Chris's cubicle. *You sure?*

Positive. Yu looked up. Chris heard his mom sigh. *I couldn't find anything about Lord...* She didn't want to spell out the name. Probably a good thing. *So I looked up castles. I found it. It was built in 1783 by a Swedish entrepreneur who bought the mountain. Get this. His name was Emerson Santa.*

Santa?

Weird, right? No one has that name. Here's another thing. That school is all about no electronics, right? No phones, no computers, buildings made of boulders. But they're heavily invested in Avocado, Inc. You know, the company with all the cutting-edge technology.

They are?

Yeah. I mean, the school tried to do it anonymously, but some blogger figured it out. They have huge endowments for research.

Chris shook his head. What could Pelz possibly be doing with cutting-edge technology? It was nowhere in the circle.

And here's another thing. Remember that weird reality show a long time ago, Big Game *and* Kringletown?

Chris started to shake his head, then sort of remembered that it had a crazy ending. Billy "Big Game" Sinterklaas was a philanthropist who fostered dozens of teenagers. Then it turned out he had some high-tech lab that was cloning them with synthetic stem cells.

Your guy was a major sponsor, Yu said. *Bankrolled the laboratory through some phony business. You believe that?*

Sis, I can believe anything. He wanted to tell her everything. But short of pulling Gingerman out of his pocket to do a dance, she wouldn't believe him.

Want to know what his name means? Yu said.

Who?

P-E-L-T-Z, she began to spell, *N-I-C-K—*

The screen went black. Chris waited. No one was looking at him. The call, though, ended. So stupid. He never should've let her spell the name. The letters weren't secret. If someone was watching, they would've known.

※

"Ready?" A slacker greeted him. She was skinny beneath a thick hood, her skin dark, smile white.

"I wasn't done."

"Oh?" She looked inside.

"I still had, like, five minutes left."

"That happens sometimes. I'll make sure you get extra time on your next call." She went to a cart parked on the other side of the dais.

"Charles brought me up," he said.

"He's busy. And I don't bite." She patted the seat. "Bundle up."

A damp, bitter wind howled through the tunnel. It stung his cheeks and watered his eyes. Chris barely heard her say her name was Gevenel and this was her favorite time of year. Christmas was almost here. Then she said she missed Thanksgiving with her family, how one year the dog pulled the turkey off the counter, and her mom cried, and they ate mashed potatoes and stuffing.

Her face was smooth, but there were wrinkles in the corners of her eyes. And tight curls of gray above her ears.

"How old are you?" Chris said.

"Excuse me?"

"I was just wondering, you know, if we were, I don't know, close to the same age. You look so young."

"That's a very nice lie. Thank you."

She didn't say how old she was. He thought she was in her forties. *Or maybe twenty-five.*

Chris thanked her for the ride. Snow was spitting across the quad. Everyone was inside.

"This way," Gevenel said.

"I've got homework."

"You've got chores."

"What?"

"We all do. The Feast is tomorrow."

He stared at his dorm. He hadn't expected to be gone this long. He'd left Gingerman with Sai. Gingerman wanted to come with him, take a ride in his pocket, but Chris wasn't comfortable with him around people. He talked too much. And what if someone saw him?

He followed her to Bixen Hall.

The cafeteria was crowded. No one was eating. They were gathered around tables. There were stations organizing plates and cutlery and groups with plants—wispy blue green juniper, stiff spruce, and bare sticks with red holly berries and boxes of pinecones—that were being arranged into centerpieces and name tags. The displays were, of course, nothing like what his mom would build. They were sprawling sculptures of natural materials.

Sai was trimming branches. He nodded.

Gevenel led him to the kitchen. It was even more crowded. The sound of chopping and boiling water, the smell of onions and spices and warm cookies. She pulled him through the crowd to a slacker with a white apron that said *Kitchen Boss*.

"Mauldin?" she said. "Got more help."

"Carrots," was all he said and pointed to a box of raw carrots that needed cleaning, peeling and cutting. Julienne. Chris washed his hands and got to work. Halfway through the load, he heard Gingerman's voice like a distant call through tin cans and a string. It was the first time he'd heard him from outside the dorm. First he could only hear him in the room, then down the hall. *Now it's across campus.*

Still, there was too much noise to understand him. And it was distracting.

Chris focused on peeling and slicing. He never minded prep work. He preferred it in a way. It was meditative. It put thoughts out of his head. Including voices. Pretty soon he smelled cookies coming out of the oven. Cinnamon, cloves and nutmeg.

Gingerbread.

"Onions." Mauldin pointed at three netted bags. "One sliced, two diced."

Chris held up a bucket. Orange shavings spilled over the sides. He was going to need more room. There were still potatoes to peel.

Greenery was piled around Sai. He'd filled a trash can with broken sticks and torn foliage. Chris got his attention. Sai said a few words, Janelle Hartford jammed a paper bag of scraps into the trash can, and he followed Chris.

They followed footprints through snow-crusted drifts, past dormant raised gardens with dried stalks poking out and small piles of mulch. Perry Nickolai and Dandy Pollerson were coming back with empty cans, heads down, noses running. Chris looked over his shoulder.

"Gman?" he said.

"My room," Sai said.

That was good. They both had hiding places in their rooms. Chris kept his window open, just in case. But a cookie falling from the second story during the middle of the day was a last resort. Besides, the snow wasn't powder anymore. Gingerman would hit the drift and shatter.

Gingerman didn't want to stay in the room. He wanted to hide in his pocket. It was risky. If someone saw him moving around—and he would—then it would be over. Chris didn't exactly know what would happen, but it couldn't be good.

"Got something for you." Sai dumped the can onto the steaming compost. He looked around then reached into his pocket. It was a wad of paper. "The pages were scattered. I can't read half of them."

Chris put the story inside his coat without looking.

"It's so strange, man. I don't remember writing it. Like a dream I forgot." Sai stabbed a pitchfork into the pile and turned it. Heat wafted up in earthy tendrils. "Do you remember?"

"What Gman did to me?" Chris said. "Every second."

There was no forgetting that experience. It was surreal and hallucinatory. A dream but something more. Like it was Chris watching the panda fight but not really. He had felt the stiffness of Gingerman's body, the panic.

Jessica Meierson and Peter McTavish added buckets of moldy strawberries and turnip greens to the pile. Sai continued turning it over. Fetid waves of steam drifted with each turn. Chris and Sai let them get ahead before following.

"Talked to my sister," Chris said. "She looked up some stuff about this place. The castle was built in 1783 by a guy named Emerson Santa."

"Really?"

"That's what she said. She also said Kogen is twenty-five years old. And then we got cut off."

"Yeah—wait. Twenty-five?"

"Twenty-five."

Sai counted on his fingers for some reason and shook his head. "They're listening. You know that. I can't believe you were talking about it."

Chris explained there was no way they knew what they were saying. Until she'd spelled out a name.

"She said Pelz invests in Avocado, Inc. You know, the—"

"Technology company, yeah. They do crazy stuff with holographics and AI. Some biological synthetics. They printed a guy's finger. Said it worked just the same. Couldn't tell the difference in a picture."

"Pelz was also somehow involved in that *Big Game* show."

"Kringletown? Oh, man. I loved that show."

"Yeah, well, if Pelz is all into that, where is it? I've never seen a lab, have you?" Chris said. "By the way, you know what Pelznickel means?"

"It's the German Santa. Wears a fur coat."

"He does?"

"I mean, not really. It's just a myth, but that's how it goes."

Chris looked around and leaned in. "Pelz was wearing a fur coat when I saw him."

"I know."

"You know?"

"He does all the time. Dude, you don't have to whisper. This isn't a secret. He wants to be Santa. Think about it. We're the gifters, it's Christmas all year, and it's pretty cold."

He had a point. "Do you think it's odd that a guy named Emerson Santa built the castle?"

"I mean, I guess. Never met someone named Santa."

Sai dragged the trash can behind him. Had he been here too long? How long would it take before Chris wasn't surprised that a man dressed like a version of Santa ran the school and phone calls were screened and students were expelled for last place?

Maybe not long at all.

The cookies were coming out of the oven. The trays were slid onto rolling shelves. Doughy confections with oversized chocolate chips and swirling sprinkles were carted off to another room where they would be transformed into edible masterpieces.

Gabby Dabral dropped a tray. The pan was still hot. Cookies scattered crumbs across the floor. Some of the gingerbread men shattered. Arms and legs broken, heads cracked. Chris helped her sweep them up and throw them in his bucket.

"Thanks," she said.

Chris went back to his station. He felt slightly nauseous. The smell of compost was in his hair. Little pinpricks stuck his eyes. It felt like an allergic reaction. But when he looked into the bucket, he heard Gingerman's voice return.

Save them.

When no one was looking, he pulled the broken gingerbread men out of the bucket.

❄

IT WAS dark when he finished.

Chris's fingers were sore. His back ached. Sai's door was closed. He had been sent to Clancer Hall to help with decorations. Chris knocked lightly in case someone was watching, then snuck inside. A mountain of loose papers had been swept into the corner. It would be easy to search the room without anyone knowing.

"Hey," Chris whispered. "Come out."

Nothing moved. Then, *A little help.*

He was inside a clay mound that was molded into the likeness of a snowcapped mountain, the details of avalanche-prone drifts etched into the sides. It was half done like a school project with a sticky note pinned to the bottom. Don't touch.

Chris found a roll of clay pressed near the bottom. He peeled it away. A crispy tan head wiggled out.

Like being buried alive.

"Can't be too careful."

He wormed halfway out. Chris pulled him the rest of the way. Gingerman didn't seem to mind. He arched back and stretched. The icing decorations were almost gone. His mouth was a thin line and his eyes misshapen. He limped along the desk.

"Your leg."

Gingerman looked down. A crack was splitting where his leg met his body. It was barely hanging on. *I might need a transplant. You got those extras?*

"From the kitchen? You saw those?"

Chris had had that weird sensation in his eyes. Gingerman wasn't just talking to him. He was picking up Chris's senses. That mind-meld thing had residual. Only it wasn't a memory.

"Don't do that again."

I didn't do anything. I just knew what you were doing. Somehow. Learn something every day.

"Yeah, well, ask next time before you..." He pointed at his eyes.

You weren't listening.

Chris pulled the gingerbread cookies out of his coat. Three of them were intact, their generic forms without decorations.

"I thought *I* had to make your body?"

Maybe. I don't know. We could use some spares. Just in case.

Sai still had the headless gingerbread cookies on his desk. They weren't in any better shape than the ones from the kitchen. He held out his hand. Gingerman climbed onto it like a platform and into Chris's coat pocket. They went to his room. Chris stacked a wall of books against the window so no one would see him put him on the desk.

"Lie down." Chris retrieved a tub of white icing and a palette knife.

What are you doing?

"Surgery."

He piled the extra gingerbread bodies next to him. He could transplant a leg, but if it didn't work, the gingerman would be hopping like a pogo stick. It was better to just fix what he had. He applied a layer of icing over the fracture.

"Stop moving."

That tickles.

It was annoying. This was all so serious and Gingerman was giggling like they were about to open presents. He wasn't sure it would work. The leg was barely attached.

"Who made you?"

Some baker, I guess. Same as these guys.

"They're not alive."

Well.

"What does that mean?"

He shrugged. *Maybe not yet. Santa works in mysterious ways.*

"Santa made you, then?"

I told you, I don't know.

Chris sculpted the icing smooth and blew on it. He turned him over carefully and began patching the back side. It didn't look as bad.

Maybe it was Mother Ginger.

"From the *Nutcracker*?"

She was a toy that came to life and became the Regent of the Land of Amusement.

"That was a movie."

It was a fairy tale written in 1816.

Chris didn't know that. It was a classical ballet before the movie.

He didn't know it was based on a fairy tale. But it was odd. Everything seemed to be happening around the turn of the nineteenth century. And he couldn't help but recall the battle of the panda bear and the toy soldier. *That was a nutcracker,* he thought.

He blew on the repaired seam. It needed more time to set. Chris grabbed a tube of white icing. He flipped him over.

What are you doing?

"Stop blinking."

He considered scraping the old icing off his face but decided to touch it up, extending the mouth and rounding out the eyes.

Gingerbread is special. Did you know that? Like hundreds of years ago, only special bakers could make us. Anyone with an oven could do it on Christmas, but the special ones could do it any day of the year.

"Is that right?" Chris muttered. "I talked to my sister today. She did some research on this place. She said a guy named Santa built the castle."

Was his first name Nicholas?

"Emerson."

That's not the fat man.

"How do you know?"

His name is Nicholas Santa. He was the first one to the North Pole.

"That was Robert Perry." Chris remembered that from history class.

History got it wrong. It was Nicholas. He met the elven and never went back.

"Then why is he called Santa Claus?"

It's a long story.

"So you're saying Nicholas Santa discovered the North Pole hundreds of years ago, and now he delivers presents?"

That's what I'm saying. Gingerman frowned, messing up his left eye. Chris used the palette knife to scrape off the mess. *He's not exactly human anymore.*

"Then what is he?"

Something else. You know any two-hundred-year-olds? It's elven magic.

"Try that."

Gingerman blinked a few times then peeled himself off the surface. He did a few deep knee bends, arms out, jogged in place. Crumbs showered the blank gingermen from the kitchen.

Chris moved them out of the way and stacked them neatly.

Can you, Gingerman looked at his front side, *you know?*

Chris grabbed the tube. He added a bowtie under Gingerman's chin. The white line of his mouth curved upward.

I got some exploring to do.

"You need to let that set."

No, I don't. He leaped onto the bed and slid down a blanket. *We don't have time, Christmas. Open up.*

Chris didn't like the idea of the gingerman stranded in a snowdrift with one leg. But he'd survived out there once before. What if someone found him? They wouldn't eat a cookie they found outside, would they?

Chris pulled the cuff on his jeans open. Gingerman climbed inside his pant leg and clung to the sock bunched at the top of his boot. This was the nightly routine: smuggling him inside his pant leg so no one would see him releasing a cookie into the wild.

Chris walked carefully down the steps.

The night was still and icy. The snow crunched. The quad was warmed by the ornaments' light. The windows of the surrounding buildings were lit. The castle was dark.

"Where you going?" Chris whispered.

Behind Clancer. I saw someone in the trees last night.

Chris went around the corner where it was dark. Gingerman scratched his way down Chris's boot. No one would see him fall into the snow. Gingerman burrowed like a groundhog. It was amazing how fast he could move for a cookie. He would cover the entire circle at that speed. He could get to Clancer, Bixen and Lasher in one night. Trupid, too. Chris thought about the other halls. There was Bonner, Stasher and Ditzen.

They were reindeer names. Sort of.

He waited outside for Sai or Joli. It was past curfew and they still weren't back. After several minutes, he went to his room. He pulled out the wad of pages Sai had given him, and started a pot of coffee. He noticed, as he grabbed the pot, some things had been moved around on the desk.

The gingermen from the kitchen were scattered.

He had straightened them into a pile. It hadn't been knocked over. It looked more like they'd crawled around. He picked one up.

"Hey."

He listened for a voice, waited for it to squirm. He bit the foot. Nothing happened. Now he was talking to regular cookies. He lay on the bed and ate the rest of it.

18

The boy was fifteen years old.

He packed a bag with enough food for three days. He brought a knife and a bow he'd fashioned from a sapling and strung with linen string, arrows shaved from cedar limbs. He left before sunrise. Gretchen was still asleep.

He followed the road upon which his father's carriage would arrive. It wound down the mountain. At forks, he would guess which way to turn. He slept in the woods, made fires to keep warm, gathered berries, and rationed his food.

Ten days later, he arrived at the port.

He had collected rocks along the way, but his pack grew heavy. He watched ships arrive and depart for two days. On the third day, he began throwing the rocks into the water.

Gretchen arrived from the castle. She and another servant found him alone on the dock. She sat with him, their legs swinging off the end, as he skipped the last of his collection over the waves.

"He loves you," she said. "As much as he can."

When they returned to the castle, the boy spent much of his time in the woods. He would stay in the wilderness for days at a time, returning for food and a warm bed. He taught himself how to set snares for small game, had even pierced a rabbit with an arrow. He would camp beneath the stars, where he would stack giant rocks in precariously balanced formations.

His father sent Gretchen to fetch him. She found him at the edge of a cliff where he'd built a camp from branches he'd chopped with an axe and lashed with vines. He smelled like a wild animal. His father was not pleased.

"Where do you go?" the boy asked.

"Enough questions," his father said. "Is it not enough to have a home? To have servants? All of this"—he swept his arms—"is for you."

He left the next day. And the boy returned to the wilderness.

He learned to fish. But he had become much more proficient at hunting. Deer and elk couldn't smell him. He waited in the trees with unflinching patience. When he felled a large animal, he would drag it back to the castle. Gretchen taught him how to dress it. They would cure the meat and bury the bones. But the boy would keep the skulls and the hide. He would wrap himself in the fur when he returned to the woods, sleep under it at night.

He began to fill the rooms of the castle. His rock collection grew. There were boxes of leaves he learned to identify, interesting branches, and the bones of small creatures—turtle shells, dragonfly wings, and cicada shells. He would spend days making things with them until he grew bored and returned to the mountain.

His father returned once again. Rarely did he go beyond his office and the kitchen, but the castle had taken on a peculiar smell. He was not pleased. The boy, now seventeen, heard Gretchen plead on his behalf. His father listened but offered no reply. He insisted the rooms be emptied of this debris and the boy properly clean himself. At dinner, they ate venison by candlelight with only the sound of their knives.

"I loved your mother," his father finally said. "But my heart is too big."

The boy lay in bed that night, looking at the pendant he'd stolen from his father, believing his father loved her. But his heart was too big.

When the boy turned eighteen years old, a horse arrived. It wasn't pulling his father's carriage. A courier delivered a letter. The boy watched Gretchen greet him. She told the boy that his father would not be returning. He didn't ask why.

That was the day he began building the wall.

It was his solitary focus for years. He would find boulders nearby and drag them back on carpets of animal hide, lever them into place with branches, and mortar them into place with crushed limestone and sand. The servants would help, but, one by one, they left the castle.

Until only Gretchen remained.

She had no family, no place to go. Only the boy. She would help him with his wall. They would toil all day in the summer sun and the winter cold, stone after stone. When she wasn't strong enough, she would mix the mortar and bring him food and water.

The castle fell into disrepair. The gardens were fallow. Walls had cracked and fireplaces needed sweeping. The rooms still full of his findings. It was cold at night. He would lie in his bed at night beneath layers of fur, listening to Gretchen sing. Her voice carried through the walls and seemed to echo on the mountain.

"When the cold winds blow, and bring the snow. On a clear winter night we will see what it's for. The year may be long, but we can sing this song, and remind us that Christmas is coming."

In the morning, the boy continued the wall until it circled the castle. And then he would begin again, to build it higher. They survived on the game he hunted and the forage she gathered.

He was a young man when the courier returned.

He sat with Gretchen at the lonesome dining table long enough to feed a small army. The letter was from a lawyer. His father had willed the castle and property to him. The boy wasn't interested in owning anything. But the letter contained more than legal inheritance. There was another name.

The name of a half-brother.

Six months later, the wall now ten feet tall, the boy packed his belongings in a bag. He slung it over his shoulder and readied a horse. Gretchen met him at the wooden gate he had built from pine branches and vines. She wasn't young anymore, but her frame was sturdy, her eyes kind.

"I will return," the boy said.

19

They arrived, two by two.

Pairing up to walk the Aisle of Giving, a narrow path between elaborate snow sculptures and ice carvings. Chris walked alongside Sai, both woefully underdressed in paint-spattered cargos and rumpled sweatshirts. Joli fit right in with a patchwork overcoat, with squares of stiff vinyl, that was retro and chic. The blustery wind blew right threw it.

Snowflakes, big and thick, were floating on the wind. No one was really dressed for the weather.

Clancer Hall was lit up with four times the normal lights, strings of large bulbs casting blues and greens and reds down the walls and across the snow sculptures. The steps were anchored by two icy nutcrackers with square mouths and spears at their sides, the ice changing colors with the lights. Among the creations, there were no panda bears.

"Not yet," Chris whispered. "Just wait till we're all in."

"What is it?" Sai said.

"Nothing."

Gingerman wanted to leave his bedroom and explore the castle.

Chris was a hard no. Everyone was supposed to be at the Feast, but that didn't mean the castle was empty.

The soft moan of a viola briefly escaped Clancer as Chris passed a sculpture of children peeking inside the lid of a large gift. Reindeer watched with icy antlers spreading like tree branches made of diamonds. These were still lifes of hungry fans honoring their presence. It was creepy.

"How long does this last?" Chris said.

"Forever," Joli said over her shoulder. "But the food is worth it."

"Pelz will be here?"

"Sort of."

Slackers stood at the entrance, handing out thick wands of twined branches with lichen tucked between them and a display of thorns at the top. Perhaps it was to symbolize the fire of nature. It looked more like a mace.

"Welcome to the Feast," Margaret Chantilee said.

Joli took a short bow. "You're welcome."

Chris and Sai each got a woodland bouquet and carried them like baseball bats. The smell of food was warm and tantalizing. It awakened Chris's taste buds despite the anxiety.

Clancer had been transformed into a wide-open space with three long tables made of gray cedar planks. A flickering candelabrum hung from the ceiling and cast deep shadows in the grain. It sparkled off the fine silverware and shiny china. All the fireplaces were stocked and flaming. Torches on the walls. And Merry Dellagrazie pulled her bow in long, mournful strokes across the viola, the acoustics sending its call around the room, embracing them. Welcoming them. Chai Bokun danced next to her in tights the color of fall.

"Let's go over there." Chris pointed at the corner.

"Sorry," Joli said. "Our seats are reserved."

She started down the middle aisle, the last place he wanted to sit. But then he saw it displayed in the center of the table: big and tan and boxy.

The winner of the fall challenge.

It was to honor the winners. Joli didn't say anything about this. Or if they'd have to stand or talk or critique their own work. Why wouldn't they? He poured water from a silver decanter into a jeweled goblet. His insides were roasting.

That's it, I'm going in.

Gingerman had seen the doors on Clancer close. Chris felt a flutter in his stomach and a slight whoosh of freedom, the sudden wind in his ears like when he and Yu would jump off the garage into a snowdrift.

"Wait!" Chris said.

"What?" Joli leaned back.

He shook his head. He didn't realize he'd said it out loud.

The raucous celebration was cut with the stroke of a small wooden stick against a chiming metal bowl. It struck three times. Ms. Grendel stood at the head table. The faculty flanked her, wearing wizardly gowns shimmering flaxen, goldenrod, umber and ash. In the room's firelight, their faces looked like weathered bark.

The slackers were conspicuously missing.

Ms. Grendel held out her arms, the wide sleeves nearly touching the table. Giddy laughter and jubilant whispers fell into silence as the last chime faded. Her eyes were as heavy as the robe's cloth. She surveyed the gathering.

Chris felt a breeze pass through the room. Although the candles didn't flicker and the napkins didn't flutter in their rings, he felt it on his face. And little bits of snow on his cheeks. Snowflakes fluttered from the dark ceiling.

"Are you falling asleep?" Joli whispered.

He was leaning on her, looking up. The snow had vanished.

"My lovely, lovely Gifters." Ms. Grendel's voice bellowed like a bassoon. A woman who could holler across a canyon with little effort. "This is the greatest day of the year. The day of gratitude. Of giving. And the first... day... of the Christmas season!"

The response was unruly. They were slapping the tables, stomping feet, fists in the air. Their roars cascaded off the domed ceiling in visceral waves. How could they be so excited? It was always

Christmas. Every single day. The free presents, the ornaments. How was this any different?

Ms. Grendel was effusive. She actually smiled. The excitement was palpable. He could feel it in his bones like he was sliding down a snowy hill on a waxed disc.

"I'm so hungry I could eat this stale house," Joli said.

"I'm so proud of what you've given us this year," Ms. Grendel said. *That sounds strange,* Chris thought. "Let us give thanks for this moment."

Everyone clasped hands with the person next to them. Sai's hand was sweaty. Joli's was cold. Some bowed their heads, closed their eyes. A brisk chill flooded the room. It went up Chris's legs. He inhaled sharply. The room dimmed. And suddenly the floor tilted. He was falling.

He grabbed the table. His plate and silverware shattered the silence. No one, though, broke their moment of thanks while Chris held on.

"You all right?" Joli mouthed.

He didn't know what he was. The candles hadn't gone out, and no one else had nearly toppled over. But he wouldn't let go. It had felt like the room rolled over.

"Let's eat," Ms. Grendel said.

Enormous curtains parted on both sides of the room. The aroma of turkey and lightly buttered baby potatoes wafted out, of fresh greens and baked squash, of cranberries and deviled eggs. Chris could smell green bean casserole, sweet potatoes with toasted marshmallows, candied yams, cheesy brussels sprouts, and cornbread.

It was a standing ovation.

The slackers wore tuxedos that were pressed and starched as stiff as their posture and carried dishes to the tables, presenting a smorgasbord of unending choices. The clatter of cutlery, the scooping of utensils filled the room. It felt like the time he went deep-sea fishing with Uncle Thomas and the room was still swimming when they returned.

"You don't look so good," Sai said.

"I'm fine." His brain tasted fuzzy.

He drank from his goblet and filled it again. He wasn't nauseous or feverish. He was just seeing things. No big deal. If he didn't close his eyes, he would be all right.

The turkey was good, not great. At least not up to the standards of the talent in that room. If it were a student project, Chef DuPont would spit it up. The baby potatoes were outstanding, and the steamed asparagus quite good. There was mac and cheese, too. Not the box kind. This was handmade noodles with rich white cheese and herbs and just enough bits of chicken.

There was no dessert. Which was odd. Then people started coming by their table. They reached over his shoulder and broke pieces off the gingerbread house, snapping off roof panels and crooked walls, dipping them in goblets of milk and calling for toasts, clicking their metal cups and slapping him on the shoulder. The second- and third-place sculptures were ravished as well. It was visceral, carnal and complete. Even the slackers joined in, crumbs down the front of their spotless tuxedos.

Merry Dellagrazie began playing the viola, the tones soothing. He resisted closing his eyes to float on her notes. His belly was full; he wasn't cold, wasn't hot. He was spot on. The world was right again.

"Hear from him yet?" Sai asked.

Swept up in the merriment, he'd forgotten about the gingerman. The worry returned. What if something happened to him? His leg broke or both of them? Or worse, someone saw him?

"Where are you?" he whispered.

When he didn't hear anything, he closed his eyes and imagined him, what he thought of as *reaching* for him with thoughts. The room spun for a moment. He opened his eyes. *Bad idea,* he thought.

"Attention!"

The viola stopped. The bell chimed. Ms. Grendel was standing again, arms out, sleeves draping over the heads of the faculty to each side of her.

"Here it comes," Joli murmured.

"What is it?" Chris said.

When the room settled, or close enough, Ms. Grendel clasped her hands together and beamed a smile across the room. He'd never seen that look on her before. Or any of the faculty. They were far too serious for joy.

"As you know..." she started.

Chris didn't hear what followed. Something drifted from the ceiling. His eyes were open, he pried them open with his fingers to make sure he wasn't mistaken.

It was snow.

Big snowflakes gracefully floated down. He watched them make their way across the room. They disappeared on the tables and floor. It was getting heavier. Sound dampened like a wintery day. It was so thick he could barely see Ms. Grendel.

"What's wrong?" Sai said.

"You... you don't see it?"

"Of course," Ms. Grendel said, "this wouldn't be a feast without..."

The table began to rattle. The cedar planks bowed and buckled. The crooked tip of a tree branch punched through it. All the tables were dancing, the splintering of wood all around, tree branches writhing from the floor, swelling with coarse bark around solid trunks.

The room rumbled.

Mossy boulders grew through the floor. They piled on top of each other like bubbles. A wall grew behind the faculty members and Ms. Grendel's sweeping announcement.

Chris grabbed Sai's arm.

"What's wrong?" Sai's breath puffed out.

The ceiling was a blackened backdrop behind the barren tree canopies, the limbs intertwining. Darkness crept down the walls and wrapped around the torches. The candles shrank.

"Lord Pelznickel!" Ms. Grendel called.

Between the stalwart tree trunks, a figure appeared. He was twice the size of a normal man. His fur coat and matted yellow trim around his neck, his cherub face got a standing ovation and raised goblets.

"We live in the stone age," Joli said, "and he's got a hologram. Great."

Chris had thought his size was part of the hallucination. He clung to Sai like he was the last knot dangling over a chasm.

Then the rope broke.

He travelled at warp speed down a long dark tunnel. Twisting and curving, his grip faded as Sai's arm vanished. He was nowhere. His eyes dry and burning. He felt the sting of snow, the sensation of a snowplow making its own path. He felt arms and legs paddling through fluff.

There were just the trees now. The trees and wall that circled campus. He looked up from the ground. It was so much higher than he'd ever seen it. Lichens were the size of maple leaves stuck to enormous boulders.

"Every year, as you know, I choose the very best." Pelz's voice called from the other end of the time warp. "The best of the best."

Christmas? Gingerman said. *Is that you?*

What's happening?

Gingerman was on the move again. There were tracks. And the smell of smoke. Then he went down into the dark. Chris felt the grind of frozen earth on his fingertips, the cold sting of frozen snow on his nose.

Look at that, Gingerman said.

He was standing on a bumpy path. In between the massive trees were small cottages of stone that looked like the gift shop beneath the Christmas Tree, warm light glowing in round windows. A hunched figure limped out of a doorway, a hooded cowl over their head. A yellow lamp swung from their hand, the flame flickering inside the glass case.

Gingerman hid against a root flare.

Chris could feel his own heart knocking. It felt so far away. He was disoriented. And frightened the hooded figure would hear his heart beating, would see the strange little gingerman cookie trying to hide.

"Without further ado," Pelz's voice called from afar, "I want to announce this year's..."

What is this place? Chris said.

Gingerman didn't answer. The figure had stopped and looked in their direction. In the dim light, he couldn't be sure, but the cowl appeared to be gray.

"Christmas Blizzard!" Pelz shouted.

It was like hitting the bottom of a bungy jump. Chris snapped back into the delirious darkness and slammed into his body with the finality of a bolt hammered through a steel plate. Sai and Joli kept him from flipping off the bench. Thunderous applause echoed in a spinning carnival ride.

"Stand up, Christmas," Pelz bellowed. "Let them honor you."

An apple lodged in his throat. His legs were dripping. Sai and Joli tried to lift him up. He couldn't hear what they were saying and thought if they let him go, he'd melt into the floor.

Christmas! Gingerman shouted.

Chris was in two places. Two minds. Two bodies. His stomach turned inside out.

The last thing he would remember was the sound of all the food he ate hitting the floor. Pelz's laughter.

Then he woke up in a room he had never seen.

20

The sky was painted slate gray. The sort of sky that felt heavy and confining, like the lid on a crate. Or a coffin. A sky that wouldn't cry or snow. It was just there. Forever and ever. So close, he could touch it. He lifted his fuzzy arm, the residue of dreams still dusting his thoughts like bits of snow.

"Hello, Christmas."

Pelz was in a chair, thick hands folded over his belly. The furry coat bunched around his wrists.

Chris was in a bed.

It was a strange room. Larger than the one in his dorm, but no dresser for clothes. Just an organized desk and small window above the bed. His elbow sank into the mattress. A bag of wet sand in his head. His mouth coated with putty.

"Where am I?" Chris said.

"Do you understand heredity?" Pelz looked like he was poured into the chair. "Every cell in the body has a blueprint, a code of DNA passed down from your ancestors that was passed down from their ancestors and so on and so forth. That code determines the color of your eyes, hair color, how tall you'll get. The sum of your genome determines who you are.

"But not all genes are expressed. Some are turned off, lying dormant inside you. Some people go their entire life without realizing the treasure hidden deep inside their cells. If they just took the time to dig."

Pelz continued talking about alleles, the dominant and recessive, how they expressed themselves. Things Chris recalled from biology class about Mendel's peas.

"But sometimes"—Pelz lifted a finger—"DNA does things science still doesn't understand. There's an entanglement between us and our ancestors. Even our siblings. We inherit their discoveries. And their gifts. Even when they're on the other side of the world."

Everything made sense. Until that. DNA didn't entangle like quantum particles.

Nausea stirred in Chris's stomach. He sat up, elbows on his knees, head down. He felt like a cartoon sketch. It was hard to remember where he had been. His stomach was empty, wrung out. He tasted vomit. There was the food and goblets of water, trees growing through tables. And cheering.

"I never said yes," Chris said.

Pelz abruptly stopped. He pushed himself upright, rubbing his round chin. "Your parents make decisions for you because you're a child, Christmas. Not because they're necessarily smarter but because they've lived longer. They've made mistakes. They know better. I've lived longer than anyone you know, Christmas."

The chair creaked.

"I know better."

The room was unsteady. A knot lodged in Chris's throat. Where were Joli and Sai? Gingerman? He'd already abandoned them when he went to the tower. *Where am I now?*

"Bring him some water," Pelz said.

Ms. Grendel entered the room, wearing a long winter coat, with a silver pitcher in one hand, condensation clinging to the sides. She poured a glass. Chris drank half of it. She put her hand on his arm.

"Slowly."

It cooled his dry throat, satisfied the ache in his stomach. His head was still fuzzy. Ms. Grendel put the pitcher on the desk. She wasn't using her cane. She didn't look like she needed it.

"Do you trust me?" Pelz said.

"I don't know."

"Good answer." Pelz slapped his knee. "Honesty. I value that, Christmas. Family secrets lead to resentment. And we are family. So trust me when I say you have hidden treasure."

Chris looked up.

"Most people never know who they are or why they do the things they do. Ignorance is the root of their suffering while the treasure of understanding remains buried." He sat on the edge of his seat. "I want to help you dig."

Chris remembered the time his mother took him to see an ear specialist. There were pointed tools on the wall and stainless-steel sinks. He sat on a table covered with a thin sheet of paper which stuck to his legs. The doctor stuck a needle in his ear. He never forgot the smell of that room.

This felt a little like that room. But it didn't smell like a hospital.

"What do I have to do?" he said.

Pelz glanced at Ms. Grendel. "It's very simple." He stood up, his girth seemingly tipping the floor toward him as he spread his arms. "Remember."

Chris waited. "Remember?"

"You need to remember what you never knew."

"I... I don't get it."

There were books and papers on the desk, pens lined up, folders on a shelf. Pelz reached into a glass jar next to the folders. It was filled with dull metal marbles. The very same marbles that Ms. Grendel had them hold. The ones Gingerman had told him about.

They bring toys to life.

"There is a creative flow in the universe, a current that exists when we let go. You felt it during the challenge. The very essence of creativity. I want you to build your inner landscape, Christmas." Pelz nudged the crown. "And we're going to help."

Inner landscape? Chris barely remembered what had happened at the challenge. It had seemed effortless at the time, but he couldn't explain how he did it. Or if he could make it happen again.

"The challenge," Pelz said as he rolled a marble, "is to drop into the current. It will take you where you need to go and show you who you are. The paradox is this: *You* are the current."

Chris nodded, but it didn't make sense. He pointed. "What's that for?"

Pelz shared a look with the old woman. Her expression was muted. Distant. It bothered Chris that she seemed uneasy. Pelz carried the marble like a robin's egg and delicately put it in Chris's hand, folding his fingers around it.

It was weighty, like before. Cold and solid. Like it would sink into the floor if he dropped it.

"You got these at the mansion. The one everyone hikes to." Chris thought that would shake Pelz. He only smiled. So Chris pushed a little harder. "Someone said these make toys come to life."

Pelz's grin only grew. He slapped his knee and let out a guffaw that sounded like Christmas Eve. "Yes, yes." He wiped his eye. "I've heard that one, too."

He was entertained to tears. Ms. Grendel less so. But he didn't deny it.

"So then why do you have them?" Chris said.

"For you, Christmas. To wake you up."

Ms. Grendel put a gold band on the desk. Like the one he wore in the castle, only this one was wider. Pelz admired it like the marble, turning it between his hands. A strange sensation hummed in Chris's head like a radar dish picking up signals. Pelz took the marble from Chris. He put the crown back on the table and the marble inside the jar.

"So you just want me to remember?" Chris said. "How?"

"Float downstream," he said, "and see where it takes you."

Chris understood. Pelz wanted him to put on the crown. Like it wouldn't hurt. Just like the doctor had said before sticking a needle in his ear.

"In the meantime, your schoolwork is here. There's no rush to remember, but I'd like you to return in a few weeks." Pelz nudged the crown, turned and smiled with a gleam in his eye. "You don't want to miss Christmas."

❄

Chris stood at the window. There was a view of a deep valley. Trees were below and as far as he could see.

There was a long hallway outside his room with doors. Chris opened them. They were more bedrooms. Empty, sterile. There was also a bathroom, a kitchen and a small gym with a treadmill and weights. No one else was there, though.

The door at the end was locked.

He wondered if there were cameras. Probably. He sat at his desk. The coffeemaker was there. The textbooks were from his room and the notes he'd spent months scribbling on notebooks.

He looked busy, flipping through the pages. The crown was waiting. He didn't have to pretend to yawn. If they were watching, they would understand he was tired. But they wouldn't know what he was doing. He closed his eyes.

And *reached*.

He was out there. Chris could feel him like a faint blip. It was so far away. A shadowy grain of sand. He tried to grab it, corral it. Hold it.

Christmas? Gingerman's voice was a whisper.

Chris strained to hear what he was saying. His head hurt. It had been so effortless before. Something had changed. Was he really that far away? Or did Pelz do something?

Where are you? Gingerman said.

Chris didn't react. He didn't want to look suspicious. He got up to pour a glass of water, looked out the window, then whispered, "I don't know."

I can barely hear you. Are you with Pelz? What's he—

"Are you all right?" Ms. Grendel was at the door.

Chris spilled water on the bed. He didn't hear her come down the hall. "Yeah. Yeah, I, uh, I was just…" He shook his head. "My head's hurting."

"Who were you talking to?"

"No one." He said it too quickly. "No, I just, I do that when I'm nervous. Can I go outside?"

"Not yet. There's work to do. Have you eaten?" She put a tray on the desk. A sandwich and an apple.

She rehearsed a smile. It didn't mean anything. Then she went down the hall and through the locked door. He realized why he hadn't heard her coming. She didn't have a cane.

And walked like she didn't need one.

❄

CURIOSITY PICKED UP THE CROWN.

A day of sitting in the room, knowing it was his choice to put it on but also knowing he wasn't leaving until he did. Pelz and Ms. Grendel were polite, occasionally stopping by to speak, ask how he felt. He was doing schoolwork in solitary confinement.

Let's get this over with.

He felt stupid, lying on the bed, wondering what Joli would say. He stared at the gray ceiling. She would do it, if she were here. Eventually she would.

The crown was weighty and snug, like a headband the perfect size. He wondered what it did. Was there a button? He was tense, expecting a jolt or a hum. It was comfortable. He closed his eyes.

He had the sense the room disappeared.

He opened his eyes. *That was weird.* The spaciousness. Like there was no ceiling or walls when he closed his eyes. No boundaries. His thoughts roamed like rabbits set loose in the countryside with nothing but hills and bramble to explore. He closed his eyes and lay there in complete peace. With no thoughts unless he chose to think.

He wasn't sleeping. He was very aware in a bed, heard the wind against the window and branches on the roof. He was just nowhere.

Images appeared.

Through no thought or will of his own, dreamy objects welled up. They were abstract and colorful, blooming from nothing, merging into each other, morphing into strange designs. Some were gruesome, the inner workings of his own biology. Others pleasant and floaty.

Float downstream.

He enjoyed the show, feeling his body press into the mattress. And then suddenly it was gone. He was falling like he'd been pushed out of a plane. He jolted up, clutching a couch cushion. The fabric was coarse, a weave of olive green and mustard yellow. It was the sofa his grandparents had given his dad. The same sofa his dad grew up on.

And now Chris was on it.

Yu was sitting at the window. Her hair was cut at her shoulders. It was dark outside. Snow was falling around the halo of a streetlight. She had her hand against the window. She liked to feel the cold.

Christmas music crackled from a small radio in the kitchen. Mom came out wearing pajamas and a floppy elf hat, standard attire for Christmas Eve. She hummed the words with her eyes closed, standing in front of the fireplace. She didn't know the verse, no matter how timeless the song, waiting for the chorus.

Dad joined in from the bedroom, coming out with flannel bottoms and leather slippers. His glasses crooked, nose red. He bellowed loud and long enough for Yu to turn around and watch them sing like badly tuned violins.

This is a memory.

But he'd never dreamed so real, but he didn't remember sitting on the couch. He remembered being in his bedroom. Staring at his laptop, scrolling through videos. It was embarrassing to watch his parents. He just wanted to sleep so it would be morning and he could open presents.

"Christmas?" Mom called through her hands. "Come out, come out wherever you are."

Chris watched his own self come out in a T-shirt and shorts and one sock. He was twelve years old. That was the year he shaved his head with the dog clippers. Mom was not happy. They were supposed to take family pictures. She was afraid people would think he was sick.

What are you doing? Yu had said to him.

Chris watched his younger self fall on the couch next to him. It was surreal. He was afraid to touch him. He looked so bored. *What's wrong with me?*

Mom and Dad started dancing that old-time dance, swaying and spinning to the sound of old Christmas music. Young Chris watched his sister join them. He didn't feel like he belonged. But he didn't even try, even when Mom pulled his younger self to his feet. All four of them turning in a circle, arms around each other.

The couch was suddenly quicksand. Chris sank between the cushions. He clawed the fabric. Once again, he was falling in the dark. His breath came in thick clouds. A ceiling of snow only inches from his face. He was in a frozen coffin. He panicked at first. Then saw that he was lying next to someone.

Ten-year-old Chris had dug a tunnel in the snowbank. Chris remembered the Minnesota Vikings stocking cap his uncle had given him for his birthday. He didn't even like sports, but he liked the way it fit. Young Chris was just lying there, breathing, thinking how good it felt.

There had been a record snowfall that year. The snow drifted up to the gutters. He and Yu had tunneled like gophers. She wanted to meet in the middle, but Chris had just stopped. It felt so good to be cold and alone.

This was where he belonged. He watched his breath spread across the ceiling and disappear, thinking if there was a way he could stay there and never come out. Make it wider, bring some stuff from his bedroom.

Yu was digging again. He heard her climb the side of the drift. Chris knew what happened next. Her footsteps punched through the snow. And then all at once, the weight of the world fell on him. His lungs desperately squeezed his last breath. He held it, knowing if he let it go, there wouldn't be another. But he couldn't move.

It was so dark.

There was the sound of thudding and more weight. Distant crying. He heard the digging. He clenched, promising not to open his mouth. And then a hand struck his chest. It scooped the snow away, and bright sunlight hit his face. His dad was there in his T-shirt. His glasses had fallen into the snow. He wouldn't find them until spring.

They pulled him out. They hugged him. Mom weeping. Dad shaking. Yu signing over and over. *Sorry, sorry, sorry.*

Chris didn't hug them back. He wanted to. He was happy but sad. The igloo was gone, and Mom wouldn't let them do that ever again.

The snow caved into a sinkhole and swallowed Chris. He floated downstream, this time not panicking, letting it take him to the next memory.

The sky was smeared with charcoal.

They were walking through an evergreen forest. The colors were a bland grayscape, the memory bleached by time and the setting sun. Dad wore a long red and white scarf that looked like a tail draped over his back. He clutched a bow saw with deep teeth on a rusty blade. Mom carried a dull green thermos. Her hair was short beneath a green elf hat. Yu was pulling a vintage rail sled their grandpa used to ride when he was little.

Chris looked five years old.

It was hard to judge the age. This was a memory clouded in youth. He was chubby, his coat unbuttoned, snorkel hood pushed back, walking far behind his family on the way to find the perfect tree. That was a tradition until he was a teen, when Dad decided on an artificial tree. Mom fought him on that. A fake tree wasn't Christmas. They compromised and bought a tree from the church.

Chris watched Dad grab a branch; Mom wanted to keep looking. She was never in a hurry. Five-year-old Chris dragged along, distracted by the falling snow. His grandma used to say they were little pieces of Christmas spirit blessing the land. Five-year-old Chris was trying to catch one on his tongue, wondering what it tasted like. It had to be a clean catch. Once a snowflake hit the ground, Grandma would say, the blessing would melt.

Pretty soon, five-year-old Chris was running through the trees.

Chris followed him. He remembered chasing snowflakes, but not getting lost. The snow was getting heavy, dampening the sound of Mom's singing and Dad's frustration. He wandered in the thickest part of the forest, but the snow found its way through the branches. The treetops swayed. The wind had picked up and the snow came down heavier. He could barely see the trees.

Five-year-old Chris didn't seem frightened.

He climbed over fallen trees and scaled a slope on all fours, his tongue chasing Christmas spirits. The weather had suddenly turned, and his younger self was oblivious.

"Hey," Chris said, "go back."

His voice had a tinny sound like speaking into a box. Five-year-old Chris didn't hear him. Chris reached for him, but his hand went through the boy like a ghost. All he could do was watch him climb a steep slope.

The forest suddenly ended.

It was a wall of trees. Their trunks so close together that five-year-old Chris turned sideways to slip between them. He stopped on the crest of the hill and stared, forgetting about the snow collecting on his head, melting on his cheeks. Beyond was a white landscape as flat as a cornfield under a blanket of snow. The horizon so wide he could see the curvature of the earth.

His parents came running, out of breath. Mom hugged him. Dad was angry, holding the bow saw like a weapon. Five-year-old Chris pointed, but they didn't see what he saw. Maybe it wasn't there, the memory distorted by wishes of Christmas spirit falling from the sky.

Chris saw it.

Out there on the crystalline horizon, a dark figure was walking alone. Trekking on the snow with snowshoes. It was too small to be a bear. Too dark. Chris watched it journey through the peaceful night, wondering why it felt so familiar. Or maybe that was part of the dream.

When darkness came, he didn't fall. He bolted up in bed, taking a breath as if he'd been under for too long. His heart thudding, lungs burning. He was shivering, couldn't feel the tips of his fingers or earlobes.

Ms. Grendel was suddenly by his side. She wrapped him in a blanket.

"What-what-what was that?" he said.

She sat him on the edge of the bed and took the crown off his head. Pelz came in, stood there with hands on his hips.

"Can you stand?" Ms. Grendel said. "It's good to walk a bit, get the feeling back."

He was weak. His bones frigid. The floor hurt his feet when he put his weight down. It felt like waking up in the recovery room, unsure of where he had been. Where he was now. Only he wasn't nauseous.

The marbles had a strange glow. They looked like they were smoking. Wisps of steam twisted off the glass jar like thin strands. Chris rubbed his eyes. For a moment, it looked like foggy strings were attaching him to the marbles.

Pelz pulled a marble out and admired the light. He looked up with a beaming smile.

"You were there."

21

Chris rolled a marble on the desk.

It was no longer dull. It contained a faint glimmer of light. The surface was etched with fine lines, an intricate webbing of fractal patterns. The gingerman said they would bring toys to life. Pelz only said one thing.

They help you remember.

But Chris felt better. Better than ever. A little weak, but his head was clear. The clutter had been blown away. Like his head had no limits for thoughts to bounce around, just endless space. The crown was on his bed with curiosity. The more he remembered.

The better he felt.

It felt good seeing those lost parts of his self. It felt like he was reclaiming them, seeing them objectively. Understanding them. Feeling the sadness, the loneliness that was always there. He wanted more. Even if Pelz was after something, he was right about one thing.

Chris wanted to know who he was.

His eyes began to itch. Then sting. A heavy wave poured through his head.

"Ging—"

Don't talk, Gingerman said. *Wherever you're at, they're listening. Just think. I'll hear you.*

Chris started to nod. Gingerman was right. The last time he spoke to him, Ms. Grendel had showed up.

You there? Gingerman said.

Chris didn't know what to do. Maybe he could take a shower and whisper with the water running or pretend he was talking in his sleep.

Try this. Picture an object. Anything at all. Close your eyes and imagine it with all the detail. The color, shape and size. The smell. I'll... an apple?

Chris was looking at the tray Ms. Grendel had left. He wondered if the gingerman had seen it. He imagined the words. Felt their weight on an imaginary page. The corners of the letters, the smell of fresh ink.

Gingerman, he thought.

Hey, buddy.

He went to the bathroom, pretending to stretch his legs, swinging his arms like Ms. Grendel had told him to do every day. He came back to his desk and opened a textbook.

Are you... you're thinking about a book?

Yes, Chris thought.

Hold on. I'm going to look.

It felt like ants crawling in his eyes. Everything was blurry, like a camera searching for focus. His ears popped.

There we go, Gingerman said. *Look around now.*

Chris casually walked around the room and looked out the window.

Nice view. Looks like you upgraded. You're not in the circle.

I don't know where I am.

We're going to find out. Go back to the desk.

Chris sat down and stared blankly at the textbook.

Is that what I think it is? Gingerman said.

What?

You've got a cookie jar of spheres.

Chris glanced at the jar, then picked up the marble on the desk.

What are you doing with them? Gingerman asked.

Chris told him about the crown and remembering, how the marbles were glowing brighter each time he woke up. *Pelz said they help remember.*

That's not what they're for, Gingerman said.

Do you have one? Chris asked.

You already asked that.

Maybe there's one in your head.

You think one of those will fit in my head? He's using you.

There was silence. Chris thought he might have lost him. No one was coming down the hall. Chris put the marble down and lay on the bed, holding the crown and thinking of putting it on.

Is Sai there? Chris thought.

He's here.

Chris closed his eyes. The stinging had turned into a mild itch he couldn't scratch. He focused on Gingerman's voice, felt it like a pebble in orbit. He imagined zooming through space like an explorer searching for a habitable planet. Then he felt the confines of thin arms and a flat head. Watery images in his vision. Enormous textbooks and paintbrushes the size of trees.

Sai. I see him. Tell him I can see him.

I can't. Remember?

Chris felt Gingerman's arm rise. Saw it waving. Sai bent over.

You talked to him before, Chris said.

One miracle at a time, buddy. I might puke.

Chris did feel a little woozy, but it was different than when this had happened at the Feast. There was so much space this time. It was pleasant. Like he was looking through a camera lens. Only he was the camera.

Hang on. Gingerman fumbled with a pencil, pinching it between his arms. He began spelling a name on a notebook. Chris wondered if Sai would know what it meant. The lines were shaky. Chris could write better with his left foot.

C-R-I-S.

That's not how you spell it, Chris said.

All right, well, I can't spell.

There's an H between the C and R. Like Christmas. You should know how to spell Christmas.

I don't know how to spell!

Start over, then. Chris was worried Ms. Grendel would check on him. *Grab that brush. No, no. That one! The one with the—*

"Chris?" Sai said.

Sai! You can hear me?

Sai grabbed his head with both hands. He had a pained look.

Sorry, sorry. Sai, I can see you. Can you hear me?

Sai nodded slowly. He bent over. "You're in there?"

No, I'm—I'm somewhere else. But I can see you.

He moved closer. Gingerman backed between the books. The gingerbread men Chris had taken from the kitchen were still on the desk. But they were propped against the wall. Like they were standing in a line.

Did you move them? Chris said.

Sai must have been playing with them. He's a little distracted.

"Where are you?" Sai said.

I don't know. Chris got up to drink some water. He was suddenly thirsty. *What did you see out back?*

Me? Gingerman said.

Behind the circle, during the Feast. What was back there?

Oh, that. Yeah. Not much. I could feel you puking, and they must've heard me moving around. A bunch of them came out. I had to get.

What'd they look like?

People. And that's not where Pelz took you. There's no views like that.

It was a little village that looked older than what was inside the circle. Like going back in time. The people were wearing the gray cloaks.

"What are you doing?" Sai asked.

Chris told him about the crown and marbles, the dreams he had that were more than dreams. Like visiting memories.

We're going to find you. Gingerman crawled over books and looked out the window. Chris worried someone would see the golden-brown head peeking above the windowpane.

The quad was empty. The snow fresh. Ms. Grendel was leaving the castle. She leaned on her cane, poking through the snow and testing her weight with each step. Chris hadn't seen her in a few hours. So wherever he was, he couldn't be far. Not at the speed she was walking. Her hip had stiffened in the cold.

I'm going in the castle tonight, Gingerman said.

The castle? No, no.

Yes, yes. I've been scouting it. Sai knows the routine. No one's around in the middle of the night. And the gaps in the doors, I can slide right under.

But I'm not in there.

I know you're not. But the answers are. Don't worry. If Pelz is in there, I'll just—

"Everything all right?"

Chris lost his balance. He collapsed on the bed, spilling water on his lap. The room was spinning. He clutched the covers and felt the water soak through his pants. The details began to come into focus. He was back in the room.

Ms. Grendel was in the doorway.

"I... I was just..." He swallowed the rest of his words.

"Careful." She took the glass and filled it with water, handing him a towel. "You need to pace yourself. Make sure you take time to eat and drink."

He sat with the towel on his lap as she looked around the room. There was nothing out of the ordinary. But she seemed suspicious.

"I'll bring new sheets for the bed." She nodded. "I'm proud of you, Christmas."

She felt different than Pelz. She cared. Pelz cared about something. Chris wasn't sure what it was.

She came back with fresh sheets and made the bed while Chris watched. The weird thing was that she was in the quad, only twenty steps out of the castle, poking the crusted snow with her cane. It was impossible. Maybe time wasn't synced with what he was seeing through Gingerman. But then he realized. Ever since he'd been in the room, she was missing something.

She never used a cane.

※

"I want to go back," Chris said.

"Mmm." Pelz fell into the chair. "I thought you preferred to be alone."

"I want to see my friends."

Pelz nodded thoughtfully, framing his chubby chin with finger and thumb. "Is that really what's bothering you?"

Chris looked out the window. Pelz had that look, that X-ray look that could see the truth. Of course, he missed Sai and Joli and the gingerman. And he did want to go back. The thing with Ms. Grendel, though. It dumped him on his head. It didn't make sense. It had to be a mistake. The person in the quad was far away. It could've been anybody with a cane.

Because Ms. Grendel is here.

"What are these doing?" Chris picked up a marble. "Exactly."

"Helping you remember."

"Then why are they glowing?"

Pelz propped his hands on his knees and looked at the floor for a long moment. "They're an aid, of sorts. They're tuning into you, giving you space to remember. In a way, they're connecting with you."

Space. It did feel like space. Like he had more room to think. And the strange thing was he did feel connected to the marbles. Felt them. And sometimes, when he first woke up from a memory, he could see the ghostly threads attached to them like spider silk waving in the wind.

"How do you feel?" Pelz said.

If he was honest? He never felt better. Light, clear. Unencumbered. He was tired, very tired sometimes, but even that didn't bother him. He just accepted whatever was in the moment. Tired or not.

"Growth is not always fun," Pelz said. "Hugs are fine, but when you're comfortable, you're stagnant."

Chris had heard that somewhere before. Was it Joli?

"You've changed since your first day on campus," Pelz said. "You have friends. And you miss them. That's good. That's the work."

Six months ago, Chris couldn't think of a friend. Acquaintances, but not friends. Joli and Sai felt like friends. *And a cookie, too.*

"I want you to go back." Pelz stood with a groan. "When the time is right."

"When is that?"

"You'll know." He dropped a heavy hand on Chris's shoulder. "Christmas wouldn't be the same without Christmas."

Pelz's laughter thundered. Chris cringed as he squeezed his shoulder. His mom told the same corny joke when he would hide in his room and she would peek inside, music coming from the front room, Dad singing.

Christmas isn't the same...

22

Curiously, the memories were always around Christmas.

They weren't always sad or depressing. There were snowball fights with Dad, making cookies with Mom, and wrapping gifts with Yu. There was also the time Mom and Dad got in a fight. Dad spent the night at Grandma's house, and Mom wouldn't come out of the bathroom.

Chris was always the observer, watching the scenes unfold. They were all familiar, even the ones he'd forgotten.

Except the time he was eight years old.

This memory was far downstream. So far, he didn't remember it at all. His younger self, eight-year-old Chris, was standing in the backyard. The stars were out and the moon so bright he could see the chocolate chip cookie print on young Chris's pajamas. His bare feet were in several inches of snow.

He was staring at the trees.

Mouth open, eyes glassy. The cold didn't bother him. There was nothing there. Just darkness between the trunks. That was where he and Yu played in the summer, building forts and catching minnows in the stream.

Chris struggled to remember this time. He recalled Mom and

Dad changing the locks that year so that they had to use a key to open the doors. And Mom sleeping on the couch a lot, even though she and Dad weren't in a fight. They said they were just being safe. Later, they said he sometimes sleepwalked.

The lights turned on in the house. Young Chris's shadow stretched between the trees. Chris's heart skipped. He thought he saw something. Short and stout, it looked like a stump. But it was looking back.

The back door slammed. Mom ran through the snow in her socks, tying her robe around her waist.

"Christmas," she said, "what are you doing out here?"

Dad wasn't far behind. He was in boxer shorts and boots, the shoelaces flicking around his legs, and carrying a small bat.

"Something's wrong," she said.

"He's sleepwalking," Dad said.

"Chris? Christmas?" Mom snapped her fingers. Young Chris didn't blink. "Do we touch him? I don't think we're supposed to touch him, when someone is... Chris?"

Dad waved his hand. Mom said she was going to call 911. Then young Chris waved at the trees and smiled.

"Okay," he said.

He turned around and walked into the house. Mom wrapped her robe around him. Dad looked into the woods and frowned. Then he followed them inside.

They never told me about this. Just made sure I never did it again. Did I?

He was sleepwalking. That would explain why he couldn't remember. *So why am I seeing this now?*

That was a legit question. He'd only visited memories, not things he wasn't present for. Young Chris was in the house. Of course, it was possible this was his subconscious filling in the blanks. Young Chris's eyes were open. He waved at something.

Chris was still in the memory, alone in the backyard. The black veil that ushered him to the next memory hadn't come for him. That didn't make sense. If Young Chris was inside...

Why am I still here?

A twig snapped.

Chris tensed. This didn't feel like a memory. What if he forgot he was really on a bed wearing a crown? Would he wake up?

He took a step.

Crusted snow broke under his foot. The short and stout stump wasn't there anymore. But something was moving farther in the forest. It wobbled between the trees. Chris looked back. The lights were still on.

He went deeper. He lost track of the movement, couldn't see if there were footsteps. It grew so dark that he thought the next memory was coming for him. He touched the trees to guide his way. He couldn't hear anything, no snapping of twigs or grunts. It wouldn't be much farther before the ground began to slope. He would go down to the stream where he and Yu would catch minnows, and turn around. Maybe that was when he would wake up.

The forest suddenly ended.

There was no hill or water. As far as he could see, it was snow. A line of trees that were bigger than he ever remembered looked like a wall against a land of ice. It reminded him of the trees when he was five years old, when he'd wandered into the forest, chasing snowflakes.

The snow glimmered like a sheet of diamonds under the full moon. And out there, where a trail was carved, the short figure wobbled on wide feet that seemed to tread on top of the snow. He was as fat as he was tall. A long braided ponytail dragged behind him.

This wasn't a memory. This didn't exist. Like the time he got lost chasing after snowflakes. *Is this my imagination?*

He watched the short figure wobble along and then, suddenly, drop out of sight. A dark hole appeared in the moonlight. Chris waited. When he turned around, the trees were gone. Ice in all directions. Alone in the middle of nowhere.

The North Pole.

The air was so clean and crisp. Imbued with a tangible sense of joy. It felt so familiar. So much like home. He wasn't afraid. He journeyed to the hole.

It was dark and deep. On his hands and knees, he peeked over the edge and heard something. It sounded like humming. He leaned a little closer, and the edge caved in. His momentum took him down a sheet of ice, the bitter wind whistling in his ears.

He shot through the dark and found himself gliding across a smooth sheet of blue ice into a cluttered room, narrowly missing a wooden bench and a leaning bookshelf. He slid all the way to the far side. The ceiling was too low for him to stand. He didn't expect to find a room at the bottom of the hole.

Or toys.

Stuffed bears, wooden soldiers, plastic dolls and metal cars. Trains on steel rails and springy slinkies and wooden blocks and rubber balls, baseball gloves and soccer balls, pogo sticks and ice skates. They were in piles and boxes and stacked on shelves. Machines were whirring. Lights were blinking. Orbs floated near the ceiling, casting eerie light on the blue ice.

The short man was on the far side.

He seemed not to notice someone had just done a belly slide across his workshop. His gray braid lay on the floor behind enormously wide bare feet with strawberry hair on the knuckles. His head was covered with a green floppy hat with a little bell on the end.

The kind his mom wore.

Chris remained still, listening to the elf (if that was what he was, what else would he be?) hum while he worked. He occasionally chuckled and said a few words, but nothing talked back to him. Slowly, Chris climbed onto his knees and crawled closer. The elf put a rolling pin down. There were cannisters of googly eyes and rivets, yarn and wood shavings. A jar of what looked like sugar. There was the distinct smell of cloves.

He filled a pastry bag and turned, muttering in some unknown language, pulling stuff from a toybox. Chris held very still. He was right next to him. His beard was reddish with streaks of gray. Cherub cheeks rosy, a stogy button nose and ice blue eyes that glittered. He smelled like warm apple cider.

"Aaaaahh-ha!" The elf's eyes widened.

It was a spice jar with cinnamon dust. At least it looked like cinnamon. The color was off. Not the color. The brightness.

"There ye go, buddy."

Chris couldn't see what was moving. A string of Christmas lights was hanging over his head, and the toybox was in the way. He could slide across the room with a quick shove for a better look, suddenly aware this was a dream and the laws of physics didn't apply. *Did they?*

Just then the elf kicked and slid on one foot. "Run, run, run... as fast as you can..."

There, lying flat and inanimate, arms and legs out, head round, was a gingerbread man. The eyes were circular. The mouth a line. The elf had made a cookie that looked exactly like Gman. But then they all sort of looked alike.

"You can't catch me..." the elf hummed.

Chris crawled closer. "Hey." His voice had an echo. *Wake up*, he thought. But the gingerman lay there like a cookie should.

The elf slid back. Chris bumped his head on the toybox, then made a racket in the string of lights. The elf didn't notice. He picked up the bright jar of cinnamon. He held it above his head. It came out like fine powder, wafting down in little points of light.

"When the time comes," the elf said, "you will find him."

The sprinkles stuck to the gingerman then melted like fragile flakes of snow. The body quivered. The eyes blinked. And, with no help at all, the gingerman peeled himself off the table. The elf slid back, hands laced over his round belly, and watched his creation look around.

Seeing life for the very first time.

He blinked at Chris. As if he was seeing the oversized young man hiding like a polar bear in a toy store.

"Off ye go," was all the elf said.

And then as quickly as Chris had seen the gingerman do before, he sprang from the table like a jackrabbit. He slid across the floor, crashed into a stack of wooden blocks, bounced through a tub of bouncy balls, and zoomed up the way Chris had come.

The elf was still smiling.

Chris expected him to say something. Like he knew Chris had been there the entire time. But he didn't. He simply straightened his green floppy hat. He took careful steps, slowly inching his way up the slope, the soles of his disproportionate feet grabbing the ice.

When he didn't return, Chris followed the exact path. He didn't know how he was going to get up the slope without momentum. But then the floor cracked. A long, jagged line was followed by another. Before he could take a breath, he fell through.

And opened his eyes in bed.

Chattering. Sweating.

The jar of marbles was as bright as stars. Sharp shadows were tossed across the room. Chris covered his eyes. The space around the marbles shimmered like the desert. The warped air was twisted in long braided cords that crossed the room. No longer were they delicate threads of silk. Now they were taut ropes.

They were attached to him.

23

His eyelashes were crimped by sleep. His throat dry, lips cracked.

He stared at the white ceiling, watched it undulate like waves, like a whale watching the world, wondering what was above the surface.

He was in bed, fully dressed. His feet fell onto the floor like lumber. Cold blew over him, cooling his fever. Something flapped like a flag atop a pole on a brisk winter day.

A bottle of water was on the desk.

He stood too fast, pulled the chair down to catch his balance. They both crashed. He lay with the coolness of the floor against his cheek, dragged himself up, and righted the chair, finding the bottle to drain it. And then he recognized where he was.

It was his room.

The textbooks were neatly stacked. Homework in a square pile. Art supplies scattered and the coffeemaker in the corner. The gingerbread men—the ones he'd taken from the kitchen—were lined up at the window, peering over the edge. The window was cracked open, loose papers flapping. They were standing next to each other, hand touching hand, all in a line.

A fresh white blanket had fallen. The quad was filled with new sculptures: icy carvings of dragons, snowy creatures, and fabric-sewn things that flapped with crusty edges of frost. There were three times as many of them since he'd last seen the quad.

This was his room. But the dreams, they were so real. It was hard to tell if he was awake. Or if this was another dream. Another memory. He stared at his hands, turning them over like the truth was in the details of wrinkles and veins. *What day is it?*

Something scratched at the door.

The doorknob turned slowly, the latch clicking. Chris watched it slowly crack open, expecting a green floppy hat and pudgy elven face to peek inside. Instead, a slender tan body slid through the opening. Round eyes of white icing widened into large circles.

The gingerman bound across the room. A skip and a hop and the cookie grabbed Chris's face, arms and legs smelling of cloves and sugar on his cheeks.

Buddy.

Sai quietly closed the door behind him. "You're back," he whispered.

Chris had just talked to them. *Was it yesterday?* he thought.

I couldn't feel you out there, Gingerman said. *You just disappeared.*

It was all coming too fast. A blizzard of thoughts with no timeline. Like scraps of paper thrown into the wind. Everything, since the day he got there, felt surreal. But now it was so... unreal.

"How'd I, uh, how'd I get back here?" he said.

"Middle of the night," Sai said. "Gman and I been checking on you, but you've been sleeping for like..." He looked at Gingerman. The cookie shrugged like he didn't know or couldn't count. "Grendel and Pelz come by every couple of hours and some of the slackers." Sai sat on the bed. "What'd they do to you?"

Yeah, Gingerman said. *What'd they do?*

"What?" Chris said.

"You look... different."

Chris spun the chair. His reflection was faint. But they were right.

Something was different. Was it his posture? His face looked weathered. *Older.*

"Am I... am I awake?" Chris said.

Sai and Gingerman traded glances. Neither of them knew how to answer the question. What could they say that he would believe? This felt as real as the dreams.

"Those weren't out there before." Chris pointed at the quad.

"We had a winter challenge," Sai said. "Grendel surprised us, just announced it one morning. Everyone had to do a sculpture with natural elements. Only rule was it had to be a creature, like mythological or fantasy or whatever. As long as it was like a creature. Just finished yesterday."

"A creature..." Chris muttered.

"You all right?" Sai said.

"Do you have something to eat?"

"Yeah, yeah." Sai went to his room.

Gingerman's legs dangled off the edge of the bed. *Can you hear me?*

"Yeah." Chris grabbed his hair. "I'm just... just confused."

Sai returned wearing a coat and with three protein bars. Chris ate two of them. He washed the third one down with another bottle of water. Sai's breath was foggy. The room was freezing. Chris still felt warm. His legs were steady. Thoughts were clicking like puzzle pieces finding their partners in a line. The memories of his parents, watching his younger selves, his sister.

"What day is it?" Chris said.

"Christmas Eve."

Chris stopped. "Christmas Eve?"

"You've been gone for three weeks. It's been two weeks since Gman talked to you. We were worried, man. No one was saying anything, and Joli—"

"I got to call my parents."

Chris searched for his boots. He hadn't talked to them in over a month. And Christmas was tomorrow. With all the memories so fresh, he knew Mom would be worried. Chris hadn't sent one single letter. And now they were probably looking at his stocking, wondering if he was okay.

"Not now, you're not," Sai said.

"No, I-I-I haven't used my call. I got to talk to them."

"Visitors' Center shut down till after Christmas. Grendel said the Christmas celebration is about the family this year. As in us. Said it was going to be special."

Special. Gingerman made air quotes.

Chris fell on the bed. He was feeling weak again. Like his body had burned up the protein bars, and the tank was tapping empty. He didn't feel bad. In fact, he felt really good. Clearheaded. Just tired.

Sai and Gingerman gave him space. Then, with his eyes closed, Chris told them what he remembered. How he had put the crown on and went into something like a trance where he visited dreams.

"It was like memories. But I was there."

That's it? Gingerman said.

Chris hesitated. "Pelz kept saying something about building an inner landscape."

What's that mean?

"I don't know. Maybe that's what made them so real."

"Why?" Sai said.

"I don't know. Pelz kept saying he wanted me to know who I am. My potential, he said. And then…"

"And then what?"

"Things got weird."

Chris took a shaky breath. He told them about the elf. How he'd sleepwalked when he was eight years old and was staring into the forest. And then Chris followed the elf to the North Pole and down into a workshop in the ice. Toys were all around and he was—

What'd he look like? Gingerman said.

"Um. I mean, an elf."

Details. Elves look different, you know, like hair and eyes and, you know, different.

Chris kept his eyes open, afraid he'd slip into the dream if he closed them. Like the barrier between waking and dreaming was a brittle sheet of ice.

"He had a long braid of hair that dragged behind him. Blue eyes, like really blue. And he wore a, uh, a floppy green hat."

The Toymaker.

"Yeah," Chris said.

No, not yeah. It was the Toymaker. *There's only one. The Toymaker is the one who makes toys special.*

"He made you."

Probably.

"No, I saw it. He was at the bench. He sprinkled dust on you and said you would find him."

Find who?

Chris shrugged. He couldn't shake the feeling that the Toymaker had known he was watching. Chris picked up one of the gingerbread men looking out the window. It was stiff and lifeless.

None of that matters, the gingerman said. *We have to find the marbles.*

"Why?"

You have some connection to them.

"Connection." Chris turned around. A vague memory of translucent threads streaming from the jar.

He wanted you to remember so you would charge them. They were glowing.

"Charge them for what?"

For something.

"For something? I need more than that."

I don't know. Pelz doesn't like Christmas.

Chris chuckled into a hoarse coughing fit. He told Sai what Gingerman said. Sai chuckled, too.

"Look out the window," Chris said. "Every day is Christmas."

The fabric sculptures looked like skinny candy cane creatures stuck to the ground.

This is just for show.

"It's a good show. We get free presents at the Christmas Tree every month."

Nothing is free. You're the one who noticed there's no Santas out there. Not one. And all those weird reindeer names for the buildings? He's got it in for Santa. He's planning something. And it's got something to do with the marbles.

Chris couldn't argue. There were so many questions with no answers. When he talked to Pelz, it all made sense. But once he thought about it, nothing made sense.

There was nothing in the castle.

"What do you mean?"

I went up to the tower, snuck under the doors. Wasn't easy getting up the stairs.

"What'd you see?"

Gingerman pointed at the bed. *Have a seat.*

Chris didn't need to sit. It was so effortless communicating with the gingerman now. But he was tired. He sat next to Sai and nodded. Gingerman nodded. Chris felt the itching behind his eyes. Double vision clouded the room; then everything was gone. He was seeing a different room from a stone floor. The walls were curved and empty. Now there was nothing but the throne where Pelz had sat when Chris had gone up to the tower.

It wasn't just that it was empty. They could've moved everything. But it was smaller, too. He remembered how big it felt, and something wasn't right. How he drank the water Pelz gave him but couldn't slake his thirst.

Is any of this real? he thought. *A talking cookie? A crown and a jar of magic marbles from a special elf? How do I even know this is real? Will I wake up later, back home, remembering a dream about a bizarre school in the mountains?*

That would explain why he'd seen Ms. Grendel in two places at the same time. Or he thought he did. He pinched Gingerman's leg to see if the cookie would turn stiff like the ones from the kitchen.

You're not dreaming, Gingerman said.

"How do I know?"

Gingerman poked his leg. *Feel that?*

It didn't mean anything. But, for some reason, it helped. He remembered the Toymaker, how real that seemed, too. The funny thing was, the Toymaker had decorated the gingerman with white icing just like Chris had, including the bowtie. Maybe that was just a detail his subconscious inserted into the dream. He recalled the sprinkles that had brought Gingerman to life.

Chris remembered something else.

There's no time to waste, Gingerman said. *Something's going to happen tonight. We need to find the marbles. Take them, hide them, eat them or something. You can probably suck the power back out of them. Tell Sai to go look at the, uh, the... Christmas?*

Chris lined up the gingerbread men from the kitchen, laid them side by side with their hands touching. Their faces were generic, the icing cracking off in places. Chris grabbed a microplane grater.

He snatched the gingerman before he could get away.

Whoa! Whoa, whoa, whoa—

"I need to try something."

No, you don't. You need to sit down and—wait!

Chris held him over the gingerbread men. When Bobby found him, he had been just a head. The body came to life. Chris pulled the grater across the Gingerman's head, seasoning the gingerbread men with dust. The gingerman howled. But it didn't take much. Just one pass, barely a notch off the top.

Something began to happen.

Chris stepped back. Sai stood up. They watched them bounce on the desk like oil on a hot skillet. And then, one by one, they popped onto their legs, swaying back and forth. Holding each other for balance.

What just happened? Gingerman said.

"The Toymaker," Chris said. "He sprinkled you with some magic dust. You remember the chocolate chip? Sai had been keeping you in his pocket. There were crumbs that spilled on his plate. They fell on the chocolate chip. And then, I don't know, it somehow jumped off the plate and hit Claibourn in the eye."

I don't get it.

"You said I threw the chocolate chip. I wanted something to happen to Claibourn, and then it did. The Toymaker said you were supposed to find him. Maybe he meant, I don't know, you're supposed to protect us."

I don't think he meant flying chocolate.

"Explain that."

The gingerbread men stood hand in hand. Waiting for something.

Why didn't I know this?

Chris and Sai squatted in front of them, looking them in their white icing eyes. They blinked like puppies. "It's a gift," Chris said, "from the Toymaker."

"How did you know?" Sai said.

"I think," Chris said, hesitating, "I think, somehow, the Toymaker is part of me."

He didn't want to say it out loud. It sounded ridiculous. But it made more sense than anything happening in the room right that second. Chris loved the cold. And that part of his DNA, the unknown part, was what Pelz wanted him to remember. Chris felt like he knew the Toymaker at some primal level. Memories locked in his being. Pelz wanted to dig it up. *The hidden treasure.*

Gingerman walked the line of gingerbread men like a drill sergeant. He shrugged his rounded shoulders. They shrugged their shoulders. He hopped and they followed. He danced. They danced.

Okay. We could've used them, like, a month ago, but let's do this. He pointed at them one at a time. *Rocko, Taco, Blocko, Socko, and Mike. Now we got names. We split up and search the place.*

He assigned them each a hall. Gingerman was going to search the rest of the castle. They were looking for marbles. If one of them found them, they would all converge. Chris didn't know how they were going to carry them. They could take two at a time, at best. And the jar was full.

"I saw Grendel at Bixen," Sai said. "There's a ton of food for tonight."

Good. Good," Gingerman said. *I'll take the high road, you take the low. Then we meet...*

Gingerman wasn't making sense. He was doing too much rhyming. But it jarred something loose. A memory of the first day Chris arrived, when his dad missed the Visitors' Center and went too far up the road. They stopped at a tunnel.

"Roadblock," Chris blurted.

What? No, you're not listening—

"Pelz isn't in the castle."

Yeah, I think we covered that—

"No, I mean he's using holographic technology to make it seem like he is, just like he did at the Feast. When I went up to the tower, it all seemed real. I even drank water, but I was still thirsty."

I don't get it.

"There's a roadblock up the mountain, past the Visitors' Center. The view I had from the room, it was on the side of the mountain."

"How far?" Sai said.

"I don't know. It doesn't matter. We can't have a pack of gingerbread cookies running around in daylight."

A pack of cookies. That's good.

"No, what I mean is—"

"You're back!"

Joli was in the doorway with a long black overcoat and a tiger-striped scarf so long its tassels dragged on the floor. She threw her arms around Chris, squeezed until his neck hurt. She smelled like coffee and clay.

The gingerbread men lay stiff on their backs. Even Gingerman.

"I told you to tell me when he was up, Sai," she said.

Sai looked into the hall then quietly closed the door. He stood as stiff as the cookies. Chris did, too. She stepped back like they were caught telling secrets. Then noticed the cookies.

"Were you, like, playing with gingerbread cookies?" she said.

Sai shook his head. Chris sighed. It was time. There was no other way to do it. He needed to sit down anyway. His legs were jelly. Sai sat on the bed next to him. Chris looked at Gingerman and nodded.

"What's going on?" Joli said nervously. "You look like—*what is that?*"

She backed up. With each step, her eyes grew until the whites were on full display. Her fingers clutched at the door. Lips fluttering.

I think she's going to puke, Gingerman said.

"We tried to tell you," Sai said. "It wasn't a dream."

She shook her head, closed her eyes. The cookies were still there when she opened them.

Let her hold you, Chris thought.

Yeeeeeah. I'm not really into that.

There's no time.

Gingerman hung his head like a child told to go to bed. Chris put his hand out. Gingerman leaped onto it. Chris carried him like a dessert. Joli was scratching the door like he was serving roasted cockroach.

"This is Gingerman."

Gingerman sat on the edge of his hand and dangled his feet. So tired of this. All the fuss, everyone freaking out. There were stranger things than a talking cookie. Flying reindeer. Toys that wanted to take over the world.

"Is this a joke?" Joli said.

"No. No, not a joke."

"Did Claibourn put you up to this? Like a remote—no!"

Chris took her hand. She pulled it away. Gingerman lay flat like a tantrum was coming. Chris tried again. This time she let him take her hand. Gingerman climbed onto his feet and lumbered onto her palm. She cringed.

Really? Gingerman said.

"This is real," Chris said.

Chris actually believed what he was saying. Fifteen minutes earlier, he'd doubted everything. *Maybe everything is a dream,* he thought.

Joli held him like a gerbil. Gingerman slowly turned to let her see it all.

"He's..." she stammered. "That's..."

"The one we made in the challenge," Chris said. "Yeah."

"How?"

Chris shrugged. "It's a long story."

"Right. Long story. Give me—ooh!"

Gingerman had plopped down to dangle his legs. Joli flinched, and he went over the edge. He hit the floor. His leg went in the opposite direction, cracking off where Chris had pasted it back on.

Great, Gingerman said, lying on his back. *That's super.*

"I'm sorry." Joli covered her mouth. "Did I hurt it?"

"It's not an *it*. It's a *he*." Chris sounded defensive.

Gingerman looked concussed. Before Chris or Sai could fetch the leg, the gingerbread men scrabbled off the desk. They charged across the floor. Even Chris would admit it was startling. They picked Gingerman up. Rocko or Blocko retrieved the leg. The others passed him up to the bed, tossed him to the chair, and dragged him up to the desk.

They began reattaching the lost appendage, pasting smooth seams of white icing like master masons. Gingerman propped on his elbows and watched. It took all of a minute before he stood up.

Didn't see that coming.

"Am I awake?" Joli said, still plastered to the door.

"If you're not, we're all in the same dream," Chris said. "And right now, we need to find the marbles."

"The what?"

He explained what had happened in the lab. The dreams, the crown, the marbles they'd held after Kogen got caught. What Gingerman had said about Pelz getting ready for something. Something not good.

"What's he going to do with them?" Joli said.

Chris didn't answer. The door began to open. Joli jumped out of the way, a shocking sound escaping her. It wasn't another cookie. It was an old woman with a cane.

"Why is this door closed?" Ms. Grendel said.

Her expression was stern. It shook their knees. Chris and Sai didn't move. Joli stuttered an explanation that made no sense. Ms.

Grendel peered past them. Chris couldn't get the courage to look at what she was seeing.

"Chris is awake," Sai said.

"I see that."

"We haven't seen him since, you know." Sai swallowed and waved his hand. "Where has he been?"

Ms. Grendel looked at each one of them, holding their gazes until their insides melted like chocolate in a microwave. Chris didn't blink. It wasn't courage. He just couldn't move. He watched her reach into her sleeve.

"It pains me to do this." She brandished three red cards. "On Christmas Eve."

They accepted the penalty, each of them holding a card by their sides. Wondering if it was for the closed door. Or something else. She walked around them like trees in a forest.

Six gingerbread men were on their backs.

Ms. Grendel frowned and nudged one with a crooked finger. Crumbs scattered on the desk. She stared at Gingerman, stooping for a closer look. Gingerman was as still as a stale cookie.

"They were left over from the challenge," Sai said. "We were just—"

"Mr. Laghari, kitchen duty. Ms. Oliveira, the Tree." She waited for them to move.

Sai stacked the gingerbread men and put them in his pocket. She didn't seem alarmed. And, thankfully, Gingerman didn't squirm.

"What about me?" Chris said.

She watched them leave and closed the door. Then she folded the sheets back on his bed, smoothed the creases, and fluffed the pillow. She fell into the chair and placed her hands over the cane.

"You need rest."

24

He was no longer a boy.
He had inherited a castle, had been raised by servants and a dedicated caregiver, and had gone to live life on the sea. He was a working pair of hands who learned the knots and scrubbed decks, slept on cots of cotton, and scrubbed his clothes in a wash bin. He learned three languages. His hands callused, cheeks sun-kissed, and shoulders baked the color of tanned leather. The boy had become lean and muscular.

A man.

Years of searching led to a strange land, where he travelled by horse and wagon, wore out soles of boots, walked roads barefoot, and ate with strangers. He stayed in villages and worked for his meals, slept in barns and tended horses. He wandered with a locket in his pocket. And then one day, he found what he was looking for.

He stood on a cobbled road, paper soft in his hand, the writing faded. The numbers blurred. The scruff of his beard was as unkempt as the hair hanging to his shoulders. After all these years, he hesitated. This was his destination.

The first drops of rain began to fall.

He opened the wrought-iron gate. A gardener looked up, wooden rake in his hand, faded cap over his eyes, watching him approach the steps without a word. To knock on the door and wait. No one answered. He considered leaving. Considered if it was better to leave questions unanswered, a quest unfinished. Answers, sometimes, were worse than questions.

An elderly woman peeked through the glass, her gray hair pulled tight. Ruffles on her buttoned blouse impeccably displayed around her neck. She cracked the door and spoke a language he understood.

"Yes?"

The man bowed his head. "Are... are the Santas present?"

"He doesn't live here anymore."

The man fiddled with the scrap of paper. Drops of rain stained the ink. He showed it to her.

"I'm sorry," she said. "Your mother passed away. A year ago."

The man clutched the locket in his pocket. "She's not my mother."

The woman was confused. She closed the door and watched him through the glass. The man stood on the top step, the patter of raindrops on his shoulders. He should have turned around. Should have lived with the questions and the answers he had imagined. That someone wondered where he was, if he was all right.

The man crumpled the paper in a ball. The paper that crossed the seas many times over. And tossed it on the ground where the rain would soak it, the ink would melt and dissolve as if it never existed. Suddenly, the weight of his journey had lifted. He had wandered all this time avoiding this moment. And now it was behind him.

He was free.

The gardener, wooden rake in hand, bent over to pick up the wadded ball of paper. His gray beard well kept; face weathered by time. He unraveled it as the man stood there, pondering where to go next. Another ship, perhaps?

"I know where you can find him," the gardener said.

"He's dead."

"The son." The gardener pointed at the name on the paper.

The man clutched the locket. The photo he had pried from it when he took it from his father's case. The woman. The boy.

"The pub, county seat, or wharf." The gardener scratched his beard, raindrops dotting the bill of his dusty cap. "He was never one to be still. Or satisfied." He squinted at the letter. "Is he your brother?"

The man left him there with the letter. How could he be his brother? Shared blood was not family.

He spent days and nights in the village, visiting local establishments, sitting in dark corners. Never asking questions, only watching faces. He found work at the docks. Week after week, he watched, sleeping on the ground when the weather was good, finding shelter in storage bins when it was not. As the months rolled past, he was certain he would never find him.

It was a morning of clear skies that he saw a portly man with a coppery beard and curly locks to match. The sun seemed to beam from his smile. He heard him laugh, a boisterous jolly that bellowed from a barrel chest. A ship named the Alexander was being loaded for an expedition to a faraway land, an adventure to the far reaches at the top of the world. He was with a boy and a woman disguised as a shy man. His wife, he guessed. But why she was posing as such, he couldn't understand.

They were posing for a photo. The flash of the camera popped. All the crew had posed, one after another. The man watched with a bag of rice hoisted on his shoulder, listening to laughter, the comradery. He stood in the middle of the walkway. And when the redheaded stranger approached, he did not step aside. Their eyes met. The same color, shape and size. The cheeks different shades but shaped as similar as their noses.

"Do I know you, sir?" the redheaded man asked.

"Aye, you do," the man said. "We've never met."

Confusion fell between them. His boy was staring, searching for the reason of familiarity. The woman disguised as a man peered from beneath her cap.

"I don't understand," the redheaded man said.

"No, you don't. You don't." The man extended his hand. "I just wanted to meet ya."

A flash popped when they shook hands. The man wanted to tell him everything about their father, whose heart was too big. The castle in another land. The nights he lay awake dreaming of the family he yearned to have. The family in front of him.

"We've never met, you say?" the redheaded man said.

"*Safe travels to ya. Hope you make it to where you're heading.*"

The man dropped the bag of rice and left the wharf. He would return sometime later to board a ship, this time as a passenger, to return to his castle. It would be many years later when he would meet his brother for a second time. He would be an old man by then.

He would be asleep in his bed when he heard a commotion outside. A scraping across the castle's roof. The snort of animals. The old man would rise from his bed, nightcap on his head, a candle in hand. He would look out the window. Gretchen was talking to someone surrounded by—

Christmas!

The word fell through the story like a rock through frozen branches. The details evaporated into a dark empty dream. Chris had fallen asleep. His name echoed distantly.

What's wrong? Chris said.

He still had his eyes closed. The bed held him in a soft embrace. A breeze cooled his face, and an odd sound clicked in rhythm somewhere in the room. He was so weak, so tired. He felt himself drifting back into slumber, wishing to see the end of the story.

No. No, no, no, no, Gingerman called. *Wake up.*

I was dreaming.

Yeah, I know. I can't think straight with your dreams blaring like a concert.

It was the story. I think I'm getting it from you.

That's great. Can you give it a rest, like, for a second? It's all fuzz and static in my head.

Chris kept his eyes closed and rolled over. *Something wrong?*

The team had to stop, that's what. Rocko is hiding in a drainpipe outside Bixen. There's enough food to feed half the world in there. And Taco is under a rock...

He named off the other gingerbread men. Chris was lulled back into a comfortable state by the clicking. It stopped for a moment then continued. Images came out of the dark like walking into a streetlight. He was looking up at a forest from a rotten stump. Gingerman was at the wall at the back of the circle. It was the village.

Stay awake, Gingerman said. *It's not safe when I got a head full of your dreams.*

I think they're your dreams.

Either way! Look, you were right about the mountain. Mike found it.

One of the gingerbread men had gone past the Visitors' Center and through the roadblocked tunnel. Chris could see it now. In the dusky light, it was dull metal flaked with lichen built into the side of a stone outcropping. Black windows punched into the walls like cookie cutouts. A golf cart was parked in front of steel doors.

How am I seeing this? Chris said.

Because they're me. And they can't do anything with you making noise. Now stay awake and we'll find those marbles.

How?

When someone comes out, Mike will sneak in.

No. No, they'll see him. He's going to have to wait—

The clicking grew louder. It was followed by humming. It was a familiar song. Chris lost connection with Gingerman, drawn back into the room and the soft bed.

They're in there, Gingerman said. *The marbles, Christmas. I can feel them. Blocko and Socko are going up there to help. They'll carry them out, hide them in the forest. Or throw them off the cliff. We just got to get past tonight.*

The clicking sounded like aluminum bats in a sword fight.

Tonight?

Don't doze on me. Tonight's the night. Whatever Pelz is planning. You fall asleep and they might freeze up in the middle of the road. You hear me?

Chris rolled onto his back and reached out. Only this time, he searched for the story. Not where he left off. He recalled the story from the very beginning, rewinding it all the way back to when the boy was a child. His mother was singing to him. That was the song Chris was hearing in his room. Only it was a different voice.

He scrubbed ahead, searching for another sound. When the boy was older, lying in his bed at night, listening to the night and thinking of his mother. And hearing the steady beat that would send him to sleep.

Chris opened his eyes.

Ms. Grendel sat at his desk. The chair creaked as she nudged it forward and back. Her hands in her lap, a ball of yarn at her side. Knitting needles going click-click-click.

"You," Chris whispered.

She stopped humming, the needles still working. He rolled over, eyes heavy. Body so warm. The familiar sound lulling him to take comfort. That all was all right. All was safe.

Just like the boy.

"Our bodies lie to us," she said, pulling yarn from her side. "Did you know that? Our brain isn't designed to know what is real. Our senses filter out what is true, show us what will keep us alive. They are rose-colored glasses we have worn from the day we were born. Without them, we would know the great injustices in the world. We survive because we believe what we are told."

She grunted. More to herself, as if she weren't talking to Chris.

"Can we choose to see the truth? I often wondered that. After millions of years of evolution, can we choose who we want to be any more than a worker bee can choose not to pollinate? I wonder."

She tugged what she was knitting. The clicking continued.

"It doesn't matter if we like the path we are given. We are on it. Like it or not."

Chris didn't know who she was talking to or what she was saying, expecting to see a phone on her lap, a conversation he was eavesdropping on. But she looked at him for the first time. Her eyes heavy and tired. Glassy. As if she'd been awake for centuries.

"Do you really believe your name is a coincidence?" she said. "A special boy born to ordinary parents. You didn't choose to come here, Christmas."

She continued knitting, stretching. Her lips pursed tightly, wrinkles creasing her chin. Eyebrows pinched in concentration or the bitter sting of a memory. He didn't understand the gibberish. Didn't understand how she could be sitting in his room. Unless the story was simply a story that never happened hundreds of years ago. Because she couldn't be here now.

But she was.

"How?" was all Chris could say. *How are you here?*

She nodded thoughtfully. Peering at the links of yarn as if the answers were buried in the pattern.

"There will always be mystery, even when the truth is right in front of us. Most people prefer the mystery. It's so much easier not to know the truth. Including me, I suppose."

She cut the string. The needles clattered on the desk.

"I want you to know this is not your fault. You didn't choose this. You were born for it. And I've waited a very long time for you to arrive."

A shiver ran through him. "What... what are you going to do to me?"

"It's what you will do. He knew this day would come. That's why he sent you help."

"He? Who's he?"

A disturbance was outside the door. A thump on the wall.

"Who are you talking about?" Chris said. "Sent who?"

She folded her hands in her lap and bowed her head. Eyes closed. She remained unfazed when someone knocked. A slacker peeked inside cautiously. His coat zipped up, snow clinging to his shiny shoes.

"He's ready for you," the slacker said.

She nodded. He closed the door. Joli was in the hall, shouting. They couldn't keep Chris in there like that. This was wrong.

Ms. Grendel stood with a groan. Her back aching, knees stiff, she shuffled over with something around her hands. Chris watched her stretch it open, let her reach for him. She pulled a knitted cap over his head, her eyes sorrowful yet kind. She touched his cheek. And he wanted to weep. Feeling the warmth of her hand flow through him, a caring that poured inside him.

"Merry Christmas," she said.

In that instant, she looked relieved. And despite the impossibilities that had been lining up since the day he arrived—talking cookies, surreal dreams and a two-hundred-year-old woman who appeared in two places at once—he felt a strange sense of relief, too. That he was exactly where he was supposed to be. He recalled what the Toymaker had said.

Find him.

"Let Ms. Oliveira in," Ms. Grendel told the slacker. "He could use some company."

Joli pushed past the slacker, careful not to bump into the old woman with her knitting needles and cane. Ms. Grendel stopped at the door, her hand on the knob.

"And, Mr. Blizzard, stay awake. You don't want to disturb your friends."

25

Chris sipped water. It spilled on the pillow.

"When's the last time you ate?" Joli said.

He shrugged. "There's food in Sai's room."

She argued with the slacker in the hall. He was leaning against the wall with arms crossed. "What is this place? You know what they did to him?"

He stared ahead like she didn't matter. There were more important things.

Chris didn't know how much he'd eaten. He'd had snacks earlier, but before that? It seemed like he just slept. And two weeks went by. He felt like a dead battery. But his thoughts were so clear. So much space in his head.

"Do you even care?" Joli said on the way back from Sai's room. "I'm closing the door. Give me a red; gimme three. I don't care. I'm leaving this nuthouse tomorrow. Bye."

She slammed the door. Chris ate what she gave him, another energy bar, staring at the ceiling while he chewed, listening to the sounds it made when he swallowed.

"We got to get to the Visitors' Center," she whispered. "They keep cell phones somewhere."

He shook his head. Even if they found a phone, there was no reception.

"I don't care about the marbles," she said. "Look at you."

"I'm all right."

"No. No, you're not all right. They're turning you into one of them." She jabbed at the door. "You can't, Chris. You can't let them."

He finished the last bite. Sighing. "She knows about Gingerman."

"What?"

"Grendel. She said he's helping me. Said someone sent him. She knows."

"Yeah, well, that doesn't matter." She shook her head. It was too much to take in. Everything that had happened, she hadn't had time to digest a pack of talking cookies. Like she was ignoring it.

"She doesn't want to hurt me. She just wants this over with," he said. "Whatever this is."

He pushed himself up and rested on the edge of the bed, then stood up. He leaned on the desk. His legs were doughy. The quad was dark. He could barely see the front of the castle.

"Where are the sculptures?" he said.

"We moved them. They all went to the Tree."

"For what?"

"I don't know, Chris!" She started pacing, twisting her fingers. Her hair was damp where snow had melted. She had stopped dyeing the tips. Now it was just tight black curls. She couldn't catch her breath.

"You all right?" he said.

"I don't know about anything, you know? I mean, flying chocolate chips and-and-and you disappearing and all of this. I just thought this place was some arty-farty hangout for outliers like you and me, and now I don't know. I never should've let them take you after the Feast. I knew something was wrong."

She stared out the window, into the darkness, looking back at how obvious it was in the rearview.

"You want some coffee?" Chris said.

"Now?"

"I could use some." He passed her the coffee pot. "We got time."

It was something to do, a ritual to settle her thoughts. She just needed a daily routine to keep the panic from shoving her off the end of the ramp. The slacker didn't say anything; she didn't argue. He looked bored, like he didn't care if she came back.

Chris prepped the coffeemaker. They listened to it drip. The smell was comforting. He brushed crumbs from papers, saw the notebook from the first day he'd arrived. The message he'd decoded when the ride had begun.

Run, run...

"You remember the story?" he said. "The one Sai wrote?"

She nodded.

"I heard the rest of it. Well, almost."

"How?"

He didn't really know. He thought it was coming from Gingerman, but it still didn't make sense. "It was about a boy, remember? He grew up in that castle. And his dad lived somewhere else, would visit every once in a while. But the boy had all these servants. They all left him. All except one. Ms. Grendel."

"What'd you mean?"

"Her name was Gretchen in the story."

"Yeah, no." She shook her head.

"I know."

"That's not her, Chris. That was, like, two hundred years ago. She can't still be alive."

"And cookies don't talk."

"What's that got to do with any of this?"

He handed her a mug. "This has something to do with Santa Claus. I know, I know. But listen. Pelz is, I mean, according to the story, he's Santa's brother. Half-brother."

"Right." She held the coffee and didn't drink. "Look, Santa isn't real. We got to get out of here."

"Where? Where we going?"

"I don't know. I've been trying to think of when this all started, you know? Like when we fell asleep and this whole crazy dream started." Coffee spilled over the edge of the mug. He took it from her and wiped her hands with a T-shirt. She stared at her hands. "Why can't I wake up?"

"Because we're not asleep."

She fell in the chair, swiveling around. Somewhere a cannon fired. The window rattled, followed by a white flash that momentarily threw sharp shadows across the quad. Joli didn't even jump.

"Fireworks," she said. "It's starting."

Distant cheers erupted. It was followed by two more explosions and sparkles drizzling over the castle. It looked haunted.

Christmas! Gingerman called.

"I'm going to lie down," Chris said.

He needed to sit down and listen, grateful she wasn't hearing the gingerman's voice. He lay down and closed his eyes.

Ready for this? Gingerman said.

Images rushed out of the darkness. Tree trunks like dark sentinels and pale snow on the ground, orange light flickering. Hooded figures were lumbering between the trees like gray-clad monks, cupping candles at their waists, protecting the flames with curled and knobby fingers. They were in a line. A gate along the wall was open.

Creepy, Gingerman said.

On the long list of things that had happened, Chris felt like that scene ranked near the bottom.

So bad news, Gingerman said. *No marbles anywhere. Pelz left the lab. Mike slipped in and looked in all the rooms. Nothing. The castle is empty, too. All the buildings. I mean, it's like looking for snowflakes in a blizzard.*

Pelz has them, Chris said.

Maybe.

Meet me at the Tree.

Why?

That's where Pelz went.

And do what, introduce myself? Hi, we're the cookie family. That might work, though. We'd freak everyone out. There would be chaos. Might throw off everything Pelz is planning.

The train of candles continued. Some of them ventured near

Gingerman. He hunkered down, his view limited to the gate. Chris couldn't make out the details aside from the orange flames.

They know about you, Chris said.

They do?

Gretchen knows.

Really? And who's Gretchen?

The story. She was the boy's servant.

Yeah. That's two hundred years ago, buddy. I don't think—

A two-hundred-year-old woman is the least weird thing happening here! You're a cookie, and Santa Claus is at least two hundred years old.

Yeah, well, he's—

He's Pelz's brother.

—made of elf—wait. What?

Pelznickel is Santa's brother. They have the same dad. But Pelz wasn't part of the family. That's what this is all about. It's in the story. You should know this.

I told you, I don't know the story...

He peeked out of his hiding hole. The last of the flames passed. The sound of grinding stone began closing the gate.

I'm going back, Gingerman said.

Stop. You can't go. What if—

I'm a six-inch cookie. There's nothing I can do out there. But if I can find the marbles, we might stop him. Just stay awake, all right. Drink some coffee. Gman out.

Chris was back in the darkness.

He sat up suddenly and looked for his boots. Joli was still in the chair, her arms wrapped tightly around herself. Winter was seeping through the cracked window. He found his boots under the bed.

"No," she said. "We're not going."

"I'm here for a reason, Jo. I want to go. I have to."

"What if something happens?"

"It already did."

He stood up and teetered. She grabbed his arm. Her hand was shivering. His coat was on the bed. He pulled it over her shoulders and she let him. Her chin was quivering from the cold and something else. He went to the door, put his hand on the doorknob.

"We don't have to go," she said.

"I know."

The slacker was gone. He'd expected someone to come for him. Maybe they didn't need him anymore. Pelz already got what he needed. Maybe he knew Chris would come anyway. He was drawn to what was going to happen. *I was born for this.*

The hallway was silent. Their footsteps loud in the stairwell. The announcement board filled with fliers and a poster for the Christmas celebration. Chris stopped outside the door. It felt so good to be out of the building, to feel the sky and the cold in his chest. He had the urge to see the horizon, to get away from the buildings and the trees, to see a flat white landscape. Just snow and ice. He took a deep breath. The stars were vivid. The north star a beacon above the castle.

"If something happens," he said, "tell my family I'm sorry."

"For what?"

He shook his head. *For all the Christmases I missed.*

26

She held his arm.

The gravel path was hidden beneath snowpack. The sky was glowing beyond Trupid Hall, where skeletal frames of metal sculptures were covered in snow. The Tree was a lighthouse, the star so bright he couldn't look directly at it.

"It's never been like that," Joli said.

"Pelz wants him to know we're here." Chris didn't say Santa. Joli didn't ask. Maybe she was starting to believe. Anything was possible now.

The Tree was covered in ornaments that glittered and shined, waved and flickered and sang from the branches. A bonfire was in the open field, its flame reaching ten feet into the air, the ground around it soft and wet. Students huddled in small groups, clutching mugs of cocoa and cups of hot cider, standing well away from the roaring fire. Their shadows danced like spokes on a wagon wheel on the outskirts of firelight where the sculptures lurked like uninvited guests.

"I need to sit," Chris said.

There were chairs in no particular arrangement, but most were facing the Tree. The faculty was seated beneath the heavy limbs, clad in dark robes and thick hats, slumped in chairs like drifts of snow while slackers marched presents out of the little stone hut to stack them on a pile like glittering logs as high as the bonfire's flames.

In the distant trees, flickering flames appeared.

Chris and Joli found chairs away from the crowd. No one seemed to notice or care. It was cold on the edge of the firelight.

"Where's Sai?" Chris asked.

"He was in the kitchen."

The presents were never-ending, like a clown car of gifts. When the last one was delivered, the slackers gathered at the fire, and the ceremony continued with dance routines and Christmas carols and string instruments. It all seemed quite normal.

An ornate metalwork sculpture resembled a clock. It was a large oval with hands attached to the outer ring pointing at the empty center. It was eleven o'clock.

Hey, Chris thought. *Where are you?*

Chris didn't want to cloud the gingerman's head with thoughts, but he was growing concerned. It had been hours since he'd heard from him. An improv performance of *A Christmas Carol* had begun. Audience participation was encouraged, shouting out lines and invitations to swap with the characters or change the story.

Joli held his hand. It wasn't the first time he'd held hands with a girl. Jenny Piccolo in seventh grade was the first. Their hands were hot and sweaty. It wasn't much fun. He'd made out with Di Frasier in eighth grade. It was exciting but strange. Neither of them knew what they were doing. He found out later she did it on a dare.

But this. This was different. Joli was nervous and cold. But the way their hands fit together was completely different than anything he'd ever done. In the middle of all the madness, he felt himself smile.

You're not going to believe this, Gingerman said.

"You all right?" she asked.

For a second, he thought she heard the voice, too. But he'd squeezed her hand when Gingerman spoke. "No, it's fine. I'm just... I'm good. Just going to close my eyes a minute."

The sounds of laughter and string instruments faded. The

warmth of the fire on one side of his face, biting cold on the other, was neutralized by the inner journey. It was like searching for a dream. He found it easy to move through tangible space he could only describe as mind.

And find the gingerman.

He was on a cobblestone path. Squatty huts had silver-gray cypress doors and wooden doorknobs. The walls were spackled with mud, with small stacks of firewood by the doors. No ornaments, no lights. A village in a thicket of trees, their trunks cracking foundations, tilting windows. Something built hundreds of years ago. Perhaps where the boy's servants had lived.

No one's home, Gingerman said. *Nothing but cots and dust.*

Who are they?

I don't know. But there's that.

The bumpy path headed straight for the mountain. The mouth of a dark cave yawned in a tangle of bare vines. Gingerman scurried like a squirrel caught in traffic. Chris didn't want to go spelunking. It would be pitch black. And Pelz wouldn't hide marbles in some dank alcove. But then he saw it. It wasn't a cave.

There was a tarnished metal door.

It was built into the mountain. Arched at the top. Thick and impenetrable. It looked like a vault.

Someone just went inside, Gingerman said. *One of those robes.*

Did they see you?

No, no, no. No. Gingerman climbed into the vines next to the door. *I don't think so.*

What?

I mean, if they saw me, they would've done something, right? I got a good feeling about this, you know? The pack is on the way. I'm just going to wait till—

The door began to move. Tiny lights, green and red, were blinking like decorations. Gingerman held still. A gray robe pushed the door open, the hood pulled over his face. Stooped, he paused to look around. Gingerman was looking up the robe. Scuffed shoes, once shiny, were inches away. The robe put his hand out to push the door closed. The gap was shrinking.

Gingerman held steady. Just before it snapped in the frame and the heavy tumblers latched into place, he slipped through the crack —the door pinching the tip off his arm.

Ow.

The room hummed with the mechanical efficiency of a large climate-control unit. The floor was clean and smooth. It was large and empty. The ceiling high and the walls covered with squares of glass. Tiny lights blinked around frosted panels.

This is it, Gingerman said. *His treasure.*

The Toy Collector, Chris said.

Right. And where does a collector put all his stuff?

In a vault.

Gingerman's steps echoed like pretzels on a marble slab. There were no ladders or stools, no tables to jump on. He wouldn't be able to reach most of the glass doors. Only the ones near the floor. And even if the marbles were in one of them, he'd have to open it. Opening the vault door was another problem.

We didn't think this through, Chris said.

Think what? He hopped to look inside the nearest glass panel.

Getting you out of there.

One giant problem at a time, buddy.

He leaped again. There was something in there. It was dark and smudgy. Maybe Chris could slip away from the bonfire without anyone noticing. But even if he could muster enough strength to walk that far, there were the gray robes with the candles and getting past the wall.

Sai, Chris said. *Maybe he can—*

Gingerman fell down and scurried to the middle of the room. The sudden shift in perspective made Chris dizzy. He almost lost the connection. A flood of cold panic filled his head.

This isn't a treasure chest.

What is it?

It's... it's a... Gingerman said. *It's a body, it's a body.*

Where?

There. There, there, there... He pointed his stubby arm. *I was wrong. I never should've come here. I should've listened to you. Pelz has the marbles, you were right. Abort. Abort!*

He called to the pack of gingerbread men.

What do you mean? Chris said.

Body. In there. What else do I mean?

Chris took a deep breath, found a calm space. *Okay. Just look again.*

No.

I just want to see.

Gingerman walked in circles, pondering the size of the trap he was in. There was nowhere to go. And Chris wanted to see for sure. Gingerman finally tiptoed closer. He gathered his courage and weakly leaped. It wasn't high enough.

I can't see anything, Chris said.

Trust me, okay?

He was shaking now. All the bravado vanished. He was now the gingerbread man. All he could think was run, run.

Just one more time, Chris said.

He did it. And this time he jumped higher than ever, high enough to see through a clear patch in the center of the window. High enough to see the gray hair, the nude body in dim green light. The eyes were closed.

It was her.

The light in the room changed. Snow fluttered over the floor like feathers blown through a fan. The vault door was open. Gingerman bolted for an escape but slipped on the snow. A gray hood limped inside and slammed the door closed.

"I knew it," he said.

Chris recognized the voice.

27

Chris was on a carnival ride.

Gingerman ran around the outside of the room, his momentum carrying him along the walls, into corners, upside down—swirling Chris's stomach. There were glimpses of the hooded figure in the center of the room, snapshots of him taking off the robe—revealing plain, soot-streaked clothing—and holding it like a matador. And then tossing it like a fishing net. It snapped like a flag.

And then it was dark.

Chris heard Gingerman struggle. Felt the heavy wool fabric. Heard thudding footsteps, a toe of one foot dragging across the floor. Light seeped through cracks as the robe peeled away. A patchy beard was knotted below his chin. White hair the color of paper. Tired pale eyes squinting, wrinkles spreading from the corners.

Kogen.

"You talk?" Kogen shook him like a broken toy. "Huh?"

He turned him around, upside down. Scratched Gingerman's head with a yellow fingernail.

"Bobby found you." He nodded. "I knew it."

His tongue darted out, brushing the whiskers curled over cracked lips.

"I told Pelznickel."

He paced the room, swinging Gingerman at his side. The view was scattered; the glass doors all had identical bodies inside.

"I told him! I told him Bobby had something. All the crumbs, the gingerbreads he was making, jabbering in his room, the poems he was writing, the run, run as fast as you can. I told him!"

He shook Gingerman, the proof wrapped in his hand.

"He didn't listen."

He held him closer. Breath wheezing. Pink tongue running across perfect teeth.

"Chris had you, too." Gingerman was cracking in his grasp. "Talk to me!"

I'm here! Chris shouted. *Leave him alone!*

Sweat trickled down Kogen's temple, seeping into a network of wrinkles. He was waiting for an answer. Gingerman nodded. A smile crept through the salty whiskers. Kogen's mouth opened, head thrown back, his laughter trapped in the empty room. The kind that trickled from a frayed mind.

"I was right," he whispered. "Can he hear me? Christmas, you there?"

Gingerman nodded again. Kogen began pacing again, panting. Mumbling to himself.

"Do you know what you've done? Huh? It was supposed to be me. Me! I was the one. I did everything he asked. I did it perfectly, every detail. My whole life. And now look at me. Look at me!"

He held Gingerman like a mirror.

"This is your fault. Your fault I'm taking care of these, these... *things*. And you don't even know why. He sucked the life out of us, and you helped him. You don't know what he is. He's-he's a taker." He looked inside one of the glass doors. "A collector."

Kogen leaned his forehead against the wall, rolling his head back and forth, then thumping it. Staring inside the glass pane.

"You promised," he whispered to the body.

Kogen clutched Gingerman with both hands. His pale eyes stared at the ceiling. Gingerman couldn't move. Even if he could escape the grip, there was nowhere to run. He was trapped.

Sai!

Chris began shouting, searching, hoping he could hear him. To get someone, Joli or everyone, lead them all to the village and open the vault. Show them what Pelz was doing. If there was enough chaos, Gingerman could escape into the trees and run far, far away.

I never should have let you go in there, Chris said.

Kogen looked down, head bobbing. A silly grin slid across his face. "But I got you, don't I?"

He wrapped the folds of the robe tighter, tucking them over Gingerman's arms, holding him like a kid with his first lollipop. He licked his lips.

No! Chris shouted.

His perfect white teeth clamped on a small portion of the gingerman's head. A crisp snap echoed inside Chris's head. It crunched between his molars, ground into small bits, dust coating his tongue. Chris could feel it spread to his cheeks, mixing with saliva, moving to the back of his tongue.

A strange sensation emerged.

Chris felt arthritic fingers and an aching back. The stiff pain in his hip. A wave of euphoria. Kogen wobbled a few steps, slapped his hand against the wall, smudging glass panels with sweaty fingerprints. His grip loosened and he almost dropped the gingerman. Then he slid to the floor.

Like poking through a thin membrane, Kogen suddenly knew the gingerman. Knew where he had been, what he'd been doing. He knew Chris was listening. The barrier that separated them had been consumed. No more secrets.

Chris knew him as well.

The puncture had spilled Kogen's thoughts. Memories spread out like oil paintings. The day Kogen had arrived at the school with his grandmother. He was so nervous that he wet himself just a little. But he quickly acclimated, excelling in classes, leading teams in challenges and almost winning. He found three marbles on his second hike and was called to the castle.

Pelz was proud.

It was the same look Chris had seen. And the same feeling he had felt. He was important. Chosen. He was there for a reason. *We've been looking for you, son,* Pelz had said.

Son.

Kogen had been raised by his grandmother, sent to boarding school, severely hazed by the older kids. He visited his grandmother on holidays. But some years he stayed at the school when she wasn't feeling well. The teachers would have him over for dinner. But most of his time was spent in his room. Alone.

He was fifteen years old when Pelz took him to the lab, put the crown on his head to find the dreams inside. He woke up to see the marbles on the shelf. They had a slight glow, barely enough to light the room. He came back to the lab often, sometimes staying months at a time. And each time the crown took a little bit more from him. Each time, he left looking a little bit older.

But the marbles eventually lost their shine.

You are important, Gretchen had told him before he left the lab the very last time. *I promise.*

He believed her. He continued to give and give, knowing he could give Pelz what he wanted if he just tried hard enough. But then time passed and he was just another student who was once promised everything. He was disgraced when he was caught vandalizing the gingerbread house. He was given the robe and, for the last time, wore the crown that turned him into an old man.

Still, it didn't light the marbles.

He was alone in a hut, assigned duties to care for the bodies inside the vault. Bathing them, feeding them, watching them sleep. He didn't know why there were so many of her or how they made them or even why. He only knew they were sleeping. And when it was time to wake one, he would open the door to let her out.

Another Gretchen exited.

She looked at him. Seemed to remember him. Held his cheek. *You are important.*

But he hardly felt those words, alone in his hut. Forgotten again. Wishing to have that feeling back. That he was important. That he mattered.

Anything but this.

Gingerman gently wriggled from his fingers. Kogen was steeped in the euphoric glow of selflessness, bathing in the expansion of mind that Chris had experienced. The loss of attachment to thoughts. Gingerman quietly walked away, avoiding clicking the floor. His legs inflexible with fractures that could break with any step.

"And where do you think you're going?"

Kogen slurred the words, crawling on his hands and knees. Sweeping Gingerman off the floor with one hand and falling onto his back. Chris was helpless. Even if Gingerman could run, he couldn't open the door. Trapped in a dead end with a man who had nothing left to lose.

Chris began to open his eyes. They had to know what was happening. What they were doing in the village. It was all a lie. All the promises were lies. This wasn't Christmas. Pelz didn't care. He was collecting them. *Why?*

He heard tapping.

Kogen lifted his head and listened. It came again, a light peck on the metal door. He checked the watch on his wrist, looked back at the instruments on the wall.

Tap, tap, tap.

He staggered to his feet and slowly regained his balance and composure, holding Gingerman tightly while he pulled the robe on and hid his face in the deep hood. He held Gingerman at his side. The world was upside down. He pushed the lever, and the door slowly crept open, snow blowing through the crack.

Someone was out there.

He was far away, hidden in the shadows. Hands in coat pockets, slouched on the cobblestone path. Too far to have knocked. Kogen squinted. His eyesight was too old and poor to see the details. He felt something scratching his ankles. They scurried over his pant leg.

Kogen shrieked, thinking what anyone would think in the woods, that mice were crawling up his legs. He slipped on the wet floor. The world went tumbling as Gingerman flew across the room and cracked against the wall.

Gingerman lay broken in half. His legs in pieces. Half of one arm and a bite from his head. He lost the ability to move. Chris just wanted to hear his voice again. Gingerman lifted his head to see Kogen rise up. It wasn't mice that had tapped on the door. It wasn't mice that scurried up his leg.

It was the pack.

Rocko, Taco, Blocko, Socko, and Mike scampered across the room. Taco had one leg and Socko had the arm. But before they could drag the body out, the scuffed sole of a once shiny shoe came down like a hammer. The gingerbread men ran. Chris felt the impact like an earthquake. Felt particles scatter into dust. The heel of his shoe stomped through the gingerman's body.

Gingerman turned to crumbs.

Chris's cries disintegrated in fractured space. He felt his presence pulverized and floating in a thousand points of light. Sounds were shrouded in watery echoes as if bouncing through a cave. Countless forms turned in a kaleidoscope.

"Come, come, little ones," Kogen said.

He had a taste of one. Now he had five. He stomped around the room. Chris was disoriented. First the slap of a hard sole on the other side of the room, then seeing it nearly crush him. The gingerbread men seemed scared, rodents evading a robe-waving, glassy-eyed madman licking dry lips. But they moved in patterns. And Chris went with them, cruising in figure-eights, drawing Kogen to one corner of the room while the others swept up the crumbs.

Absorbing them.

Crumbs stuck to their legs and arms, vacuumed like bits of metal shavings to magnetic cutouts. Kogen was winded, coughing into his fist. Sweat stung his eyes. He hadn't noticed that the door was not latched. Or that they had cleaned the floor. Not a speck of Gingerman was left.

He brandished the robe as a matador once again, expecting to corner them, to capture at least one. He lunged for Blocko—Chris knew their names now—and the heel of his shoe slid over the snow-specked floor. His legs split like a cheerleader's finale. Much wider than a man his age could or should do. His mouth opened in a soundless gasp, writhing onto his side. The door very quietly opened. The gingerbread men, however, didn't escape.

Sai.

Kogen was in tears. A wounded animal letting out mournful howls. A babble of nonsense, scratching at the floor, clutching the ruptured muscles between his legs. Sai knelt on the ground, hands out. The gingerbread men scrambled into his arms like a mother collecting her cubs. He looked down at Kogen one last time. And then began running through the forest.

Sai!

He didn't hear Chris. If he did, he wasn't listening. He ran from the village, away from the gathering at the Tree toward the other side of the circle.

Toward Bixen Hall.

28

"No!" Celebration was all around. The bonfire blazing. No one heard Chris shout.

"Hey." Joli put her arm around him. "You all right?"

His gums were numb. A wave of pins and needles pricked his senses. It took a moment to recognize her. The memory of being crushed beneath Kogen's shoe lingered. *How long have I been gone?*

Something exploded.

The sky flashed white hot. Crackling trails whistled over the Tree. It was ten minutes till midnight.

"We have to go." He tried to stand. "We have to—"

A figure sat down beside him, her comforting hand on his arm. Gretchen smiled warmly. "It's okay."

"He's not okay. Look at him. Look what you've done to him."

Joli's anger was drowning in the unruly celebration. When Gretchen sat down, he momentarily forgot about Sai and the gingerbread men. There was a palpable presence about her. It surrounded him, held him. Joli felt it too, her anger trailing off. He felt completely reassured everything was exactly as it was supposed to be.

"What did he do to you?" Chris said to Gretchen.

It was her. All those bodies. Or they looked like her. Who was he talking to? Was this Gretchen? Or something that looked like her? She took his hand in both of her hands.

"We all have a purpose," she said.

The bonfire suddenly blazed nearly twice as tall, its flames reaching for the stars. Chris felt its warmth. The sculptures danced in the flickering light. The crowd scrambled back, their cheers reaching another level. The faculty were standing, hunched over, applauding. A figure entered the firelight, clad in a long fur coat that dragged the ground, a thick fuzzy hat upon his head.

Lord Pelznickel raised his arms. "Gifters!"

They huddled like penguins, giddy with anticipation, eyes on the mountain of presents towering behind him. He silenced them with a gesture, glassing the mob with an expectant eye and a secret on his lips.

The clock ticked closer to midnight.

"This is the greatest time of year." His voice was gravelly, mysterious. "This will be a very special Christmas, boys and girls. A night to close your eyes and watch sugarplums dance, to listen for a fat man and his reindeer with hope and desire churning your stomachs."

They snuggled closer, their breath steamy.

"This year will be different." He raised a finger. "A Christmas of truth and things well deserved. A season of things magic."

He pulled a bag from his pocket. It wasn't small; it wasn't large. A bag just the right size. He fished inside it. They oohed when a golden light cast over his broad grin.

A marble between his finger and thumb.

Chris wilted. Gretchen held him tighter. The marble drew from him like a lamp pulling electricity from an outlet. *He sucked the life out of us*, Kogen had said.

"A very special Christmas," Pelz said, "indeed."

He flicked the marble like flipping a coin. Instead of dropping into his hand, it streaked like a firefly. People gasped; someone shrieked. It struck an ice sculpture of a mythical creature with a pointed beak and oversized talons.

It didn't shatter.

The marble left a hole and nestled in its chest like a burning coal. Light crackled in jagged veins. It began to crack as if, at any moment, it would shatter into a pile of ice cubes. Frosty chips began to flutter. The beginning of a very special Christmas started with a simple gesture.

It unfolded its wings.

There were more gasps and muttering. No laughter. An ice carving was coming to life in front of their eyes. It stretched its wings like a pterodactyl. The head swiveled with an icy glare in each eye. It bent its scaly legs, lifted wings of ice, and looked to the stars.

It launched like a rocket.

Snow swirled in its wake. Embers circled the fire. Chris felt a tug like a cable pulling his insides. He couldn't feel his legs anymore. It glided like a bird of prey, cruising over a column of hot air rising from the fire to lift it higher.

Pelz brandished two more marbles. One went into a metal thing that resembled a reindeer with sharpened antlers. The other went into a glass sculpture of a robed figure with angelic wings. Each glowed to life. Each launched. Each of them pulled from Chris.

I'm powering them.

It was impossible. He had some connection with the marbles, a real physical connection. It looked like an ethereal cord twisting from their circling bodies like kites, swaying down to the ground. He wasn't holding a reel of string. It emanated from his chest. Part of him was inside the marbles now animating the sculptures to life. *Just like the toys.*

Chris's breath was shallow. He heard Joli, the worry in her voice, the pleading with Gretchen. No one heard. They watched in amazement.

"A Christmas," Pelz bellowed, "the world won't forget!"

They cheered. They applauded. They stamped their feet and hugged each other. This was going to be the greatest Christmas of all.

The clock struck midnight like a hammer on a church bell. It shocked some of them into fits of giggles. Chris felt it in his chest as the sensations faded. He was useless now. A numb shell of a person.

Joli was on her feet, shouting at the others to come to their senses, didn't they see what was happening? But they were overwhelmed with joy. Each time the gong struck, their cheers grew louder. They danced in circles, hopped in place. Hugged and wept and sang. Pelz watched the sky.

It was on the twelfth and final gong that everything changed.

It sounded like lightning. Electric fingers reached across the mountains and tickled the stars, then ripped the sky open. The white light momentarily blinded them. They shielded their eyes, with ghostly images hovering in their vision. The soaring sculptures had converged.

They were battling.

Twisting in the night, they yanked back and forth as bells grew louder. They were coming down fast. The students ran. Joli wrapped her arms around Chris and dragged him away. The sculptures crash-landed like a boulder breaking off the mountaintop. It was followed by a stampede of hooves. Plumes of snow cascaded over them, descending like glittering diamonds in the firelight. As it settled, there was something there.

It was a sleigh.

The sculptures were latched onto the golden rails. Reindeer were tangled in reins slumping from the front of the sleigh. And a very fat man sat up in the seat, pushing his red hat upon his head. He looked out in surprise that was matched by those who looked back. There was no other explanation for who it was. Even the most rational mind would know who it was.

He's real.

Snorting and stamping their hooves, the reindeer swung their wide-reaching antlers. The one in front was larger than the rest, his eyes glowing, steam firing from nostrils like broken pipes. Santa tossed the reins and pulled a lever. The harnesses fell from the reindeer in a shower of bells.

"Take them to safety," Santa said with a bellowing tone.

He pointed at the tight group of students and the faculty trembling beneath the Tree. The reindeer lowered their broad spans of antlers. They dispersed the stunned group, herding them like cattle, gently prodding those attempting to stray for another peek. The reindeer ushered them all very far away.

Chris wondered, in his dizzy state, why he was still there. Joli and Gretchen, too. And one reindeer.

The biggest of them all.

He was nearly the size of an elephant, with antlers as broad as a truck is long. His black eyes narrowed, nostrils flaring. Santa climbed out of the sleigh and patted the reindeer's hindquarters, muscles writhing beneath the hide.

"Easy, boy," Santa muttered.

Pelz had lifted the bag. The marbles clattered inside. Santa looked at the sculptures still clinging to the rails. Heat waves radiated from the back of the sleigh where a large sack was loaded. One of the sculptures had damaged it in mid-flight. It sparked and smoked.

"What have you done?" Santa said.

"I've come to collect," Pelz said.

Santa looked at Chris, his eyes softening. Joli attempted to pull him away. "You've taken from a boy."

Strange translucent cords braided the air, connecting Chris to the bag of marbles, to the sculptures clinging to the sleigh. And to Pelz. It was a ghostly web anchored to his chest. He passed his hand through them. They momentarily scattered like columns of smoke.

"All these years," Pelz said, "I've watched and waited, taking what I needed, Nicholas."

Santa seemed to understand. His expression of anger and confusion softened. He held out his arms. "I'm not perfect, Kris."

"No!" Pelz's voice echoed. "You're not. You've had everything. Did you ever think of me? You and all of this, passing over year after year and never looking back. Not once."

The sleigh popped. Smoke rose from the back. A piece of equipment fizzed. Santa cast a glance to the sky.

"You and all your little ones, all your technology, keeping it to yourselves. I've been very patient, brother. No one is coming to save you."

"What do you want?"

Pelz gestured to the sleigh. "What I am owed."

"I don't understand."

"Step aside and give me the reins. You stay here with all of this. I want you to feel what it's like to be forgotten. To be nothing more than a mistake."

"The reindeer won't take you. There's not going to be—"

"I don't need them." Pelz rattled the bag. "I just want you... to be here. And I'll take what I deserve."

Santa took a step forward. Pelz raised the bag of marbles. The big reindeer snorted. Santa pulled off a white glove. The cuff of his coat hung from his wrist.

"I'm sorry, Kris." Santa offered his hand. "For what our father did. For the life you were given. Come with me. Give back what you've taken from the boy and the others. It doesn't have to be this way."

The bag bathed Pelz's face in golden light. He plucked out a marble. Held it between finger and thumb. Chris felt it in his chest, saw the air bend around it, reaching for him. Drawing from him.

"There is no other way."

Pelz dropped the marble. It hovered in midair, then shot into an abstract sculpture of logs and limbs tied together with multicolored rope. It began to quake. Then assembled itself into a woodland creature with bulky legs and clunky arms, a head folded from boughs of spruce. Heavy logs stomped holes into the frozen earth.

An orb popped out of the sleigh. It was the size of a softball and deeply etched. Gravitational waves warped around it. A magnetic field resonated like a weapon.

"There it is," Pelz said. Chris could feel him smile.

Snow began to swirl toward it until, layer upon layer, a massive snowman materialized. Head like a turret, a body of gyrating snow, it stood lightly touching the ground. Pitted eyes stared at Pelz.

The reindeer roared. In a long leap, he soared over the ground and jerked his head, slamming antlers into the log creature. Branches cracked in a shower of splinters. A second toss of the antlers swatted the thing into chunks of confetti.

The marble rolled into the snow, its light never dimming.

In the melee, the snowman snatched the bag from Pelz's hand. It happened too fast to see. One moment he was holding it, watching the woodland sculpture almost reach the heavy sack in the back of the sleigh; the next moment his hand was empty.

Pelz didn't resist. He was in awe of the snowman. "Beautiful," was all he said.

"It didn't have to be this way," Santa said.

Pelz was surrounded by debris as the reindeer stomped an ice sculpture into icy shards that rained down into the fire, hissing. Pelz kicked a twisted rod of iron.

"No," Pelz mused. "No, it didn't."

He reached into his pocket to retrieve another bag. It was smaller than the one Santa was holding. Chris felt it sway in Pelz's hand; felt it tug inside his chest. Saw the atmosphere twist in a braided rope. Santa opened what the snowman had taken, dug inside for a handful of dull granite rocks.

Pelz tipped the bag he was holding. The marbles—all of them—spilled in a glowing shower. They fell abnormally, like watching a time-warped video, slowing as they neared the ground, like gravity reversing. Then they scattered.

Chris groaned.

He felt thinner. Transparent. Like a string of taffy pulled to its limits. The fire dimmed. The glowing marbles shot through the dark. Each one hit a target.

Sculptures shuddered.

One by one, they moved in unnatural ways. Fabric wings and pointed limbs, metal torsos and glass spheres began to shine. Smaller ones climbed on top of each other, combining into grotesque objects. Some tall, some stout and grinding. Others long and stringy.

The snowman swelled to twice its size, inhaling snowdrifts beyond the Tree. Arms like tree trunks, the bulk of an automobile, it leaned forward and began to soar. It would crush everything in its path. But just as its feet lifted off the ground, something popped out of its chest.

The metallic orb ejected like a cannonball.

It struck a sculpture of writhing ropes. At first, it appeared to be intentional. Some sort of weapon the snowman had fired. But then the snowman fell into a pile like the work of a snowplow. The reindeer reared up and let loose a cry that shook the ground.

Santa put his hand on the reindeer's flank.

The ropey sculpture spit the etched orb out. It rolled through the snow, leaving a track that reached Pelz's feet. He bent to retrieve it, holding it with both hands, tracing his fingers over the engraving.

"Beautiful."

Night was falling like a palpable veil. Chris could barely see through the cloak of darkness. The two men, the reindeer and sleigh were vague forms. It was the ethereal cords that appeared tangible. The way they curled and twisted like conduits of energy flowing from Chris. There was only one cord that didn't feed the marbles.

The one connected to Pelz.

He could feel the old man's heart patter, his pulse quicken. All the years of anticipation bubbling in his chest.

"Sacrifices were made," Pelz said, entranced by the orb. "With time, they will be forgotten. You understand, brother."

The reindeer broke from Santa's grip. He shattered a glass replica of a toy soldier. The marble swatted into the dark like a shooting star. It was a tiny dot that began to arc above the trees, circling around and boomeranging toward the debris. The glass shards reassembled into a crude form of what it had been. The marble pulsed.

The reindeer ignored Santa's pleas. The viney sculptures slithered around the muscular legs and sprawling antlers, snapping as he tossed his head. Little by little, they slowed him down and tangled him in a writhing net.

Chris sank into the darkness.

At first, he was numb. But then sensations began to rise. He could taste them. The sour tang of fear, the sweet allure of power. They were thrilling at first. Beneath them, though, was bitter resentment and salty greed that emerged from a bottomless pit of wanting. It was a strange and groundless experience that had no form. They were primordial. When images began to appear, the sensations took shape. Chris knew what they were. He had witnessed this in the lab.

These were memories.

Pelz was in the castle's tower, looking down on a winter courtyard illuminated by a full moon. There was a sleigh tethered to a team of reindeer. And a stout man in a red coat talking to someone. Chris felt the burn of Pelz's anger and the anxious flutter of anxiety.

He followed him down a dark stairwell, Pelz sliding his hand along the cold wall. His footsteps echoed. He rushed through the castle in time to hear the bells jingle and slushing of rails. The reindeer pedaled thin air toward a pale moon.

Gretchen was there. Alone.

She was an old woman trembling in the cold, her cloak pulled tightly over hunched shoulders. She looked up with tired eyes and a weak smile. Pelz approached timidly. Almost frightened. He looked so much younger than her. She was older than him, had raised him from infancy. She was there to greet him when he returned from his journey overseas.

He looked exactly the same as when he'd greeted his brother at the port. DNA has a magical quality, Pelz had told him in the lab. Sometimes it knows when something fundamental has changed. And it changes, too.

Chris clung to a sliver of doubt. If that was Santa, he wondered, then he would be over two hundred years old. Pelz, too. Just like his brother.

"What did he want?" Pelz asked as she shivered. It wasn't pleading or hopeful. It was bitter.

"He said," Gretchen said, "difficult times would come."

"He wanted you to leave."

"He did."

Pelz was stolid. Hands clenching. Gretchen shuffled toward him. She took his hands in hers, pulling his fists open.

"I will never leave you," she said.

She put her arms around him, rocking back and forth. Humming his mother's song. Pelz remained rigid, staring at the moon. The silhouette long gone in the Christmas night.

Chris was ejected from the memory, tossed into a dark nothingness again. *Out!* he heard Pelz shout, shaking off the parasite leeching his memories. Santa's pleas to stop were tiny and fading.

Joli held him and Gretchen looked over her. But Chris couldn't find his way back. His body felt foreign, an object he could no longer occupy. If he did, the marbles would take the rest of him. He sought refuge in the space of mind. He looked for the gingerman. He was broken, but he was out there.

And Chris found him.

29

A dust storm of video feeds streamed ten thousand viewpoints. He was weightless. He was everywhere.

Sound waves broadcast from a single location in a room, vibrating each speck of vision, reverberating off the walls and ceiling like visual sonar. It was rhythmic. Pulsing.

A dark form swung in the mist. The edges fuzzy, the core dark. Like an apparition of radio waves. Chris surrounded him. Felt the figure's muscles contract as he swung something heavy.

Sai! Chris thought.

Sai looked around. He said something, but his words were stretchy and warped. He scraped dust into a pile, shoveled it into a bowl. Then slid an object on the counter. *Bang.*

A gingerbread man shattered.

Two more of them stood on the edge of a steel prep table and watched Sai swing again, the surface shuddering. Watched him steamroll the pieces into dust, the crispy bits crunching beneath a wooden rolling pin.

Sai, what are you doing?

He swiped the debris into the bowl. He didn't reach for another gingerbread man. Rocko voluntarily lay down. Arms and legs out.

Bang!

There was nothing Chris could do. He was a witness. It couldn't be Sai. Why would he destroy them? Why would they let him?

This was the end. His parents would be devastated. His sister would never use their secret language again. Joli would be distraught. Even Kogen, the thought of him all alone made Chris's heart ache. Christmas was over.

And it was his fault.

If he never came to the school, if he didn't win the challenge or listen to Gingerman, he never would've gone to the lab. Never would've given the marbles power. He could've stopped this from happening if he just never existed.

You were born for this, Gretchen had said.

Sai scooped the remains of the last gingerbread man. He pulled a box fan from under the counter and switched on the ceiling fans. Space began to swirl. Sai's dark form shifted in the current. He pushed the tables out of the way and cleared a space on the kitchen floor, then began dumping buckets of food—potatoes and carrots, bags of flour and sugar, tubs of margarine and candy. Entire boxes of produce and tray after tray of cookies and cakes and ice cream. He opened all the cabinets.

Then he sprinkled a handful of dust into the fan.

It dispersed like powdered sugar, coating the food, the flour-dusted counters, trays of cupcakes and bowls of pudding.

The mist began to clear.

Chris's vision crystalized. Details sharpened; colors deepened. Sai looked pained, gutted. But determined. He tossed another handful into the fan. Another cloud spread throughout the kitchen.

The tan specks of gingerbread were absorbed into oily globs of butter, soaked up by moist cake, disappeared into vegetables. The edges of the mound began to creep like a sea creature exploring the ocean floor. Bits of food flew off the counters. Jars tipped off the shelves and shattered. Blobs of jam slurped like slugs; pickles sacrificed themselves to the growing pile.

Sai dumped the rest of the bowl. A sweet haze permeated the

room. He coughed and sneezed and ran. The food pile rose like dough.

Chris no longer saw the room from ten thousand points. He was seeing it from all directions. Felt the cold hard floor. Felt utensils swallowed up. Food flew from beneath the cabinets, soared from the tables in the dining hall. He squeezed through tiny openings, squished through the doorway.

Tables and benches splintered under his weight. The windows shattered. Chris oozed into fresh air where Sai watched from the shadows.

Chris slithered out of Bixen Hall like a doughy organism, through cracks and busted windows, under doors. Each segment merged with the rest. He rose on two legs until he was looking at the tip of the castle.

The frozen ground shuddered.

Snow exploded beneath a heavy footfall. He swung his arms to keep his balance and clipped the castle. A chunk of granite hurtled toward the ground. Sai covered his head. It narrowly missed him, thudding through the snow.

Hang on, buddy.

Chris heard the voice. The gingerbread men had swept up Gingerman from the vault. Sai hadn't been destroying them. A conglomeration of jams and jellies, sweets and breads, meat and vegetables and cakes and cookies and candy lumbered like a newborn dinosaur.

Chris was along for the ride.

Their momentum carried them too quickly around the castle. They ran to keep from falling. Snow shook from the buildings. Ice cracked on the walls. The full extent of the Tree came into view. The bonfire. Joli and Gretchen. Santa. The reindeer snared in rubbery bands.

Pelz was in the sleigh.

The sculptures turned like nightmare playthings to see a giant lean back and, for a long moment, stand still. Pelz looked up, confused. He lifted one arm, the matted sleeve sliding to his elbow, and pointed at the kitchen creature vaguely resembling the shape of a gingerbread man. Nothing happened. There was no ball inside the gingerman, nothing to pull out like he had done to the snowman.

The sculptures charged.

Chris couldn't control what he and Gingerman had become much more than a lumbering gait. The sculptures would have crawled over them like ants, slashing and biting off one piece at a time until they were scattered across the snow and fed to woodland creatures.

But Chris felt the marbles inside them.

The translucent cords twisted the atmosphere. He felt energy pulse, saw them grow brighter inside the sculptures, watched them pounce like otherworldly creatures. The ethereal tethers emanated from Chris. They were luminescent and vibrating, singing when he reached out with thought. He was connected to them. All of them.

Including Pelz.

He didn't know how he did it. He couldn't explain much of anything that had happened or how he latched onto the marbles. Like his mind was an invisible hand that plucked them like instruments. Yanked the cords like fishing lines.

The marbles popped out.

They shot from the sculptures like bullets. It looked like weapons fired, musket balls sinking into the lumbering doughy giant. Every impact made the world a little brighter. Chris could see the onlookers' expressions. The surprise, the shock. The rage. The sorrow. One marble after another hit the giant gingerman with a dull thud. The darks of the world became lights. The lights became whites.

One by one, the sculptures fell like abandoned puppets.

Sounds faded in a bleached world. The bonfire cast eerie blue light on a fur-clad figure. Pelz was on his knees. Mouth open in a cry that faded into the light. The final translucent tether twisted from his chest. Chris felt it pump like an umbilical cord. Until the world was blank.

Little by little, the whiteness coalesced into tiny crystals drifting in random patterns, finding their way to a soft blanket across a flat land. Chris didn't know where he was.

But he wasn't alone.

30

The castle was gone. The mountain and the Tree, everything. Snap of the fingers.

They were replaced by an endless white slate. There was nothing else. Except Pelz.

He looked like a wounded animal, shuffling through knee-deep snow, his hands clenched into fists. Even from a distance, Chris could see the tendons stretch from his neck.

"Nicholas!" Pelz shouted.

He raged at nothing. Stomped holes in the snow, swung at the air. Steam rose from his scalp.

He turned with wide eyes.

Like a bear in the cold of winter, he charged. The strength drained from Chris's legs. He couldn't outrun him. There was nowhere to hide. He closed his eyes and braced for impact. Felt the furs brush his cheek as the wild man ran past him.

"Where are you?" Pelz shouted.

The old man kicked snow and cursed the sky. He spun in circles, falling down and getting up dusted white to do it again and again.

"He can't see you."

Chris spun around. A short man was behind him, his wide feet treading the soft snow. A long beard lay over small hands laced over a very round belly. A long braid over the hair over his back.

"Where am I?" Chris said.

"This is you."

Chris shook his head. Everything was so real. "Then who are you?"

"That question is not simple. Nor is the answer. Now, this moment, I am you. But he"—he pointed a stubby finger—"is not."

Pelz's shouting devolved into raspy sounds interrupted by desperate wheezing.

"I don't understand."

"This is your world, Christmas." The elf gestured, which didn't help whatsoever. "Your inner landscape. Do you remember?"

Inner landscape. That was what Pelz wanted him to find. The crown helped him remember, but it was more than that. He was bringing an inner landscape to life. Thoughts and emotions displayed an inner reality, a dream that was more than a dream.

"He wanted you to build this," the elf said. "What he didn't realize was that you would bring him here."

The transition to this place was foggy. Everything before this—the reindeer and Santa, Joli and Gretchen, the gingerman—now seemed like a dream. This was as real as anything. Yet it couldn't be. There was nothing but snow. Before this was the mountains and the school. Joli and the students and faculty, Santa Claus and reindeer. Sculptures had come to life. Chris had merged with the gingerman, had pulled the marbles out of the sculptures.

Gingerman was different than the toys and the sculptures. A marble didn't give him life. He was special. He was made for this. And so was Chris.

He stared at his hands. "Impossible."

"Possibility," the elf said, "starts with an idea. That idea is fed creativity. It is groomed and loved until it takes on a life of its own. But sometimes we lose track of where the idea begins and ends." He turned his attention to Pelz. "And we can't tell the difference between ourselves and what we believe."

Pelz was consumed by his past. He lost himself in the idea of what he was supposed to be, what he couldn't have. And now there was nothing for him to do in this barren winterland. If this place was truly Chris's inner world, then Pelz was somehow in his mind.

"How did I get here?"

"You contain infinite possibilities. In his blindness, he didn't know what you contained."

"Am I talking to you, really? Or am I talking to myself?"

The elf blinked heavily. "This, Christmas, is your true nature. Who you are. You see everything here. I am part of you. You are part of me."

"I'm the... the Toymaker?"

"We all are." He chuckled. "If we look close enough."

Pelz had fallen to his knees. His anger dissolved into ramblings. Snot ran from his nose.

"You've given him the greatest gift of all," the elf said. "He sees himself."

Pelz's eyes were blank, hopeful and mad. Chris didn't shape this place, but maybe Pelz didn't see the same thing. Chris was at home in the cold and open. The endless sky and flat horizon. In Pelz's eyes he saw the vast emptiness, the loneliness. The void he'd sought to fill his entire life.

He was seeing it starkly now. The pain and rejection, cursed with an inner life of cold, seeking to warm himself the way a child does. To take, to possess. To collect at all costs. And in the end, he found himself still shivering.

"What am I supposed to do?" Chris said.

The elf faintly smiled. It was like asking the mirror a question and expecting an answer.

"I know you're my imagination," Chris said to the elf, "or maybe you're part of me. But you're not here."

The Toymaker didn't answer. Chris took a knee.

"I don't know what to believe. The school, Pelz, Joli, Sai or... or a gingerbread man."

Pelz palmed his face. He stifled sobs, his chest convulsing.

"Dream or not," Chris said, "this man tried to take it all away. He took from everyone. What he did... he deserves this. Do you hear me?"

Chris wished Pelz could see him.

"What you did to Gretchen, what you did to the grays, the faculty, the slackers. To Kogen. The promises you made and the lies you told. Do you hear me?"

Rage warmed Chris. He walked around the heap of sobbing furs.

"You took!" Chris screamed. "And my parents? How were they going to find out about me? How much more were you going to take? How much? My mom and dad—"

"Christmas."

Mom and Dad were knee-deep in snow. They were wearing Sunday church clothes. Dad in his beige Dockers and a polo shirt buttoned up. Mom in a fuchsia blouse and black skirt, twisting a string of pearls around her neck. And Yu. She wore jeans and a concert T-shirt, her bare arms crossed.

Chris felt a lump in his throat. They weren't real. But still, he wanted to hug them. He hadn't seen them in so long. And he'd only called once, or was it twice? Did it matter? He didn't want to call them at all.

"I'm sorry," he said. But they didn't answer.

He didn't want to have a conversation. It felt easier to blame Pelz. But he was sorry. Sorry for everything he missed. Sorry for everything his family offered and he wasn't there. But he couldn't go back and change it.

"There's nothing more dangerous," the elf said, "than a child in adult clothing."

Pelz curled up on his side. Knees to his chest. The sobs were uncontrollable now. The coat looked too big. He was smaller. Younger. A young boy wailing in a lonely, lost world. Pelz couldn't change his past, would never find the brother he wanted, the father he deserved. A mother who passed too young. He was a boy clinging to Gretchen in a big, big world.

A child in an adult world trying to fill the hole the only way a child knew how.

Chris fell on his knees. He knew how it felt not to belong. Not to matter. The dark corner of his closet. The confines of an igloo dug in a snowdrift. He just wanted to feel like he belonged to the family that loved him. *Why do I feel this way?*

Chris began to hum.

It came to him spontaneously. He didn't think about it, just let the vibrations fill him. He swayed back and forth, drawing out the notes longer and louder.

Pelz grew quiet.

Chris began to sing familiar words. He felt silly at first, his voice low and cracking.

"When the cold winds blow and bring the snow."

The world rang like tiny bells. The ice shook below him.

"On a clear winter night we will see what it's for. The year may be long, but we can sing this song."

He hummed the refrain. It was all that he knew. Perhaps that was all there was to the song. It was all that mattered.

"And remind us that Christmas is coming..."

Snow began to rise off the ice. It floated like diamonds in a spotlight. The horizon grew fuzzy. The elf disappeared. Pelz was a child in a bundle of furs, his eyes closed.

"The year may be long, but we can still sing this song..."

The world was filled with magical static that clung to his cheeks and clouded his vision. Pelz faded in the rising blizzard. Chris didn't understand how any of this was possible. If this was just a strange dream, as strange dreams were, or if Pelz was really there. Maybe this was just a story he told himself. There was no gingerman or school. No sculptures or Santa Claus. But none of that mattered. So he sang as the blizzard thickened.

"And remind us that Christmas is coming."

31

It was a silent night.
Something was pressing against his forehead. There was an ache in his neck. Chris sat up. A page stuck to his forehead. It fluttered to the desk. He sat there blinking, trying to remember.

What day is it?

His mind was a whiteout. A snowy day obscured his thoughts; memories eluded his grasp. Something had happened, a big event that lurked in the webbing of his mind like an abominable snowman playing hide-and-seek.

A frosted window was lit with morning sunlight, traces of crystallized patterns spread across the glass. His desk was organized. His room was a mess of clothing, but the textbooks were squarely stacked. Notebooks neatly arranged. The coffee pot empty. A list of homework assignments checked off.

He leafed through loose papers tucked into a folder: a letter to his parents he never finished and endless notes with doodles in the margins and tired scribbles. He picked up the page that had been stuck to his head. UNRUAFASASUCN.

What did that mean?

Through the foggy window, faculty was exiting the castle. Their heavy robes were crimson and green, as were the floppy hats they wore. One of them leaped off the steps, sculpted a snowball, and bombed the ones loitering near the door. Chris thought it was a prank, a student pretending to be one of them.

But they all jumped off the steps.

They scattered in the field, scooping snow, taking cover behind the holiday sculptures that were rigid beneath a fresh layer of snow. Something wasn't right. Maybe they were all students pretending to be faculty. It looked like Ms. Faber riding on Mr. Paulowski's back and Mr. Picquery tossing handfuls of loose snow and Ms. Ralter dancing like a child on a snow day when school was out.

The slackers followed them out of the castle. They were wearing the usual attire, pressed pants and puffy coats, and threw snowballs of their own. They hugged, slackers and faculty, like family. They shook each other's hands, slapped each other's backs, and called to each other with a wave, dispersing in different directions. Chris was trying to sort through the confusion. Something wasn't fitting. Then he noticed one of the slackers walking toward Bixen Hall.

He was limping.

A thought rose through the memory fog. Chris didn't bother tying his boots. He ran down the hall as he struggled into a sweatshirt, tripping down the stairs. He slipped on the icy steps and nearly fell.

"Merry Christmas, Mr. Blizzard," Mr. Papikan said. "Up early this morning, are ya?"

Merry Christmas? The lights on the castle were blinking, the tinsel glittering, the ornaments turning. Mr. Papikan waved and smiled. He wasn't hunched over or shuffling through the snow. He hopped on the path and sang loud enough to wake the entire campus.

What's happening?

Chris sprinted across the quad, snow packing into his boots. His ankles were stiff and nearly numb. He slowed to a stop, breathing foggy clouds, nose leaking. The square peg still trying to fit into the round hole.

Bixen Hall was bustling.

Faculty and slackers held the door open as they came with trays of food and left with buckets of compost. The windows were frosted; icicles hung from the eaves. The walls weren't buckled. Every stone in its place. Chris didn't know what it was supposed to look like.

Just not this.

He opened the door to the smell of fresh pastries and wooden tables with pitchers of milk and juice and centerpieces of holly and pinecones. Slackers worked in the kitchen, wearing white aprons with flour on their cheeks, licking icing off their fingers, flicking bits of food at each other.

They were young.

Like a group of college-age camp counsellors enjoying the moments before the kids woke. The floor was sinking and rising at the same time. His memories moved out of the fog, but their edges were still fuzzy. He remembered the sound of snapping furniture and breaking glass. Chris turned for the door.

"Whoa, hey." A young man with perfect teeth caught him.

Chris backed away, shaking his head, trying to fit the memories in the right slots. It wasn't matching what he was seeing.

"You're up early," Kogen said. "Breakfast isn't for another hour. I can get you something if you're hungry."

Chris swirled in a whirlpool of vertigo. Kogen was beaming. Welcoming. A hand out to shake.

"Something in my teeth?" Kogen limped to the door.

He was limping badly, much worse than before. Something had happened to him. Kogen turned around. Chris could only stare.

"You get everything you need for Christmas?" Kogen said.

"What?"

Kogen picked his teeth. "You know, it's not about what you want. It's what you need." He threw his head back and filled his lungs, exhaling a white cloud. "It's a new day, Christmas. Perfect just as it is."

He smacked Chris's arm.

"Come on, I'll sneak you in for an early bite. You must be starving."

Chris's stomach was inside out. The world upside down. He felt like he was in a play and had forgotten his lines. Where was the audience? Someone was going to tell him this was a joke. He'd slept so long he'd forgotten where he was.

The first rays of sunlight touched the tip of the castle. Icicles dripped down the rough-hewn stones, trickled between the seams like tiny streams and dribbled from a missing chunk. A stone had been broken off. Chris moved closer to a memory.

"Merry Christmas," Kogen called.

Chris barely heard it. He remembered looking through the spire's window as if he were as tall as the castle. Swinging his arm like a wrecking ball that clipped the castle and shook the ground. A snowdrift was perfectly sculpted at the foot of the wall, the surface glittering. He waded through it, plunging his hands into it until he couldn't feel his fingers. His foot hit something solid. He pulled out the missing piece of granite with frozen hands.

He lugged the broken piece like a divining rod leading him to a treasure trove of memories. The Tree was heavy with ornaments, limbs weighted with snow. The ground was charred with remnants of a bonfire. His memories rushed through the veil and nearly knocked him over. He dropped the granite and staggered. He fell on his knees.

This is where I woke up.

There were large animals and short, fat people with thick beards and bushy eyebrows. Wide feet. They were gathered around one of the animals with antlers as wide as his bedroom. Three of them—they looked like identical triplets—were helping someone onto the reindeer's back. He was slumped over, tired. Bundled in snow-crusted furs.

Pelz.

A shell of what he had been. A deflated version of the man who ran the school. And now he was on the back of an enormous reindeer. The reindeer's belly began to swell like a balloon. Someone called out to clear. The reindeer snorted and growled, then, crouching low, launched off the ground like a catapult slinging a payload.

Ronin.

That was the reindeer's name. Chris didn't know how he knew

Ronin's name or that he was the biggest reindeer of them all, the one that protected the herd. And now he was carrying Pelz away. But moments after his hooves left the ground, he suddenly froze in midair. He was suspended twenty feet from the ground like an animated sculpture hung from a wire.

He had passed through a shimmering veil that smudged the details of the trees, turned the stars into watery lights. A translucent dome emanated from the back of a large red sleigh. It had been damaged, but now it was working, casting a sort of warped forcefield. Ronin with Pelz and the triplets on his back had gone through it and just... stopped.

"I'm fine," a deep voice said. "Yes, yes, I know."

A fat man in a red coat had his hand to his ear. His beard was long and curly and as white as his gloves. His fuzzy hat flopped to one side. The short, hairy people moved around him like worker bees. More of them popped through the overhead bubble like it was raining elves. Ronin was still frozen.

"Everything will be taken care of, I promise. We've got a long night ahead of us, yes. Don't worry."

Humid breath was on Chris's face. Nostrils on a furry snout nudged him. Antlers like tree branches, the reindeer pushed him again. Chris was at the edge of the dome. And just on the other side, Joli was a still life reaching for him. Her hand outstretched, mouth open as if calling his name. Gretchen pulling her away. They were like wax statues. Like time outside the dome had stopped.

"What are you doing?" someone called.

Chris snapped out of the memory. He was on the ground, exactly as he remembered it. Joli was walking toward him, wearing a long black coat with technicolor tassels dangling from the sleeves. Sai followed in his puffy coat.

"You sleep out here?" She looked down at him.

Chris didn't know what to say or if he should say anything at all. He wasn't sure if he was still remembering until he took her hand. She swatted the snow off his back.

"You looking for lost presents?" she said.

"That's a good idea, actually," Sai said. "You find anything good?"

Chris looked around. The snow was perfect around the charred bonfire. Didn't they see that? If everyone was there last night, it would've been trampled, even if it snowed last night. But it was pristine. Like no one was ever there.

"You don't remember?" Chris said.

"I remember you snoring. Wasn't he, Sai? Curled up on the ground like a puppy. We basically carried you to your room. Well, Sai did."

"I did."

"You don't..." Chris pointed. "Look!"

Ms. Taiga was dancing with Mr. Kolodzie. Her head thrown back in full-throated laughter and her hair dark and thick. She was lithe and nimble, flowing with grace. Joli and Sai looked at each other.

"She's young!" Chris said.

"Yeah, no," Joli said. "She's, like, forty. I mean, that's not old, but it's not exactly—"

"They're all young. The faculty, I saw them this morning. They were in the quad throwing snowballs and-and-and running around and hugging. And singing!"

Joli and Sai traded glances. "I don't get it," Sai said.

"I saw Kogen," Chris said. "He looks twenty years old, or twenty-two or something. Basically a college kid."

"Thaaaat's because he's twenty-two or something," Joli said. "Am I missing something?"

"But he's back. Don't you get it? He didn't go anywhere, like nothing happened. He's at Bixen right now. I'll show you."

"Back from where?" Sai said.

"Back from... you know, sabotaging the gingerbread house. We got Grendel to catch him. And then she, she..."

The marbles.

The marbles were heavy and warm and glowing. They were sucking the life out of him. They had long translucent strands. And then he pulled them back. Yanked them out of possessed sculptures because he'd become this enormous thing with—

"Where's Gman?" Chris said.

"Who?" Sai said.

And then it was clear. Chris refused to believe it. After everything that had happened. He walked around the burned patch and told them everything. The more he talked, the more he remembered. The sculptures coming to life, Pelz sending them into the sky to pull the sleigh down. Santa Claus and reindeer.

"He was using me," Chris said, "to power the marbles. Somehow he-he-he had this crown and it connected some part of me. And Sai, you were in Bixen. You took all the gingerbread men and smashed them into pieces and sprinkled them on the food. And then it all kind of mushed together into this giant gingerbread man like a-a-a monster. Not a monster but a, I don't know. Something. And I was there; I was in it. It was me and Gingerman. And then…"

He trailed off. After that it was all white. Something had happened he couldn't quite remember. *What was it?*

"The inner landscape," he said.

"The what?" Joli said.

"You remember the inner landscape Pelz wanted me to create? To make the memories real. I went there. And somehow I pulled Pelz into it. And the elf was there. The Toymaker, just like Gingerman said. He told me what it was. And then I woke up right there." He pointed. "There were elves and reindeer. And then Santa, he…"

Chris didn't wake up in his bedroom, not the first time. He remembered the big man approaching him after the reindeer had nudged him away from the bubble's edge, away from Joli's catatonic reach from the other side. The colors of his red coat blurred. The white gloved hand reached for him. And Santa said one last thing. It was faded in those final moments.

"You won't remember this," Chris repeated.

Joli was frowning. Sai's mouth hung open. Chris looked for a hint, a spark that might incinerate the veil hiding their memories. They were there, too. They had to be.

"That," Joli said, "is a wild dream, Christopher."

Christopher.

"What punch were you drinking last night?" she said. "Are you allergic to, like, pineapple or something? I binged on Ding Dongs one night and dreamed the tooth fairy was riding a chopper with the Easter bunny on the back and—"

"It happened, Jo."

"Oh, yeah. Yeah." She nodded at Sai, then took Chris's hand. "Except the part about Pelz."

"He was there, too. He started the whole thing. He had this bag—"

"Pelz is gone," she said.

"That's what I'm saying. He's—"

"No, I mean he wasn't even here last night. He left yesterday morning. That's what the big celebration was all about. He retired, said it was time."

"Yesterday?" Chris said.

"Yeah," Joli said. "He said it was time to move on. He'd been doing this forever and needed to work on some things. He seemed a little sad."

"He seemed a lot sad," Sai said. "Ever seen a grown man cry?"

Chris had. It was in a land of snow, curled up and wailing. Only he wasn't a grown man. *There's nothing more dangerous than a child in adult clothing.*

"Before we get frostbite," Joli said, "can we get breakfast? Najean said she'd sneak us in early. I say we grab a bag of sticky buns, take them up to your room for some coffee, and eat ourselves into a Christmas coma."

Sai was already on his way. Joli pulled Chris along.

"No," he said.

"What's wrong?"

"I just need to, uh, need to think a minute."

Sai turned around. They looked worried.

Chris held up his hand. "I'm okay. Seriously."

They nodded. "Maybe you should write that stuff down," Sai said. "It's a good story."

He slapped Chris's chest. Joli threw her arm around his neck and kissed the side of his head. They said merry Christmas and started off. They weren't going to remember. No one would.

But that didn't mean it didn't happen.

❄

Chris stood in the trees, recalling the way the candles had flickered in the dark spaces between the trunks, the way the grays cupped the flames. Now the door between the circle and the village beyond wasn't just open. It wasn't even there.

The wall was so much taller when he'd seen it through the gingerman's eyes, hiding in a rotted stump. The huts were stark reminders of lives time had forgotten. But now the tiny structures were looped with garland. Wreaths hung on the doors, strands of lights hooked to the thatched roofs.

Slowly, carefully, Chris walked down the cobblestone path. Presents were stacked next to the buildings. Some of the doors were open. Laughter flowed out like smoke from the chimneys. It was some of the faculty. When they saw him, they raised their mugs, called out merry Christmas, and then continued singing.

None were wearing gray.

They wore colorful coats of magenta, turquoise, sapphire blue or hunter green. Heavy beads around their necks, large loops in their ears, and sharp hats upon their heads. They were young—if forty was young—and sang their songs, told their stories and stoked their fires.

It was Christmas morning.

The cobblestone had been swept. Snow packed into the crevices. The rising sun found its way through the trees. Occasionally, snow would fall from the branches and drift down in silent descent. As if carried by the songs. All was light and weightless, happy and serene.

But the cave ahead was dark.

The arching vines couldn't hide the heavy gleam of the vault door. Chris had seen it from the ground. He imagined what it was like to merge with the gingerman. As he stood in front of the steely door, he reached out for his friend, trying to remember how he did it before. It was like casting a net of thoughts. But there was nothing out there to catch.

Gingerman wasn't there.

The door was slightly open. The festive air turned cold. Anxiety filled his legs and pumped his heart. The rush of familiarity, of being here before, of the things inside. This was where bad things had happened. He wanted to turn around and go back, find Joli and Sai, forget any of this had happened. Why didn't he forget, too? They seemed to be happy. Why couldn't he? But he would always wonder if he turned around.

It took both hands to pull the door open.

The exact memories of what had happened surfaced. There were glass panels on the walls like a futuristic mausoleum. The soles of his boots squeaked. His pulse quickened. It felt like the moments before opening a treasure chest. He took a deep breath. With his hand on the glass, he peered inside one of the panes.

It was empty.

It was narrow and deep, like a rectangular hole. Chris walked around, his footsteps echoing. He was relieved. Maybe the things he thought happened didn't happen after all. Maybe none of this had happened. They were all empty. All except one.

He attempted to pry the door open. The seam was smooth and perfectly fit. He felt a spring give way. The door opened like a filing cabinet. There on a platform was a stick figure. It was branches gathered from the woods and lashed together with twine. The legs stout, the arm reaching out for an embrace. The head a bundle of braided whips laced to the shoulders.

"Hello." Gretchen darkened the doorway.

The sterling knob of her cane was gripped tightly, supporting her weight. It tapped the slippery floor. She shuffled inside with a kind smile. A heavy smile. She wasn't like the others. She looked no different than he remembered. She was old and tired.

"It was open," Chris said. "So I just, I was looking around."

"Ah, yes. Not much we keep here anymore. It's okay." She shooed him forward. "Look all you want."

Chris looked through a few more glass panes. No stick dolls. Just deep empty pockets and a clean floor with beads of melted snow.

"Are you looking for something?" she asked.

"I don't know." He shook his head. "What was in here?"

"Well"—she rubbed her chin—"it was something Lord Pelznickel valued very much."

"What?"

She shrugged. "It doesn't matter now."

"Where'd he go?"

"He's in a better place now."

"He died?"

"No. No, no, no, no." She chuckled with a wave. "No, he travelled north. To stay with family. Everyone will be happier. Don't you think?"

He was unsure what that meant. He was nervous to tell her what he remembered or where to start. She had been in his room last night. She'd sung the song to Pelz when he was a child. The same song Chris sang.

"Can I tell you something?" He looked at the floor.

It was difficult to look at her and sort the memories. They were already different than when he'd told Joli and Sai, blending together like thoughts that didn't have clear boundaries. Tainted with doubt.

"Santa came last night."

He stalked the room and spilled the rest of the details before they faded completely. The sculptures, the marbles. How he'd stopped Pelz and what had happened when he sang the song. How everyone had been old and now they were young.

"Why are you still old?" Chris said.

Her laughter was scratchy. She coughed into her fist and held out a hand. "Well," she said, catching her breath, "I'm exactly who I am."

He felt foolish. Everything sounded so silly. He paced to the back of the vault. People don't get younger, and buildings don't repair themselves. Santa's elves couldn't do that. *Right?*

Debris had been swept into the corner. A few twigs that looked like the ones he was holding. But something else. He pinched a crumb. It wasn't much bigger than a bird seed.

"I can't hear him anymore," he muttered.

"Are you listening?" She didn't ask who he was talking about. She wasn't smiling, but she looked kind.

"Do you know who I'm talking about?"

She shrugged. "We all have someone in a time of need." She took a tentative step and pointed with the cane. "What do you have there?"

He carried the crumb like a gemstone. But Gretchen took the stick doll from his other hand. Her demeanor transformed like a cloud passing through a blue sky. Eyebrows creased, chin jutting out, she saw something beyond the semblance of sticks and twine.

"There once was a boy in a castle," she whispered.

A wave of chills rode down Chris's back. He knew that line. It was the opening sentence to the story Sai had scribbled down. The story Chris had pulled from Gingerman. But Gingerman didn't know the story and swore he hadn't told it to Sai. Gingerman didn't know a lot of things or, if he did, how he knew them. Like how Kogen was cheating.

"Life is full of surprises," she said. "It never goes as you expect."

She closed his hand around the stick doll and walked away, the tip of her cane finding its way between the stones, her steps careful on the uneven surface. As if she'd walked that path many times. She did the things that needed to be done. She was always there for Pelz. When he was a child. When he was an adult.

"It was you," Chris said.

Gretchen was the one. She knew the gingerman was there. Could she talk to him, too? Was she telling the story? Did she know Kogen was cheating and how to catch him? But even with the crumb between his finger and thumb, the memories were fading. He doubted these things had happened. Really, a cookie that talked and walked? Santa Claus and reindeer? Every minute that passed made them seem more and more like a dream.

He caught up to her. "I think this is for you."

There once was a boy in a castle. But without the woman who

truly loved him, he was just a boy without a home. She cradled the stick doll.

"Never forget the ones who love you," she said.

Those words would change him. The memories that had come to the surface evaporated like snowflakes on a summer day. One day, a long, long time from now, they would surface again. He would remember a time when magic was real and Santa was snatched from the sky, when reindeer battled sculptures and elves repaired a village. But right now, he was just a boy at a school.

He sprinted across campus, past faculty wishing him merry Christmas, through the quad of still life sculptures until his lungs burned. The iron gates were wide open, never to be locked again. Up the winding path and through the woods, he ran until his legs were noodles.

The Visitors' Center was empty. A cubicle was lit.

He fell into the chair, sweat streaming down his cheeks. Dizzy and huffing, he wiped his eyes to see someone already on the monitor. His mom wearing her elf hat, Dad with a cup of coffee, Yu in a sweatshirt. There was so much to say, so much to explain. Why he hadn't written or called. He wanted to say that he wished he were home right now. But he didn't feel that way. He didn't want to be there.

"I really wish," he huffed, "you were here right now."

32

Memories fade. As all memories do.

They gently walk into the fog, edges blurring, colors bleaching until they're distant familiar forms. And then one day, they slip into the mist and become nothing more than a story. But always, somewhere out there, I knew they were there.

I can't explain why I remembered. It was one Christmas Eve I heard footsteps on the roof and the scuff of metal rails. There was no one to be seen, but the sound was enough to clear the fog. I lay in bed that morning recalling humid reindeer breath and the tinny sound of bells. The way time froze inside a bubble.

I remembered the Arctic.

Did any of it happen? Memories are that way, rinsed in the desire to make it so. But I choose to believe. There's no other explanation for why I am here today.

"Grandpa?"

A little girl peeked around the door. Her black hair bound in rows. Her dark eyes as big as sugarplums. Her mocha cheeks flushed with cold.

"Yes, my dear?"

She ran across the room and climbed onto his knee. He pushed the chair back, groaning as an old man does. Scarf around her neck, she looked at his desk.

"Why do you use a feather?"

"Because it's my favorite. Want to try?" He dipped the quill in the inkwell.

She scribbled her name in blocky letters. *Raiya.* The sound of the tip was grating, but Chris had grown fond of it. It was sounds that ushered his memories back.

"There's a lady here," Raiya said, dipping the quill.

"Well then, we should go talk to her."

He tickled her ribs. She jumped off giggling, dropping the quill. Chris closed the leather book. He pushed off the desk and leaned on an old mahogany cane with a sterling silver handle. The metal tip tapped the stone floor. Beams of sunlight cut through the clutter.

Raiya held the door open and held his hand as they descended the stairwell. Lights had been installed on the ceiling, illuminating the sooty walls that once held torches. She talked about her sisters and brothers, what they were doing, how they were going to hike that afternoon and she wasn't old enough because the house was haunted. Chris had told them many times the mansion wasn't haunted.

But that was another story.

Chris took one step at a time, holding tightly to her little hand. With the cane hooked through a coat loop, he clung to the bannister. His knees protested all the way to a heavy oak door. Raiya leaned into it.

A woman was looking at a photo on the wall, her hair pulled back in a ponytail, black and shiny. Eyebrows sculpted; cheeks full. She beamed at the little girl.

"Thank you, Raiya." The little girl ran out of the room to join her brothers and sisters. "Precious," the woman said. "Your great-great-granddaughter?"

Chris held up three fingers.

"Great-great-great?" she said. "And you still take the stairs?"

"Keeps me young." His laughter bellowed in the room with

surprising tenor. And, as usually happened, brought laughter to the ones around him.

"Juana Gonzalez." She offered her hand. "Thank you for meeting me. I know it's a special day and you're busy. It's been hard getting our schedules lined up."

"Well, I hope I'm not keeping you from family."

"This is a very remote place you live. It's so authentic. I don't think I've ever been in a real castle." She looked around. "I love these photos. They must be hundreds of years old. Are they replicas?"

"No, no. Everything is what you see."

"Is this you?"

She went back to the photo on the wall. He leaned on his cane, slightly winded. The photo had captured three students hard at work. One of them was applying a bead of white icing to a wall on a gingerbread house. The other two were watching, their cheeks smudged with flour.

Chris smiled. This photo always brought that reaction. It was followed by a sentimental wave of emotion. Sometimes his eyes misted. It didn't feel like him in that photo. Like it was another life with people he missed dearly.

"How long ago was that?" she said.

"I don't have enough fingers and toes to count that high."

"I can't imagine." She leaned closer to the photo.

"You'd be surprised by what you can imagine."

"Oh, I'm sorry." She tapped her temple. "I'm using Neurolink. I should have told you. If you're not comfortable, I can—"

He raised a hand. The world was light-years ahead of him. He wasn't opposed to the visual and audio feeds uploading her cortex to a cloud server. Of course, the reception was poor out there. He assumed she'd cleared space in her internal drive to store the data till she was back in the real world.

"Do you want to sit?" She gestured to the old table.

"I'd rather walk. Please."

She followed him into the hall. Her reaction was like most visitors seeing the high ceilings and rough walls for the first time. It was so spacious. Sounds were amplified by the solid surfaces.

She was bundled in an Arctic coat fresh off the rack. It was rated for subzero temperatures. She wore multiple sweatshirts beneath it. Chris wore a thick sweater with a long green scarf. The scarf wasn't something he usually wore, but Rocko, his great-great-grandson, had given it to him for Christmas.

"I don't think I could live in the cold," she said.

"You adjust."

They entered the foyer to the sounds of shouting and screaming. When they opened the door, it sounded like school had let out. Children were running in a field. There were snowmen with sticks and carrots. Dominic was flying a kite. Pyruvate was building a snow fort. And dozens of other children were hurling snowballs, hiding behind intricate sculptures that adorned the front lawn. Some of the parents joined in. Others watched from the sidelines with mugs of coffee.

"Do you know all their names?" Juana said.

"Of course." He grunted with a smile. "Eventually."

She laughed from the belly. He could name every one of his children and grandchildren. The great-grandchildren took a little more time. The great-great-great-grandchildren required some help.

"I see you're going on a hike." Erica, his granddaughter, climbed the steps. She wrapped the scarf around his neck and insisted he put on a coat, making sure his beard didn't get caught in the zipper. "He still thinks he's eighty years old."

"Just going out back," Chris said. "Not far."

She reached into his pocket and pulled out a floppy green hat. The material was thin and had been repaired many times. He'd been given new hats for Christmas, but he preferred this one. It was an inexpensive hat from a department store and didn't keep his head warm. It was nothing special. But a special person once wore it at Christmas. So did he.

Erica put a walkie-talkie in his pocket. "I know what not far means, Poppy. Don't let him climb," she said to Juana. "And be careful. Dinner is in three hours. We're setting up in Dancer Hall, okay?"

Juana looked surprised. She had been prepared for an interview in a castle, not hiking. Not in this weather. And not with him.

"Don't climb?" Juana asked. "Is she serious?"

"I don't know." He chuckled.

The paths had been cleared. His cane sank firmly in the gravel. They started around the left side of the castle when a snowball landed a few feet away. Chris turned his shoulders. His neck was stiff.

"Would you be so kind?" He pointed the cane.

She knew what he meant. Juana scooped snow and packed it. Not bad for someone who lived in a warm part of the world. He aimed the cane at his great-great-granddaughter Joli. Juana had played sports growing up. She hit the teenager on the run. The other kids came running.

"No, no!" Erica shouted. "Stop."

Chris and Juana got off a few close calls before the parents herded the children away. Juana smiled. The joy was like a whirlpool that sucked her in. He could tell she wanted more. He did, too. But he knew his limitations.

"I don't get it," she said. "How do you do it?"

He took her arm. "Longevity is a gift."

They made it around the castle without another snowball. The children's shouting would stay with them until they reached the trees. Chris named the buildings they passed, how they were renamed decades ago.

"Santa's reindeer," she said. "That's good. I'm writing an interest piece that will—"

Chris began to laugh. His beard had turned white many years ago. He used to laugh like that when he played Santa for the children. And then, with enough time, it just became part of him. And when he found something really funny, it came out almost like it was written on the page.

Ho-ho-ho!

"What's so funny?" She couldn't help but laugh. "You're perhaps the most interesting person in the world. And a medical marvel to kick."

The stories of the world didn't often reach him. His family would sometimes print them. They left their phones at the Family Center—what used to be called the Visitors' Center—and turned off their enhancements. They didn't always turn them off, he knew. But they couldn't airdrop the stories to him anyway. He was unmodified. Or, as the kids called it, *an organic*.

"How did you inherit the school?" she asked.

"Kris Pelznickel had no family."

"So you were just lucky? There had to be a reason."

She was angling. He didn't inherit a mountain for good grades. He had been forty years old when an attorney called him. He was teaching culinary classes at a local college while running a bakery.

"There were certain... events that made me a good candidate."

"Gretchen Grendel chose you."

He remembered the call well. Gretchen had passed away and named him heir. He hadn't been in touch with her since graduating. And now she was gone. He'd hung up and wept. He never should've let time get away from him. Then again, he never really believed she would pass.

"Yes," he said. "Ms. Grendel."

"Was she family?"

"She lived almost her entire life here."

"There's no records of her. No birth certificate, no history. No one really knows who she was."

No one really did. Perhaps not even Pelz. Chris did, though. She often told him that he was special. She wasn't entirely wrong, but it was only half the story, and she was too modest to tell the rest. *She was special.* As Chris recalled, she was the one who saved Pelz from himself. Chris was only helping her, unwittingly. At least, that was how he remembered it.

"Things were different back then. Watch your step."

They left the path. The snow was almost to their knees. The Tree was heavy with ornaments. The branches were touching the ground. The store beneath it was hidden in the shadows. There wasn't much in it these days. Some things of storage, but no presents. Gretchen had shut it down sometime after Chris had graduated. Nothing was free.

The Christmas clock was new this year. The winter challenge had been to replace the old one. There were winners and losers. It was a challenge after all. The school hadn't lost its edge in that respect. But no one was expelled for losing.

This clock was twenty feet tall on fiberglass posts. The intricate metal ring appeared to float. The hands rotated around the perimeter. He recalled the tradition of counting in Christmas morning with students. Now it was just family who stayed to watch the sky.

Students went home for Christmas.

The area was adorned with sculptures made of glass, iron, and stone. They were permanent installments that were added to from time to time. Some were more abstract than others, but the spirit was evident. There were reindeer and sleighs, giant snowmen and elves. Santa Claus, of course. And a figure most people wouldn't recognize in fur pelts.

"This is amazing." She glassed the area, capturing the images through retinal imaging. "Do the students do these?"

"Yes."

"Where are they?"

"Home. With their families."

"It wasn't always like that."

"The school has changed. Come, this way."

They trudged out of the snow to a path leading through the woods. Shadows obscured the narrow stretch leading to the wall.

"What made you come back?" she asked.

Curious question. "Young minds are a gift to the world. The mission of the school still honors that."

Juana recited the successes of the graduates since Chris had returned. They were technology titans, industry leaders, celebrated artists, and award-winning teachers. "They say a lot of good things about you. But not all of it good. Some make this place sound like a boot camp."

He chuckled. He liked to blame the arthritis in his hands on the sleepless nights he'd spent here as a student. That had not changed. "Art is work, Ms. Gonzalez. Growth occurs on the edge of hardship."

It dropped a few degrees in the shade of the trees. Juana hunched her shoulders. Her voice was beginning to tremble.

"Kris Pelznickel left when you were a student. Did you like him?"

"I understood him. He was brilliant, really. But like many people of his caliber, he was complicated. Troubled."

"How so?"

Chris shrugged. How could he explain the strange and sordid history of the man they called Lord Pelznickel? First, he'd have to convince her that Santa Claus existed. That Pelz was his half-brother and that, somehow, against all of what humankind knew about physics and the human body, his longevity had been gifted to him when Santa met the elves. There was no explanation for it. Perhaps what Pelz had once said, that his DNA was synced to his half-brother, was in fact true. There was no evidence for it. But neither was there evidence for flying reindeer.

"This is the Village," Chris said.

The gate had been removed. The wall that still surrounded the school had many such openings now. This one led to a series of huts with a cobblestone path. The structures were well preserved. No one lived there anymore. Staff and faculty lived among the students. But, like the students, they were with family.

"This is like walking back in time," Juana chattered. "Everyone went home for Christmas. What about you?"

"This is home."

Chris had uttered that response many times when students asked where he was going for Christmas. What they didn't understand was what he meant. It wasn't the castle or the walls that was home. It was the cold.

A stone bench was at the end of the path. It had been carved by students from a slab of marble with beautifully crafted inlaid ironwork. The edge had been inscribed with the graduating class. The surface, once polished, was slightly worn from time.

Juana shivered. Chris took off the coat Erica had put on him.

Juana refused, but she could see the perspiration on his temple. She would be doing him a favor by carrying it. A lone beam of sunlight found its way through the trees. Tucked under an eave of vines, the air was still in a recessed alcove hidden in shadows.

"Do you know the urban legends surrounding Pelznickel when he left?"

Chris nodded. He wasn't the only one who had begun to remember. Time seemed to be the steel wool that eroded the barrier hiding others' memories as well.

"That night, many of your classmates said the faculty had suddenly become younger," she said. "And Santa Claus appeared with flying reindeer and elves and a giant snowman. The reports are amazingly consistent and corroborated. Everyone talked about a giant cookie."

Chris laughed from his belly. He slapped his knee. It sounded so funny to hear someone say it out loud. And so serious. Juana laughed, too, but waited for an answer.

"Yes, well." He wiped a tear. "Those are good stories."

"You don't recall any of that?"

"I recall many things. But, you know." He shrugged with a gleam in his eye.

"I get how impossible it sounds, but maybe he staged some kind of dramatic exit?"

"Let me show you something."

He pushed up with the cane and held out his hand. A narrow path led up the mountain. Steps of timbers had been laid into the earth, with a railing made from branches, the surfaces polished from decades of use. He climbed one step at a time, assuring Juana he was fine. It was far less of a climb than the tower. Although that many steps in one day was taxing.

They reached the top where branches formed a twining tunnel. He leaned with both hands on the cane.

"Are you sure—"

"Yes." He raised his hand with an assuring smile. "It's just a little farther."

She hooked her arm around his elbow. The wind whistled briskly down the corridor. She cinched the collar around her neck.

"Pelznickel was screening his students when you were here. Did you know that? He illegally accessed genome databases. There's speculation he was looking for someone. Or something."

"Like what?"

She shrugged. "A particular gene. There's a rare sequence that companies still haven't traced. Did you have it?"

"We don't do that anymore, Ms. Gonzalez."

"You know Pelznickel had heavily invested in technology before you came here as a young man. Avocado Inc. was a primary beneficiary. And then there was the controversial ranch called Big Game he funded. It's well documented that he supported the advent of synthetical stem cells. Some even speculated he was manufacturing artificial bodies."

"Really?" Chris frowned. He'd been asked that before. His response was well rehearsed. "Where did he do that?"

"Here. At the school. Are you not aware of it?"

"Oh, I've heard the rumors. Santa Claus also visited, remember."

"The medical technology industry attributes many of their breakthroughs as a result of his investments. There's no doubt he had some stake in it."

Chris paused. "Who are you talking about?"

"Pelznickel."

"No. Who was he cloning?"

"I didn't say cloning, Mr. Blizzard." She stopped. "I was hoping you could tell me."

"Ah." He nodded. "You've come all this way, Ms. Gonzalez. Surely you have a guess as to who it was."

She smiled coyly. "You."

"There you go."

"Are you denying it? You're a hundred and thirty years old, Mr. Blizzard. You're hiking up a mountain that you inherited for no discernible reason. Pelznickel was a smart man. He wanted to ensure his legacy before he died. It only stands to reason that if he was, in fact, manufacturing people, he would *create* an heir."

The ground was frozen, knobby roots bulging on the path. He wondered how many times he'd walked this way, wondered often when would be his last hike. And still he kept going. So yes, he'd asked himself that very same question.

Am I who I think I am?

There was so much that had happened during that time he couldn't remember. So many dreams he could not untangle from reality. The barrier had never been thinner than when he was young. Was there a secret he kept from himself? Because she was right. Pelz had been at the frontier of creation. The bench where they sat was right outside the entrance to his laboratory, now grown over and, as Gretchen once said, used to store something he cared about.

But his creations were not for the reasons anyone expected. He was creating someone over and over. Someone who cared about him, someone he couldn't let go of, not while he was alive.

"I'm sorry to disappoint you, Ms. Gonzalez. If Pelznickel was, as you say, creating artificial bodies, it was not me."

"You've been tested?"

"You're not the first to ask. An independent lab can verify your answer. I am just like you. Without the"—he whirled his finger around his head—"the neuros."

She wouldn't be satisfied. Test results could be falsified. But Chris had volunteered to test himself long before anyone had asked. His longevity was a modern miracle. When asked what his secret was—rising early? eating healthy?—his response was always the same. Somewhere in his DNA was a sequence handed down from a very special elf. Or so he liked to believe. How it happened, he couldn't say. There was much he didn't understand. But one thing was scientifically certain.

He had good genes.

The end of their walk reached a sharp edge of the mountain. Juana stopped short, shaking her head. Too many steps and it was several hundred feet to the bottom. The view was expansive. The valley lay below. Chris sat on a log a few steps from the edge. Slowly, she worked her way next to him. She'd forgotten all about the cold.

Chris had discovered this area shortly after he'd gotten the call of Gretchen's passing. It had grown over many years ago. He'd found it by accident and thought it was a great place to meditate. He'd found heavy stones still stacked with carvings on their surfaces. He'd searched for stick dolls in a small cut of rock, but time would have weathered them to dust. Still, he knew it was very special. He imagined, hundreds of years ago, a boy coming here to spend his nights under the stars, warming himself by a fire, and wondering where his father was.

"I believe there are many things we don't understand," he said. "Is this beautiful? My senses believe so. But this, out there, is only being what it is, nothing more. The beauty, Ms. Gonzalez, is created here." He tapped his head. "Our minds create the magic in the world. This is why the school exists."

"You believe in magic, then?"

"It's all around us. We just have to see it."

She couldn't see it quite like he could. Thoughts and questions clouded her perception. One day, though, she might find herself awake at night to hear the tinny bells.

"You believe in flying reindeer and giant cookies, then?" she said.

Chris looked around. "Not at the moment."

She laughed, agreeing, shivering uncontrollably now.

"You're cold. Head back, please. Warm yourself by the fire. And stay for dinner. You're welcome to stay the night. Tell your friends you slept in a castle, mmm? Maybe if you're lucky," he said, leaning into her, "you'll hear bells on the roof."

"Ha. Well, I can't leave you here."

"Please. This is my home. I do it all the time."

"Erica will be upset."

"She's used to it. Besides, she'll be furious if I let you freeze. Please go. I'll be right behind you. I don't get up here as often as I used to, and who knows how many more trips I've got. I won't live forever. I promise."

She stripped the coat off and draped it over his shoulders. Erica was certain to be angry if she returned without Chris and wearing his coat. But Erica knew what to expect. Juana stood to hug herself. Her lips were pale.

"Your daughter said you're writing a book about this place, about what happened when you were a student."

"Ramblings of an old man. Who knows if it's true."

"I'd like to read it."

She left in a hurry. Chris was alone on the perch. It was true he savored the moments he reached this pinnacle. How many more were there? Beauty should not be so hastily ignored. Chris wouldn't live forever. Good genes were one thing, but they were not immortal. He could feel the tenure of his life in his joints, when he woke in the mornings.

He bundled the green hat in his hands then shirked the coat and opened his sweater, letting winter embrace him. He breathed in the icy air. The sun was still behind him. On any other day of the year, he would remain until it breached the mountain and settled over the valley, until the shadows were long and his belly grumbled. But his family was waiting.

He reached into his pocket and propped a golden-brown gingerbread man on his lap.

"Merry Christmas, buddy."

TOYMAKER: RETURN OF THE LOST TOYS (BOOK 9)

Get the Claus Universe at:
BERTAUSKI.COM/CLAUS

❄

Toymaker: Return of the Lost Toys (Book 9)

CHAPTER 1

"What's this?" Mom said.

The gift was under a pile of wrapping paper. Mom reached for it, the sleeve of her brand-new robe sliding down her arm. Avery watched her examine the expert wrapping, the corners sharp and the folds precise. The dragons tussled on the back of her mom's brand-new robe. The robe Avery's dad had bought on a trip overseas, the white silk matching her mom's pale white skin.

"Who's it for?" Avery asked.

There wasn't a tag or a name scribbled on the paper. Mom slid the loose end of the ribbon between her fingers, where a name had been typed.

"Bradley," she said.

Avery's brother didn't answer. He was on the couch, his hands on his thighs. A certain sparkle made his eyes look like emeralds.

"Bradley?" Mom's pale cheeks were suddenly rosy. "Please tell me you are not working, son."

He was in deep. Didn't even blink when she said it. He thought gift-giving was over, activated a virtual connection. His lenses glittered with fractal images.

"Avery, please." Mom's lips drew thinner than pine needles.

Avery crawled to the couch and smacked his leg. "Hey!"

He started, then looked around. The optic glitter faded from his virtual lenses. "I thought we were done—"

Mom threw the gift on his lap. He struggled to catch it. Dad sipped his coffee and sighed. Avery smiled. He totally deserved it.

"Who's it from?" he said.

"Secret Santa," Mom said.

"I thought we weren't doing that anymore." He looked at Avery. "Are we doing that?"

They weren't doing Secret Santa anymore, but she wasn't going to help him out of the hole he'd dug. He knew the rules. And, if she was honest, she wanted to watch him squirm.

"Bradley." Mom tapped her temple. "How many times have I asked?"

The answer was five. It had been five years since he'd finished college. Five years he'd been caught working while they were opening presents or eating Christmas dinner. And five years Mom had tried to move him out of the house. If Dad had his way, Bradley would live with them forever.

"Be right back," Dad said. "Don't open without me."

Mom creased wrapping paper into neat piles while they waited. Her legs were folded beneath her, her posture perfect. She grew up in a wealthy family that, according to Avery's friends, was sort of like royalty. Avery knew where her mom grew up. It wasn't royalty. But it was hard to ignore her perfect manners and impeccable posture. She knew the proper etiquette at formal dinner parties, which fork to use. Things Avery didn't care about.

Avery counted her gifts. A dream journal was on top, the cover with white floating bubbles containing tiny figures. Nana Rai gave her one every year. *Never forget your dreams,* Nana would say.

She had been wanting a sensory jack kit since she was in grade school. Her friends all had looker kits. Avery would watch them go virtual while she waited for them to come out. She hoped this was the year she would join them.

This was not the year.

Instead, Santa brought her a high beam laptop with virtual projection and thought manipulation. The flat chrome plate with expandable multi-fold capability, magnetic keying and temple strobe linkage. Images could be pulled with three-dimensional scaling and holographic mining. It was first class. It was not a virtual looker kit.

"Do you like it?" Mom said.

Avery tried not to sound disappointed. Mom knew. Discussions had been had at the dinner table. It was unfair Bradley had had a blaze gamer kit with wraparound lens slicks when he was ten. *Blaze kits aren't immersive*, Mom would say. But they were. Just because they didn't transport, they were still immersive. And that was why he was the best virtual striker at Avocado, Inc. Why? Because he'd started gaming at ten.

Avery's phone buzzed. "I'm going to the bathroom. Don't let Bradley open it till I'm back."

"Hmm."

Iona sent a photo of her Christmas haul. Clothes and accessories and, of course, immersive add-ons because her parents didn't say no to first-rate technology. *Look what my mom got,* Iona added. It was a new virtual looker kit, of course, but not a brand Avery had ever seen. Maybe it was a fancy hiwire sensory jacker that co-opted *all* the senses. Lookers grabbed sight and sound and, sometimes, smell. Hiwires added touch and taste. They were things of rumor, the complete and total immersive experience that was always being promised to the general public.

Iona's mom's lookers were sleek black. Like polished obsidian. Feathered wraparounds to entwine around the head; convex eyeblades with a logo embossed between them.

"I know what you're doing." Bradley thumped on the bathroom door.

She flushed the toilet and ran the water in the sink. He was waiting. His eyes were muddy green without the lenses, the whites tinted yellow.

"You should take notes." She hid her phone in her waistband.

Dad was on the couch, running his finger along the sharp edge of the mystery gift. Mom had pressed all the Christmas paper flat.

"Who's it from?" Bradley picked up the gift. "Seriously."

Dad didn't know who half the gifts were from. "Only one way to find out," he said.

Avery assumed Mom really was playing Secret Santa, which gave Avery hope there was another present under those squashed piles of wrapping paper.

Bradley fell on the couch. Dad spilled his coffee. Add a touch of creamer and it would match her dad's complexion. They waited for him to clean up. Bradley examined the perfect wrapping. It was like a machine had sealed the seams. A work of art that deserved a pedestal. It would be a shame to tear it open. He found a tab at the bottom.

Dad came back with a brown robe with pockets in the front and the Avocado, Inc., logo above the right breast. Bradley didn't wait for him to sit down before pulling the tab. It was impressive what happened next. It unfolded like origami in reverse. The top flipped and the sides dropped. A clear plexi box was inside.

"Wow," Bradley said. "Thanks, Mom."

"It wasn't me, darling." They traded glances. Mom wasn't playing this time.

"Dad?"

He shook his head, his attention on the display box. The plexi sides fell like mechanical walls. Bradley picked up what was inside. Dad leaned in for a closer look. "Who is this?" Dad pointed at an inscription inside the wraparound band. The engraved letters were almost microscopic. "BT and Company?"

"A start-up?" Bradley said.

They were intrigued and concerned. It was flawless design. Avocado was the top-line company in virtual environments. Everyone copied their designs. But this... this was an original. And elegant.

"Iona's mom got one," Avery said. "Looks just like that."

"She did?" Mom said. "How do you know?"

"She texted when I was in the bathroom."

Bradley and Dad examined the sleek black finish, the seamless eyeblades, the integrated sensory pads. This was like driving a brand-new sports car into a car collector's living room. One no one had ever heard of.

"Who was it from?" Mom asked.

Avery shrugged. Later that afternoon, she would find out that Iona's family was just as perplexed as they were. A mystery gift that hadn't been there the night before. A tightly wrapped gift with Iona's mom's name stamped on red ribbon.

"Think it was Jerri?" Bradley said.

Dad grunted. The Avocado CEO was generous. She'd lavished the employees with gifts before, but always at the company party. Never delivering secret packages. *Besides, why didn't Mom and Dad get one?* Mom had been with the company for ten years. Dad had been there twenty, had gotten Bradley his internship. Bradley had only been full-time for two years, and Iona's mom had been with Avocado for three.

"What's that?" Mom said.

The logo between the eyeblades was etched in simple green lines. Bradley ran his fingers over the engraving. "Bird Time and Company?"

"Bird time?" Avery said.

"It looks like a bird eating a giant seed," he said. "Maybe Jerri sent out prototypes."

"I haven't heard anything." Dad would know. Products like this took ten years to design and trial. How could they produce this without him knowing? Besides, it said BT and Company.

Bradley and Dad discussed the possibilities. Maybe they should reach out to Iona's mom first, find out if anyone else in the company got one. It would turn out quite a few people did. And not just Avocado employees. People all over the world. Same box, same ribbon. Same black looker kit.

Avery picked it up. It was heavier than she expected. Like some sort of metal that was never at room temperature. The surface didn't smudge. Her fingerprints disappeared. There were no external controls, no override button or external power feed. She looked inside the eyeblades. They looked like black holes in a dark room. Dense. No reflection. It would have to be paired in order to find a line. She slid the bands over her ears, felt the feathered ends crawl through the tight curls along her scalp. Even though the material was heavy and solid, it flexed and molded around her head. The eyeblades cupped her eye sockets.

A deep hum gonged between her eyes. A mysterious distant bell that never faded. There were no images, just a strange sense of falling. Floating in nothingness. Bodiless. But she wasn't alone. Something was out there.

"Hey, no."

Bradley stripped the lookers off. It pulled small hairs from her head, brought sharp tears to her eyes. Avery teetered off a speeding merry-go-round. A slight wave of nausea quickly settled. Dad wasn't on the couch. He had gone to the kitchen. And Bradley was wearing a different shirt. *How long was I wearing them?*

"You can't just put these on," Bradley said. "We don't know what these are."

"They're immersives."

"Not what I mean, skunk. We don't know if these are neuronet enabled or just projectors. You can't just pair up. Think. What if these plant a bug in your brain?"

"*Please.*"

But he was right. She'd seen the movies where minds were hijacked by rogue immersives. They were movies, sure. But those things had happened. They didn't exactly make zombies, but she could end up with programmed thoughts that weren't hers.

Bradley took the looker kit down to the basement. Mom warned him not to work. It would be eight months to the day before anyone knew what the mystery gift did. The whole world would find out.

And the hunt would begin.

Click here to get Toymaker: Return of the Lost Toys (Book 9)

YOU DONATED TO A WORTHY CAUSE!

By purchasing this book, you have donated 10% of the profits is annually donated to **Ronald McDonald House Charities.**

ABOUT THE AUTHOR

My grandpa never graduated high school. He retired from a steel mill in the mid-70s. He was uneducated, but a voracious reader. As a kid, I'd go through his bookshelves of musty paperback novels, pulling Piers Anthony and Isaac Asimov off the shelf and promising to bring them back. I was fascinated by robots that could think and act like people. What happened when they died?

Writing is sort of a thought experiment to explore human nature and possibilities. What makes us human? What is true nature?

I'm also a big fan of plot twists.

BERTAUSKI.COM

Printed in Great Britain
by Amazon